Louise Douglas was born in Y
merset for the past twent
autiful sons and a partner who works in construction.
She earned her living through writing for years, firstly
a journalist and more recently copywriting for a
riety of clients, but only achieved her lifetime's
nbition to become a fiction author in 2008 when her
rst novel, *The Love of My Life*, was published. It was
nglisted for the Romantic Novel of the Year award and
e Waverton Good Read Award and has been widely
inslated.

Two years later, *Missing You* was published and went
n to win the Romantic Novelists' Association People's
hoice award by public vote. It was also shortlisted for
e Brit Writers' Award 2010.

The Secrets Between Us is Louise's third book. Her
nspiration came from the beautiful Somerset country-
ide, the county's ancient association with the natural,
nythical and spiritual aspects of life, and from some of
ouise's favourite classic novels.

When she's not writing, Louise is usually reading,
valking with the family's dog, Lil, and spending time
vith her amazing family and friends.

Also by Louise Douglas

The Love of My Life
Missing You

For more information on Louise Douglas and her books, see her website at www.louisedouglas.co.uk

The Secrets Between Us

Louise Douglas

TRANSWORLD PUBLISHERS
61–63 Uxbridge Road, London W5 5SA
A Random House Group Company
www.transworldbooks.co.uk

THE SECRETS BETWEEN US
A BLACK SWAN BOOK: 9780552777339

First published in Great Britain
in 2011 by Bantam Press
an imprint of Transworld Publishers
Black Swan edition published 2012

A CIP catalogue record for this book
is available from the British Library.

Addresses for Random House Group Ltd companies outside the UK
can be found at: www.randomhouse.co.uk
The Random House Group Ltd Reg. No. 954009

The Random House Group Limited supports the Forest Stewardship Council (FSC®), the leading international forest-certification organization. Our books carrying the FSC label are printed on FSC®-certified paper. FSC is the only forest-certification scheme endorsed by the leading environmental organizations, including Greenpeace. Our paper-procurement policy can be found at www.randomhouse.co.uk/environment.

Typeset in 11/14pt Giovanni Book by Falcon Oast Graphic Art Ltd.
Printed and bound by CPI Group (UK) Ltd, Croydon, CR0 4YY.

4 6 8 10 9 7 5

For Chris, Nick and Mark,

with all my love

CHAPTER ONE

I first met Alexander in the walled garden of the Hotel La Fiora in a secluded part of the southern coast of Sicily.

I was swimming in the pool and had been there for a while, half an hour maybe, long enough for the skin on the pads of my fingers to wrinkle. I floated on my back with my arms spread wide. From above I would have looked like a crucifix spinning slowly on the surface of the water. My eyes were closed against the needling brightness of the sun. It was the middle of August and the temperature was well over thirty degrees, and at that time of day, early afternoon, most Italian people were asleep indoors with the shutters pulled to. My sister, May, had gone to the room she shared with her husband, Neil, for a lie-down. She was much fairer than me and struggled in the heat. I was not sleepy. I preferred a swim to a nap and, anyway, I found it best to keep myself occupied, because in quiet moments my mind tended to drift back to Laurie standing at the doorway to our bedroom a week earlier, watching me pack and begging me not to leave him. His hair stood on end. He was holding his glasses by one of the arms, waving them. He wore his faded-to-grey trousers and his feet were bare. My bag was on the bed and I was stuffing it with clothes. Behind me, Laurie had said: 'Sarah, this isn't helping. We need to talk about our problems. You can't just run away.'

I had replied quietly: 'Watch me.'

The most pressing of our problems, at least as I saw it, was that Laurie had slept with my friend Rosita in that very bed, our bed, not just once but several times. It wasn't the actual infidelity; it was the fact that Laurie had taken his lover, my friend, into our bed, our most private place, that disturbed me most. I don't think I'd have minded so much – at least it wouldn't have hurt so badly – if they'd simply rented an anonymous hotel room and fucked one another stupid there.

After they'd had sex, he must have lain on the bed and watched her dress, seen the private angles of her shoulder blades and elbows as she reached backwards to marry the hooks and eyes of her bra. Laurie was probably already beginning to feel guilty, because that was Laurie's way. Even so, he took trouble to cover his tracks. After Rosita left, he must have showered and made the bed; patted out the pillows; checked for any stray long dark hairs. He must have plumped the duvet, turned and straightened it, and, later, he let me sleep in the same place where Rosita had lain.

I could not forgive him that.

As I packed, Laurie had pleaded with me. He blamed his infidelity on me – no, not blamed exactly, but he intimated that I had driven him to it. He was distraught, his face distorted with contradictions. 'You've been so distant lately,' he'd said. 'I didn't know how to reach you.' And I had replied: 'Believe me, Laurie, this wasn't the way.'

Rosita was a distraction, a salve, according to him – that was all. She was a symptom of the unhealthy condition of our relationship since we'd lost the baby. He always spoke in terms of 'we' and 'us' when talking about the stillbirth to show that he saw it as a mutual loss in which equal pain but no blame or responsibility was apportioned.

Sleeping with Rosita was stupid, he had said; it was nothing. It meant nothing. I didn't remember if I'd said anything out loud, but the words cannoning through my brain making my eyes hurt were: Oh but, Laurie, you did not change the sheets. You took her into the bed where our baby was conceived, that sacred place where we talked to him, and you measured his progress with the palm of your hand every night on my belly. You took her there, to our most private place, and then you let me sleep where she had lain. You betrayed us all. You lied, your body lied and you did not change the sheets.

In the swimming pool in the garden of the Hotel La Fiora, I paddled with my hands a little, to make myself rotate in the sunlight. I was heavy with my thoughts, weighed down by them. I floated but I felt as if I were made of lead.

It was hot and quiet in the hotel gardens. The blinding white concrete of the main building was staggered down the cliff-face so that every bedroom window overlooked the bay. Dark-leaved citrus trees, palms and spiky plants in terracotta urns cast patterned shadows on the grass, and a sprinkler quietly and methodically watered the beds. People dozed on their loungers in the shade and a tiny grey kitten pounced on a spider on the footpath. Even the man who sat behind the bar in the kiosk by the pool was struggling to stay awake, his face cradled low in his hands, his upper eyelashes yearning to meet the lower ones. He flicked away an insect with the back of his hand; yawned. A motorbike drove by on the pot-holed road beyond.

Most of the hotel guests around the pool were resting on their sun beds with their eyes closed, or reading airport thrillers. They were older than me; middle-aged Italian and German holidaymakers with short, grey hair and sunglasses, wrinkled chests and hard, round bellies. I dipped underwater and swam a length, and at the far end of the pool I turned. Under the trees, a little boy was climbing out of his trousers, holding on to the side of the sun bed for balance. Beside him, a man in faded Hawaiian shorts and sunglasses was sitting hunched, elbows on splayed knees, blowing into an armband. I hadn't seen any children at the hotel before; it wasn't the kind of place for young families. None of the other guests seemed to have noticed him.

I slid beneath the water again and swam a few strokes. When I broke the surface, I wiped my eyes with my hands. There was a splash, and a rush of water, waves. I turned to see the same child doggy-paddling towards me with his chin held high, his upper body made buoyant by the inflated orange armbands. His white-blond hair was cut very short, which made his eyes and ears seem very large and his face too small, and streaks of sun-protection cream on his nose and cheeks glistened in the sunlight. I headed for the steps at the far end. I did not want to share the pool with a child. The man was standing on the second step, hesitating. A phone was ringing, its tone piercing the somnolence of the afternoon. The sleepy people were disturbed. They raised their heads and pushed their sunglasses up their foreheads and frowned at the noise. The man glanced from the child to his phone on the lounger and back again. He caught my eye.

'Would you watch him for a moment?'

I hesitated; I half-shrugged, half-nodded. What else could I have done? The man gave me the thumbs-up and stepped out of the pool, the wet hairs of his legs black and flat against the skin. I moved towards the child, who was concentrating on his swimming.

'Hi,' I said.

'Hi.' He looked as displeased by the supervisory arrangements as I was.

I struggled for a straightforward question, and eventually asked: 'Who taught you to swim?'

'I don't need armbands,' he replied. He had a slight lisp. His two top middle front teeth were missing.

'Oh.'

'Mummy said I didn't need them but my dad makes me wear them.'

The boy looked towards his father, who was standing facing us but leaning into the telephone, listening earnestly.

'What's your name?' I asked the boy.

'Jamie.'

'That's a nice name. How old are you?'

The child looked at me. His eyes were the same blue colour as the tiny square ceramic tiles that lined the swimming pool. The irises were outlined in a darker colour and there were drops of water on his lashes. His face was delicate and small, babyish, but his expression was almost adult in its seriousness.

'Six and three quarters.'

'Oh,' I said. 'Good.'

I wondered if my son would have been anything like this boy if he had lived six and three quarter years. He'd have been darker in his colouring, certainly, and less intense. I always imagined a sunny, cherubic child when I thought of my boy as he might have been; bright-eyed with rosy cheeks and sticky fingers squirming solidly in my arms as I hugged and tickled him, demanding kisses.

No, he would not have resembled this child at all.

Jamie, pale and solemn, his legs pedalling beneath the ice-blue water, held my eyes. He said: 'Watch.'

He put his palms flat on the surface of the pool, dainty little fingers with seashell nails splayed, and moved them slowly as if he were playing the piano, or the guitar. On the floor, the sunlight was reflected in the patterns of the water Jamie choreographed above. It danced on the little tiles, rippled, shimmied and waltzed, and made flowers, spirals and circles. Jamie had turned the bottom of the pool into a kaleidoscope. I watched, as he had told me to, and after a few moments he looked up at me, expectantly, and I realized he was waiting for praise.

'That's clever,' I said. 'Who showed you how to do that?'

'Mummy.'

'Where's Mummy now? Is she having a rest?'

Jamie shook his head. His eyes were glassy in the light and the pale, freckled skin on his cheeks and nose was slightly sunburned. He gave a little sigh as if he were tired of answering this question, tired of being asked.

'Mummy's gone,' he said, and from the way he said it I knew he did not mean 'to the shops' or 'for a lie-down'. He meant 'gone for good'.

CHAPTER TWO

When his phone call was over, Jamie's father came into the pool. He walked down the steps and pushed off underwater, surfacing beside me. I studied him as if he were a figure in a painting. He had taken off his sunglasses and his eyes were deep set, brown, hidden behind his lashes as he squinted in the light. His hair was long; it reached his shoulders and was almost black. He had not shaved for a few days and his skin was a sallow colour, as if he were recovering from an illness. Something was not as it should have been. As he drew closer to me, I pulled away.

'Thanks,' he said.

'You're welcome.'

'Listen . . .' he said, and at exactly the same time I said: 'Anyway . . .' and we both smiled at our mutual clumsiness.

'I'm Alexander, Alex,' he said.

'Sarah.'

I didn't know what else to say and I had no

inclination to share the pool so I gave a little shrug and I said: 'I have to get out now.'

He said: 'OK.'

I was relieved he didn't try to engage me in conversation. I dreaded being asked friendly questions about myself, and having to lie because the truth would make the other person uncomfortable. Having so much to keep hidden made me feel ashamed; I was contaminated by my situation and I far preferred to be left alone.

I moved away towards the steps. Jamie and his father watched me. When I reached the end of the pool, Alexander sank down under the water.

I climbed out and went to stand on the wooden slatting beneath the pool-side shower. I arched back my neck to run the clean water through my hair and felt the sunshine warm on my face. Then I straightened again and opened my eyes and saw him watching. He gazed at me while Jamie splashed around him in the pool. Alexander's face was expressionless and composed. Flashes of light refracted from the water on his cheeks and chin. I paused, for a moment, with my hands in my hair, to watch him back, and he caught my eye and held it for a moment. Why was he staring? Could he tell something was wrong?

I broke the eye contact and turned away. I wrung the excess water from my hair and wrapped myself in the big yellow hotel towel that I'd left on the fence beside the shower, tucking it in at my chest, and then I picked up the purse that had been hidden beneath it and headed back across the lawn. The grass was prickly against the soles of my feet. The mobile was ringing again on Alexander's sun bed. As I walked by, I could see the name of the caller illuminated in the window: Rowl. At the side of the lounger a small blue teddy bear lay face down in the grass. I leaned down to pick it up, and make it sit, propped against the pile of clothes, looking out over the swimming pool.

I asked the man in the kiosk for a glass of lemonade and drank it at a table in the shade. A little lizard ran up the wall beside me and stopped dead still at eye level. It was a pretty little thing, the pads of its toes like sequins pressed against the whitewash of the wall. I gazed through the hedging that bordered the sea edge of the garden at the blue, blue sky that canopied the bay and the hazy outline of the coast on the other side of the water. I tried to lose myself in the colours and the distance but was distracted by the movement in the pool, and by the sound of Jamie's father calling him out.

I passed them on the way back to my lounger. Alexander was rubbing the child's head with a towel; the boy was whining, complaining that his father was too rough. Jamie stood on one leg, scratching the back of his knee with his toes. He wrapped his skinny little arms about his chest, and shivered. Alexander had his sunglasses on again; I could not see his face, but his back was an arch of muscle and bone and the hair in the hollow of his arms was long and dark. A nasty scar, still gleaming slightly purple at its perimeter, dissected the place beneath his arm just under his lowest rib. The swimming shorts were stuck to his buttocks.

I kept my back to them while I wriggled my sundress over the top of my damp bikini and packed my stuff into my bag. I put on my sunglasses, stepped into my sandals and clipped across the paving stones set in the lawn back through the conservatory doors into the air-conditioned cool of the hotel.

I held my head high and did not look back.

CHAPTER THREE

In my room, I arranged the pillows at the foot of the bed, and lay on my front with my face resting on my crossed arms. I watched some Italian television, but I must have fallen asleep. When there was a knocking at the door, I didn't know where I was. For one giddying moment, I thought I was still in the hospital coming round from an anaesthetic and that maybe everything I thought had happened had not. Perhaps when I opened my eyes, there would be a healthy, dark-haired baby swaddled in the cot beside my bed nuzzling his fist and blinking back at me. My heart accelerated at the thought and I felt a squeeze of hope that it might be true and at the same time a rush of panic in case it was not.

I rolled on to my side and opened my eyes and recognized the colour of the paint on the hotel-room wall and the gilt-framed still life of fruit and wine, and I struggled to contain the disappointment, heavy as a boulder inside me.

The knocking came again, a little more loudly.

I rolled off the bed and tried to arrange my face into a

normal expression before I opened the door. It was May, my lovely sister, all flushed from her shower and made up beautifully. She smelled of shampoo and baby powder. I saw a flicker of concern cross her face when she saw me, and I smiled, but my lips didn't feel as if they were in the right place.

'You're not ready yet?' she asked. I looked down at myself. The damp imprint of my bikini was silhouetted on the sundress and I knew my hair must be wild where I'd lain on it. May reached out and smoothed my hair with the palm of her hand. 'Are you OK, Sarah?'

'Mmm.' I nodded brightly. 'I must've dropped off.'

'You've got pillow creases on your cheek.'

'Sorry.' I reached up to touch the hot ridges in my skin. 'I'm sorry.'

'Shhh,' said May.

She was wearing a floaty, pale-green top over white jeans that were a little on the tight side.

'You look lovely, May,' I said. 'Is it late?'

'We booked the taxi for eight,' she said. 'Remember? So there's time for a drink in town before the restaurant?'

I remembered.

'What time is it now?'

'Quarter to. It's OK, don't worry. Neil's gone down, and if the driver won't wait we'll find another. You take your time.'

May walked over to the open window and gazed out at the sunset on the sea. Inside, a mosquito hummed. I reached down to scratch a trio of bites on the back of my left calf, then I opened the wardrobe door and took out a navy maxi-dress. In the mirror fastened to the inside of the door, I could see May, reflected, watching me, rubbing her lower lip with the tip of her index finger like she always did when she was worried.

'You were thinking about the baby again, weren't you?' she asked.

I shook my head. 'I was dreaming, that's all.'

'Has something happened?'

'No.'

'You haven't spoken to Laurie?'

'No.'

I pulled the damp dress off over my head and folded it over the bed-frame to dry.

'Did he text you? I thought he might text you. I know you told him to leave you alone but I thought . . .'

I shook my head.

'No, he didn't.'

I turned my back while I took off the bikini top and slipped the blue dress over my head.

'Well, anyway, you're looking better,' May said so brightly that I knew the opposite was true. 'Are you feeling any better?'

'I'm fine,' I said.

'Sarah . . .'

'Honestly, I am.'

'I shouldn't have left you by yourself in the garden earlier. I knew I should have stayed with you.'

I wriggled the dress down until it hung properly with the straps crossing my back and sitting in the dip in my shoulders.

'Actually I was glad you left me. I had a nice time by

the pool,' I said. 'I swam and I sunbathed. I met some English people.'

'Oh yes?'

'A man and his little boy.'

I sensed May tense. I knew what she was thinking: that the man and his child had reminded me of what I had lost. I knew her concern was borne entirely of love, but at the same time I hated being the cause of her anxiety. I carried on quickly, as if the obvious parallel had never entered my mind: 'He's not that little, the child, he's nearly seven. I watched him for a few minutes in the pool while his father took a phone call. He's called Jamie, the boy.'

'And what about his mum? Did you meet her?'

'No, she isn't with them. Jamie said she'd gone away.'

'Maybe she's visiting friends or had to work while they're on holiday,' May said.

'Maybe.'

May stepped back to look at me.

'You're a bit burnt,' she said. She picked up her bag, rummaged inside and passed me the jar of expensive after-sun cream she'd bought in the airport duty-free shop. 'Use this.'

Obediently, I unscrewed the lid and dipped my finger into the lotion. It was cool and sweet-smelling. I smoothed it on to my sun-hot face, concentrating on the half-circles of parched flesh above and beneath my eyes. I tried to smile at May and this time I must have been more successful because she smiled back at me.

'I shouldn't have left you by yourself,' she said softly. 'I should have looked after you better.'

CHAPTER FOUR

The next days passed slowly. During daylight hours, May and I stayed in the hotel grounds. I would have been happy to spend every moment beneath the trees by the pool, but the heat always became too much for May and she didn't want to leave me on my own so, every afternoon, when she began to puff and flag, we both went inside.

We ate oily fish, olives and tomato salad in the chill of the air-conditioned dining room and then sat on reclining chairs in the deep dappled shade of the terrace, listening to piped music – an Italian tenor singing love songs that we didn't understand. We sipped iced water, switched away the flies and talked of this and that, nothing much. A large fan blew warm air towards us, turned its face away, and then returned in a soporific rhythm.

As the afternoons wore on, and the heat became a little less intense, May and I followed a steep, winding footpath cut into the cliff at the back of the hotel. It led down between waist-high walls of sharded grey, volcanic rock with little silver and lavender-coloured plants creeping and growing in its crevices to a private bathing area. A wooden platform stuck out over the green-blue sea that lapped against the rockface. The sea was teeming with busy little fish. I liked to sit on the edge of the platform, with my legs hanging down over the cool water, watching the way the sunlight dazzled the waves, its patterns fragmenting and dancing. I liked the smell of the sea and the feel of the lively air immediately above it. May lay on a towel on the platform, reading her book. I stared at the facing coastline across the bay. Sometimes it was very clear, I could make out trees and buildings; at other times the heat haze over the water obscured it from view.

It was so peaceful, and I didn't have to talk to anyone or explain anything or even think too much about my situation.

May's husband, Neil, was a journalist with the Manchester-based news and features agency NWM. He had been sent to Sicily to work on the shoot of a drama that was being filmed there. Neil's role was to interview the stars, the producer and director and write background features to distribute to the media, generating publicity in advance of the film's release. It was easy for me to be in Sicily with him and May. I didn't want to be anywhere else. I certainly didn't want to go home.

Home was the house I shared with Laurie. Home would mean endless talking, negotiations and explanations and, in Laurie's terminology, turning the spotlight on the issues that were affecting our relationship. He, I knew, would be suffering from a combination of guilt and frustration that would manifest itself in a stream of tiny accusations towards me, pinpricks of anger disguised as expressions of concern. Because, what he would be thinking was that, if I had let him look after me, if I'd shared my feelings with him after the baby, none of this would have happened.

In all the time I was with Laurie, which was all my adult life, I had been regarded more as his girlfriend than as an individual in my own right. We were Laurie-and-Sarah. He didn't mean to be demanding or controlling, but there was more of him than there was of me. He was older, cleverer, more knowledgeable and gregarious; I was quieter, shyer, less educated, and I was happy to swim in his wake. I couldn't remember how I was supposed to look, or be, or even what my voice sounded like when I was on my own, without him. Laurie had always looked after me and looked out for me, but something changed after our son was stillborn. I hadn't wanted to analyse my feelings as he did; I'd just wanted to be left alone. And he, feeling abandoned, had turned to Rosita.

I was too tired to deal with Laurie. Sicily felt safe. It felt distant. It felt like a bubble, and I would have been happy to stay there for ever.

CHAPTER FIVE

Then suddenly everything changed. The lead in the film Neil was working on collapsed on set and was hospitalized. The official line was that he had suffered heat stroke but Neil suspected it was more serious than that. The actor was flown back to America, the film was put on hold and Neil was free to go back to Manchester.

That meant May and I would have to leave, too. We only had a few days left, and Sicily became even more precious to me. I could not bear the thought of leaving.

On one of our last evenings we decided, for a change, to eat at the hotel. May and I went down together. The terrace was illuminated by fairy lights and candles in the necks of empty wine bottles centred on the tables. Large, pale moths danced in the areas of light and then disappeared. The swimming pool glowed an artificial blue in the black garden and far away across the bay the lights of isolated villas and farms twinkled like stars. I stood for a moment and gazed out. Moonlight trickled on the sea and a small boat bobbed along the coastline, dropping nets by lamplight.

Neil was waiting for us at our table. He stood when he saw us and smiled.

'Hello, you,' he said, and he stepped forward to take my sister's hands. They kissed quietly, and without fuss, and I looked at my feet.

When they drew apart they were still smiling into each other's eyes like lovers who hadn't seen one another for years, rather than the twenty minutes or so they had been apart. It wasn't their fault, but their intimacy humiliated me.

We sat down, scraping the metal feet of the chairs on the paving slabs. Within moments, a waiter was at our table, putting down a chilled glass jug of iced water, a little wicker basket of bread and a bowl of flavoured olives.

'How did work go?' I asked Neil. 'Did you get everything you needed?'

'More or less.' He pulled a sardonic expression. May and I exchanged smiles. Neil was always self-deprecating but I knew he was good at his job. There was a big demand for the stories he generated, which weren't always the kind Laurie approved of. Sometimes there had been friction between the two men when they met at family gatherings or social occasions. I'd tried to stay neutral, but had felt I ought to side with Laurie, out of loyalty. Having dinner with Neil every night in Sicily had made me realize what a gentle, funny person he was. I was glad my sister was married to such a lovely man. I wished I'd realized sooner.

He and May began to talk about something else, some friend of theirs who was having family problems. I tried not to listen to their conversation. I concentrated on watching people come and go inside the hotel. My eyes followed an incoming couple, a frail man wearing a fedora and a younger man – his son, perhaps – who accompanied him. They exchanged a few friendly words with the concierge, picked up their key and walked over to the elevator shaft. As they did so the lift doors slid apart. Out stepped a small boy with large ears. It was the little boy from the pool, Jamie. I hadn't seen him since that day. He was wearing clean but crumpled trousers and a T-shirt that was rather too big for him. He looked as if he had been woken when he would have rather slept on. Behind was his father, wearing jeans and a baggy shirt with the sleeves rolled up. Alexander was followed by a tall, smart, skull-faced man in a cream linen suit who carried, under his arm, a leather case, about the size of a laptop.

The two men stopped in the foyer. The skull-faced man patted Alexander on the back and they spoke privately for another moment, their heads close together, and it was clear from their faces that their discussion was serious. Jamie sank against his father's thigh and tugged at his shirt. Eventually, the men pulled apart. Alexander took an envelope from his pocket and gave it to the other man. He opened the envelope, looked inside, shook hands with Alexander, ruffled the top of Jamie's head, and left.

Alexander watched him go and ran a hand through his hair. He looked exhausted. I could see the child's mouth moving. He pulled his father's hand in frustration and the man looked down at him as if he had forgotten he was there.

He checked his watch and had a word with the concierge. She gestured towards the garden, suggesting they ate in the hotel restaurant. I watched as they came through the glass doors. The maître d' went over to them. He shrugged his shoulders apologetically, turned the palms of both hands towards the sky and raised them. What could he do? All the tables were taken or reserved.

I saw Jamie's face fall. He sank a little into himself. The poor child was tired and hungry, and I couldn't bear the thought of him having to wait any longer to eat. It was late enough already.

I glanced at May and Neil. I wanted to ask if they'd mind, but they were still engrossed in one another, so I took matters into my own hands. I stood and crossed the terrace, between the tables and the overhanging lights, to where the man and boy stood. I steadied myself against the back of a chair, cleared my throat to attract their attention and said: 'There's room at our table. You could join us, if you like.'

Alexander turned to look at me. I could tell from the slight dilation of his eyes that he remembered me. I pressed my fingers into the cool wood of the chair.

'No,' he said. 'Thank you, but no. We'll walk along the road. We'll find a pizzeria.'

'But I'm hungry now,' said Jamie.

'There are plenty of places near by.'

The maître d' raised his eyebrows. The closest

restaurant was a couple of kilometres away and the roads were unlit, without pavements, and were race-tracks for Sicilian young-bloods in the dark.

'Dad, my legs are *tired*.'

Alexander glanced at me then over to our table.

'We couldn't intrude . . .'

'It would be no intrusion. It's just me and my sister and brother-in-law.'

He opened his mouth to raise another objection.

'It's up to you,' I said.

The waiter, tactfully, studied the list attached to his clipboard. The boy swung on his father's hand and pleaded. He said he was going to die of hunger. He said he didn't want to walk another step. He said Mummy would have given him something to eat by now. That seemed to be the deciding argument.

'OK,' said Alexander. 'If you're sure, Sarah.'

I was surprised he remembered my name, but I said yes, I was sure, and took them to the table.

May and Neil looked up and exchanged glances as we approached.

I introduced everyone and explained how I had met Alexander and Jamie at the pool and that there was nowhere else for them to sit. May said, as I had known she would, that of course they should join us. She said it would be lovely to have some company for a change. She made such an effort to make Jamie feel welcome that I knew she was thinking about his missing mother, and I wanted to hug her.

May, Neil and I shifted our chairs a little to make room. The waiter brought more cutlery, bread and water and, after a few moments, we all settled in our new places. I felt a little nervous. I sat up very straight and couldn't think of anything to say.

Jamie slumped down in his chair and put his thumb in his mouth. He seemed different from the self-assured little boy I'd spoken to in the pool, much younger and more vulnerable. Alexander said: 'He's ready for bed. It's my fault – we've driven a long way today and we haven't had anything to eat since breakfast.'

'Where've you been?' asked Neil.

'Inland. I had some business to attend to.'

'Oh yes?' May asked, but Alexander didn't elaborate.

'You've been away for a while,' I said quietly. 'I haven't seen you in the hotel.'

Alexander nodded.

'Over a week,' he said. 'But I've done all I can now. We're here to relax for a couple of days before we fly home.'

'It's a beautiful spot,' said Neil.

'It is.'

'I'm hungry,' Jamie whined.

May smiled fondly at the boy and said she always hated it if she didn't eat, especially after a long drive, and Jamie frowned.

'I was bored. Dad was talking to this stupid man for ages,' he said.

'That's normally my prerogative,' Neil said, 'talking to stupid men.'

'And I *told* him I was hungry,' said Jamie.

May pulled a sympathetic face.

'But still they kept on talking. And they wouldn't let me sit with them on the balcony.'

'Oh dear.'

'They were drinking beer. And the man was smoking. My mummy says smoking makes you die.'

'Eat some bread,' Alexander said. 'Here, you can dip it in the oil.'

'I don't like oil.'

May smiled.

'You're here on your own?' she asked innocently.

Alexander nodded.

The table shook. Jamie was swinging his feet, kicking the table leg.

'Jamie, stop that,' said Alexander.

'Mummy's gone away,' Jamie said. 'She went away and she hasn't come back.'

'Oh, I'm sorry,' May said.

'She didn't want to live with Dad any more because he was so mean to her. That's what my Grandma Ginny says.'

Alexander put his hand on Jamie's knee.

'Stop it,' he said, more sharply.

'And now Daddy's always cross and we never have proper dinner and everything's shit.'

'Enough.'

Just one word, and Alexander did not raise his voice but he said it with such authority that I caught my breath. There was a silence. Even the insects seemed to go quiet. Jamie stopped kicking and looked up at his father. The man looked down at the boy. They held one another's gaze. I hoped the child was not going to cry. I noticed Alexander's fingers were trembling, casting shaky shadows on Jamie's knees.

'What shall we have?' May asked breezily. 'I fancy a pizza.'

During the meal, Neil and Alexander talked about their work. Neil played down the high-profile aspects of his career to draw out Alexander, who told us he was a stonemason who ran his own business. He shared Neil's passion for geology and they had a mutual admiration for many of the classical Greek and Roman architects. They discussed the ancient buildings on Ortygia, and Alexander was interested in hearing which had been modified with false façades or other artifices for the film. I tried to engage Jamie, but he made it clear he did not want to talk to me. Still, it gave me pleasure to watch him eat. He wolfed down his pasta and then fell asleep, curled up like a puppy in his chair, orange-coloured sauce smears all over his cheeks and chin. Alexander covered him with his fleece and then he and Neil resumed their conversation.

I listened attentively, but Alexander gave away very little about himself outside his professional life and did not mention the gone-away wife. He didn't say where he and Jamie had been for the past week or so either, nor did he elaborate on the 'business' to which he'd had to attend. The less he said, the more I wanted to know. I had ordered spaghetti alla Norma. The tomato and aubergine sauce was peppery and delicious, but it went cold on my plate because my attention was with Alexander. Waiting staff moved around us like ghosts, bringing food, pouring wine, clearing dishes. The other guests faded into the evening, the murmurs of their conversations dissolving into the night air. It felt as if we were on our own little island at the table. May dabbed her lips with her serviette and undid the button on her trousers. The top of her arm was wide, cream-coloured. I rested my face against her shoulder and felt safe in the talcum and vanilla scent of her. From that pure place I looked across the table to the darkness that was Alexander. He swallowed his wine and sliced his calf's liver. He ate his meat before his vegetables, enjoying it like a true carnivore. He must have sensed me watching him, because he looked over.

'What about you, Sarah? What brought you here?' he asked as he wiped his plate with a piece of bread.

This time, when he said my name out loud, I jumped.

I'd been asked this question several times in Sicily and thought I'd become immune to it, only now my cheeks burned hot. May stepped in to explain, as she always did. 'I invited Sarah to join us, to keep me company while Neil was busy working,' she said. 'I know how lucky I am to come to these lovely places with my husband, but it can get awfully lonely for me, being on my own all the time.'

Alexander nodded.

I was grateful to my sister, but felt compelled to put the record straight. I wanted to be honest with Alexander, even though the truth was awkward.

'Actually,' I said, 'my partner has been having an affair with a friend of mine, and May and Neil went to a lot of trouble to arrange for me to come out here for a break, so I could get away from them both.'

My voice sounded strange, brittle and panicky. May tensed. Across the table I saw Neil's smile fade into an expression of discomfort. Had I spoken too loudly? Had I said too much?

'Sarah' – May whispered so quietly that the word was really just a breath in my ear – 'don't . . .'

I pretended I hadn't heard her and smiled brightly to show that I had not said those things because I wanted, or expected, sympathy. I took a good drink of wine and exhaled, a little shakily.

'Oh.' Alexander gave no indication of being either surprised or sympathetic. 'So you're here to decide whether to swallow your pride?'

He looked at me. I saw the waxing and waning flame of the candle reflected in his eyes.

'Nothing's decided yet,' said May. 'Sarah needs time to think.'

I wound my serviette round my fingers.

'You can't go back,' Alexander said. He was looking directly into my eyes. 'When something like that happens, you should never go back.'

The waiter came to take our plates and May turned the conversation to less controversial matters. I stayed silent. I sipped my wine. I thought about what Alexander had said.

Until that moment, there on the restaurant terrace of the little Sicilian seaside hotel, I had not seriously considered leaving Laurie for good. I hadn't seen it as an option and I was certain he hadn't either. I'd assumed, as everyone else assumed, that there would be an awkward few months of reconciliation culminating in some kind of reordering of our lives. Laurie would make some grand gesture. Perhaps we would marry or move house; perhaps we would do what everyone said we should do and try for another child to help us move on from the one we had lost. None of these alternatives cheered me. The future with Laurie was like a hill I was too exhausted to climb.

But now I realized there was another option. Alexander had shown me. Leaving was easy; I had already left. So long as I did not go back, I would not even have to endure a sad and painful breaking-up conversation with Laurie or another tearful scene with Rosita. If I stayed away, there would be no possibility of my succumbing to their entreaties or worrying about the years that were already behind us having been wasted time. My emotions tipped like a seesaw suddenly weighted on the other side, the heavy end hitting the ground with a thump.

I felt a rush of adrenaline, a shocking, pure thrill like the sensation of jumping into cold water. I had been liberated. There was no decision to be made. I was free.

I finished my wine and held my glass out to Neil. He half-filled it.

'Steady on,' said May. 'Don't forget we have to be up early to catch the bus.'

'Where are you going?' asked Alexander.

'Taormina. It's a hotel excursion.'

'I've heard the amphitheatre is incredible.'

'It's a must-see,' said Neil. 'They shot some daybreak scenes up there. It's stunning.'

'We have to make the most of our time,' said May. 'We won't be here much longer. We've been so lazy, we've been here for weeks and haven't done anything cultural, and now we're having to pack everything we want to see into the last few days.'

'It's always the way,' said Alexander.

He checked his watch. The backs of his hands and his forearms were covered in dark hair. His clothes were baggy on him. He must have lost weight recently. He looked down at his sleeping child. Jamie's pale hair stuck up and his eyes flickered beneath their lids. I felt a pang of something deep and tender: he needed someone to keep him company when his father was doing business, somebody to make sure he ate regularly and slept when he needed to sleep. The maternal urge I felt towards the little boy made me deeply uncomfortable. I longed to touch him, to pick him up and hold him and comfort him, but he wasn't mine to hold. I had no child to hold and there was no way, for me, to relieve the tug I felt towards Jamie. He had a mother of his own, even if she wasn't there with him. He was none of my business. I drank my wine as if it were water, hoping it would anaesthetize me.

Alexander yawned. 'Thank you for your hospitality,' he said, 'but it's time I put my son to bed.'

'Stay and have some more wine,' I said, reaching across the table for the bottle. I didn't want him to take Jamie away.

Neil said: 'We normally finish with a Limoncello as a *digestif*. You'd be most welcome . . .'

Alexander shook his head. He took a number of

notes out of his wallet and put them on the table. May and Neil made a token protest, but he waved it away.

'Thank you, all,' he said. 'It was a very pleasant evening.'

He stood up, and as he did so he rested his hand on the bare skin of my upper arm and squeezed. He touched me for a moment; it was merely a 'goodbye' less formal than a handshake, less intimate than a kiss, and perhaps it was also a small gesture of solidarity. Either way, it moved something in me. It was only a tiny movement, like a leaf falling to the ground, but it was the first time in months that I felt myself relax a little. My body softened as if something hard and solid had been released from inside, and with the exorcism came a sense of relief. I wanted to sigh and lean forward and rest my head in my arms. I smiled up at Alexander.

'Good night,' I said softly.

Alexander took the child in his arms, a bundle of skinny limbs, cropped hair and shoes that seemed far too big for his ankles, and he said good night.

I watched him cross the garden and the hotel foyer, Jamie's hand swinging like a flower in the wind beside his father's thigh. The maître d' opened the glass door into the hotel and Alexander passed through with a nod of thanks. I watched the light of the lift enclose them and the doors close behind them.

May topped up our glasses and then put the empty bottle upside down in the cooler. We were quiet for a few moments.

Then May said: 'Poor little lad. He should've been tucked up hours ago.'

'He'll be OK,' Neil said. 'He'll be right as rain in the morning.'

He scraped some semi-molten wax from the base of the bottle that held the candle with his fingernail and moulded it between his fingers.

'Alexander seems a decent sort,' he said.

May picked up her cardigan and pulled it around her shoulders.

'Didn't you think it was a bit awkward when Jamie said those things about his mother leaving? I didn't know what to say.'

'I expect it was Grandma Whatever-her-name-was putting ideas into his head,' said Neil. 'Some people always have to find someone else to blame.'

May nodded. She glanced at me and glanced away again.

'It's a shame when families break up like that. Especially when there are little ones involved.'

'Perhaps it'll sort itself out in time,' said Neil.

'Perhaps. He didn't want to talk about the wife though, did he?'

'Maybe he's been so hurt by her he doesn't feel he *can* talk about her,' I suggested.

'Well, that's a possibility, certainly,' Neil said.

'Definitely,' said May.

There was silence again. It felt as if our little private table-island were adrift, miles from anywhere.

May pulled her cardigan tighter across her chest.

'It's a bit cooler tonight,' she said. 'Do you think the weather's turning?'

'Oh, I doubt it,' said Neil.

We all watched the candle flicker and die in the slightest of breezes and, as it did so, a chill ran through me.

'Ooh,' said May, giving me a little hug. 'I felt that. Did somebody just walk on your grave?'

CHAPTER SIX

I was up early the next morning and in the pool by 7 a.m. Each time I reached the far end I promised myself that, when I turned, Alexander would be there, watching, but he wasn't. There was no sign of either him or Jamie; only one of the gardeners was out, cleaning the paths. After thirty lengths I gave up and went back to my room to shower, and then May and I had a good breakfast of bread, cheese, fruit and coffee before queuing up in the foyer for the tour. Next to the volcanic Mount Etna, Taormina was the most famous attraction on that side of Sicily.

May was chatty; I was tired. I hadn't slept well. My hair was still damp when we climbed aboard the minibus. Our driver, who was called Salvatore, took us in and then out of Siracusa on a long, straight road through some forgettable countryside, reclaimed marshland and then past massive factories and chemical works, with Etna gradually dominating more of the skyline ahead of us. I closed my eyes and drifted for a while. I had a dream I'd had ever since the baby was born. I was in the playground, at primary school. I was eight or nine years old and wearing a grey tunic and a polo shirt that was itchy under the armpits and short white socks with brown sandals and I was skipping, jumping over a long rope that was being turned by two of my friends. I loved skipping and I was happy. The other girls were turning the rope in time to the rhythm of the words they were chanting: *Sarah and Laurie sitting in a tree, K–I–S–S–I–N–G. First comes love and then comes marriage, then along comes Sarah with a baby carriage.* They chanted and turned the rope faster and faster and I jumped faster to keep up and I was laughing and breathless and flushed with joy. Then the singing faded and the playground and the children disappeared and there I was grown up, alone somewhere, standing with my hands on the handle of an old-fashioned hooded pram. The pram was well sprung; it rocked on its big wheels. I bent down and leaned forward and pulled the blanket gently back, a smile on my lips and a clutch of pleasure in my heart, anticipating seeing my sleeping child snug in his little blue sleep-suit.

But the pram was empty.

I'd had the same dream a hundred times and the pram was always empty and each time it shocked me.

I must have cried out, because May nudged me.

'Hey,' she whispered, shaking my arm. 'Sarah, shhh.'

I struggled to fight off the dream and remember where I was.

'Were you having a nightmare, love?'

'Mmm.'

May pulled a sympathetic face, then took my head

between her two hands, pulled me close to her and kissed my forehead.

'You'll be all right,' she said.

'I know.'

'You've been through a lot. It takes a while to get over these things is all.'

'Yes.'

'Look,' she said, nodding in the direction of the window. 'There it is.'

I followed her gaze and, through the windscreen of the bus, beyond the cedar trees and the red-roofed villas, saw the town of Taormina, clinging precariously to the top of a high, impossibly steep-sided hill like icing on a very tall cake.

'Spectacular, eh?'

'Oh it is; it's like something in a fairytale.'

May smiled. 'We're going to have a good day,' she said.

The bus crawled steeply upwards along a winding road into the centre of the pretty little town, one-time home of D. H. Lawrence, according to May's guidebook. It was obvious why he had chosen to live there. It was, despite the tourists and the cars, exquisite. May and I drank Orangina and ate slices of salty mozzarella and spinach pizza at a table outside a shaded café surrounded by trinket and postcard shops. We fed a little pregnant ginger cat that was about our legs. We strolled through the light and shadow of the gardens where Lawrence liked to walk and sat on a bench dedicated to him. The trees were full of starlings, the fountains splished and tinkled and painted railings gave way to precipitous views over the roofs of hotels and apartment blocks. We took some photographs and walked further uphill, along a narrow road lined with shops and canopied kiosks selling puppets and souvenirs, to the gate that led into the amphitheatre park.

We bought our tickets and followed the climbing path into the amphitheatre, walking up its slopes and sitting on the ranks of benches carved out of the hillside. Neither of us said much. The place was too beautiful for words.

We were a few rows down from the upper rim of the theatre. My clothes pinched my flesh and nipped at my sunburn. I eased my thumb along the length of my bikini strap. We gazed down at the stage and beyond, through a partly fallen back-wall, to the bright haze wrapped like a shawl around Etna's shoulders, and closer, to the little villages tumbling down the slopes of other mountains, the windows of their buildings illuminated by the sun. Everything was apricot, sand-pink and gold.

May put her sunglasses on top of her head to keep her hair out of her eyes and took some more photographs.

'People won't believe this back home,' she said. 'They simply won't believe it.'

We watched a group of children down on the stage many feet below us. They were wearing plastic gladiator helmets and carrying swords. A couple of young adults in blue T-shirts were organizing the children in an excitable and noisy fashion, with the help of a megaphone. I shaded my eyes with my hand. One of the children, a skinny, fair-haired boy with sticking-out ears who was hanging back, reminded me of Jamie. I squinted but I couldn't be sure. I looked around, but there was no sign of Alexander. I told myself not to be ridiculous. If he'd been planning to come to Taormina, he'd have mentioned it.

'I'm too hot,' May said. She stretched out her legs. 'I need a drink.'

'I don't think there is anywhere here.'

'I'll walk down into the town. They'll let me back in again if I keep my ticket, won't they?'

I supposed they would.

'Are you coming?'

I shook my head. 'Do you mind if I stay? It's so lovely.'

'Will you be all right?'

'May . . .'

'OK, sorry. I can't help being a big sister.'

'And I'm very glad you're mine, but stop worrying.'

May gave me the guidebook. 'I'll meet you back here in an hour,' she said. 'Shall I bring you a Coke?'

'Yes, please.'

I watched her make her way back down to the bottom of the amphitheatre. There were few tourists around because of the time of day. After a while, the sun burning my arms and legs, I stood up and went the other way, climbing to the very top of the enormous bowl carved out of the hillside. My feet were dusty and my heart beat with the exertion. I wandered into the wooded area beyond, seeking shade.

It was deserted.

The area was rimmed by railings, marking the edge of the park. I stepped forward carefully, one foot at a time. I didn't want to get too close in case the drop on the other side was sheer, but when I reached the metal barrier I was reassured. The ground did not fall away steeply but sloped downwards, and was interrupted by sprawling cacti with huge, plate-shaped leaves and red flowers, and scrubby trees. I leaned on the fence and when I looked over, way, way below was an idyllic little island surrounded by sea so clear and perfectly blue it made my heart ache. I stared out and was lost in the day.

It was pleasant to be alone. I drifted like a feather on the breeze, my mind full of blues and whites, and when he came, it was as if he had come from nowhere. I didn't hear his footsteps but suddenly he was beside me; I jumped and dropped the guidebook. It spun as it fell on the other side of the fence and landed spread-eagled amongst the pebbles and dirt a little further down the hill.

'Sorry,' said Alexander. 'I didn't mean to scare you.'

'It was my fault,' I said.

'I could climb over and fetch it back.'

'No!' I cried, then said more quietly: 'No, really, it's all right.'

He took off his sunglasses. He looked exhausted. He said: 'I saw you come up here. I was pretty sure it was you.'

'It was.'

'I just . . .' he said, and then he swallowed and turned his head away.

I waited a moment, but Alexander didn't collect his thoughts. He seemed to be lost somewhere.

'Is that Jamie on the stage with the other children?' I asked.

Alexander nodded and checked his watch. 'He tagged on to the group. He's fed up being with me all the time. He wanted to be with other kids. They're doing a little play in fifteen minutes.'

'Then we have fifteen minutes,' I said.

I didn't know what had come over me; that was not the kind of thing I ever said. I was the shy one, the quiet, introspective one, I never took the lead at anything, but the words came from nowhere into my mind and out of my mouth. Being with Alexander was imperative. Since the previous evening, since he had squeezed my shoulder, my mind had been full of him.

He licked his lips and I wondered if already I had gone too far, or if, maybe, he had not understood what I meant.

'Are you sure?' he asked and I stepped forward.

There was an irresistible pull between us like two magnets hefting together, defying gravity. You couldn't see it, but it was real, it was there. We fell on to and into one another in the deep shade on the wooded hilltop. It was not something that could be refused or denied. It was inevitable.

CHAPTER SEVEN

It was over in moments. He groaned and his breath burned hot beneath my ear and I was weak in his arms; I was spent. I felt as if I were bruised all over. I had never felt so healthy. I was giddy with my own daring. I felt brazen and desirable and strong and alive.

I felt *so* alive.

I breathed into his neck. I breathed him in. My back was pressed against the railings. I knew that when I looked over my shoulder in the bathroom mirror later, a narrow, horizontal bruise that stretched the width of my hips would exactly match the diameter of the metal fencing behind me. I slid my legs down his legs and found my balance. The dusty soil was warm and soft beneath my feet and the insides of my thighs were raw and slippery. I wiped between my legs with my dress and straightened it and he stepped back, away. Alexander took another step backwards, wiped his mouth with the back of his hand. He watched me.

'Are you all right?'

'Yes, I'm fine.'

He picked up my sandals, dusted them off, passed them to me and held my elbow as I stood on one foot and then the other to put them on. Now I felt shy, a little embarrassed.

'Let's walk,' he said.

We walked very slowly, very closely, with propriety, like a couple who have been together for decades. I could smell him in the heat that came up from his skin; a smell powerful with intimacy. To other people we must have looked like husband and wife, not people who hardly knew one another. I put my sunglasses on. I wanted to press up to him, fall into him, feel his hands over me like the sea.

We stopped at a viewpoint over the cliff, close to the tour party. The voice of the guide drifted over to us. He was explaining the disparity between the levels of the two seas that met below us. One was higher than the other. It made no sense, this tidal step in the water, and the ancient people explained it by telling a story of a giant clam which, twice a day, swallowed the water of one sea and then spat it out again. The Americans chuckled. I was interested in the story but I could not concentrate. I was prickly with Alexander. We gazed out at the horizon. I half-wished for the world to end there, right there, when we were still strangers and everything was perfect between us.

Alexander ran the back of his fingers down the curve of my neck. He was exploring me.

He said: 'I've been thinking about what you told me.'

'Mmm?'

'About your man and your friend. What they did.'

'I probably made it sound worse than it was,' I said. I did not like to be reminded of Laurie, especially not then. 'You don't know the whole story.'

'I know enough. Don't go back to Manchester. When somebody lets you down like that . . .' He sighed. 'My wife, Genevieve, when I met her, she was in love with someone else. She told me; she was honest about it. I married her anyway. I thought I could make her change how she felt but I couldn't.'

'She loved you enough to have your child.'

He didn't reply but gazed out into the distance.

'There was never going to be a happy ending for Genevieve and me,' he said. 'I see that now. And she's gone. It's over.' He rubbed his hand beneath his ribcage. 'It was all a waste of time. It was all pointless.'

'You've got Jamie.'

'Yes. Yes, I have. He's the only good thing to have come out of it.'

I couldn't think of anything to say that wouldn't sound insincere or clichéd but it didn't matter because Alexander had gone into his thoughts again.

'What do you do, Sarah?' he asked eventually. 'For a job, I mean.'

'I work for an engineering company. I'm a secretary.'

'Do you like it?'

'It's all right. Only, Rosita works there too. My friend. The one who . . .'

'Oh. So you won't want to go back there?'

'I don't know. I haven't really thought it through.'

Alexander nodded and was silent for a moment. Then he said: 'I can't do it all on my own, not work and still be there for Jamie. I need someone to help me.'

'Of course you do.'

'What I mean to say is . . .' He paused a moment, then he said: 'You could come and live with me.'

I laughed. Honestly, I thought he was joking. I laughed for a moment, then I stopped and I looked at Alexander. The fingers of his left hand were moving over the place beneath his right arm where he was scarred. He wasn't joking. He was serious.

'I thought it would be better without her, but since Genevieve's been gone everything has been difficult,' he said.

'Is that why you came to Sicily? To get away?'

He sighed and a shadow passed across his face.

'No.'

I waited. He did not elaborate. He seemed to lose himself and when he spoke again he had lost his train of thought or else he had chosen not to say any more about why he had brought Jamie to Sicily.

He said: 'It'll be the same when we go back unless . . .'

The fingers of his left hand made a claw and scratched at the wound beneath his shirt. I tried not to watch.

'Unless you come,' he said. 'Then things will be different.'

'You don't know anything about me.'

'I know enough. I think you're honest. I like you. I can't afford to pay much but I can offer you a roof over your head and you can help look after Jamie and the house and . . .' He stared away into the distance. 'It could be a fresh start for you.'

I nodded.

'School starts again in a couple of weeks. It's going to be hard for me to get back from work in time to pick Jamie up. I have to know that somebody I trust will be there to meet him. If you were there . . . If you came . . .'

A tiny stain of blood seeped from the scar into the fabric of his shirt. It hypnotized me. I watched and it spread, making the shape of a crescent moon. His fingers finally relaxed.

He said: 'What is there to lose, Sarah? If it doesn't work out you can go back to Manchester. And you never know. We might be good for one another.'

I leaned forward and, even though I didn't know him very well, I kissed his lips as gently as I could.

'OK,' I said.

Back home, my family and friends thought it was a terrible idea.

They said I was overreacting to the situation, that I shouldn't risk myself on a stranger, that I would be vulnerable on my own, away from everyone I knew and everything I held dear. They said I wasn't thinking straight – it was my hormones, they were still all over the place from the pregnancy; it was depression; it was grief. Even considering moving in with a man about whom I knew next to nothing was stupid and dangerous and so completely out of character that maybe I was having some kind of breakdown. What if Alexander was a conman, or worse? Even if he had not actively abused his wife, she had her reasons for leaving him – and to leave the child, too, he *must* have done something awful. He may be one of those Jekyll and Hyde characters, a charmer on the surface and an insecure and possessive control-freak on the inside. Those types always isolated their victims and then dominated them. If the abuse was not physical, it would be emotional and verbal.

It wasn't only my family. I hadn't been back to work since the baby, but my line manager, Shelley, came round and took me out for coffee. She told me that Rosita had handed in her notice so I could return to my post without having to see her. It was her decision to go. She was entirely aware of how badly she'd behaved and had done the noble thing by removing herself from the picture. Shelley reached across the café table and took my hand in hers.

'Coming back to work might be the best thing. When you're feeling a bit low, you're better off being with people you know and trust,' she said. 'I know it'll be difficult, hon, but I'll be there to help you.'

I did not point out that the person I knew and trusted better than anyone else in the world was the one who had hurt me the worst.

I refused to see Laurie. I was afraid, if I saw him, my resolve might be softened. I deleted his emails and his texts but I did speak to him once, on the telephone. He was calm, gentle and perfectly frank. He said he would do whatever it took to repair the damage and to heal our relationship. He did not demean either of us with cheap excuses or apologies. His sincerity was clear and I understood that he was finding the situation at least as painful as I was, but I was strangely unaffected by his words. I felt neither sympathy nor regret. My mind was made up and my ticket was booked.

My mother begged me to reconsider. She insisted I see the doctor, who prescribed a slightly higher dosage of anti-depressants despite my insistence that I was recovering – in fact, I had not taken a single pill since Sicily. Mum, or maybe Laurie, must also have mentioned to Dr Rooney that they were worried about my behaviour because he recommended I seek counselling. I listened politely, but saw no point going down that route. Surely it's natural to be sad when your baby is stillborn? Wouldn't there be something wrong with me if I *hadn't* been a bit out of sorts? He said he'd contact the hospital and they'd get in touch with me directly to arrange an appointment, and I concurred, thinking that letters are easy to ignore.

My father said the whole idea of running off down south was bloody stupid and he'd give it a week, fortnight at best. May, the only person who knew the whole story, said it was sex that was pulling me towards Alexander and a maternal instinct with no outlet that attracted me to Jamie, and neither misdirected incentive was the basis for a successful fresh start. I listened to them and appreciated their concern, but would not be swayed. I apologized to my parents, wholeheartedly agreed with my sister but took no notice and, two weeks later, I moved out of May and Neil's spare room and into my new life.

CHAPTER EIGHT

Alexander and Jamie met me at Temple Meads station in Bristol. I'd spent the whole journey fearing that Alexander would not be there, that nothing that had happened between us was real. All the things the people who cared for me had said over the past weeks about me living in a dream world came back to worry and poke at me. I dreaded having to go creeping back into the arms of my family for another dose of kindness, recuperation and told-you-so's.

But it was all right: as the train slowed at the station they were there underneath the electronic sign at the far end of the platform, exactly where Alexander had said they'd be. Alexander, newly bearded and with longer hair, stood taller and leaner than I remembered, and beside him was the small, serious, blue-eyed boy with the big ears. They cast long shadows across the grey platform in the early September sunlight. The train juddered to a full stop. Alexander and Jamie had come to bring me home. My heart was pounding. Knowing they could not see me, I watched for as long as I dared, then joined the queue to haul my bag from the rack by the door.

They came forward to meet me, Alexander first and Jamie hanging back. I tried to relax but it was awkward. Alexander leaned down – I thought he meant to kiss me and held up my face, but he only took the bag from me. People swarmed around us like ants around an obstacle. We stood there, quiet in our own space, and they went round us.

'You look good,' he said, after what felt like for ever.

I could not, in truth, say the same of him. He looked dishevelled, exhausted and drawn. He stroked his chin.

'I like the beard,' I said.

'My grandpa says he looks like Jesus,' said Jamie.

'Oh yes?'

'And Grandma says he looks a disgrace.'

'Come on,' said Alexander. 'This way.'

We were at the end of the queue to go down the stairs that took us to the tunnel beneath the platforms. I couldn't think of a single thing to say. I tried to make myself relax, but I couldn't. We weren't in Sicily any more, we were back in the real world.

Alexander's dusty old Land Rover was in the car park at the front of the magnificent station façade. I opened the door and climbed up to the passenger seat. The footwell was littered with sandwich cartons, empty cans and parking tickets. I spotted the lid of a lipstick tube amongst the clutter. This small piece of silvery tat made me uneasy. I was sitting where Alexander's wife used to sit. This was her place, at her husband's side. She must have sat here thousands of times, next to Alexander.

My face felt hot, as if I were doing something wrong.

I pulled the door to and wound down the window. Alexander helped Jamie into the back, clearing space amongst the tools and overalls, then climbed in beside me and started the engine. The vehicle juddered and shook. He fiddled with a knob just beneath the steering wheel until the rattling subsided.

'OK?' he asked.

'Yes, I'm fine. Is it far?'

'About an hour to Avalon.'

'Avalon?'

'That's the name of the house. Here.'

He delved into the back well and passed me a plastic bottle that had once contained ginger beer but was now half full of tap water. It was warm, but still I drank. Alexander glanced at me, and then pulled the car out of its space, into the stream of taxis and buses queuing to leave the station.

I gazed out at Bristol as the Land Rover bounced through the city. I asked a few questions, but Alexander's answers were monosyllabic; he seemed to be entirely lost in thought, so I gave up, and just watched.

We crossed the River Avon via an ugly road bridge at a spectacularly beautiful spot, and Jamie pointed to the suspension bridge to the right of us high above the wide, brown river that curled away between the sheer cliff-faces of the gorge, the forest to the left blooming with colour; a thousand different shades of green dropped into their mirror images in the water. I'd had no idea that Bristol was so breathtakingly dramatic, so lovely.

'People jump off that bridge,' Jamie said.

I glanced over my shoulder at him. He was playing with a toy action figure. He held it upside down by its feet and dropped it as a demonstration.

'They used to,' Alexander corrected. 'They used to bungee. We saw it on telly, didn't we?'

'It's a terribly long way up.'

'Or down,' said Alexander. He turned his head towards me, but I couldn't see his eyes, only myself reflected in the windows of his sunglasses. 'Are you afraid of heights?' he asked.

I nodded. I couldn't tell him that it was only since my pregnancy. Before that, hardly anything scared me. Since my baby was stillborn, I had realized how frightening and unpredictable life could be. I saw danger where previously I had only seen possibility.

It wasn't the pain of childbirth. I had expected that. When the persistent ache that had been squeezing me deep inside for a few days developed into a definite pain I was thrilled. I phoned Laurie to call him home from work and fortunately he was in the office and not out with clients. Then I ran upstairs to check I had everything in my hospital bag: newborn nappies, cotton mittens, vests, talcum powder, sleep-suits, toothbrush, toothpaste, flannel. It was an unnecessary exercise. I knew everything was where it should be. I'd been checking for days.

I put one hand in the small of my back – it was a pose I thought I should adopt – and with the other I stroked my hardening belly while I gazed out of the window in my best coat and shoes, waiting for Laurie to come home.

I had never been so excited in my entire life. I had never looked forward to anything as much as I looked forward to the coming few hours.

In the hospital delivery suite I threw myself into the rhythm of childbirth with enthusiasm. I had been warned how much labour hurts but nothing had prepared me for the physical violence of it or the way my body would take over. I was shocked but I knew it was what women had to endure if they were to be mothers. I was too busy breathing to listen when the medical staff explained they were changing the monitor strapped around me because it wasn't picking up a heartbeat and they thought there might be a problem with the machine. A different midwife came in and then a doctor. The atmosphere in the room changed, but I ignored it. Laurie tried to talk to me, to prepare me, but I shook him away. I had a job to do. I carried on delivering. Laurie, the midwife, the doctors and the nurses were following the wrong script and I wouldn't listen to them. I wouldn't look at their faces, I wouldn't believe what was happening because if I didn't believe it then it couldn't be true.

Bristol ended suddenly, just the other side of the river, and almost at once we were driving through countryside that was lush and green. Cattle grazed, heads down in fields; little villages went by. The hedgerows were drooping with the weight of an abundance of late summer flowers and leaves. Ahead I could see the looming silhouettes of the Mendip hills and they were glorious, purple in the light. We drove up a busy section of road and on past pubs and farm shops and fruit stalls. There were fewer and fewer villages, more farm tracks, the occasional all-night garage. As the sun began to set to our right, we turned off the main road and went uphill along a narrow, winding lane. Hills rose out of the gloaming green and shadowed landscape below us. Alexander pointed out Glastonbury Tor in the distance as a low Somerset mist settled over the valley. Scrubby blackberries weighed down the brambles that wove through the hedgerows, and the bracken was already dying. A huge flock of rooks, two hundred or more, cawed overhead, disturbing the calm of the wide, pale sky. For the first time that year I felt the promise of autumn in the air.

'Here we are,' said Alexander, turning sharply into a gap between the trees. We rattled over a cattle-grid and went up the track that led to Avalon. The Land Rover bounced and bumped over pot holes as we wove through a tunnel of trees, until the trees gave way to fields and up ahead I saw the house.

The light was fading but was still strong enough to illuminate the front face of the building. It was larger, older and more substantial than I'd imagined. It had been there for so long that it seemed to be part of the landscape that surrounded it, an organic thing of stone, red-clay roofing tiles, wood and plaster. Alexander parked the car at the end of the track, next to a semi-derelict barn overrun with bramble and ivy, a couple of empty stables and a double horse-trailer, tilted forward to rest on its towing bar. Bales of hay were stacked at the back of a big old shed. Swallows darted in and out of the bucolic clutter of buildings and into the orchard beyond, swooping fast as arrows close to the top of the long grass. Black and white cows grazed beneath the tree. The orchard boundaries were defined by nettles, tall as my shoulder, that leaned over with their own weight.

The house sat in its own gardens, separated from the orchard by walls at the front and a barbed-wire fence at the back. A substantial wooden porch, overwound with honeysuckle so old that its main stems were as thick as my wrists, stood slightly lopsided before the front door. There were windows on either side of the porch and above it. It looked as if the original house had been extended to the side and backwards, or maybe it had just been built in a ramshackle way, with extra rooms added on as afterthoughts. A couple of tiles had slipped from the roof and the dun-coloured plaster that rendered the old stone walls was peeling in huge, papery flakes. The flower beds in the garden were untidy and overgrown but it was clear from the faded blooms on the stems of the roses and the colours and shapes of the shrubs, now jostling for light and space, that at one time the garden had been beautiful.

'It's a mess,' Alexander said, following my eyes. 'Genevieve was too busy with her horses to bother with the garden and I haven't had the time.'

'She's a rider?'

'Yep.'

'She might be in the Olympics,' Jamie said.

I laughed. I thought he was joking, then I remembered that Jamie was not a frivolous child. He looked at me crossly and immediately I tried to make up for my reaction by saying: 'You mean she's a really good rider?'

'One of the best,' said Alexander.

'Oh. Does she do show-jumping?'

'Eventing,' Alexander said. 'Dressage, show-jumping and cross-country. A lot of people are into it round here.'

'You don't get much of that in Manchester,' I said.

Alexander smiled at me.

'Where are the horses?'

'Genevieve's mother's looking after them for the time being. She . . . well, I'll tell you later. This way,' he said.

I followed him through a wooden gate and up a small, flagstoned path to a side door that opened into a whitewashed room full of boots, stacks of newspapers, empty wine and vodka bottles and other things waiting to be recycled, unwashed laundry and cobwebs. One whole wall was covered with shiny rosettes, mostly red, and a couple of rope horse-collars hung from a metal hook beneath the window. Grooming equipment and a rusty tin of hoof oil were packed into a blue plastic pail. Riding coats and boots were heaped in one corner together with an assortment of heavy-duty rope, metal and leather kit that must have been something to do with horses. A misshapen cardboard carton of washing powder lurched on top of a washing machine in the far corner of the room and an old dog bed lay beside it.

A second door led into the kitchen, which was large, warm and untidy. Soiled crockery was stacked in the sink, and a cat stood on the counter eating the remains of a chicken carcass. The floor looked as if it had not been washed in weeks and the windows were grimy.

Alexander put my bag down, shooed the cat from the

chicken and turned the dish round. There was little meat left.

'Bollocks,' he said. 'I was going to make us a sandwich for dinner.'

The cat had a self-satisfied look on its face. It jumped on to the kitchen table and cleaned its paws, licking its fur with its tiny pink tongue.

Alexander sighed. 'It doesn't even belong to us. It just comes in and steals our food.'

Jamie went over to the cat and stroked it. The cat ignored him.

'I'm sorry,' said Alexander. 'This isn't much of a welcome. We were going to have a tidy round, weren't we, Jamie?'

Jamie scowled and put his head on the table. He watched the cat.

'Only I had to work late so Jamie had tea round at his cousins' house and between us we got nothing done.'

'It's OK,' I said. 'That's why I'm here, isn't it? To help sort things out.'

Alexander looked bone tired. 'Yes,' he said. 'That's why you're here.'

CHAPTER NINE

Alexander made a pot of tea. I was touched that he went to the trouble of the teapot rather than simply putting teabags in mugs, and I drank my tea while he made toast for Jamie. When the boy was settled at the table, he took hold of my bag.

'Come on,' he said. 'This way. I'll take you to your room.'

I followed Alexander as he hefted my bag through a small door built into the wall of the dining room, up some narrow stairs.

Mine was a smallish room at the back of the house, in the eaves. The ceiling sloped so steeply that I could only stand up straight by the bed-head wall. There was room for the bed and a rickety old chest of drawers with a dusty Tiffany-shaded lamp perched on top. I had to stoop to open the drawers. The window on the far side of the bed was small and square, divided into four equal panes. A cobweb stretched across the top left-hand pane and dead insects dusted the ledge. Still, somebody had made an effort. A small glass vase stood on the sill and in the vase were three roses, their petals the yellow and pink of ripe pomegranates and their scent faint, but sweet.

'Will this do?' Alexander asked, setting down my case.

'It's fine,' I said. Then a little more enthusiastically: 'It's lovely.'

It wasn't lovely though. It felt like a servant's room. I was certain it had never been used by the family because it had a lonely, unloved feel to it and there was a faint smell of damp and must, as if the door and windows were rarely opened. I'd been hoping for something different. I didn't know what exactly, but something better than this, something more welcoming.

Alexander and I had spoken on the telephone several times since we'd returned to England. We had been careful with one another, avoiding awkward topics such as his wife and where she'd gone and Laurie and what he'd done, instead making practical arrangements – agreeing my wage and so on, and exploring one another's tastes in books, music and films. I knew that he came from the West Midlands but was not close to his family; he would not talk about them at all. I also knew that his father- and mother-in-law, Genevieve's parents, were well off and lived in a big house on a hill close by. The family fortune had come from the rock that was quarried from the heart of the hill. Alexander said the family had dug into it like a child would dig into a favourite pudding. The original Victorian quarry had been exhausted years ago, and a new, enormous, state-of-the-art one had been opened closer to the main road. I knew that it was Alexander's job and Genevieve's father's fortune that had brought and kept them together, in ways I did not yet understand. We both liked Merlot but Chardonnay gave us a headache. Neither of us had a sweet tooth. We were both better at listening than talking. As such, our conversations tended to go for some time with neither of us actually saying very much. Despite this we had, I believed, achieved an acceptable level of intimacy.

Now I was thrown into a well of insecurity and anxiety. I'd learned not to assume how life would turn out, but it scared me, this small, dark room with its sloping ceiling and its tiny window.

Alexander scratched his forehead. The situation was horribly uncomfortable. Coming here, so many miles from Manchester, and escaping that awful, all-encompassing emotional intensity, all those people walking on eggshells trying to avoid talking about the myriad subjects they thought might upset me, had seemed such a good idea, it had looked like the easy option. I'd never been to Somerset before, nobody knew me or Laurie or what had happened and I thought that would make it much easier for me to put it all behind me. Also, I'd been looking forward to helping Alexander and caring for Jamie.

Instead I felt as if I didn't belong there. Nothing felt right. It felt as if it might never be right.

Alexander and I both looked at the bed that was to be mine. I realized that, just as I was wondering if I had made a mistake by coming, he was wondering if he'd made a worse one in inviting me. I sat down on the edge of the mattress, bouncing as if to test the springs.

'It's really comfy,' I said.

Alexander sat beside me and the mattress tipped me towards him. I had to clench my stomach muscles to avoid rolling into him.

'Sarah,' he said gently, 'there are things I need to tell you. This situation . . . it's more complicated than you realize. Genevieve . . . she . . .'

I pushed my hair out of my eyes and hooked it over my ear.

'It's all right,' I said. 'You don't have to explain.'

'But I have to tell you. The thing is, you've come from Manchester, where I guess you could pretty much be who you wanted to be. People don't judge one another so much in cities because there are so many different kinds of people there.'

I nodded.

'Now you're in Burrington Stoke, population less than a thousand people. Everyone knows everyone else and everyone thinks they have the right to know everyone else's business. It's like being part of a big family and I know that sounds cosy but it's not always a good thing.'

'You mean they'll speculate about why I'm here?'

'Just a bit!'

I smiled shyly.

'That's all right.'

'But you don't know what it's like to be the centre of attention in a place like this.'

I shifted my weight a little and shrugged.

'I don't mind people being curious about me,' I said.

He shook his head. 'You're not the point.'

'Then who is?'

'Genevieve.'

I felt a prickle of unease. I looked down at my hands.

Alexander exhaled.

'I need to tell you about her,' he said.

'OK.'

He began to talk about his wife and, as he did so, his voice became slower and heavier and his head hung forwards and his shoulders became rounded like an older man's. I listened as he told me about their relationship and felt as if I were being included in something huge and important.

He told me that Genevieve was very precious to her parents because she was her mother's only child, and her father's only true love child. He said both her parents would do anything for their brave and talented daughter. She had, from a very early age, shown a prodigious talent for riding and this had been nurtured and encouraged. She'd had the best education, the best of everything, and the investment had paid off.

Alexander didn't tell me how he and Genevieve met, but he said, when they married, she was on the rebound from an intense affair. She told Alexander that she would do her best to forget the man she had been seeing, but that he was the love of her life. For a while – several years – Alexander and Genevieve had managed. But lately, their relationship had foundered. Genevieve was clearly unhappy. The two of them had begun to bicker, then argue, then fight. They kept up appearances for the sake of her family, the village, Jamie, but no matter how hard they tried, they both knew it was never going to work. Their marriage had been over for a long time before Genevieve left. He said he was resigned to her going; in a way it was a relief to him. But nobody else knew quite how bad things had become or how unhappy they were together. So while Alexander expected it, everyone else, including her parents, had been shocked when Genevieve went away.

I stared at the old-fashioned floral pattern on the quilt and pulled at a loose thread. She was special, he said. She was the best rider in Somerset and that made her a local celebrity. Her parents were influential and respected. And because everyone felt as if they knew her, they were all concerned when she left and they were still concerned now.

I nodded and nibbled at the cuticle of my thumb.

'It's all anyone talks about,' said Alexander. 'They want to know where Genevieve is and what she's doing, why she left so suddenly. There are a lot of rumours. That's why it's best for everyone if, for now, we make it very clear that you're my housekeeper and Jamie's nanny, nothing more than that.'

He scratched his head. The light outside was fading and the room seemed darker and colder. A black beetle scuttled between two of the huge black roof beams.

'You don't mind me telling you all this?'

'Of course not,' I replied, rather too brightly. 'It's best I know.'

'Genevieve's family owns most of the land around here. A lot of the people in the village are their tenants. And . . . well, they're devastated.'

'Doesn't Genevieve call her parents?'

'No.'

'She doesn't write?'

'She left letters for me and for them the day she went away. She told her parents not to worry if they didn't hear from her for a few weeks and that she'd be in touch once the dust had settled. Since then, we've heard nothing.'

'I expect she'll contact them soon,' I said cheerfully.

Alexander didn't smile.

'We parted badly, Genevieve and I,' he said. 'I said some things . . . we both said and did some things we shouldn't have.'

I nodded.

'You never met her so you can't understand what she was like,' he said, and his voice sounded terribly sad. 'To me she was . . .' He trailed off and stared at the wall as he tried and failed to find a word to sum up his feelings for Genevieve.

'Why do you say "was"?' I asked. 'Why do you talk about her in the past tense?'

He shrugged. 'I meant when she was here.'

CHAPTER TEN

He left me to make myself at home. I lay across the bed to reach the window, unhooked the catch and opened it. It overlooked the orchard. The very last of the sunlight stained the top leaves of the trees a brilliant gold; their branches were weighed down with apples, and mistletoe bloomed a darker green in their crooks and elbows. I could not imagine anyone wanting to leave this place nor how it would feel to own it, to have been born into it. It was so beautiful. It seemed so perfect.

I thought I heard footsteps on the landing and the door moved a little; the metal latch tapped against the chimney breast. I turned, but nobody was there. I went over to the door to see if it was Jamie, spying on me. The landing was empty. I waited a moment to make sure he wasn't hiding somewhere. I was certain someone was there, but nothing moved, there were no creaks or sighs. I supposed it must have been a draught from the window disturbing the door. Old houses made noises; it was their way. I knew that.

I had promised to call May, but there was no signal on my phone. I wrote a text and held my arm out of the window, but it didn't send. That made me feel very alone. I tried not to remember what my mother had said to me about men who isolate women. It was hardly Alexander's fault there was no network coverage.

I made up the bed with the linen stacked at its foot, and unpacked my bag, putting all my things into the chest of drawers. The wood smelled a little musty and I balled up the paper liners, which were damp, and as I put them in the waste basket I remembered the clothes I'd left in my drawers at home: baby clothes. I hadn't bought much before the baby was born, because we had asked not to be told if it was a boy or a girl – we wanted to be surprised. I had anticipated the pleasure of shopping with my new child snug against my chest in the sling, choosing clothes specifically for him – or her, if he'd been a girl. And when that pleasure was taken away, well, I'd been drawn to the infant sections of shops anyway. I spent hours in the department stores, hovering over the pale-blue jumpsuits, pretending, to myself at least, that I was a real mother. I picked up little coats and hats, tiny pairs of socks and gloves, and I'd feel the fabric, checking it was soft and warm enough for my son. Other women, clearly pregnant, looked at me. I smiled at them and they looked away. I wondered if they could tell, if they were worried I would jinx them. The assistants were kind to me, though.

'It's for my son,' I would say as I laid my purchases on the counter to be paid for and bagged. 'He's so gorgeous. He's going to look lovely in this.' And the assistants smiled and they didn't ask where my baby was. Nobody ever asked.

So I bought nappies and vests, and hundreds of pounds' worth of clothes. I filled up my drawers with baby-boy clothes and toys and, when I was alone in the house, I took the clothes out and laid them out on the bed, and I talked to my son as I held each item to my cheek.

Laurie knew about the clothes, but he didn't say anything; not to me anyway. But I knew he knew, because sometimes I'd catch him staring at me with concern in his eyes, as if I were an alcoholic and he'd found a half-empty bottle of vodka hidden in the laundry basket.

In the bedroom at Avalon I pushed the drawers shut; they were stiff and creaky. I stood up and wiped my cheeks with the back of my hand.

I supposed this part of the house hadn't been used for ages. The radiator was icy cold. The room needed airing; that was all. It needed somebody to live in it and open the windows and bring it back to life.

I washed my hands and face in the bathroom further up the landing, put on some fresh mascara, brushed my hair and went back downstairs.

Jamie was lying on the sofa in the living room, with his head hanging over the side, watching TV and eating cubes of cheese and crisps from a bowl on the carpet. The kitchen door was closed but I could hear Alexander's voice beyond.

'Is your dad on the phone?' I asked Jamie.

He nodded, without taking his eyes from the television.

I sat down beside him, picked up his feet and put them on my lap. His socks were sticky and smelled of trainers and sweat.

'He's talking to Grandma,' he said.

Genevieve's mother, I presumed.

'She didn't want you to come,' Jamie said. 'She thinks it's a scene.'

'A scene?'

'A *bus* scene.'

'Oh. Obscene.'

'She says you're a hole-digger.'

'I think she meant gold-digger.'

Jamie looked up at me, caught my eye and looked away again.

'What's a gold-digger?'

'It's a person who pretends to be somebody's friend because they want the other person's money.'

Jamie stared at me while he thought about this information.

'No, I think Grandma did mean hole-digger,' he said.

I tried to hide my smile but I wasn't quick enough.

'Grandma doesn't think it's funny,' said Jamie.

'No, of course not.'

'Nor do I.'

Jamie fished the remote control from the carpet and turned up the volume on the television. He pulled his feet away from me.

I stood, stretched, switched on the light and drew the curtains. I wandered to the far end of the room and studied the spines of the books in the case. Amongst a plethora of Jilly Cooper novels, books on horse management and eventer biographies were a couple of Italian language dictionaries and guidebooks and a number of books on law. Framed photographs stood on top of the case. Most were of Jamie at various stages of development but in amongst them was a portrait of a woman. It had to be Genevieve. I picked it up and held it to the light.

She didn't look as I had imagined her. She was smiling in that bashful way that the most attractive people do – as if they know how beautiful they are and are faintly apologetic about it. She was standing beside a railing in some foreign country; beyond, a range of slate-grey cliffs towered over a perfectly green sea. One slender hand rested on the railing and her face was turned towards the camera. Her hair, the silver-gold-buff colour of ripe wheat, was shoulder length, well cut. She wore a yellow vest-shirt, shorts, a wedding ring. Her shoulders were smooth and tanned. Her composure and grace reminded me of an old-fashioned celebrity but her look was contemporary. She had a heart-shaped, symmetrical face and dark eyes beneath long, dark lashes. She was beautiful; there was no denying it. Genevieve was lovely.

'That's Mummy,' said Jamie.

'She's very pretty,' I said, and I heard the note of jealousy in my voice.

'Mmm.'

I smiled at the child and was struck by how very small he was; too small to be motherless. I had no right to attempt to fracture his already bruised loyalties. I put the photograph back in its place.

'Do you miss her a lot?' I asked.

Jamie nodded. He sat up and wriggled deep into the side of the settee. He put his thumb in his mouth. The blue teddy was tucked into the crook of his elbow.

'I wish she would come back,' he said.

CHAPTER ELEVEN

Despite everything, I settled down to sleep that first night feeling a little more normal. Nothing had been quite as I'd hoped. I'd been naïve in underestimating how difficult things had been, and still were, for Jamie and Alexander. Still, I was relieved to be away from Manchester. For the first night in ages I didn't hold my breath waiting to hear May's footsteps as she ritually crept to my bedroom door and listened to make sure I wasn't crying. I no longer had to keep a perma-smile glued to my face to prove to the people who loved me that I was all right, and I didn't have to worry about what I said. I could just be, and it was soothing. I hoped I'd be trusted to look after the house and the child without too much supervision. While Jamie was at school, I'd be on my own, and I was certain I'd be able to pull myself together if I had the time and space and didn't have to deal with people looking at me and talking about me when they thought I wasn't listening.

That weekend, Alexander showed me around the village. The late-summer light made everything appear strangely artificial, like a film set. The country air was soft on my face, it tasted different from city air, and I soon became accustomed to the agricultural tang of cut hay, mud and manure that suffused the whole area.

We walked down Avalon's drive and turned left, going perhaps half a mile before we reached the new quarry junction. It seemed out of place, set, as it was, beside this quiet country road. There were traffic lights at the entrance and large double white gates protected by cameras pointing in and outwards. The whole area was surrounded by a high, spiked metal fence. The road was wide enough for load-bearing lorries to turn and exit with their heavy cargo. The entrance was guarded by a lodge and I could see the uniformed guard inside. He had his feet on the counter and was staring at a television mounted on the wall. I could not tell if he was watching a programme or monitoring security cameras.

'This is Jamie's inheritance,' Alexander said. 'Genevieve's family owns all this, the quarry and the land behind it.'

'Do you work for them?'

He shook his head. 'I work for myself. Sometimes I come here to look at a piece of stone, see if it's suitable for a particular commission. Mostly I work at the yard in Castle Cary. That's where I've got my gear and where people come to see me.'

We watched as the gates swung open and a truck pulled out on to the road, its engine grinding under the weight of the stone it carried. It shed a fine white dust as it rumbled and groaned on towards the village.

'Don't the people who live here get fed up with the noise?' I asked.

Alexander shrugged. 'They're used to it.'

We walked on into Burrington Stoke. It was not much of a place, just a few shops on either side of the road, a pub that was still hung with baskets of colourful trailing flowers and which advertised Sunday lunches and Butcombe beer, and a run-down hotel. A number of unassuming former local authority houses lined the far end of the road and some lovely old cottages and country houses were set further back. At the far end of the village, close to the memorial cross, was the entrance to a farm. Small, shaggy cows stood by the gate feeding from a bale of hay, bothered by black, buzzing flies. A lane at the side of the farm led up to the village primary school. Alexander nodded to a couple of young women coming down the lane on horseback. I backed into the hedge to make way as they passed. The animals were huge. Their big feet clopped and they swung their heads as they went by, eyeing me suspiciously. The young women with their big shoulders and bare arms made no attempt to hide their curiosity. As soon as they had passed, one said to the other, loudly enough for me to hear: 'Who's she then?' And the other said: 'No idea,' and then added more quietly, 'But did you see her shoes?'

I looked down at my feet. I was wearing purple ballet pumps made grey by the quarry dust.

'You'll need proper boots,' Alexander said. 'It gets muddy here when it rains. I'll sort some out for you.'

He showed me where the entrance to the school was, a little way up the lane.

'I'll drop Jamie off on his first day back on Tuesday morning, and Claudia will pick him up when she fetches her girls,' Alexander explained. 'She'll show you the ropes. After that I need you to be there to meet him every day. He mustn't come home with anyone else. It's important.'

'OK.'

'And, Sarah, you can't be late. You have to be at the school gate before three thirty.'

'I won't let you down. Who's Claudia?'

'Genevieve's half-sister.'

'Won't she mind me being here?'

Alexander shook his head. 'She knows I need help. She's been a rock these last few weeks. In fact, she was the one who suggested I get a nanny.'

'Are her children at this school too?'

He shook his head. 'They go to St Margaret's in Montacute.'

'They have to go to school on Saturday morning,' said Jamie.

I pulled a face. 'How awful.'

'But they have riding lessons and longer holidays.'

'That's not so bad then.'

'Uncle Bill says he has to pay an arm and a leg for them to have longer holidays.'

'That's the beauty of independent education,' said Alexander.

We walked a little further, past the run-down hotel

and what was probably once an old ducking-pond, and soon were at the far end of the village.

'Isn't there a church?' I asked.

'It's up on top of the hill. Close to where Genevieve's parents live.'

I smiled at Jamie. 'Do they have a nice house?'

'It's big!' he said, widening his eyes and holding out his arms in an exaggerated fashion.

Over his head, Alexander nodded. 'I'll drive you up,' he said. 'I'll show you.' After lunch we got back into the Land Rover. Once again, we turned left at the bottom of the drive, drove along the main road for a while and turned right into a narrow lane about a hundred metres before the entrance to the new quarry. In places the lane was little more than a single track, winding upwards between high hedges. We drove through a narrow tunnel formed by the branches of overhanging trees, climbing steeply through twists and turns until we came to a fork.

'That's the entrance to the old quarry,' said Alexander. He slowed the Land Rover. 'They shut it down thirty years ago.'

The quarry's gates towered above the lane. They were locked together by a thick chain secured by a padlock. Barbed wire was threaded between the metal bars of the gates. A gurning skull and crossbones gleamed from the blood-coloured background of a weathered DANGER, KEEP OUT sign that hung at an angle from the gates. Another sign said: TRESPASSERS WILL BE PROSECUTED.

I shivered.

'Why did they close the quarry?' I asked.

'It was inaccessible for big wagons. It was more commercially viable for the Churchills to open the new one at the bottom of the hill where the trucks can get out on to the main road without any problems than it was to build a new road up here.'

'Why is it all fenced off like that?'

'Kids kept coming up here in the hot weather to swim in the pit. Teenagers. They ignored the signs and jumped off the cliff. One lad drowned.'

'That's awful!'

'It was years ago,' said Alexander. 'Before I met Genevieve, but she remembered him.'

'He shouldn't of been in there,' said Jamie solemnly.

'No, he shouldn't,' said Alexander. He was silent for a moment. Then he said very quietly: 'Nobody goes there any more. People have forgotten it exists.'

We drove on.

At the top of the hill, the lane opened out. On either side were fields bordered by hedges and fences. I noticed a pair of handsome liver-chestnut horses standing beneath a small clump of trees at the centre of a gently rolling meadow to our left. Alexander nodded his head without taking his eyes from the road.

'Genevieve's,' he confirmed.

The first building we reached was set back from the lane and surrounded by a high fence and electric gates, so all I could see was the roof and a huge, arch-shaped window. It was clearly a large barn that had been beautifully and extensively converted. Laurie and I used to be addicted to home-buying and restoration television programmes and I could tell that no expense had been spared. Everything was perfect.

'That's where my cousins live,' said Jamie, leaning over me to point.

'Wow!'

'Classy, eh? Mixture of Claudia's old money and Bill's new,' Alexander said. I looked at him. Was he being sarcastic? Was that jealousy I'd heard, or resentment perhaps?

'And here's the church,' he said in an ordinary voice. 'If you're interested, there's loads of Churchill family history inside and in the graveyard.'

'Oh, OK.'

'And just over there,' Alexander continued, nodding his head to the other side of the lane, 'you'll see the roof-tops of Eleonora House.'

'They live here? Almost on top of the old quarry?'

'The original Mr Churchill wanted to build his house as close as he could to the source of his wealth,' Alexander said. 'I suppose it made him feel proud; connected. Plus, he could keep a close eye on things.'

'It must've been tough on the workers,' I said quietly. 'They wouldn't have been able to get away with anything.'

Alexander smiled.

He pulled the Land Rover up at the entrance to the drive to Eleonora House, and left its engine running.

The house was bigger and grander than anything I could have imagined. It was a real old-fashioned country pile, with wisteria curling up a façade that was set a good way back from the lane at the end of a straight drive lined with topiary bushes shaped abstractly like clouds and waves. A life-size statue stood on an ornate pedestal just outside the gates at the entrance to the drive. It was a Victorian-style child-angel, with a lovely face and downcast eyes. One hand held a rose to her breast, the other was extended, as if to draw visitors into the drive.

'That's Eleonora,' Alexander said. 'She was the original Mr Churchill's youngest daughter and the one he loved best.'

'She died young?' I asked quietly.

Alexander nodded. 'Some kind of masonry accident while they were building the house. The sculptor used her death mask as a model for the statue.'

'How morbid!'

'Gen thought it was romantic. She was the image of the statue when she was a child.'

I would have liked to know more, but at that moment Jamie, who was sitting behind me, shouted: 'There's Grandpa!' and I was distracted.

The Land Rover's window was open. I could see, quite clearly, the figure of a tall, aged man in a hat just outside the house. He was stooped over a cane and was examining something, a rose bush perhaps.

'Can we go and see him? Can we go and say hello?' Jamie asked.

Alexander glanced at me.

'I don't know,' I said. 'Perhaps it would be better if we waited.'

'Too late,' Alexander said. A thin woman had come to stand beside the man. She was shading her eyes with one hand and, with the other, she beckoned us down the drive.

'Virginia,' Alexander said, almost under his breath.

'Couldn't you pretend you didn't see her?' I asked.

'That would be lying,' said Jamie.

'Come on,' said Alexander. 'Let's get it over with.'

CHAPTER TWELVE

We sat on comfortable, solid garden furniture on a circular terrace beside a perfectly manicured lawn in what Virginia Churchill called the 'family' garden. The lawn was square, surrounded by flower beds, and each bed contained a profusion of different plants. I was no gardener, but I recognized the skill that had gone into the planting; the tumble of contrasting colours was not accidental but designed so that each patch of flowers complemented the next, and behind the flowers were hedges that acted as a perfect backdrop. The centrepiece was a huge old pond, its stoneware overgrown with trailing plants and the dark green water heavy with pale, waxy lilies. Dragonflies black as jet buzzed amongst the water plants. The overall effect reminded me of a romantic painting and, if I had not been so nervous, I would have enjoyed simply sitting and looking.

As it was, Alexander and I were carefully avoiding one another's eyes while we were served tea by a middle-aged woman called Mrs Lipton. Mr Churchill – I could never imagine calling him Philip – sat awkwardly on his chair, with one leg stretched out in front of him. He wore worn brown corduroys and a cotton shirt with a cravat. The rim of his hat covered his eyes, but I could see a wide jaw and a chin that was faintly stubbled. His skin was weather-beaten. Veins bulged on the back of huge, bony hands that were spotted with age.

When the tea was poured, Mrs Churchill asked Mrs Lipton to fetch some toys for Jamie, and she returned with a child's archery set. She set the target up at the far end of the garden and, after making sure we had everything we needed, joined the boy to help him put the arrows in his bow, and to retrieve them when they fell short. Within a few moments of Jamie leaving the group, Mr Churchill's jaw relaxed and his mouth fell open. He began to snore rhythmically.

The whole situation made me feel awkward and tongue-tied. I could think of nothing to say, so was quiet apart from thanking Mrs Lipton for the refreshments and complimenting the Churchills on their beautiful home and garden.

'It's very good of you to come and introduce yourself,' Mrs Churchill said to me. Her voice was clipped and there was more than a hint of sarcasm or perhaps irritation. She passed me a cup of tea. The china was pretty if a little fussy.

'Virginia, I'm sorry, we didn't mean to turn up unannounced like this,' Alexander said.

She made a swatting motion with her hand.

'No, I'm glad you came. You know how anxious I was to find out who this person was you'd engaged to look after our grandson.'

I smiled and shuffled a little in my seat.

'Well, here she is,' said Alexander.

'Here I am,' I said like an idiot.

'You're not what I imagined,' Mrs Churchill said.

'What did you imagine, Virginia?' Alexander asked.

Virginia ignored him. In a pleasant but loaded voice she said: 'I know my daughter would never have dreamed of leaving her son in the care of a stranger.'

Alexander started to object but Mrs Churchill held her hand up to stop him.

'Things being as they are, perhaps, Sarah, you'd be kind enough to tell me what exactly are your childcare qualifications?'

'I . . .'

'The main thing is that Jamie likes her. And I trust her,' Alexander said.

Mrs Churchill leaned forward. Her eyes were blue, pale blue like ice, and her face, although etched with the anxiety and distress she'd endured over the past few weeks, was still strong and determined. It was so close to mine that I could detect a staleness of breath amongst the late-summer warmth of the air. She must have had a bad tooth in her mouth or an infection.

'Do you have *any* relevant qualifications?' she asked me.

'Not exactly.'

'Have you worked as a nanny or an au pair before?'

I glanced at Alexander but he was staring up at the ornate chimneypots on the roof of the house.

'No.'

'And you don't have any children of your own?'

The quiet, still face of my son came into my mind. His perfect little lips. His eyelids. His tiny fingers that closed around my little finger, not gripping like a normal baby, but touching; his fingernails delicate as cowslip petals; the unique design of his fingerprint that would always be a secret.

'No,' I said.

'In other words, you have no valid professional reason to be here!'

'Virginia, please . . .' said Alexander.

'What were you thinking?' Virginia asked him calmly, but in a voice that was so cold it made me ache inside.

'Sarah's only looking after Jamie while I'm at work, a couple of hours a day at most. If there are any problems she's perfectly capable of asking for help. When I come home, I'll take over again.'

'And what's she going to do with herself while Jamie's at school and you're at work?'

'She'll be acting as housekeeper.'

'Acting?'

'You know what I mean.'

Virginia put her cup delicately on her saucer and turned back to me.

'Alexander told us he met you in Sicily,' she said.

'That's right.'

'And that your relationship is purely a business one.'

'Yes.'

'Sarah,' she said, 'can you look me in the eye and assure me there is nothing going on between you and Alexander?'

I hesitated. Alexander stepped in. He did his best. He

insisted to Virginia that there was nothing untoward between the two of us. He argued that, in Genevieve's absence, he was best placed to decide what, and who, was best for Jamie and himself. Virginia said that, in Genevieve's absence, his position was debatable. There was some undercurrent going on, something I didn't understand. The two of them argued politely, bitterly and coldly, without once raising their voices, until Philip from beneath his hat and without opening his eyes growled. 'That's enough.'

I apologized to Alexander for my lack of quick-wittedness as we drove back to Avalon. He had the window open, and rested one elbow on it. He drove with his left hand, and gnawed at the knuckle on the forefinger of his other one.

'Don't worry about it,' he said. 'Virginia can think what she wants.'

I did not know how to respond to that.

He turned his head slightly and smiled at me in a resigned fashion.

'Let her do her worst,' he said. 'We'll survive.'

CHAPTER THIRTEEN

I don't recall dreaming that night. I don't remember anything about it until something disturbed me in the early hours.

I lay for a moment with my eyes closed. My heart was thumping, but I didn't know what it was that had woken me. Gently I eased myself up on one elbow and with shaky fingers and my breath catching in my throat I drew back the edge of the curtain. A weak light was seeping into the field. There was nothing there. I tried to calm myself; it was just nerves. I exhaled and relaxed. I closed my eyes. And then I heard a distinct noise, and it wasn't coming from the window, but from the wall, just behind my head.

I sat up straight, clutching the eiderdown to my chest. My heart was beating so fast it hurt. I could hardly breathe. It was a scrabbling noise, loud and insistent, as if something bricked into the wall was trying to fight its way out. It was a desperate noise, like the clawing of fingernails. It went on for several seconds, there was a pause, and then it started again.

'Alexander!' I called, but no sound came from my mouth; I was gagged by my panic. I could not formulate the word; the only noise I could make was the catching of my breath. I slid my feet out of bed and crept from the room, too frightened to look behind me. In the almost-light, with my fingers on the wall to my left, I crossed the black tunnel of the landing, round the corner to the door that opened into Alexander's bedroom, and I knocked with my knuckles. My hands were so shaky and my arms so weak with fear that I hardly made a sound, and there was no answer.

Almost crying, I leaned on the door and I called: 'Alexander! Alexander! Please wake up!' and I heard the creak of bedsprings, a rummage of covers and a grunted: 'Hmm?'

I pushed the door open a little and stepped forward. It was dark in the room but, through the gloom, I made out Alexander's shape as he propped himself up on one elbow and squinted at me.

'What is it? Are you OK?'

'I'm sorry' – my voice was fragile – 'only somebody . . . there's something . . .' I paused and listened. I could still hear the noise, the rattling and scrabbling in the wall down the corridor, fainter now but it was there. I had not imagined it. I wrapped my arms around myself.

'Something's inside the wall, Alexander. Something's trapped. It's trying to get out . . .'

Alexander swung his legs out of the bed. My eyes had become accustomed to the gloom and I could see his face was screwed up as he struggled to wake. I could smell him more strongly in the mustiness of the warm air that came up from the bedclothes.

'It's the squirrels,' he mumbled. 'I should have warned you.'

'Squirrels?'

'They're in the roof. They chew the wires. I put a trap up. It must have fallen into the wall cavity.'

'Oh!'

'They go berserk in the cage trying to get out. It'll have rocked it off the rafter and knocked it down.'

'Can you get it out?'

'I'll try. Pass me my shirt, would you?'

Alexander pointed and I turned to reach out for a T-shirt hooked over the back of a wicker basket in the corner of the room behind me.

I sensed Jamie at the door before I saw him. The child stood just behind me, barefoot in his pyjamas.

He was standing on tiptoe, one arm extended, and I couldn't work out why but then there was a click and the room filled with light.

Jamie rubbed his eyes with his fist. The blue teddy bear was tucked under one arm and his pyjama bottoms sat low under his skinny little belly. He smelled of wee. He looked from me to Alexander and said: 'Grandma said you would be together in Mummy's bed.'

'No, Jamie, no, it's not like that,' I said.

'What about Mummy?' he asked. 'If you're in Mummy's bed where will she go to sleep?'

'Oh, honey, no, I just came in because . . .'

'Sarah had a nightmare,' Alexander said firmly.

'That's right,' I said.

Jamie looked at his father with suspicion.

'She's going back to her room now,' said Alexander.

I nodded.

'I'll see you later,' I said to Jamie.

'You're a hole-digger!' Jamie said. The dismay in his voice cut me, and I realized why he thought a hole-digger was worse than a gold-digger. I saw myself through his eyes: a stranger to the child whose mother had left him only a few weeks previously, an intruder in his parents' house, a female stranger, lank-haired, pale-faced, standing barefoot in his parents' bedroom, *their* private place. And then, worse, I saw myself as he imagined his grandmother saw me, a hole-digger with a spade in my hands, a good, solid shovel, standing shoulder-deep in a grave-shaped pit, the mud piling behind me. From nowhere the image of something grey and broken lying ragged and open-eyed on the ground beside me came to mind and I shuddered.

'Come on, soldier,' Alexander said. 'Let's go back to your bed for a bit.'

He swooped Jamie into his arms and I heard his footsteps go back along the landing.

I couldn't bear to go back into my room. I didn't want to hear the desperation of the poor trapped squirrel. I reached round the door to pick up my bag and crept into the bathroom to shower. I was careful to slide the bolt shut; even so, I felt shivery when I took off my nightshirt. I felt peculiarly bare. Oh, it was stupid, the squirrel noises had spooked me and everything was still strange. Nobody was looking, nobody could see.

I stepped into the shower and pulled the curtain to.

The cubicle was greasy and the water only lukewarm. It trickled sullenly through my hair and down my back. I had trouble working the shampoo into a lather and it didn't fill the room with its usual fruity fragrance. There was an underlying smell. I poked with my toes at a crust of matted hair and soap scum around the plughole. The vinyl curtain stuck to my backside and as I turned to peel it off I thought I saw a movement beyond. Holding my breath, I peered around the edge of the curtain, but the bathroom door was still closed and locked, and the cold little room was still empty. It must simply have been steam swirling that I glimpsed from the corner of my eye.

CHAPTER FOURTEEN

Breakfast the next morning was strained. I tried to jolly Jamie out of his misery and keep him distracted while Alexander went up into the attic and fished the squirrel trap out of the wall cavity, but I was jumpy. I dropped a glass and broke it and I couldn't ramp up the Rayburn to warm the last of the milk for Jamie's breakfast. It stayed resolutely cold in the pan but, when I put my hand on the hob a few minutes later, it burned me and, as I snatched my hand away, I knocked over the pan and the milk went everywhere.

Jamie was pale and sulky. Alexander came down with the trap hidden beneath a towel and disappeared outside with it for a while – I assumed he was releasing the animal somewhere far from the house – and when he returned he smelled of the cold and of fresh air. He put a pair of leather gauntlets down on the counter, washed his hands under the kitchen tap with Fairy Liquid and then wandered through the downstairs rooms searching for lost pieces of paper, his telephone charger and various other paraphernalia.

Jamie sat at the table in his school uniform – long grey trousers and a blue sweatshirt – swinging his legs and spooning dry Coco Pops out of a cereal bowl. All there was for him to drink was orange squash. It was not a nutritious breakfast for a growing boy on his first day back at school. I resolved to stock up with fruit and other fresh food.

After Alexander and Jamie left in the Land Rover, I spent an hour or so in the front garden, pulling up weeds by the handful. I worked hard and soon my hands were filthy and a huge pile of weeds was heaped on the lawn by the top flower bed, but when I stood back it was clear that I had hardly scratched the surface of what needed to be done. The garden was large, far too big to manage without the help of a gardener. In the past, somebody must have come in.

Already half-exhausted, I went back inside and made myself a mug of black coffee and some cheese on toast. I ate outside, watching the birds and the squirrels busying themselves burying hazelnuts. I enjoyed their quickness, the way they sat on their bottoms, looking this way and that with their nut-shaped, bright little eyes while the breeze riffled through their grey-brown fur. Every so often they would chase one another hectically along the lawn, up a tree and through the branches, dropping twigs and making the boughs sway and dip. I wondered which was the squirrel that had been trapped. In the sunshine, it seemed ridiculous that something so small and cute could have scared me so.

A stream ran along the bottom edge of the garden; it attracted insects that shimmied in the sunshine and ducks, and I was sure I glimpsed a kingfisher. The garden was beautiful and full of life but all the time I was aware of the house behind me, those tall old windows looking out as if they were watching. I should have been happy; at last I had what I had craved in Manchester: peace and quiet and time to myself. Instead I was nervous as a sparrow.

I wasn't used to the countryside, I told myself. That was all.

I looked back towards Avalon. It was just a big, empty house and it was my job to clean it. If I was to prove my credentials as housekeeper, it was imperative I did some actual housekeeping.

I found a bottle of bleach, some cleaning fluid and a couple of worn cloths amongst a tangle of carrier bags in the cupboard under the sink, put my iPod in my pocket, plugged in the earphones and went upstairs.

I started with Alexander's bedroom. It was a mess. Clothes and towels were strewn everywhere, empty mugs and glasses crowded the surfaces and empty beer bottles littered the carpet. A riding crop was hooked over one of the wardrobe door handles, and a muddy black jacket over the other. A pile of *Horse and Hound* magazines had been untidily stacked beside the dressing table. Photographs of Genevieve's two horses had been tucked into the rim around the mirror's edge. I picked up the T-shirt that Alexander had worn that morning, and held it to my face. It made me feel better. I put it on over my jumper, like a talisman, and began to collect the dirty linen and pile it on the landing ready to wash. I wasn't sure what to do with the jacket but thought it would be pointless to leave it there, dirty, so I picked that up and put it on the pile too. A single blond hair was stuck to the collar, so fair that it reflected the sunlight. It was longer than Genevieve's hair had been in the picture downstairs, about the same length as mine.

As the room became clearer, my mood began to lift. I sang along to the music on my iPod and was almost relaxed, almost enjoying myself, when, on the other side of the room, I thought I glimpsed somebody watching me. I saw a slight, fair-haired woman crouching as if in fear, holding out her hand to me, pleading. Her lips moved. I heard her say: Help me.

'Genevieve?' I whispered, pulling the earphones free, raising myself slowly to my full height, and as I did so the woman stood too and I realized that all I'd seen was my own reflection, distorted in a mirror that was slanted away from me. The outstretched hand had been mine, reaching forward for a pair of discarded jeans. The slightness and blondness of the image must have been an illusion, a trick of the light. And the words, they must have been something I'd been singing along to, that was all. I stood there for a moment or two, staring at myself, but I could not recognize the woman in the mirror; it did not look like me.

I felt nauseous and a little giddy.

I took off Alexander's T-shirt and left the room quickly.

I did not give myself time to dwell on what had happened. I turned up the volume of the music and went straight into Jamie's room. It was smaller, but just as untidy as his father's. The walls were patterned with a paper that showed the moon and stars and, at various intervals, spaceships with smiling green aliens sitting in pods. There was a low child's bed and a wardrobe, its open doors and drawers spilling clothes and toys. There was also a small desk and chair and a golden hamster in a cage that needed cleaning out. The cage was perched on a little wooden chest next to the window. I refilled the hamster's water bottle and made a mental note to buy new bedding for it the next time I went into the village. I picked up all the clothes to wash, stripped the sheets from the bed and piled them on the landing, beside Alexander's.

There was another door on the landing. It opened into a long, narrow room with a small window at the far end. It was a walk-in wardrobe and it was full of Genevieve's clothes.

I ran my fingers over the fabrics. They were beautiful to the touch, expensive, lovely, and all size eight. They made me feel big and unwieldy. Genevieve's competition coats, jackets and shirts were covered in protective polythene, obviously fresh from the dry cleaner's. There was also a range of hunting jackets, breeches and silk stocks in different colours. Boots polished to a mirror-like shine and a range of different kinds of riding hats took up most of the space below. A small part of the room had been given over to a dozen or so evening dresses and designer suits. Beneath these was a rack of shoes. I picked one up, a beautiful, light, Italian heeled sandal with a leather sole and gladiator straps. It was pretty and a dainty size three; like the clothes, far too small for me.

A full-length mirror stood by the window. This house was full of mirrors, I thought. It was full of mirrors and memories. Why had Genevieve left so many of her clothes behind? Had she been in such a hurry to leave?

I remembered the day I packed for Sicily, how I had stuffed random clothes into my bag, not really caring what I put into it; it was the act that was significant, not the packing. Maybe Genevieve had felt like that too. I wondered if Alexander had been standing behind her, begging her to stop and talk to him while she packed. I didn't like to think of him like that. I'd rather imagine him angry and proud than belittled and humiliated.

He'd said he was resigned to her leaving, that their relationship had been over. Then why had they parted so badly? And why did he still seem so bewildered and so lost?

I told myself to stop speculating. Their marriage, what went on between them, wasn't my business. These things that happen are private between man and woman.

I backed out of the room, closed the door quietly and set to work cleaning the bathroom. It took ages but eventually everything was spotless and shiny. The tiles and enamel-ware gleamed and the room smelled of soap and lemon. As an afterthought, I buffed the mirrors and opened the door of the little medicine cabinet that hung on the wall beside the window. It contained an assortment of old pill bottles, razors and hotel toiletries and I picked up what was obviously out of date and put it in the bin.

Half-hidden at the back of the cabinet was a small, dark-blue silk make-up bag. I took it out of the cupboard and opened the clasp. It contained a lipstick tube without its lid, a pair of tweezers and two small cardboard boxes. I knew what they were. I used to keep similar boxes in my make-up bag. I opened one box and took out the long, slim blister-pack that was inside. About half of the blisters had been popped.

It could only have belonged to Genevieve.

I could think of no reason why she would have left her contraceptive pills behind. Surely she'd have remembered to pick them up before she left?

CHAPTER FIFTEEN

At half past four, a rackety old Volvo estate pulled up on the drive and Jamie and two lanky, identical-looking girls in grey and maroon school uniform with their socks around their ankles clambered out. The girls wore old-fashioned straw boater hats. They saw me standing at the gate and stood still, close together, watching, whispering. They were about nine years old.

A large, hot-looking woman with long brown hair streaked with grey climbed out of the Volvo's front door, opened the boot to let out two panting black Labradors and the three of them led the children up the drive. The younger, larger dog bounded towards me and leapt up, almost knocking me over with his huge paws. He was all muscle and must have weighed at least as much as me.

'Blue, get down!' the woman bawled. The dog ignored her and tried to lick my face. I pushed him away and he jumped up again, and when, for the third or fourth time, I pushed him down, he ran around my legs, wagging his tail and making playful feint jumps, his big pink tongue hanging out of his chops.

The older dog was heavy on its legs. So was the woman. Her hair was held back with kirby grips and she wore Jesus sandals on her big, grubby feet. She was wearing a long, shapeless dress that reached to her ankles. She huffed to the gate and smiled. I greeted Jamie, who pushed past me with a scowl.

'Jamie . . .' I called.

'Fuck off!'

He ran off down the garden, and the willowy twin girls, shocked and impressed, followed gracefully in his wake. I tried not to mind or to let my humiliation show in my face.

The woman shook her head as she came through the gate and she held out her hand to me. The smile on her face was genuinely warm.

'I'm Claudia,' she said. 'Genevieve's half-sister. How do you do?'

'I'm Sarah,' I said. 'Alexander's housekeeper.'

'Oh, you don't need to introduce yourself. Everyone knows who you are.'

'I've only been here a few days!'

'The jungle drums never sleep.'

From the corner of my eye, I saw a movement down the garden. Jamie was throwing stones into the stream. The ducks quacked and flapped up into the sky. The twins squealed and turned away.

'He shouldn't do that,' I said. 'He shouldn't throw things at the ducks.'

'He's showing off,' said Claudia. 'It's for your benefit. Best to ignore him.'

'I'm not very good with him,' I said.

Claudia patted my arm. 'He'll come round. You need to be patient, that's all.'

For a moment we stood and watched the children. Jamie had taken off his shoes and socks, and was ordering the girls to do the same. The younger dog bounced around them, begging them to throw the sticks they were collecting.

'What are they called?' I asked.

'The dogs or the twins?'

I laughed. 'Twins.'

'Petra and Allegra. And the dogs are Bonnie and Blue. She came from the dogs' home and is a lady. He's a full-flight, locally bred pedigree who set us back six hundred smackers and is completely out of control. The postman's threatened to sue us if he knocks him off his bike again and we were expelled from dog-training classes after he impregnated a German Shepherd. You don't mind if I put the kettle on, do you? I'm parched.'

'Oh, I'm sorry, I should have thought!'

We went into the kitchen and I filled a bowl from the tap for Bonnie while Claudia made tea.

'How are you settling in?' she asked.

'Fine, thank you.'

'Don't you find this house a bit of a nightmare? Always seems to be something leaking or breaking or falling apart – that's what Genevieve said. Not that I'm trying to put you off or anything.'

'I'm still getting used to it,' I said. 'We drove past your house at the weekend, the converted barn. It's beautiful.'

'Yes, yes it is. We're very lucky.'

She leaned her bottom against the kitchen table and

smiled at me. Bonnie lay on the floor and watched her adoringly.

'I heard you met my father and my wicked stepmother.'

'Can't a person do anything in private round here?'

She shook her head. 'Abso-bloody-lutely nothing. Did Virginia give you a hard time?'

'A bit. She thinks I'm under-qualified to look after Jamie.'

'That's because you scuppered her plans.'

'I did?'

'Mmm. She wanted Jamie to go and live with her at Eleonora House until Genevieve comes back.'

'I didn't know that.'

'She likes to be in control, does Virginia. Alexander has been struggling here on his own and Virginia was most insistent that she'd take Jamie. Plan A was that he'd move in with her when term started so that Virginia could meet him from school and generally look after him, at least during the week. When Alexander came back from Sicily and said he'd found help her nose was very much put out of joint.'

I was shocked, although I tried not to show it. That put a completely different slant on everything that had happened between Alexander and me. So he had an imperative to find somebody to help him. Would anyone have done? Had he simply been searching for an available, easily manipulated woman he could persuade to take the role of housekeeper/nanny at desperately short notice?

'Does Virginia suspect my motives?' I asked brightly.

'Of course she does. But Alexander assured us that your relationship is strictly business. She told me you didn't give her a straight answer when she asked you directly but I expect that's because you were embarrassed.'

'Yes.' I nodded.

'But that's right, isn't it? I mean, there isn't anything between you and Alexander?'

'No,' I said, with as much conviction as I could muster. 'No, there isn't. All he thinks about is Genevieve. She's all he talks about.'

It was only when I said the words out loud that I realized they were true. I had a sudden, desperate pang of homesickness. I wanted to talk to May. I wanted to be back amongst people who loved me. My eyes felt hot. I'd spoken to my family since I'd come to Somerset, but briefly. I'd made out it was Nirvana and had told them how wonderful it was here, and how much better I felt, how all I'd needed was a change of scenery. Now I realized how selfish I'd been and how hurtful those words must have sounded to the people who had done so much to try to help me.

Claudia didn't notice my discomfort. She smiled in approval at what I'd said about Alexander.

'Well, that's exactly as it should be. So there's nothing for Virginia to worry about. She always sees the worst in people, I'm afraid. Really, she should be grateful to you for helping the family out in a crisis.'

I stroked the top of Bonnie's big head.

'Do you get on well with her, Claudia?'

'Virginia? So so.'

'Oh.'

'Her heart's in the right place, I suppose. Did Alexander tell you the story about Genevieve and me?'

'No.'

'You might as well hear it from me,' she said, spooning tea leaves into the pot. 'Because if I don't tell you someone else will and they'll make far more of a meal of it.'

'Tell me what?' I asked quietly.

She sighed. 'Virginia is my father's second wife, obviously. She swanned into our lives when I was about twelve – it was some hunt ball or other – and my father was besotted at first sight. You couldn't blame him. Mother was like me. Overweight, bit of a sight, none too bright, and Virginia was . . . well, she wasn't at all like that.'

I didn't know what to say to this.

Claudia smiled. 'To cut a long story short, Daddy and Mother divorced so he could marry Virginia and things all went a bit pear-shaped for my brother and me after that. We're civilized together, she and I, but we're not exactly best friends.'

'You have a brother?'

'I might as well not have. He's disowned us.'

I waited but she didn't say any more. She rubbed the bottom of her nose with her knuckle.

'What about your mother? Does she still live in Burrington Stoke?'

'No, she passed on a long time ago.'

She put the lid back on the pot and a different expression came into her eyes. She smiled as she gazed out through the door into the garden.

'I have a sister, though,' she said, and the tone of her voice had changed; it was gentler now, lower. 'Genevieve was my compensation for having to put up with Virginia as a stepmother.'

She fanned her face with a copy of the village newsletter. Her skin was pasty, beaded with sweat, but she was still smiling.

'We've always been very close,' she said.

'I'm glad,' I said. I thought of my own sister and how she cared for me. I would ring her the moment Claudia was gone. I would tell her how much I appreciated her.

'Do you know where Genevieve is now?' I asked gently.

Claudia shook her head.

'I'm sorry,' I said. 'It must be an awful worry for you.'

Claudia shrugged, picked up the packet of biscuits I'd put on the table and unwrapped the paper.

'The thing is . . .' Claudia sighed, and took out a biscuit. She looked at it and then broke it in two, and fed half to the dog. 'Genny has always been an "act first, think later" kind of person. Since she was a little child she's been impetuous and I just hope . . . Oh, I hope she's not in any kind of trouble.'

I thought of the abandoned, or forgotten, or deliberately left-behind contraceptive pills. I thought of the image in the mirror. I shivered a little and turned away.

'Am I talking too much?' Claudia asked. 'I'm sorry. You're probably wondering what kind of family you've ended up working for!'

'I'm sure Genevieve's all right,' I said, and I was trying

to reassure myself as much as Claudia. 'If she's the sort of person who does things on the spur of the moment, then . . .'

'But she's never gone away like this before. Well, once . . . She went off the rails for a while when she was at university, but that's not unusual, is it? Virginia was always so protective, it was no surprise that Genevieve kicked her heels up when she had the chance.'

I nodded.

'That's why Daddy and I were so thrilled when she took up with Alexander. He calmed her down. He was a positive influence. Virginia didn't think he was good enough for her, obviously, but my father adored him from the start. And Jamie came along and it was all perfect!'

I smiled as best I could.

Claudia put the other half-biscuit into her mouth.

We were both quiet for a few moments. Then Claudia said: 'I always seem to end up talking about Genevieve. It's a beautiful day. We won't have many more like it this year. Why don't we go and drink our tea outside?'

We sat on a blanket on the overgrown lawn in the front garden, Claudia and I. I sipped tea and breathed in her secondhand cigarette smoke while the children played and bees fed on the lavender stems and the songbirds gorged on blackberries. Claudia chatted about village life, and what it was like growing up in Eleonora House, the calendar governed by horse shows, trials and competitions and social events: balls, charity dinner dances, birthday parties. It was a different world from the one

I'd known and I enjoyed hearing her stories, although I did not envy her. It wasn't only that I felt sorry for her and her brother. I imagined that it must have been difficult growing up in a family where everything was so managed and organized. There could have been very little room for rebellion. No wonder Genevieve felt suffocated. I rubbed the inside of the old dog's ear with my knuckle and she groaned with pleasure.

Later, when Claudia had left with the twins and the dogs, and Jamie was inside the house watching television, I picked the mugs up and emptied the dregs over the wall that separated the garden from the orchard beyond. I disturbed a crow. It flapped away lazily with blood on its beak. I looked down over the wall. The crow had left behind a small, silvery-brown mess of blood, fur and jaw: the remains of a squirrel. Its skull had been smashed into fragments.

The crow could not have done that. The sleeve of my cardigan caught on the top of the wall, and as I pulled away I looked down.

I wished I had not.

On top of the wall was a smear of blood, and caught in the roughness of the grain of the stone was a circle of silvery hairs and one tiny shard of bone. Leaning up against it was a wooden-handled mallet with a metal head.

I dropped the mugs and backed away.

Alexander had killed the squirrel.

There was no other explanation.

CHAPTER SIXTEEN

The squirrel-killer breezed in later smelling of a dry, scorched substance that I came to recognize as stone-dust, and of sweat. He had shrugged off the top half of his overalls and tied the arms around the waist. He went straight to the sink and washed his hands, then he turned to smile at me. I was sorting out the laundry I'd washed earlier.

'Hi,' he said. 'Something smells good.'

'Lasagne.'

'You don't know how great it is to come in to the smell of home cooking!'

'It's nothing special,' I said.

He glanced at me. I did not let him see my face.

'How was your first day in service?'

I smoothed the towel I was folding.

'Fine.'

'Any trouble from Her Ladyship?'

'Virginia? No. But Claudia stayed for a while when she dropped Jamie off. She's lovely.'

'Yep. She is.'

'She told me a bit about her family.'

'Did she mention Damian howling at the moon?'

'Damian?'

'Her brother.'

'Oh . . . No, she said . . . well, nothing really. She told me how much she and her father like you.'

Alexander had his back to me, so I couldn't see his face. He made a noncommittal noise.

'She asked about us,' I said. 'I told her there was nothing between us.'

He pulled up a chair and sat down.

'Thank you,' he said. 'It's for the best. Though there's no love lost between Claudia and Virginia. Claudia's loyalty is with Genevieve.'

I noted that we had managed less than two minutes of conversation before Genevieve's name was mentioned. I snapped a pillowcase.

Alexander unlaced his boots, one after the other, and when he eased them off his feet I could smell the hot wool of his socks. I found it endearing. If I had known him better, if I hadn't known about the squirrel, perhaps I would have gone to his chair and stood behind it and rubbed his shoulders. As it was, my heart had hardened slightly.

'Hey,' he said, 'are you all right?'

'Yes,' I said.

Then I said: 'No. Actually, I'm not. Did you kill the squirrel that was trapped this morning?'

He didn't apologize or shrug or look remorseful. He said: 'Yep.'

'Why? Why didn't you let it go?'

'Because it would have been straight back in the roof. There'd have been no point trapping it in the first place.'

'You could have taken it somewhere else and released it.'

'You can't do that. Squirrels are territorial. They fight and they spread diseases amongst themselves. It would be cruel.'

'More cruel than smashing its head in?'

He reached out and took hold of my hand and squeezed. I looked down at my hand in his. It looked all wrong.

'It's a country thing,' he said. 'It's what you have to do. It's kinder than poisoning them.'

'It's horrible.'

I withdrew my hand and rubbed it with the palm of my other.

'You're a city girl,' he said. 'You've got this Beatrix Potter idea of fluffy squirrels and rabbits in jackets and . . .'

'Don't patronize me, Alexander.'

'I'm sorry,' he said. 'But it's true. Squirrels are vermin. Real life isn't like a romantic novel.'

Now there was anger in his voice, and I didn't know him well enough to push it any further. I turned away so that he wouldn't see the heat in my face, and I took the cucumber from the colander of washed salad on the counter and a sharp knife, and began to peel it.

'This is stupid,' he said, in a more conciliatory tone. 'Don't let's fall out over this.'

I nodded, but I didn't say anything.

'If it upsets you,' he said, 'I'll find a different way to get rid of the squirrels.'

'OK,' I said. 'Thank you.'

Alexander had a shower with his son while I finished making the dinner, and then the three of us ate together at the large, dark, wooden dining-room table. I'd given the room a cursory clean but, from the amount of dust and debris, I was pretty certain it hadn't been used for its original purpose in months. Piles of paper, unsorted washing, riding paraphernalia and other mess lay in little heaps on the seats of chairs and on the sideboard. The huge oil painting of two horses in a field that dominated one side of the room was dull with dust. Genevieve couldn't have been bothered with housework for a while before she went away. Or maybe she never cleaned the house. Why would she want to spend time polishing and vacuuming when she could be out riding in this beautiful countryside with the wind in her face, knowing she was one of the best in the country?

I ate slowly and watched Jamie. He had forgotten his previous surliness and wriggled excitably in his chair. His delighted responses to Alexander's constant, gentle teasing made me relax and feel happier. The blue teddy sat on the table beside Jamie's plate. I was relieved to see the boy animated and cheeky, like a child his age should be.

Alexander had lit waxy yellow candles on the big old mantelpiece that ran almost the length of the room above a cavernous fireplace, and there were candles on the table too, flat paraffin tea-lights, and one stuck into the neck of a wine bottle that reminded me of our first dinner together, that night in Sicily. I watched the father and son, and listened to them, and after a while I almost forgot about the squirrel. I almost forgot about Genevieve too. Almost. But she was there, in the flickering shadows; she was in the pattern of the curtains and the weave of the rug, crouching behind the pile of books that cast strange shadows in the candlelight. I felt a draught on my face, and was convinced, for a moment, that it was Genevieve returned, but of course it wasn't; it was just the door gently closing itself.

The candles burned down and, outside, the night dimmed and darkened. Alexander drew the curtains. Shadows flickered cosily on the walls. Jamie's chatter slowed. Alexander wiped his plate with a piece of bread and put the bread in his mouth. He took a drink of his beer. I tried to relax, but my uneasiness was pervasive. I was aware of eyes in the walls; I heard whispers. The whispers were telling me that I did not belong at Avalon, that Alexander was right: I was not a country girl; it would be for the best if I left and went back to where I belonged.

I told myself not to be silly; I was homesick, that was all. It was bound to take a while for me to settle in. I wished I knew where I stood with Alexander. I had felt uneasy lying to Claudia, but maybe it hadn't been a lie. Maybe there *was* nothing between Alexander and me.

The best thing, I thought, would be if Genevieve sent a postcard, preferably from somewhere far away, saying she was blissfully happy. Then people wouldn't mind if Alexander and I ended up together; they might even be pleased for us. They'd say: It turned out all right in the end.

I stacked the plates and took them into the kitchen. The cherry cheesecake I'd made earlier was in the fridge, its jelly and soft-fruit topping glistening. I tried not to notice the colour or the consistency. In the poor light it reminded me of congealing blood.

I took it out and was slicing it free of its tin with the blade of a knife when I saw, through the kitchen window, headlights drawing up on the drive. The white-yellow beams swept through the darkness and picked out the rambling stalks of unchecked brambles and failing nettles in the borders. The tyres made a soothing, crunching noise on the gravel and stone. I thought, at first, that it was Claudia returned – maybe she'd left something behind – but when the passenger door opened I distinctly heard the disembodied voices of people speaking over a radio. I'd heard that sound before. It was the police.

CHAPTER SEVENTEEN

I had time to call a warning to Alexander and to rinse my hands under the hot tap. I checked my reflection in the window and opened the door with a tea towel in my hand.

There were two police officers – a man and a woman – and they were friendly enough, brisk and apologetic. They came inside wrapped in a cloud of colder air that was blanketed with moisture. I shivered. The man was in plain clothes; the woman held her black, banded hat in her hands like a schoolgirl. She had dark shiny hair and a round, pretty face. She must have seen the worry on mine because she was kindly and assured me that nothing was wrong; they hadn't come with bad news, they just needed a quiet word with Alexander.

Jamie was fascinated by the police. He stood barefoot in front of them and gazed at them, awestruck.

'Have you got a gun?' he asked the woman.

She laughed. 'No! But I have handcuffs.'

'Handcuffs!' he whispered. 'Can I hold them?'

'I can do better than that. If you're a good chap and

let us have a few words with your dad in private, I'll let you put the lights on in the car.'

'The police lights?'

'Yes.'

This was good enough for Jamie. He stayed in the kitchen with me like a lamb while Alexander, ashen-faced and with a new bottle of beer in his hand, took the police into the living room and shut the door. I stacked the dishwasher, cleared the table, wiped everything down, only half-listening to Jamie, who was rabbiting on and on about the police he'd seen on television. I should have been glad that, at last, he was talking to me, but I wished he'd be quiet so I could hear what was being said behind the closed door. It had to be something to do with Genevieve. It had to be.

When I'd finished tidying up, I poured myself a glass of wine and Jamie and I went to sit in the garden, to look at the stars.

It was country dark outside, but already I knew the physiology of the garden: I knew which tree was where and how the walls went and where the overgrown kitchen garden was bursting out of its boundaries, the sage, mint and rosemary gone wild and thuggish. The lawn was overgrown, its ruggedness interrupted with fallen apples that I had meant to collect. I sipped my wine and pointed out the few constellations I recognized to Jamie. His mother had told him that stars were wishes. I could tell, from his voice, that he knew that wasn't exactly true, but we didn't know one another well enough to argue the point.

The police talked to Alexander for nearly an hour.

When we heard the living-room door open and their voices, Jamie and I went back into the kitchen. He huddled next to the Rayburn, I switched on the kettle, but nobody wanted tea or coffee. The policeman shook Alexander's hand and thanked him for his time and cooperation. He called him 'Mr Westwood'. Alexander looked pale and dreadful. The woman police officer smiled at me and fiddled with the radio at her shoulder. She kept her word and took Jamie outside to let him work the lights on the police car. They turned the garden into a fairground. I thought there was something obscene about them. Jamie liked the lights though. He was truly impressed. I jollied him along but Alexander did not even come out into the garden to watch.

When the police left and we went back inside Jamie became withdrawn and subdued again. He put his thumb in his mouth and sidled up to his father. Alexander's face was stony-cold. He hardly seemed to notice the child was there.

'Did they come to talk about Mummy?' Jamie asked around his thumb.

'Yes.'

'Is she in trouble?'

'No, Jamie,' Alexander said. 'Nobody's in any kind of trouble. Not yet.'

After Alexander had put Jamie to bed he came into the living room barefoot, his shirt hanging over his too-loose jeans and with a bloodstain in the region of his kidney, where he'd been picking at his scar again.

His beard was like pencil strokes drawn on the skin of his cheeks.

'Jamie wouldn't settle,' he said. 'He's all wound up.'

'It was an exciting evening.'

'We read *The Gruffalo* four times.'

'Is that a record?"

'Oh no. No, some nights we got into double figures after . . .'

'Genevieve left?'

'Yep.'

I uncurled myself from the settee and followed him into the kitchen.

He took a bottle of vodka from one of the cupboards, half-filled two small glasses and topped them up with ice.

He sat on a chair at the table. I sat back on the settee and pulled the throw around my shoulders. I took a sip of my drink and enjoyed the alcohol rush in my bloodstream.

'Go on,' he said. 'Ask.'

'It's not my business.'

'It is now; it's very much your business.'

'Then tell me why they came. What did they want?'

Through the open door that led into the living room, I could see the portrait of Genevieve on the bookcase. I could feel her eyes watching me, smiling at me. I shivered and tucked my legs up underneath myself.

Alexander rattled the ice in his glass.

'Virginia has reported Genny missing. As in "missing person"'.

'Why would she do that?'

'She's been threatening to do it for a while.'

'But why now? Why has she done it now?'

He looked at me and raised his glass.

'Because I'm here?'

'She suspects you are my mistress!' He gave a splutter of laughter. '"Mistress"! That's what the police said. I bet that wasn't the word *she* used.'

'Oh.'

Alexander put his glass on the table and hung his head.

'Virginia's come up with this story about me wanting Genevieve out of the way so we could be together, you and I. She knows I can't afford to pay a qualified nanny's wages and doesn't believe you'd have agreed to come unless there was already something between us.'

I stared into my glass.

'What did the police say?'

'They asked questions mainly. I told them the truth: that you wanted to get away from Manchester and I needed someone to live here to look after Jamie in return for board and lodging and the paltry sum I could afford to pay you. They asked if we were sleeping in separate bedrooms.'

I shuddered.

'Did you have to give them a tour of upstairs?'

He shook his head.

'Do they want to talk to me?'

'Not at the moment.'

I took a sip of my drink. 'Did you show them the

letter Genevieve left for you saying she was going?'

'No.'

I waited for him to tell me why he hadn't produced this irrefutable evidence that Genevieve had left of her own accord, but he said nothing more. Something moved at the periphery of my vision – the cat returned maybe, or a curtain in the draught. I wrapped my arms around myself.

'Why didn't you show them the letter?'

'I don't have it any more.'

Again a movement caught my eye. It was distracting me. 'Where is it?'

'I burned it.'

'You *burned* it?'

I struggled, for a few moments, to come to terms with the fact that Alexander might have disposed of the only evidence he had to support his story. Then I told myself not to be stupid. Why would he need evidence anyway? It wasn't as if he'd done anything wrong.

'I was drunk,' Alexander said. 'It was a few days after . . . I couldn't get hold of Genny. I kept calling her, begging her just to let me know she was OK, but her phone was always switched off and I . . .' He trailed away into his memories. 'Every time I heard her voice on the answerphone . . . it was driving me mad. I was out of my head for a while.'

I stood up and went to check the door was closed. Perhaps the draught was coming through the cat-flap.

'I don't suppose it matters,' I said gently, struggling to maintain my stream of thought. 'She wrote to her parents too, didn't she?'

'Yep. And apparently in that letter she went on about how unhappy she was with me and what a heartless bully I was.'

We were quiet for a moment or two. Then I asked: 'Are they going to look for her? The police?'

'I suppose so.'

Something about his voice bothered me. I took another sip of my drink.

'Are *you* worried about her, Alexander?'

'No,' he said, in the same quiet, stony voice I'd used the last time I spoke to Laurie. 'No, I don't give a toss about that woman now. I'd be glad if she was dead. She can go to Hell for all I care.'

I looked at him, and he looked so distressed I had to look away again.

'Fuck her,' said Alexander. He wiped his nose with his wrist, put down his glass and walked out of the room into the garden.

I waited for a while, but he did not come back inside so I finished my drink and went quietly to my bed.

CHAPTER EIGHTEEN

I should have left then. I should have returned to Manchester, but I didn't, even though it was obvious that Alexander and I were careering towards a disaster. Nothing was as I had imagined it. My romantic and, in retrospect, ridiculously naïve dream of setting up home in the country with a beautiful but damaged man and caring for his charismatic, tragic child seemed a million miles from the reality I now faced.

For days after the police came Alexander retreated right back into himself. I felt sorry for him and my instincts were to reach out and coax him out of whatever dark place he was in, but the truth was I hardly knew him at all. I was afraid of making things worse, of adding to his distress or making him angry. I couldn't think of any words of reassurance or comfort because, whichever way I looked at the situation, it looked the same. Genevieve was gone and nobody knew where she was, and until she returned, or at least let her family know she was safe, we would continue to live under the huge shadow cast by the cloud of her absence.

Part of me wished she would return.

Part of me hoped she would not.

If such thoughts were going through my head, they must have been haunting Alexander too.

When he was in the garden and I was inside, I watched him, searching his body language for clues. He moved like a man with a burden, always; when he was alone his fingers moved to the scarred place on his side and worried at it like a dog with a sore. Sometimes he would stand for ages simply staring out across the fields; maybe he was watching the birds or the clouds but I believed he was lost in thoughts of Genevieve and interminable 'what if' scenarios. It seemed to me that his sense of foreboding was worse than mine.

At dinner I studied his face while he ate, or when he was listening to Jamie's chatter and, although I searched, I found no trace of deceit. Alexander was evasive – often he refused to answer questions, even Jamie's questions – but he did not lie. He would rather say nothing than tell a lie. I was sure of that. I was as sure as I could be.

One day I asked him why he did not move away from Burrington Stoke if he was certain Genevieve was never coming back. Why not up sticks and start again somewhere else where nobody knew him or his history or what had happened? He told me he owed a debt to Genevieve's father and that he could not leave until it had been repaid.

'What kind of debt?' I asked.

'The money kind,' he replied.

And that was that. I already knew that, if I pushed, he

would simply withdraw. So I was quiet, and I waited.

I told May about Alexander's debt during one of our regular telephone conversations while I was waiting outside the school for Jamie. It was one of the few places where I had a signal for my phone. I was looking for reassurances; I didn't get them.

May recounted several horror stories about people she had heard of who had been in debt and then rounded off with the statement: 'Owing money is not a sign of good character.' She said it in a manner that implied that was a gospel fact.

'That's a bit harsh,' I said. 'What about people who have money problems because they're ill? Or because they've lost their jobs?'

'Does either of those reasons apply to Alexander?'

'I don't think so.'

'Then stop being so defensive.'

'Anyway,' I said, 'Alexander's working all hours to pay it back.'

'It's just one more thing, though, isn't it? One more thing that's wrong. Something else to add to the growing list of reasons why you shouldn't stay in Somerset.'

'I like it here,' I said brightly, reverting to my preferred script. 'It's doing me good being away from Manchester.'

'You don't *have* to be there, though, do you? You could be in London or Edinburgh or Dublin or Leeds. You could be anywhere. You're just infatuated with that man. He's got some kind of hold over you. What's it going to take to convince you to come home?'

Then we went into a conversation we had already had many times. May tried, for the hundredth time, to persuade me to return to Manchester and, for the hundredth time, I refused to budge. She told me that Laurie had called her to ask how I was; he'd been trying to contact me directly but the phone was always switched off.

'It's not switched off,' I said. 'I just don't get any signal at Avalon. And, anyway, I don't want to talk to him. Why would I?'

'He just wants to know you're OK. And also, Mum said the doctor's written and . . .'

'May, I have to go,' I said. 'The children are coming out of school. I'll speak to you soon.'

After that I made a vow not to tell May anything else about Alexander that could possibly be construed as a sign of bad character, and hurried through the afternoon to reach a point where I could relate the conversation to Alexander and reassure him that Genevieve had probably not been ignoring his phone calls but was simply in a place where there was no network coverage. When I told him he looked at me as if I was an idiot.

'Don't you think I thought of that?' he asked. 'I must have left a hundred messages.'

'But you can't retrieve messages without a signal!'

'She's not using her phone any more,' he said. 'The bills still come here but no calls are listed. She hasn't used it in weeks.'

'Oh.'

Then I said: 'Alexander, if Genevieve's calls used to be listed . . .'

'I've done that. I called every number on the bill I

didn't recognize, and asking Genny's vet and hairdresser if they knew anything about the whereabouts of my wife didn't get me anywhere apart from convincing people who were already suspicious that I was paranoid.'

He scratched his head with both hands, furiously.

'Sorry,' I said quietly.

'Look' – he sighed and took hold of my hands, and he held them tight in his hands, his thumbs squeezing down – 'I know you're trying to help, Sarah, but please stop. It's not your job to find Genevieve. It's nothing to do with you. Let it be.'

'OK,' I said.

He turned away, and that was my cue to leave the subject alone and never go near it again.

CHAPTER NINETEEN

One day followed another.

About three weeks after I'd come to Avalon, I was eating my lunch in the garden when I heard a clattering on the gravel of the drive. Over the top of the wall I saw the top half of a white horse and a girl in a sweatshirt waving at me. I picked up my empty mug and plate and walked over to the gate. The girl dismounted on the other side and walked the last few steps, holding on to the reins so that the horse had no choice but to follow. We faced one another over the gate.

'Hi,' she said. She was about my age, with ruddy cheeks and strings of brown hair hanging down on either side of her face beneath a shabby riding hat.

'Hi,' I said.

'Is Genny in?'

'No,' I said. 'No, she isn't.'

'Oh!' The girl frowned. 'But she knew I was coming today. We planned it ages ago and I've come a long way.'

She looked at me as though waiting for me to give her a reason why Genevieve had missed her.

'Perhaps she forgot?' I suggested tentatively.

'Well, obviously. Where is she?'

'I don't know.'

'Out riding?'

Behind the girl, the horse delicately extended one front leg like a ballerina, leaned down, and rubbed its cheek against its knee. The flies were bothering it. It had darker grey freckles on its face.

'No, I don't think she's riding,' I said.

The girl looked at me with exasperation.

'Sorry,' I said, 'but, really, I don't know where she is.'

'Who are you exactly?'

I realized that she had probably seen me sitting by the stream at the bottom of the garden as if I owned the place.

'I'm the housekeeper.'

'Genny didn't say anything to me about getting a housekeeper.'

I shrugged helplessly. The horse shook its head and blew air out of its nostrils. It made a whinnying sound. The girl turned to it and calmed it with her hand.

'When are you expecting her back?' she asked. 'Is it worth me waiting?'

'I don't know when she'll be back.'

The girl frowned again.

I grasped for something to say that would make me credible.

'Do you know Mrs Churchill? Virginia?'

The girl pushed the horse backwards away from the gate.

'Of course I know her.'

'Perhaps you'd better speak to her.'

She grabbed the front of the saddle with one hand, found the stirrup with her left foot and hopped effortlessly on to the horse's back.

'I will,' she said, and she made the horse turn and start cantering down the drive, sending gravel skittering this way and that.

I exhaled as she went, and turned back into the house.

She wasn't the only visitor. The farrier turned up just a few days later wondering why Genevieve hadn't brought the horses down into the loose boxes for their regular appointment. He had also come a good distance and I went through a similar conversation with him. There was a flurry of enquiries from the organizers of various major equine shows and events, which I politely deflected. I even answered a telephone call from the manager of a horse and donkey sanctuary in Taunton asking if Genevieve would be available to turn on their Christmas lights. I said I didn't know.

'She's such a lovely person, she's always helped us out before,' the woman said.

'I'm sure she'd love to do it, but . . .'

'We thought she could arrive on horseback to turn on the lights. Don't you think that'd make a good photograph?'

'I'm sure it would,' I said. 'Only the situation here is difficult.'

'Can I pencil her in? Then she can either confirm or not when she's ready.'

I didn't tell Alexander about any of these things. I

didn't see the point. I knew he would pretend they meant nothing, but they would remind him of Genevieve and how she had stepped out of her life, and his, and I didn't want anything to cause Alexander any more pain than he'd already been through.

September was drawing to a close. The days grew shorter, and I bought myself some warmer clothes one Saturday when Alexander took me into Castle Cary to show me where he worked. I used to be drawn to the fashion items; now, I picked up practical sweatshirts, fleeces and jeans. Alexander bought me a waterproof coat and a good pair of boots.

'You're turning me into a Wurzel,' I complained.

'I like Wurzels,' he said, and I smiled and said: 'If you're happy, I'm happy.'

Alexander smiled at me then and I saw something new in his eyes. He moved his face towards me as if he were going to kiss me, but Jamie was looking up at us with curiosity, and nothing happened. We did not touch physically, but something had changed between us; the connection was stronger. I was sure of it.

I worked hard. While Jamie was at school I cleaned the house thoroughly, one room at a time, not just the floors and surfaces but inside the cupboards, the skirting boards, the windows. Gradually, Avalon became less dark and gloomy. I cleared out the spiders, vacuumed up the dust and worked away at the stains. I carried out minor repairs and organized a handyman to deal with more substantial problems. Lights whose bulbs had needed replacing now illuminated the darker corners of the house, radiators gave out warmth and draughts were blocked. I paid with my own money for a builder to come and fix the holes in the roof so that the squirrels could no longer find their way in.

I found a photograph beneath the plastic cutlery tray in the kitchen drawer. It was a picture of Genevieve, with her hair long, like mine, standing beside the statue at the entrance to Eleonora House. Genevieve was mimicking the pose of the statue, one hand at her breast, the other reaching out and turned towards the gateway to the drive, inviting visitors in. Her face was downcast, like the statue's, and the resemblance between them was striking. It was an old photograph, watermarked and dirty. I thought it was creepy. I couldn't understand why I couldn't see the shadow of whoever had taken the picture. Surely it should have fallen across the grass, in front of Genevieve. And why had she posed like that, knowing the tragic story behind the statue? Was it a joke, or was she trying to underline her blood heritage by showing how alike she and her unlucky ancestor were? Either way, I didn't like it.

I didn't know what to do with the photograph. I couldn't bring myself to throw it away, but I didn't want to have to find somewhere safe to put it. In the end, I slipped it back beneath the cleaned tray, where I had found it.

In all my cleaning, I never went again into Alexander and Genevieve's room. If I went past and the door was open, I would pull it shut. The empty space inside the room scared me. I knew, rationally, that all I'd seen that day was my own reflection – that was all it could have been. But what I remembered seeing was not me but someone else altogether, and the more I thought about it, the more the fear in the eyes of the face in the mirror seemed to haunt me.

I did not mention any of this to May during our daily phone calls. The last thing I needed was May telling the rest of the family I'd had a supernatural experience, that I was obviously having trouble coping with my situation and that my mental health was deteriorating. No, I didn't want them to start down that route – it had been difficult enough persuading them that I didn't need specialized 'help' after the baby – so I said nothing about the image in the mirror, nothing at all.

CHAPTER TWENTY

Autumn was settling in, and so was I. There hadn't been a frost yet, but the morning air was cold and mists hung low over the valley. As the colours of Somerset mellowed into pale greens and browns, I felt calmer and less anxious. When I spoke to May on the telephone, I must have sounded more like my old self, because our conversations were more normal. I still had nightmares about losing the baby, but they weren't as regular as they had been. Looking after Jamie and Alexander took up so much of my time and energy that I dwelled less on the past. I did my best to shut out the thoughts and memories I didn't want in my head and, by keeping busy, I generally succeeded.

I was becoming used to the countryside. I had begun to appreciate the seasonal changes that you don't see in a city, or at least not to the same extent. The light and temperature used to change with the seasons in Manchester, but in Somerset everything was slightly different every day. The hedgerows were full of berries, the bird droppings around the house were purple with blackberries, and my boots crunched hazelnut shells already broken by squirrels and littered along the pavements.

By now, the people of Burrington Stoke knew I was Jamie's nanny and that I lived at Avalon. They always asked if there was any news of Genevieve, and they told me things about her.

Midge Taylor in the Spar said her sister used to be in the same branch of the Pony Club as Genevieve and that Genevieve had run her parents ragged as a teenager.

'It was Mrs Churchill's own fault, my sister said,' said Midge. 'She kept such an eagle eye on Genevieve that, the minute her back was turned, Gen would be up to no good! She used to climb out of her bedroom window and *ride* into the village to get to the Young Farmers' parties, tie the horse up outside and ride it back again when the party finished! All the boys had a thing for her, and all the girls wanted to be like her. She was so much fun!'

'Why wasn't she allowed to go to the parties?' I asked.

Midge shook her head. 'Boys,' she mouthed.

Joyce Hope, the teaching assistant at school, told me that Genevieve had contrived to get herself expelled from two of the best and most expensive boarding schools in Britain because she couldn't stand the regimentation.

'Heaven knows how she managed to get into university,' said Joyce. 'I think the Churchills paid for some private cramming, or else they must have pulled some strings, because that girl was far happier outside with her horses than she was inside with her books.'

I smiled at the stories of Genevieve's courage and daring. They made me more curious about her. Alexander never told me anything much, so I had to put together what bits and pieces of information I could gather. When I was on my own, at Avalon, I tried to imagine how Genevieve must have felt. She was living in the same house as I was, drawing the same curtains, cooking in the same pans. I tried to make myself feel like Genevieve, in order to understand what she had come to dislike about her life so much that she had walked out of it. She lived in a house that was big and unruly but which must have suited her lifestyle. She had a beautiful, healthy son and was married to Alexander, and even if things weren't perfect between them, surely they couldn't have been *that* bad. She was a champion rider, who had access to the best horses and could exercise them in some of the loveliest countryside in England. Why would anyone in her right mind walk away from all that?

There were only two people who could answer that question. Genevieve wasn't there; and Alexander refused to talk about his marriage although he sometimes, inadvertently, told me some small detail about his life with Genevieve.

He showed me how to recognize a sloe berry and made me bite into one, and I was horrified by the way it dried my mouth, thinking I was poisoned. He laughed and said: 'Gen used to love collecting those!'

'What for?' I asked, tapping my parched tongue against the inside of my cheek.

'Sloe gin. She made it every autumn so it was ready in time for Christmas.'

'Sloe what?'

'You just need berries and sugar and gin. It makes a liqueur that's better than anything you can buy in the shops. It was one of her little rituals.'

The next day, when I was alone in Avalon, I took down the recipe books from the shelf beside the Rayburn. Alongside a very tattered Mrs Beeton and two Jamie Olivers that looked as if they'd hardly been used, I found a homemade book. Inside were hand-written recipes for soups, pies and pastries and, sure enough, glued to the back cover was a piece of lined paper with instructions for making sloe gin.

On the way home from school that afternoon, Jamie and I duly picked a bagful of the tight little black berries with their silvery bloom. He solemnly pricked the fruit and poked it through the necks of well-washed empty squash bottles while I measured out the sugar and the gin. It felt right to be doing something that Genevieve always did, carrying on the tradition.

Another day Jamie asked if we could go to the conker tree.

'I don't know where the conker tree is,' I told him, and he said he would show me. It was at the back of the village hall, a huge, old horse-chestnut with leaves that were browning and curling, and branches ripe with seed-pods. We collected conkers, dozens of them, from the grass beneath the tree. I watched Jamie, who was always happy when he had a task to undertake, and I felt a little sad for Genevieve that she was not here to see her son.

Later Alexander sat for hours at the kitchen table, skewering holes through the middles of the biggest conkers and threading string through. Jamie sat opposite him, with his head in his arms, watching his father and swinging his legs. When one conker had been successfully attached to its string, Jamie would select the next from the pile and slide it across the table. Neither of them said a word but they were so alike in their concentration on the task in hand. Jamie could not have had a more attentive father.

I had dropped Jamie off at school one day and was walking back to Avalon when I met a tall, thin, gypsy of a man with deep-set eyes and yellowy dreadlocks. Even though it was a warm day, he wore a long coat and worn old boots. He was leaning against the garden wall of one of the village houses, smoking a roll-up. Behind him, scraggy chickens scratched in the soil of their pen and washing flapped on a line stretched across the garden. He raised a hand in greeting when he saw me.

'Hi,' I said tentatively. I thought he might be just passing through. People who looked like him sometimes did, on their way to Glastonbury.

'Hi,' he said. 'I'm Jamie's uncle, Damian.'

I recognized him at once. This was Claudia's brother. I could see some likeness between the two of them; although he was so thin and she was the opposite, they had the same slightly hooded eyes and an identical jowliness about the chin.

'Hello,' I said. 'Pleased to meet you.'

'And you're the infamous nanny.'

His voice betrayed his origins. He tried to disguise the public-school consonants behind a lazy West Country burr, but it didn't work. He said the word 'nanny' with a slight sneer, as if being hired help was something to be ashamed of. For all his hippy pretensions, he was still, at heart, an upper-class snob.

I smiled in a businesslike way.

'Yes, I am.'

'I've been watching you,' he said.

I was determined not to let him have the satisfaction of scaring me.

'I expected you to be less conventional, Damian. Everyone's watching me,' I said.

He laughed.

'OK,' he said. 'And fair play to you for standing up to Virginia.'

'I don't stand up to her,' I said. 'I just keep out of her way.'

He laughed again, a slightly nervy, high-pitched laugh.

'Do you mind if I walk with you for a while?' he asked.

The pavement wasn't wide enough to accommodate us both, and the road was busy with school traffic, so I went in front, with Damian following behind. I found his presence unnerving. I hoped he wasn't looking me up and down, sizing me up.

'Are you staying in Burrington Stoke?' I asked when the pavement widened at the new quarry junction and he came alongside me.

He shook his head.

'I'd rather cut off my right hand than stay here. I just came back to see if it was true about Genevieve being missing.'

'I'm afraid it is,' I said.

'How perfectly karmic,' Damian said.

'I don't understand.'

'A life for a life, Genevieve for my mother.'

I thought maybe Damian really was slightly unhinged.

'Nobody's suggesting she's dead,' I said quickly.

'I think she is. Don't you?'

He was making me uncomfortable.

'How did you find out she was gone?' I asked.

'The old bill found me. They tracked me down. Fair play to them.'

He looked around him at the neat, mown grass verge beside the quarry entrance and exit. The grass was pale with stone-dust.

'We could sit here for a while,' Damian suggested. 'Have a smoke and a chinwag.'

'I ought to get back to Avalon,' I said. I delved for an excuse. 'I'm expecting a delivery.'

'OK.'

He looked over to the gatehouse. The guard had spotted him. He was speaking into his phone.

'I'm not exactly Mr Popular round here,' Damian said, grinning. 'In fact, they don't like me at all.'

Out of the corner of my eye I saw a white van heading down the track inside the quarry. The gatehouse guard had put down his phone and put on his cap.

The last thing I needed was to be caught up in a

scuffle between Damian and the quarrymen. I imagined what Virginia would have to say about that.

'Why don't you come back for coffee at Avalon?' I suggested.

'I don't know . . .'

'We'll just sit outside, in the garden.'

The long red and white pole that formed the barrier across the quarry exit was slowly rising. Any moment now and the gates would swing open and the van would come through.

'Go on then,' said Damian. 'If you insist.'

He was a good few years older than me, but still, of the two of us, I felt like the adult. I could feel how uncomfortable he was in the world. It was sad that his life had been derailed by his parents' divorce when he was so young, and I was sorry for him but, at the same time, he gave me the creeps.

He followed me up the track that led to Avalon, but hung back when we came to the garden gate. I asked if he was not familiar with the house.

'I've never been here before,' he said.

'Why not?'

'When I was a kid this house was rented out to tenants. We weren't encouraged to fraternize with the peasantry.'

'Oh. But surely when your sister lived here . . .'

'Half-sister.'

'You never came when Genevieve was here?'

'Didn't anyone tell you I'm persona extremely non grata in these parts?'

'I heard the exile was self-inflicted,' I said.

'Even if it was, I'd never have set foot in any house where darling Genevieve lived,' he said. The bitterness in his voice stopped me from asking any further questions.

Damian asked for decaffeinated tea. I didn't have any. In the end he settled for a glass of tap water and I drank instant coffee. We sat in the garden, and the mournful sound of the sirens drifted across the fields from the quarry. I heard the sound at least three times a week; it was a warning that there were going to be blasts at the rockface, and I wasn't used to it yet. It seemed to go on for ages, and although I realized its purpose was primarily to ensure no living thing remained in the area that was about to be dynamited, still the sound seemed sinister to me.

Damian had noticed my discomfort.

'Know what? That noise is so familiar to me that I quite miss it,' he said. 'When I was a kid, I used to run down the hill when I heard the siren. There's a point at the edge of the woods where you can see the blast and, a few seconds later, there's this deafening sound like an air crash, and the rush of air hits you. I used to find it exhilarating.'

He laughed, but there was a note of cynicism in his voice.

'Why don't they like you being up at the quarry?' I asked.

He shrugged self-deprecatingly and cleared his throat, and I knew he was going to tell me something about himself that made him proud.

'It's my life's ambition to close it down,' he said. He

turned his glass in his dirty fingers, waiting for my response.

'Why?' I asked.

'Because it's wrong. Everything about it is wrong. The Churchills are pillaging one environment for the raw ingredients they can sell on to destroy another.'

'I don't follow you.'

'They take stone from here, and it's used to build roads, executive houses, shopping centres, whatever, elsewhere, fucking up the environment all over the place while they get rich on the profits.'

'Oh.'

Damian's voice was sounding less self-conscious now. As he became more passionate about his theme, the upper-class vowels made themselves clear despite his best efforts.

'The whole thing stinks,' he said. 'What right does the Churchill family have to blast into that hill and profit from their vandalism? They have no more right to the land than anyone else.'

I picked a stem of grass that had grown a seedhead.

'I suppose they own it . . .' I said, stripping the seeds from the stem.

'How can they "own" something that took millions of years to form?' Damian asked. 'It doesn't belong to anyone. It belongs to us all. Up until a few decades ago, that land was a perfect hill. It was covered in woodland, ancient woodland that was home to all manner of flowers and trees, butterflies, animals, and now it's all being blasted away for the commercial gain of my family. Once they've finished with it, they'll be wealthier, but nothing will be able to grow there. It'll just be another abandoned quarry. Another eyesore. A dead place, a murdered place. Do you think that's right?'

I could not reply. If I sympathized with his point of view I would be being disloyal to Alexander's in-laws, Jamie's grandparents, yet I could not argue with what Damian said, because it was true; he was right. I realized that inviting him back to Avalon had been a mistake. It wasn't that we had nothing to talk about but that there was nothing we *could* talk about. I pretended to be worried about the non-existent delivery and was relieved when Damian said he had other places to be.

I asked if there was any way to get in touch with him, in case there was news of Genevieve.

'No,' he said. 'There's no way to get in touch.'

'At least tell me where you'll be?'

He shrugged. I felt a twinge of frustration.

'Damian, what if we need to contact you?'

'You won't,' he said. 'If Genevieve's body turns up, I'll read about it in the newspapers.'

'There is no body,' I said. 'She's not dead, Damian, she's gone away of her own accord.'

Damian raised an eyebrow. 'Do you really believe that?' he asked.

I wondered if he was being deliberately weird and melodramatic, but thought maybe it was a symptom of the mental distress Claudia had hinted at and Alexander had mocked.

'She left letters saying as much,' I said calmly. 'She said she wouldn't be in touch for a while.'

'If she was alive, she'd have contacted Claudia by

now,' he said. 'We all know that. Those two were always so close. Claudia could never see Genevieve for what she was, despite what happened to our mother.'

I could see the memories crowding into his head. He licked his lips like a nervous dog and his hands trembled.

'You mean the divorce?' I asked gently. 'I know that must have been awful for you, but . . .'

'Not the divorce!' Beneath the hair and the grime, his skin had paled and tiny bubbles of sweat appeared on his forehead. He wiped them away with the back of his hand.

He said: 'You don't know, do you?'

I shrugged helplessly.

'Well, here's the big news,' he said. 'My mother hanged herself the day Genevieve was born.'

I clasped my hands over my mouth. 'Damian, I'm so sorry, I had no idea, I . . .'

'When father married the hugely inaptly named Vir-gin-i-a' – he dragged out the four syllables with bitterness – 'Mother, Claudia and I were relegated to a cottage on the edge of the estate. Mother couldn't bear it. People were talking about her, her friends pitied her, she wasn't eating, she wasn't sleeping and when she heard about Genevieve, it was the last straw.'

'That's terrible.'

'And I found her,' he said, looking up, into my eyes. 'I was six years old and I found her.'

'Oh, Damian!' I leaned forward to touch his hand, hoping to comfort him a little, but he pulled away and shook his head. I didn't know what to do, so

I sat beside him until he had composed himself again.

'It fucked me up,' he said at last.

'Well, it would.'

'I didn't speak for two years. Couldn't. Father sent me to different shrinks, but nothing worked. And all the time Virginia was swanning round Eleonora House with her cute little Churchill baby on her hip, treating Genevieve like a princess and Claudia like shit and acting as if nothing had happened. That's why I went away; that's why I'll do whatever I can to shut the quarry down; and that's why I never wanted anything to do with my half-sister.'

I exhaled slowly and waited, but Damian didn't say anything else. After a moment or two he leaned back, taking his weight on his extended hands.

'Are you going to go and see Claudia while you're here?' I asked as gently as I could.

He shook his head.

'Won't she be upset if she finds out you were in the village and you didn't at least go and say hello?'

'Claudia knows what I'm like.'

'Should I tell her we met?'

'Tell her whatever you want. I don't give a toss.'

'Damian, you know she cares about you.'

He nodded. 'I know.'

Then he uncurled his long legs, stood up and stretched.

'Well,' he said, 'good luck, nanny. You're going to need it.' And he was gone with a backward wave of his hand, banging the gate so hard it rattled on its hinges.

I watched until he disappeared into the tunnel of

trees at the far end of the track, the hem of his coat flapping around his worn old boots, then I went inside and locked the door with the big metal key. I kicked off my shoes, went into the living room, and curled up on the settee. I stayed there for the rest of the morning, thinking about Damian being the same age as Jamie when he found his poor, dead mother, and how that must be one of the worst things that could happen to a child and how it would stay with him for the rest of his life.

CHAPTER TWENTY-ONE

I told Alexander about meeting Damian and he said he thought it would be a good idea to steer clear of him if I saw him again.

'He's not staying in Burrington Stoke,' I said, and Alexander said that was definitely for the best.

Still, a couple of times, I was almost certain I glimpsed Damian; one morning I thought I saw him leaning against a tree at the far end of the orchard, with his coat wrapped around him and his chin tucked into its collar. I wondered if he had slept there, watching the house, but when I looked again, I realized that what I'd seen was probably just a displaced branch, felled by the hedge-cutter that had been along the lane the day before. Another time, from the car window, I saw someone with long, messy fair hair walking along the high street, with their hands in the pockets of a long coat. I only saw the back of the man, and could not be certain it was Damian. I had a few bad dreams, and then I forgot about him, but I never forgot what he had told me.

* * *

Certain aspects of my life in Burrington Stoke were continuing to improve. I had become friendly with a nice young woman from the village called Betsy. She was marginalized, like I was, only in her case it was because her three children all had different fathers. She lived in one of the small line of council houses that fronted the far end of the high street and she painted ceramic plaques saying things like 'Drink up thee zider' which she sold to the tourist shops in Wells and Bath. I was glad to have a friend of my own age, who was unconnected to the Churchill family.

Another positive was that Jamie and Alexander seemed happier now that Avalon was cleaner and tidier. Keys, shoes and schoolbooks were less likely to be lost or misplaced, so we were all less stressed.

It never went away, though, the wondering about Genevieve. The more I tried not to think about her, the more she was in my mind. I sometimes found myself having imaginary conversations with her about certain aspects of the house or about her early life. I wondered how old she was when she realized that her coming into the world was what had driven Claudia and Damian's mother from it. I wondered what it was like to be in Eleonora House on her birthday when she was a child. It didn't matter how pretty, bright, talented and rebellious she was, nor how adored and beloved; still her birthdays must have been terrible times for the whole of that disjointed family. Their money could do nothing to make things better. Genevieve couldn't have had parties – not on the anniversary of the death of the mother of her half-siblings. The candles on her cakes would have counted the years since the suicide. Did the Churchills work out some respectful compromise? A visit to the cemetery to lay flowers on the grave in the morning, Genevieve's presents in the afternoon? No wonder Damian was still angry. Thinking about the situation made me shudder.

It must have been awful for all three children.

I couldn't ask Claudia about her family. I didn't want to remind her of bad times. She was missing Genevieve terribly, and she seemed so lonely. Some days, she brought the twins round after school, and Jamie and the girls lay on the living-room carpet playing board games while she sat with me in the kitchen and taught me recipes to make the most of the produce that grew in the orchard and the garden. We were comfortable and easy together. Despite the awkwardness of the situation and the difference in our social status, we became friends. Perhaps Claudia liked being in Avalon, doing some of the things she used to do with Genevieve. Maybe being there with me made her feel closer to her missing half-sister. She had many acquaintances but no real friends and confided in me all the time. I told her very little about myself. I was more than happy to be the listener, to hear what Claudia had to say. Her loneliness was like a millstone around her neck; Genevieve going had left a huge hole in her life. And although it was Genevieve's disappearance that had brought Claudia and me together, I was always glad when I heard the barking of the dogs on the drive signalling that she was coming in for a cup of tea and a chat.

She taught me things I did not know. She explained that people in that neck of the woods were stoic. They respected restraint, in behaviour and emotion. She said locals expected people to maintain their dignity at all times, even when the world was falling apart around them. People who didn't demonstrate this degree of self-control were mistrusted. That was why her brother had found it so difficult to fit in. I prompted her to explain.

'Damian's one of those people who can't help but wear his heart on his sleeve,' Claudia said. 'He never got on with Genny. He never made any effort with her and he was awfully jealous. It wouldn't have mattered if he'd learned to hide it, but he didn't. He hated her but he was sort of obsessed with her at the same time. And he used to do spiteful things.'

'What kind of things?'

'Horrible things . . .' Claudia looked out of the window and sucked in her lips. 'Once, he poisoned her pony, fed it yew. I don't think he meant to hurt it badly, he only meant to disable it. Genny was due to go to London with the Pony Club the next day – they were through to the finals of something or other at Wembley and there was an awful lot of fuss getting ready. She was so excited and happy. He wanted to stop her going.'

Claudia sighed. 'Cracker, the pony was called. Poor thing had to be put down.'

'Oh, Claudia, how awful.'

'People tried to feel sorry for Damian; they were always cutting him slack, and I think he found that humiliating. He preferred them not to like him so he developed this odd persona,' Claudia said. 'It's a shame. He could have been anything he wanted to be. He could have been a hero but he chose to be a drop-out, a misfit. He doesn't belong anywhere.'

'Don't you worry about him?' I asked.

She smiled and shook her head.

'Every so often I read about him in the newspapers or see him on the television,' she said. 'He's always up to something, being controversial, making people uncomfortable. I believe it's his way of letting me know he's all right. Or maybe he's just trying to get on Virginia's tits. Either way, he succeeds!'

I didn't tell her that Damian had been in the village, or that he had been to Avalon and talked to me, because I thought she would be hurt. I thought I was doing the right thing.

I listened to Claudia, and I learned.

Whenever I was in the village, I kept myself to myself. I didn't give away any information apart from the absolute basics, no matter how much anyone tried to draw me. I always smiled and was polite, but I never discussed the situation at Avalon.

There were a few exceptions. I told Betsy everything and was friendly with the postman who continued to deliver letters for Genevieve; bank and credit-card statements, invitations to equestrian events and fashion-house previews. I put the letters into a pile on the counter, and when Alexander came home he put them straight out into the green box for recycling.

'Don't you think you should keep those?' I asked him once, and he shrugged and said: 'What for?'

CHAPTER TWENTY-TWO

Late in September, Virginia invited Jamie to stay overnight at Eleonora House the following Friday. She said she had a surprise for him.

Alexander went to speak to Virginia and Philip about the arrangements. He told me he wanted Philip's personal assurance that Jamie would be allowed to return to Avalon after lunch on the Saturday. He seemed, to me, to be taking the invitation rather too seriously. Despite all the family's problems, Virginia and Philip were Jamie's grandparents; it was obvious they had his best interests at heart and it didn't seem unreasonable for them to want to spend some time with the boy. Part of me thought it would be a good thing, because Jamie would be able to reassure Virginia that Avalon was a cleaner, calmer, happier house now. He would be interrogated, for sure, but since the squirrel morning I hadn't been into Alexander's bedroom. Jamie knew that and, given that his father and I had not so much as looked at one another with desire or spoken an inappropriate word since I had come to

Avalon, there were certainly no crimes of passion to report.

I tried to make Alexander see that the overnight visit might be a good thing but his reaction was strange.

'I have to be sure they'll let me have him back,' he told me.

'Of course they will! What else would they do with him?'

'You don't understand,' he said.

'Then tell me what it is that's bothering you.'

But he wouldn't.

I wasn't worried about Jamie going to stay at Eleonora House for a night, but I was jealous. I didn't like the thought of Genevieve's mother having our boy all to herself. I imagined her dusting him down, metaphorically, and wiping any trace of me from him. I imagined her wrapping him up in Genevieve again like a lamb wrapped in the bloodied fleece of another to disguise its smell.

Conversely, I also looked forward to that Friday night with intense anticipation and more than a little dread. For once, Alexander and I would have the house to ourselves. If he acted with his usual circumspection, then I would know that what had happened that day in Taormina had been a one-off, something that only served to bring the two of us together in a practical way. Sometimes I wondered if that breathless, glorious sex in the shade of the trees had not been the romantic catharsis I remembered but something else altogether.

Then I remembered how Alexander had explained

the situation when I arrived at Avalon. He had said it would be best if people thought I was 'just' the nanny. 'For now,' he had said. He had been right. It would have been wrong for us to have behaved with even the slightest impropriety, not least because it would have been cruel to Jamie. But he had been letting me know that there would be a time when we could be together, openly. I was sure that was what he had meant.

Most of the time I was certain there *was* something between Alexander and me, something unresolved.

I felt it. It was strong as the tide.

Still, in darker moments I had my doubts.

The bottom line was that, if there was no seduction while Jamie was with his grandparents, there never would be. The stakes could not have been higher and the anticipation was thrilling and terrifying.

During the afternoon, I made a tagine, slicing the onions and peeling tomatoes, garlic and peppers. While the meat simmered and tenderized I opened a bottle of red wine and left it in the pantry to breathe.

When Alexander brought Jamie home from school, I gave the boy a tuna and mayonnaise sandwich and a glass of milk, and made sure he changed into decent clothes before helping him pack his rucksack. Jamie was nervous about staying away from Avalon and his father. He had never been separated from both parents at any one time and was concerned about practical matters such as where he should brush his teeth and what he would be given to eat for breakfast.

'I don't like eggs,' he said, as I tightened the straps on his rucksack.

'Don't worry, Daddy will tell Grandma,' I promised.
'I might be sick if I have to eat eggs.'
'You won't have to eat anything you don't want to.'
'Are you sure?'
'Absolutely.'
It would have been easy for me to exacerbate Jamie's anxiety and persuade him that he should not go, but I didn't. I was kind and reassuring. I imagined his grandparents would be nervous too and it would be best for everyone if the visit was a success.
When he was ready, Alexander drove Jamie up to Eleonora House. I waved them off. Then I checked the dinner, ran upstairs and made up my face, sprayed perfume on my wrists and throat and threaded silver hoop earrings through my ears. I didn't change into anything tight or sexy. That would have been too obvious, but I put on a clean top and my favourite jeans.
By the time Alexander returned, I was curled up on the kitchen settee with a glass of wine in one hand and a paperback in the other.
'Hi,' I said, smiling and swinging my foot prettily. I had painted my toenails. 'Whatever that is,' Alexander said, crossing straight past me and opening the oven door, 'it smells bloody fantastic.'
'It's spicy lamb casserole.'
'My all-time favourite. How did you know?'
'Because last time I made it you told me.'
'Oh yes.'
He shut the oven door, turned to his right and opened the fridge door. He had not looked at me once.

'Do we have any beer?'

'There's wine.'

'Yeah, but I feel like beer. I was going to go up for a bath.'

I fetched him a cold beer from the rosette room, handed it to him crossly and sulked in the living room while he went upstairs. I heard the noises of the bath filling, and Alexander scrubbing the grit from his fingernails in the bathroom sink overhead. I switched on the television.

'Sarah!' he called down.

'What?'

'Would you bring me a glass?'

'What did your last servant die of?' I muttered.

I didn't move for a few moments.

'Sarah?'

'All right, I'm coming.'

I stood up, fetched a glass from the kitchen, and went back upstairs.

The bathroom door was open and I could hear the splashing of the water from the taps, but I couldn't see Alexander.

'Where are you?' I called, turning the glass between the palms of my hands.

'Just put it on the window ledge, would you?'

I stepped forward and put the glass down. Night was falling beyond the window and the pane was misty with condensation. I rubbed a little circular gap in the chill moistness with the palm of my hand and felt, more than heard, the sudden movement behind me.

I didn't have time to work out what was going on.

Alexander lifted me up from behind and dropped me like a child into the bath. Water and foam slopped over the side and I laughed and squealed as he, naked and unrepentant, climbed in on top of me.

I was so relieved. More than anything, I was relieved.

He *did* want me; he wanted *me*. I hadn't been mistaken, it was more than business between us, and the relief I felt was overwhelming. Inside my head was a profound joy: I should not have doubted Alexander, I should have trusted my instincts from the start.

It had taken so long for this to happen because this was the first time we had ever been alone together, the first time we had had a chance to drop our reserve. We made the most of it. Every moment of the propriety with which we'd behaved up to that point fell away as we splashed and kissed and explored one another in the bath. Alexander peeled wet clothes from me, his hands, at last, were everywhere, and he, being naked, was entirely accessible to my mouth, my tongue, my fingers. He held my face between his hands and kissed me this way and that and in those warm, wet moments with my eyes closed and heat everywhere I lost track of what was me and what was him and what was the fabric and water between us. And all the time we were laughing, smiling, delighting in one another. I had never been happier; it far surpassed anything I'd ever experienced with Laurie. If there was a slight shadow in the sunlight of my joy that evening, it was the conviction that I never would feel quite this way again.

'I've never seen you with no clothes on before,' I

whispered as we were lying, uncomfortably, side by side in the bath, which was, by this time, almost empty. The bathroom carpet was sodden and I feared for the living-room ceiling below. I shivered a little, and ran my fingers down his chest, through the curly hair at the centre of the breastbone, to the scar beneath the ribcage that had, once again, scabbed over.

'What do you reckon?' he asked, making a fist and flexing his arm.

'You'll do,' I said.

Then I said, 'What if inviting Jamie to stay the night was just a ploy by Virginia to see what we would get up to if we were alone? What if she's lurking outside with a crack team of police and any minute now the house is about to be raided?'

'Shut up,' he said softly, kissing my hair.

'What if she's got the place bugged? Hidden cameras?'

'I told you to shut up.'

'How did you get that?' I asked as I fingered the edges of the scab. 'Was it an accident?'

He reached backwards, awkwardly, with his hand and moved my fingers from that place. He lifted them to his mouth and kissed them, gently, one by one.

'Don't let's waste time talking about the scar,' he said.

So we didn't.

We never ate the casserole. By the time we went downstairs it had dried out in its dish, the lid fused to the base by charred juices. The jacket potatoes were withered and hard as stone. I was wrapped in one side of the duvet, Alexander in the other. He was a new Alexander to me, that night. He was a relaxed, funny, charming Alexander who joked and laughed and who made cheese and crisp sandwiches entirely nude, having relinquished the duvet, in a gentlemanly fashion, to me while I lit the fire in the living room. I watched him covertly, enjoying the way his muscles moved beneath his skin and the shape of his thighs and his buttocks and his back.

We never made it to the freshly laundered and aired sheets and pillowcases of my bed. We fell asleep on the settee, watching the flickering of the fire, our bodies touching all the way down, his front fitting into my back like we were two halves of the same something, something that was better intact than it was when it was the two of us, apart.

I was certain then that May was wrong, Virginia was wrong, anyone who doubted Alexander's integrity was mistaken. How could a man who held me so close, who laughed so long and so openly, who kissed me so gently, be doubted? How could he have done anything to hurt anyone?

CHAPTER TWENTY-THREE

Alexander went to pick Jamie up after lunch the next day. While he was gone I chipped pieces of desiccated lamb from the casserole dish. I was interrupted by the telephone. I answered, and a female voice said: 'Hi. Is that the nanny?'

'Yes.'

'It's Phoebe here, Gen's friend. Could I speak to Alexander?'

'I'm sorry, he's not here at the moment,' I said. 'Can I take a message?'

'Yes. Ask him to call me, would you? Tell him our new au pair has let us down . . .'

'Oh dear, I'm sorry.'

'Silly girl. Ukrainian. I knew we should have stuck with a German. But in the meantime, I wanted to ask Alexander if we could use you for a few hours a week, come to some sort of nanny-share arrangement?'

I opened my mouth and closed it again.

'It's so hard to find decent help,' Phoebe continued. 'At least we know you're reliable.'

'OK,' I said quietly. 'I'll pass on the message.'

I replaced the receiver and took a deep breath.

Jamie came running in soon enough. His cheeks were flushed and his eyes were bright and he looked as healthy and as happy as I'd ever seen him.

'Hello, you!' I said. I did not hold out my arms to him in welcome; he had made it clear from the start that such familiarity was inappropriate except when he decided he needed some kind of physical comfort. I respected his boundaries.

This time, however, he ran to me and launched himself at me, so I had to catch him. He wrapped his arms around my neck and his legs around my waist and said: 'Sarah, guess what? Guess what?'

'Ummmm . . . You had a nosebleed?'

'*No!*'

'You were allowed to stay up to watch a film?'

'*No!*'

'I give up.'

'I got a pony!'

I pulled my face back to look at his face. Close up, the blueness of his eyes was astonishing; it took me by surprise like a sunset sometimes does, or a birdsong – something routine but extraordinarily lovely. Those fair, almost-white lashes that blinked at me were always unfamiliar, so unlike his father's dark ones.

'You got a pony?' I repeated stupidly. I couldn't take my eyes from his face.

'Yes! He's exactly the same as the one Mummy learned to ride on. And Grandma says I can go there every Friday and ride him and when I'm good enough I can go to competitions with my cousins!'

Behind Jamie's back, Alexander came into the kitchen carrying his bag and raised a lascivious eyebrow at me.

'A pony! Jamie! You are *so* lucky.'

'He's called Luc,' said Jamie, wriggling out of my arms. 'Short for Lucozade, which Grandma says is a drink the same colour as him. The proper word for it is palomino. And already I can make him walk and stop and he knows he's mine.'

'Of course he does,' I said.

'And Grandma says if I work hard I can be as good a rider as Mummy and then when Mummy comes home she'll be proud and we'll be able to go riding together.'

He went to the fridge and pulled the door open.

'What can I have to eat?' he asked.

'Whatever you want,' I replied.

I worried about Virginia's true motives for buying a pony for Jamie and I'm sure Alexander did too, although, as was usual with uncomfortable subjects, it was not something we discussed. Perhaps we were being overly cynical. Certainly his paranoia was rubbing off on me. Maybe all Virginia wanted was to encourage her grandson to share his mother's passion for riding. But I wondered if she was subtly making Jamie feel that Eleonora House was his home, at least as much as Avalon, so if ever he should go to live there, for whatever reason, it would not be too much of an upheaval. My main concern was that she might be planning some kind of legal action to remove the child from his father's care. In the end, this possibility worried me so much that I called Neil, who knew a little about law, to ask his advice. He said there was no reason at all why a child would be removed from his natural father simply because his grandmother suspected the father might be sleeping with the housekeeper.

'And is there any truth in that rumour?' he asked in a friendly voice.

'That's absolutely none of your business, Neil,' I said.

Neil put on a newsreader voice and said: 'When asked about the relationship, Sarah refused to confirm or deny the affair, which will only lead to further speculation on her sister's part.'

'Stop it,' I said, but I smiled with a pleasure that was a combination of tentative pride and embarrassment.

'Listen, Sarah, we don't care what you're doing,' Neil continued in his normal voice. 'Well, we do, but mainly we just want to know you're OK. We want to know that Alexander's OK. May's still worried about you.'

'She's blowing everything out of proportion. As usual.'

'She wants you home. And she's not the only one.'

I held the phone close to my cheek.

'So you definitely don't think there's any danger of Alex losing Jamie?' I asked quietly.

'As long as the child is being well cared for and the wife doesn't turn up demanding custody, then no.'

'Thank you, Neil,' I said.

'You're welcome, Sarah. You're welcome any time.'

* * *

So I tried not to worry, and I tried not to allow myself to think up conspiracy theories. Those nights, the handful of precious Friday nights we had that autumn when Jamie was with his grandparents, Alexander and I fell into one another, and each successive Friday it was as if our relationship had intensified. Each time, I made something special for dinner and, each time, we did not eat it, we were so eager to make the most of one another. On Friday morning I washed and dried the bedsheets, and later Alexander came into my bed and we behaved with absolute hedonism, twitching and gasping and laughing and arching and groaning and pleading; I was desperate to please him and to give him pleasure and I loved his beautiful body, all its muscle and bone and hair and even the scar that never healed. He gave himself to me, he abandoned himself and I devoted myself to him, committed to making him come once, twice, three times, until we were both sticky and spent. Then we'd wrap ourselves in the duvet like we did that first night – it was our ritual – and we'd go downstairs to sit in front of the fire, picking at cold food. Eventually we would go upstairs, always to my bed, the spare bed, where we clung to one another like children. We never went to the bed he used to share with Genevieve.

I loved those nights, I loved every moment of them, but at the same time I was afraid. I did not know how they would end, or when, but I knew our Friday nights at Avalon were finite. And because of this, I could not give myself wholly to Alexander the way he gave himself to me. I held something back so that, if everything came to be lost, I would still have something of myself in reserve.

CHAPTER TWENTY-FOUR

Everything was more or less all right, we were managing, and then Claudia and Bill invited Alexander and me up to the Barn for dinner.

'Friday . . .' I said, when Alexander told me. It was impossible to keep the disappointment from my voice.

Alexander was hunched down in front of the Rayburn, which had gone out. He reached up to me and put his hand on my thigh. I slid into the warmth of his fingers.

'Claudia thinks she's doing us a favour because we won't need to arrange a babysitter,' he said cheerfully.

'Oh.'

'Pass me the wick, would you? That white thing there, on the table. And don't look so worried.'

'Why would they invite you and me? Do you think Virginia has put them up to it?'

'You're more paranoid than I am. No, it's nothing like that. Claudia likes you, you know she does. She just wants to give you a nice evening to say thanks for everything you're doing to help the family.'

'Alex . . .'

'It's OK,' he said. 'You haven't done anything wrong. If Gen was here . . . I mean, if she knew about you and me she'd be pleased. She'd be glad I was moving on.'

'But Claudia doesn't know that and . . .'

'Claudia knows you're doing a brilliant job with her nephew. That's what she cares about. And how can we refuse to go? How can we turn down such a generous invitation? Think how that would make Claudia feel.'

I nodded, but I felt miserable. When I was alone with Claudia, I could be myself because our relationship was genuine. But to be with her and Alexander and to have to disguise everything I felt for him would be a travesty of our friendship. She trusted me and I would be lying to her at a time when she was being more kind to me that she ever needed to be.

'You'll like Bill,' Alexander said. 'And he'll like you. He likes everything Claudia likes.'

'She doesn't know me very well, does she?' I said.

Alexander looked up at me and smiled.

'Claudia's a very good judge of character,' he said. 'Remember that.'

I returned his smile, but it didn't make me feel any better about myself or the situation.

'And there's another couple going too,' Alexander said. 'Somebody who wants you to do some work for them or something.'

'Oh lord, not Phoebe? Alex, she called here wanting to speak to you about me helping out with her kids but I forgot all about it, I . . .'

'All right, all right, don't get stressed!' Alexander said,

standing to take me by the shoulders, and squeezing with his big strong hands. 'Don't worry. I'll tell them it was me who forgot to call them back.'

Still, I dreaded the evening.

When it came, we drove again up the steep, winding lane, past the chained gates to the old quarry, up to the converted barn. The lane was very dark. All we could see was what was illuminated by the Land Rover's headlights. When we arrived at the Barn, the fancy wrought-iron gates to its drive were closed.

'That's unusual,' Alexander said. He wound down his window and pressed a button on the intercom which was housed on a wooded post at the side of the drive.

'It's me,' he said, and I heard the crackle of a man's voice coming through the speaker and the sound of the dogs barking furiously in the background. The big gates swung slowly open.

Alexander parked the Land Rover, which looked embarrassingly scruffy on the neat drive paved with pinky-coloured blocks in a fishbone pattern and lined with containers of plants, all beautifully maintained. As we stepped out of the car, the gates closed behind us. We heard the click as the lock slotted into place. Three other cars – Claudia's Volvo, a big, glossy four-wheel drive and a slinky BMW – were already parked on the drive.

'No escape now,' Alexander said. He reached over and took my hand and then dropped it as we approached the porch. My teeth were chattering.

One of the girls, Petra, opened the door to us and was almost immediately bowled over by Blue, who charged past her and leapt at my chest, planting his two huge paws painfully on my breasts and reaching up to lick my face. He would have knocked me over if Alexander hadn't been there to catch me.

'Down!' Alexander said in the voice he sometimes used to reprimand Jamie, and Blue dropped at his feet and gazed up at him, grinning and thumping his tail on the ground.

'You stupid dog,' said Alexander fondly.

Bonnie waddled around Petra and leaned against me, wagging her tail. I fondled her ears, and said hello to the little girl. She looked like Alice in Wonderland, in a blue nightie and white socks. Her straight hair was held back by a band.

'Sorry about Blue,' she said. 'He doesn't know how to control his emotions.'

'It's OK,' said Alexander. 'That's a good fault in a dog.'

'Please come in,' said Petra.

'I wish some of your beautiful manners would rub off on Jamie,' Alexander said, and Petra smiled and slipped away to find her twin. I followed behind Alexander.

I couldn't see anyone else inside, and my spirits lifted for a moment: maybe Phoebe and Ted had cancelled.

The Barn was huge, not quite open-plan, modern in design and beautifully furnished. It was the antithesis of Avalon. Everything was new. A set of floor-to-ceiling picture windows looked out over the fields that sloped down the hill, their perimeter lined with tall trees and hedges that hid the view of the new quarry way down below. It was cosy and homely and reminded me of a nest – an expensive, tasteful, luxurious nest. The walls were covered with family photographs, mostly pictures of the twins; snapshots that had been blown up to fit their frames were interspersed with professional portraits. There were also pictures of Genevieve. Mostly they were of Genevieve riding, either going over jumps or standing beside one of her horses, holding the reins, a red rosette fastened to the animal's cheek strap. She looked breathtakingly elegant and athletic in her competition riding clothes. When she was jumping, leaning forwards over the horse's neck, going over impossibly high jumps, it was obvious she was enjoying herself, and she looked so graceful, so exactly right in space and time.

The photographs irritated me, and I knew what I was feeling was jealousy. Genevieve was so perfect in every way. No wonder everyone loved her; no wonder her leaving had left such a big, boring, empty space in everyone's lives. People never would stop talking about her and missing her and speculating about where she was and when she would come back, until she did. I could never be like that. I wasn't that kind of person. I was the sort of person people tended to forget.

I realized that when Genevieve came back to Burrington Stoke – if she came back – and I had to leave, there would be no pictures of me, no anecdotes, no anything to remind them that I'd ever existed.

'Do you ride?'

I turned to see a tall man with a pleasant smile on his face and a champagne flute in each hand.

'Bicycles,' I said.

'Me too. Never saw the attraction of horses myself. Flighty animals with big feet and no brakes. I'm Bill.'

'Sarah.'

'I'm very pleased to meet you at last.'

Bill took my coat and put a drink into my hand in return.

'And this is our good friend Ted,' he said, introducing a portly, youngish man with bad teeth and sweat blooms beneath the underarms of his shirt.

Ted nodded at me, but did not hold out his hand.

'Claudia won't be a moment,' said Bill. 'Take a pew.'

I sat down on the edge of a big, squashy chair and clutched my glass. I could hear the sound of chattering beyond and recognized Phoebe's low-slung voice.

'What's with the gates, Bill?' Alexander asked.

Bill glanced round quickly to make sure his daughters weren't in earshot.

'Someone's been hanging around,' he said quietly.

'Do you know who it is?'

Bill shook his head.

'A few things have gone missing. And the dogs keep barking in the night.'

'Foxes maybe?' said Alexander.

'Travellers,' said Ted. 'It's always travellers. Or teenagers from Wells.'

'Yep, it's a rough old place, Wells,' Alexander said, with a wink to me. I smiled.

Bill shook his head again.

'I don't think it's either. Whoever it is sneaking around seems to be deliberately trying to put the wind up us. Poor old Claude's beside herself with worry. We're thinking about getting CCTV installed.'

'Shit,' said Alexander.

'Are you all right, Sarah?' Bill asked. I felt very hot but suspected that, for once, I had gone pale.

It was Damian. It had to be Damian who was hanging around the house. I should have told Claudia he'd been in the village. I tried to find a way to bring this possibility into the conversation, but Allegra materialized at my shoulder offering me a bowl of pistachio nuts and then Phoebe came into the room, all lipstick and elbows, and monopolized the conversation. I thought I must mention my concern to Alexander as soon as we were alone together. He could then perhaps have a quiet word with Bill.

Bill wasn't what I'd expected. I'd pictured Claudia married to someone shaggier. I knew Bill taught at the university so I'd had a rather unkempt professorial type in mind – a beard, glasses held together with Sellotape, missing buttons on his shirt and a pot belly.

In real life, Bill was taller even than Alexander, with the ranginess of his daughters. He spoke with a pleasant American accent. His hair was closely cropped to disguise the fact that it was receding, and he was attractive, but in a subtle way. I thought at first that he was considerably younger than Claudia, but later concluded that, while she looked older than her age, he did not.

Bill was funny and self-effacing, one of those people whose intense intelligence shines through without their ever showing off. Best of all, he was kind. He did everything he could to put me at my ease, especially when it became clear that Phoebe and Ted did not know how to talk to me. He sat opposite me balancing his bony wrists on his knees, and the twins sat at his feet doing a jigsaw puzzle and we talked about the countryside and how, in Bill's eyes at least, once you became part of it, it was impossible to go back to the city.

Bill was originally from Boston and more lately from London. He said he did not miss it. He had been a university professor, an expert in medieval French literature, and after he'd married Claudia he'd taught at various universities for some years. Now he devoted himself to his writing. He had travelled extensively, researching and publishing a number of books, one of which had been hugely successful and used as the basis for a popular television series. He claimed this was just a fluke.

'It paid for the swimming pool, though, didn't it, Daddy?' said Allegra, and we all smiled.

The old dog, Bonnie, came and leaned up against my legs and I petted her. I felt safe amongst these kind people in their lovely home. I didn't like the thought of Damian creeping round outside, peeping through the windows, disturbing the dogs and stealing things.

I tried not to look at the pictures on the walls but my eyes were drawn to them. Genevieve was so vital, so *alive*. My eyes lingered on a picture of Genevieve and Claudia, standing with their arms around each other. Genevieve was resting her head on Claudia's shoulder and Claudia was laughing unselfconsciously. The half-sisters were like chalk and cheese, Genevieve so petite and neat, Claudia huge and scruffy. Only their smiles were similar.

'She's a cracker, isn't she?' Ted asked, following my eyes. He wasn't talking about Claudia.

I smiled and nodded.

Ted cleared his throat.

'Is there any news?' he asked Alexander.

'No.'

'The police came to talk to Phoebe, you know.'

'No, I didn't know.'

'They asked me all kinds of questions,' Phoebe said, pursing her lips. 'It was very upsetting.'

I felt Alexander tense with irritation.

'I guess they're only doing their job,' said Bill.

'They haven't come up with anything yet then?'

Alexander shook his head. Ted sighed.

'Bad business,' he said. 'They were asking Phoebe about Gen's – er – social life. Did it ever cross your mind that she might have been—'

'Ted!' Phoebe said. 'For goodness' sake. Now is not the time or place.' She glanced meaningfully at me.

Ted held up a hand in apology.

'Oh, don't mind Sarah,' said Alexander. 'She's very discreet.' Gently he touched the back of my hand with the back of his, in the gap between our two chairs, and I relaxed.

Claudia came into the room during this last exchange and my heart ached for her. She was such a good person. Her whole life had been devastated by the actions of Genevieve and her mother and still Claudia bore no grudge, not an ounce of resentment. The pictures on the walls were like a shrine to celebrate Claudia's enduring love for her half-sister. I looked up and caught her eye. We smiled at one another and I didn't look at the wall again.

After a while, the cooking smells coming from the kitchen became irresistible. Bill took the girls upstairs to bed and then we ate our meal around a beautiful, round wooden table in the dining area. The table was polished to a gleam that reflected the candlelight and was laid with silver cutlery and fine bone-china crockery.

Claudia looked noble. Her hair had been put up so that wisps of grey-brown fell down around her face, and she wore a long dress that was Grecian in influence. It didn't make her look any more slender, but it suited her shape entirely. Diamonds sparkled at her earlobes and her throat. I never normally thought of Claudia as being rich – she was just big, posh, kind Claudia – but that night her class and her wealth and her breeding were apparent. She was a wonderful hostess. We ate hot wild-mushroom salad for a starter, followed by the most delicate white sea bass in a lobster and saffron sauce with baby potatoes, asparagus and tiny carrots. The wine was amazing, far stronger than I was used to, and we drank a good deal of it. At least I did. As the evening wore on I stopped feeling so shy and began to join in the conversation, even though Phoebe made it clear that she didn't find this entirely appropriate.

'Do you cook, Sarah?' she asked as we ate our main course.

'Yes.'

'She's very good,' said Alexander.

'And where did you train?'

'Sorry?'

'Where did you learn to cook?' she asked, leaning forward encouragingly as if talking to someone who didn't understand basic English.

'She's just naturally talented,' said Alexander.

'You must have gone to college,' Phoebe persisted. 'Or even university! I understand that people do degrees in just about anything these days. Even childcare!' She looked around the table, but only Ted laughed.

'Yes, I went to college,' I said. I felt very small. I didn't know what to do with my face.

'You see, we're still looking for some part-time help,' Phoebe said. 'We've got a girl from the village but she's not really the right sort, and what with the horses taking up so much of my time . . .' She looked expectantly at Alexander. He ignored her.

'Cut to the chase, Phoebe,' said Ted.

'All right. Alexander, we were wondering if we could borrow Sarah every now and then?'

Alexander shook his head.

'Sorry, Phoebe,' he said. 'Sarah's not up for hire.'

He said it in a friendly way, but a decisive one.

'Oh,' said Phoebe. 'Maybe just on an ad hoc basis when we're desperate?'

'No,' said Alexander.

There was a slightly strained silence. I was taking very tiny mouthfuls of food. My fork scraped on the plate.

'This is delicious,' Ted said cheerily, raising his glass to Claudia. 'Never mind skinny horsey girls like Phoebs and Gen. Give me a woman who can cook any day!'

Claudia smiled but suffered a little at the same time. 'That's what finishing school in Switzerland does for you,' she said.

'You went to finishing school?' I asked.

She nodded. 'Virginia and Daddy sent me there as soon as it became clear that brains weren't my strong point.'

'Really?' I said. 'I've never met anyone who's been finished. I sometimes feel as if I've hardly been started!'

I thought it was quite funny, but nobody laughed. Alexander looked down at his plate. Phoebe inhaled deeply and slowly and Ted just went redder and drank more wine. I felt slightly hysterical. I'd been containing myself for too long.

'You've gone all Lancashire on us, Sarah,' Bill said.

'Sorry,' I said. 'It must be the wine.' I picked up my glass and took another drink.

Claudia smiled at me. 'If I'm the finished product, Daddy should have asked for his money back.'

I giggled, but Bill frowned. He reached across the table and squeezed Claudia's wrist. 'She's always putting herself down,' he told us. 'Always she insists on this tiresome self-deprecation.'

Claudia turned her arm over to take his hand in hers. He gazed at her with a sincerity that I couldn't watch; it felt voyeuristic. I looked down at my lap. How secure Claudia must feel, how safe in the cocoon of love woven by her husband, her daughters, her home. Did that make up for her terrible childhood, her suicidal mother and her damaged brother? Was that enough for her?

'I can never quite believe that somebody as perfect as

Claudia could agree to marry somebody as flawed as I am,' Bill said quietly. 'It's a fact that constantly surprises and delights me.'

'Stop it,' said Claudia, but her pleasure shone through her embarrassment. She was twisting an emerald bracelet around her wide wrist.

'Well said!' Ted joined in. 'Well done, Claudia!'

Alexander was staring at his plate. I knew him well enough to know he would not enjoy this display of affection, this talk of emotion.

'Where did you two meet?' I asked Claudia, to change the subject slightly and relax Alexander.

Phoebe and Ted exchanged glances.

'Oh, sorry,' I said brightly. 'Shouldn't I have asked that?'

'No, no, it's fine,' Claudia said. 'We met just a few hundred yards from here, at Eleonora House. At one of Virginia's infamous hunt balls. It's where everyone in this neck of the woods meets their partners.'

I took another drink of wine. My glass seemed to be empty, and then full, almost at the same time, but I never noticed anyone filling it up.

'Everyone gets terribly drunk and randy,' Claudia continued.

'Come on, Claude, it was a bit more romantic than that,' said Bill. 'There were stars and champagne and dancing and moonlight.'

Claudia smiled at the memory. 'Yes,' she said. 'Yes, there were.'

There was a moment's pause while we all pictured the scene in our minds.

'Virginia's balls are legendary,' Ted announced wistfully.

I snorted. I couldn't help myself.

'Sorry,' I choked, as Alexander passed me his napkin. Everything, all the tension I'd been holding in, was struggling to get out. I was well aware of the others trying to ignore me but I felt as if I were about to explode with nervous energy.

Claudia took her hand out of Bill's and stood and began stacking the plates.

'We're a bit of a romcom cliché,' Bill said, heroically trying to divert attention from me. 'Falling in love at a hunt ball when neither of us is interested in blood sports.'

'Not as much of a cliché as us,' I chimed in. 'We're a holiday romance!'

There was an immediate silence, and everyone paused, as if we were in a film. Claudia stopped rattling the cutlery and Bill froze with a wine bottle half-poised over her glass. Ted slowly went a deeper shade of puce.

I laughed brightly. 'I mean, that's what everyone thinks!' I said. 'Only of course it's not true. Our relationship is strictly professional, isn't it, Alex? Just because we met while we were on holiday people assume we had a fling, but we didn't, we talked and obviously we got on well together and . . .'

'Sarah, shut up,' Alexander said under his breath.

'Pass me your plate, Sarah,' Claudia said.

I passed my plate.

There was another silence. It seemed to last for ever.

I saw Phoebe raise one eyebrow at Ted in a knowing way. I pulled my skirt down and fixed my eyes on the picture on my place mat.

'Let me give you a hand, Claudia,' Phoebe said in a voice as sticky as treacle.

'Me too,' Ted said. He obviously couldn't bear to sit at the same table as me a moment longer. I screwed my napkin in my hand as the two of them made a big performance of helping Claudia.

'How's work?' Bill asked Alexander.

'Good, thank you.'

'Still putting in all the hours God sends?'

Alexander nodded. Bill took off his glasses and scratched an eyebrow.

'You must have made enough to pay the old man back by now, surely?'

'Bill, please!' Claudia interrupted. 'Let's not talk about business at the dinner table.'

'Sorry,' Bill said. 'Sorry.'

'Is there anything I can do, Claudia?' I asked.

'No, thank you,' she said in a cold, hard voice. 'You've done more than enough already.'

I said very little for the rest of the evening.

CHAPTER TWENTY-FIVE

The next day I woke with a migraine and a head full of regret. I didn't know how much damage had been done by my comment. I valued Claudia's friendship. Now, the truth – or a strong suspicion of the truth – would be between us, and I felt, as I had before, that it would be wrong not to be entirely honest with her. I asked Alexander what I should do, but he refused to talk about it. He closed himself off from me. I would have preferred it if he'd shouted at me – brought his feelings out into the open and dispersed his anger – but I didn't have the courage to initiate an argument.

Phoebe, I suspected, would have promised Claudia not to breathe a word about what I'd said but would tell everyone she knew. The news would be all over the village by now, galloping through the horse-riding sorority like wildfire.

I was desperate for reassurance so I went to see Betsy. I had not told her everything about our relationship, but she knew most of the story and, like everyone else in the village, she was well aware of the domestic politics of the Churchill family. Her mother went up to Eleonora House twice a week to collect and drop off the Churchills' ironing.

We sat in the kitchen of her chilly council house and dunked no-frills ginger biscuits into mugs of milky coffee. I told her exactly what had happened and she rolled her eyes.

'Well, honestly,' she said. 'It's Alexander's fault, making you keep secrets like that. What does he expect? If you'd been honest about everything right from the start, people would've been used to the situation by now.'

I explained about Alexander knowing his relationship with Genevieve was over ages before she left, but that other people wouldn't see it like that. They'd think, like Virginia, that it was obscene to begin a love affair so soon after she was gone.

Betsy didn't see it that way. 'It's just covering up one set of lies with another,' she said. 'What's the point? The truth always comes out. Always, sure as God made little green apples. The more you try to push it down, the stronger it tries to bob up.'

Betsy leaned over to the baby, who was sitting in her high chair, and wiped her nose with the cuff of her shirt. The baby turned her round, red face away and squirmed.

'Do you think I should call Claudia and apologize?' I asked.

Betsy pulled a face. 'I should wait for her to come to you,' she said.

'What if she doesn't?'

She shrugged. 'Then don't take it personally. Blood is thicker than water and all that.'

'Do you think she'll tell Virginia?'

'I don't know,' Betsy said. 'You've gone and put her in a very awkward position. She won't want to be keeping things from Virginia, not with the situation with Genevieve being how it is. And if Phoebe's going round spreading the news, it won't be long before it gets back to her anyway.'

I groaned. 'Oh lord,' I said, 'could it be any worse?'

'Yes,' Betsy said cheerfully. 'It could. And it probably will be.'

It was immediately apparent that Claudia wanted to sever her friendship with me. She sent a message via Jamie to cancel a trip we had arranged to take the children to the cinema and she didn't call in to Avalon any more. I called her several times, but each time was connected to her answerphone.

I didn't leave a message. How could I explain in a few seconds all that I needed to say? I couldn't bear the thought of Claudia being hurt because of me. At the very least I wanted to explain why I had lied. Also, I missed her.

One morning, one of those glorious mid-October mornings when the autumn hangs on by its fingertips and anything still seems possible, I collected two basketfuls of the best of the apples from the huge old mistletoe-laden tree in the front garden, and I walked up the hill, all the way up the lane past the old quarry, to Claudia and Bill's house. My shoulders and arms were aching by the time I reached the Barn. The dogs heard me before I reached the gates and came running from the back garden to greet me, barking madly through the wrought iron, their paws skittering on the paving. Claudia could not pretend she was not in. She opened the gates remotely and then came to meet me at the door, drying her hands on a tea towel. I held out the baskets.

'Tell me to go away if you want,' I said. 'The apples are for you, anyway.'

Claudia pulled at the neckline of her shirt. Blue ran around me in circles, still barking. She waved her hand at him to make him sit and he ignored her, bouncing up at me. Through the mayhem I said: 'I have to tell you how sorry I am. It's the least I can do.'

Claudia didn't say anything. Her eyes seemed redder and more watery than the last few times I'd seen her. She looked older.

'I'll go,' I said. 'Take the apples. You told me you liked to make apple sauce at this time of year.'

'Genny and I always spent a day at it,' Claudia said. 'It was one of our traditions. Come in.'

She stepped aside and I went into the house past her, through the hall and living room, into the huge, beautiful kitchen. I put the baskets down on the slate-tiled floor.

'Alex said I shouldn't say anything,' I said. 'He said whatever I said would make things worse.'

Claudia shook her head. 'My sister is missing. Whatever you and Alexander get up to is not going to make the situation any worse than it already is,' she said. 'What I find difficult is that you deceived me.'

'I'm sorry.'

'I thought you were my ally, Sarah. I don't have many people to talk to round here, but I thought I could rely on you.'

I felt my eyes grow hot. I looked into her dear face and wanted to weep and beg her forgiveness, but I remembered her rule about being dignified.

'I only meant to protect you,' I said. 'I'll tell you anything you want to know.'

Even to me, the words sounded hollow; too little too late.

Claudia shook her head. 'I don't want to know anything,' she said.

'Then what can I do . . .'

'Nothing,' she said. 'You can't do anything. You only get one chance at being trusted, Sarah. You should know that as well as anyone. It's a fragile thing and when it's gone, it's gone.'

It was true. We stood together in silence for a few moments. I felt terribly ashamed.

Then Claudia said: 'Well, you're here and you've brought a ridiculous amount of apples. You're going to have to give me a hand.'

'Thank you,' I said.

It was a pleasant afternoon. As time went by, so we both relaxed. The apples floated in the sink and I peeled with a sharp knife while Claudia stood at the stove stirring the cut pieces of white apple flesh in two large pans with water and sugar. I put the cores and the damaged flesh into a colander to go back out to the compost bin and, covertly, I glanced at Claudia. Her round shoulders were hunched over the steaming pan. She was stirring the apple sauce with a wooden spoon, and then transferring it with a metal ladle into sterile jars fresh from the oven. I could hear the gentle popping of the hot, sweetened juice. The kitchen smelled of cooking sugar. Claudia had a tea towel over her shoulder.

'This is nice, isn't it, Gen?' she said distractedly. 'Just you and me.'

Her voice was softer than normal, full of affection.

I did not want to spoil the moment for her, so I said nothing at all.

CHAPTER TWENTY-SIX

Rumours and innuendo spread through Burrington Stoke almost by osmosis. Phoebe had been at work, and she'd been diligent in her tale-telling. I soon came to the distinct impression that people were avoiding me because they had heard my involvement with Alexander was more than professional and could not condone it. There was a coolness about the shopkeepers and villagers when it came to their dealings with me that had not been there before.

When I took a bag of tatty old books and DVDs into the charity shop, the lady who was manning it said: 'Are these Genevieve's?'

'I don't know,' I answered truthfully. All the items had been dusty and squashed under furniture or at the back of cupboards. They were clearly unwanted.

'Why are you getting rid of her things?' the woman asked, and her expression became hard. 'Aren't you expecting her back?'

I felt my face colour.

'We were just having a clear-out. Don't you want them?' I asked.

The woman shook her head. 'I don't want anything that rightfully belongs to that wonderful girl,' she said.

That wasn't all. Several times, the phone rang, but when I answered there was nobody there. Three days in a row I found a single dead magpie by the hedge at the bottom of Avalon's garden. I knew some of the villagers shot the birds, but it seemed too much of a coincidence that they should all fall in the same place. I couldn't forget the words of the magpie rhyme: one for sorrow. Alexander picked the birds up and threw their carcasses into the orchard to make a meal for the foxes and the crows and told me to stop being paranoid. I could not understand how he could remain so calm.

I would have felt terribly isolated if it weren't for Betsy and Claudia, who, although our friendship had cooled, still needed me as I needed her. Bill aside, there was nobody she could talk to openly and honestly and I was beginning to understand how difficult it must have been for her to be a motherless girl in a small village with a brother damaged beyond repair, a father who owned everything, a glamorous, celebrity half-sister and a stepmother who was feared and revered in equal measure.

The second time I met Virginia Churchill was by accident, during the last week in October. I was in the Burrington Stoke Spar-cum-post office, filling a wire basket with milk, bread, coffee and ingredients for the pasta dish I had planned for dinner that evening. It was an old-fashioned, family-run shop; you could buy everything from a newspaper and a loaf of bread to jump leads, aspirin and bird seed. Everything was packed together and there was only room for one person in any particular aisle.

I was reading the list of ingredients on a packet of stock cubes when I heard Alexander's name mentioned in a clipped female voice that I recognized at once. I put the packet back on the shelf and moved to the end of the aisle.

Virginia stood at the far end of the store, at the post office counter, with her back to me. She was paying in cheques from the estate's tenants.

Mr Taylor, the shop's proprietor, was making a note of the cheques, and Virginia talked to him as he worked. From his stance, and the way he sometimes glanced up at Virginia over the top of his half-glasses, I had the feeling that he had heard her story, or versions of it, many times before. His shoulders were hunched and he kept nodding as if in agreement, without concurring with anything she said. He knew what Virginia didn't: that I was in the shop.

'What nobody seems to be taking into account is that Genny always was incredibly sensitive to how other people were feeling,' said Virginia. 'I told the police. She simply would not go and live somewhere else without letting her family know where she was. She wouldn't! It's twelve weeks since she disappeared and they continue to procrastinate.'

'They say that the police are overstretched . . .' Mr Taylor said.

I couldn't see Mrs Churchill's face, but I imagined her expression.

'It's outrageous,' she said. 'Their complacency is disgusting. Ian Twyford told me they were keeping an open mind but they can't *do* anything unless there's a good reason to suspect something is wrong.'

'There you are then,' said Mr Taylor. 'If Inspector Twyford doesn't think there's anything to worry about then there probably isn't. He's always kept an eye out for your daughter, hasn't he?'

Virginia huffed. 'But there is reason for suspicion now! We know that Alexander and that girl *are* more than just good friends. And that they're both consummate liars.'

Mr Taylor swallowed, and rubbed his lips with the palm of his hand. He was trying not to catch my eye.

'To be fair,' he said in a careful voice, 'Alexander must have been lonely.'

Virginia snorted. There was a pause as she rummaged in her bag.

'And maybe he had the whole thing planned all along. We all know what that man's capable of,' she said.

I couldn't bear to see Mr Taylor suffer any longer. I summoned all my courage, stepped forward and cleared my throat.

Mr Taylor scratched at the corner of his mouth. His daughter-in-law, Midge, was sorting greetings cards behind him. She too stopped what she was doing and waited. There was panic in her face. I smiled at them both and stood a few feet behind Virginia.

'Good morning,' I said.

'Good morning, Sarah,' said Mr Taylor.

'Hiya,' said Midge.

Virginia turned. I held on to my breath.

Her appearance took me by surprise. With make-up, the resemblance to her daughter was striking, only Virginia was a distorted version of the Genevieve I'd seen in so many photographs: older, harder and tireder. Virginia looked exhausted. Her silver-gold hair was pulled back from her face painfully tightly into a ponytail and the skin of her thin neck was crêped. Her eyebrows had been harshly plucked. Her beauty was still there, but it had been spoiled by time and worry. My fear of the woman was tempered by pity. I remembered that it is a terrible thing to lose your only child. Virginia looked me up and down.

'Sarah,' she said eventually.

'Mrs Churchill.'

I held out my hand but she did not take it, so I let it fall to my side. Minutes seemed to pass. I didn't know what to say next. I didn't know what to do. I could hardly start to justify myself to Virginia while standing there in the Spar, with the Taylors watching us from behind their counter and a small, intensely interested queue forming behind me.

Virginia said: 'You and I need to talk.' She glanced over my shoulder and the people in the queue immediately looked at the contents of their wire baskets. 'In private,' she added.

I paid for my shopping then we went into the Swan Hotel at the end of the high street and sat in deep, cracked-leather armchairs in the lounge while a waiter fetched over-brewed coffee served in bone-china cups so old that the pattern had almost entirely worn away. The lounge was dark. Dust motes danced in what little light came through the leaded windows, the carpet was worn and the room smelled of pea and ham soup. Hunting memorabilia hung over the huge stone fireplace and pictures of the hunt lined the walls. The murmur of a smattering of guests, all elderly, was like a buzz behind us. At first Virginia said nothing; she watched me like a hawk. I tried to look as if I were at home in the place, although I was so far down in the chair that I could not reach the armrests with my elbows, so they were clamped to my side. I tried not to fidget. I needed to go to the lavatory but could think of no dignified way to excuse myself.

When our coffee came Virginia took her time stirring in cream and sugar. She passed me my cup by the saucer then said: 'Let's not beat about the bush. I need to explain my position.'

'No,' I said. 'No, you don't. I realize how me being with Alexander must look to you, and I am sorry if we hurt you, I didn't mean any harm, I—'

She held up her hand. I stopped speaking.

'How long have you known Alexander?' she asked. 'The truth, please.'

'We met in Sicily.'

'Alexander told you he was married?'

I struggled to remember what he had told me.

'Yes.'

Virginia winced, and I realized that the truth painted

me in a worse light. I had known Alexander was a married man and still I went with him.

'What did he tell you about Genevieve?'

'That she had left him.'

'And you believed him?'

'Of course.'

Virginia stared at me levelly.

'You had a holiday romance,' she said. Now it was my turn to wince. 'He moved you straight into his home. Don't you think that's strange behaviour for a man whose wife had' – she made sarcastic inverted commas with her hands – '"left him" only a couple of weeks earlier?'

'Alexander told me . . . He said his marriage had been in trouble for a long time before Genevieve left. He needed help with the house and with looking after Jamie.'

'He had all the help he needed here.'

'Perhaps he felt he could do with somebody who was on his side,' I said quietly.

Virginia picked up her cup, took a sip, put the cup down on the dark little table that stood between our two chairs and patted her lips with a paper napkin. When she spoke, her voice was icy.

'What will you do when Genevieve comes back?' she asked.

'If she comes back . . . I don't know.'

Virginia looked at me, and her look was cold as death.

'You think you're so clever but there's so much you don't know, Sarah,' she said. Her voice was low and threatening. 'You don't know, I assume, that Avalon is my daughter's house? It belongs to Genevieve, not Alexander; it was a gift from her father.'

I had not known that.

'And it was her father's money that set Alexander up in business.'

'But he's paying back the loan.'

She shrugged as if that were not the point.

'Alexander was penniless when he married Genevieve. He was jobless. He had nothing. Ask him. Everything Alexander has now – all the luxuries, the lifestyle you're enjoying – by rights belongs to my daughter.'

I stared at the cup and saucer on my lap. More than ever I felt as if I were terribly in the wrong, although I didn't know what I had done. I did not like the insinuations and the implications behind Virginia's words and, worst of all, I did not like being told so much about Alexander that I did not know.

I shifted a little to ease the pressure on my bladder.

'Do you trust him?' Virginia asked me.

I looked up, into her eyes. 'Yes, of course.'

'Even though it must be clear to you now that he hasn't been entirely open with you?'

'He's told me everything that I needed to know.'

'So you know he's been in prison?'

That shocked me. The trembling in my fingers made the cup rattle in the saucer on my lap and for an awful second heat engulfed me and I was afraid I might collapse. It took all my energy, all my will, to maintain my composure. Virginia must not see how upset I was by this revelation; she must not. I raised the cup to stop the rattle and sipped the coffee. It was lukewarm.

'You didn't know, did you?' she asked.

I put the cup back down in the saucer. The coffee had left a horrible taste in my mouth.

Virginia leaned forward and took the cup and saucer from me.

'Sarah,' she said, almost gently, 'you might think you know Alexander, maybe you think he loves you or he needs you or that you can help him, but what you're dealing with is a fantasy; a romantic fantasy. The truth is different. You don't know what kind of man he really is. You have no idea. I suspect your fantasy is stopping you from seeing the truth.'

Tears were prickling at my eyes and my bladder now was so uncomfortable I felt faint. I was too hot.

'It's not Alexander's fault Genevieve's gone away,' I said. 'Genevieve left because she wanted to, not because he did anything wrong. Perhaps she was seeing some-one else.'

Virginia froze when I said this. She seemed shocked, but not surprised, and I realized that I had, in-advertently, hit a nerve. Her discomposure gave me strength. If Genevieve's own mother suspected her of adultery, then there must be a strong possibility of it. It would explain everything. And if she and her lover had run away together, then no wonder they had covered their tracks so carefully, no wonder it had all been so sudden. It was the obvious explanation. I felt myself flush as possibilities raced through my mind, but before I could put them into any sort of order, Virginia spoke again.

She leaned forward so her face was close to mine, so close that I tasted, for the second time, the sourness of her breath.

'Who is this other man, Sarah? Do you have a name for him?' she hissed.

I shook my head, alarmed by her intensity.

'Has Alexander told you anything about him?'

'He doesn't know anything.'

'Are you sure?'

I nodded.

Virginia sat back a little. She pursed her lips and considered me in the same way a snake might consider a mouse. When she spoke next, her words were slow and precisely measured.

'Here's something else you don't know, Sarah,' she said. 'When Genevieve told Alexander she wanted to leave him, a little while before she disappeared, he said he wouldn't let her. He told her he'd rather see her dead.'

'People say things they don't mean when they're upset.'

'And sometimes they say things they do mean.'

'Yes, but—'

'How "upset" do you think Alexander might have been if Genevieve told him she was leaving him to be with someone else? Somebody who would treat her better than he did? Somebody who cared for her?'

I swallowed.

'Hmm?'

I could not answer.

'What do you think he might have done, Sarah?'

'I don't know,' I said, but the words came out so quiet I don't think Virginia heard.

She seemed drained now. She sat back in her chair, looked up at the wood panelling on the ceiling and sighed.

'If Genevieve has come to any harm,' said Virginia, 'I'll make sure Alexander pays for it. And you. I don't think you're evil. I think you're naïve and easily led, but if he's guilty and if you stand by him, you're just as culpable.'

We were silent for a moment. Across the room an elderly man in a wing-chair snored. A fly batted at the window behind us.

I tried to keep my voice steady and calm. 'I trust Alexander,' I said.

'Then, Sarah,' said Virginia, 'you're even more stupid than you look.'

The day, the week – everything had been tainted.

After Virginia stood to pay for our coffees, I went into the ladies and sat on the toilet for ages, until I was quite composed. Then I came out of the cubicle and washed my face in the basin with cracked, heavily scented soap that dried my skin. I had no make-up with me, so had to go back out through the lounge with my face swollen and blotchy. I could feel the eyes of the staff on my back as I made my way through the dark reception hall with its huge fireplace, and out of the front door. I was barely across the threshold before the murmur of their excited voices set to gossip and speculation. I went into Burrington Stoke's tiny library and spent an hour or so browsing the shelves and looking at leaflets about ploughing contests and bell-ringing until I was certain Virginia would have left the village and there was no danger of bumping into her again. I tried not to think about what she had told me, but her words were inside my head. No matter how I tried to pretend they were not there, their presence was pervasive.

The handles of the carrier bags dug into my hands as I walked along the road back to Avalon. I did not even notice the car pulling up beside me until the passenger door opened. It was Bill.

'Penny for them,' he said.

'You don't want to know.'

'Hop in. You look exhausted.'

I climbed into the seat, putting the shopping in the footwell. I rubbed the palms of my hands on my knees to restore the circulation.

'Has something happened?' he asked gently, moving the car forward.

I shook my head, but then the tears gave me away.

'Oh dear!'

Bill turned the car into a lane and stopped on the verge beside a gate. He passed me a handkerchief and sat quietly beside me while I cried, and when I began to feel a bit better he said: 'If I had to bet who had upset you, my money would be on Virginia.'

'How did you guess?'

'Because the woman can be an absolute class-A bitch.'

I sniffed.

'Also I was in the post office just now and Midge told

me Virginia had whisked you off to the hotel for a dressing-down.'

I smiled feebly.

The windscreen was steaming up. We both stared out of it across a green and brown landscape. The crop-fields had been ploughed and long dark lines of churned mud stretched up to the horizon.

'Listen, Sarah,' Bill said. 'I don't like Virginia. I can never forgive her for what she's done to Claudia, but it seems to me that, right now, she's very close to a breakdown. The stress of all this, not hearing from Genevieve, she can't cope with it and she's looking for somebody to blame.'

'I know.'

He said gently: 'Ironically, it's easier for her to believe Alexander has done something unspeakable to Genevieve than it is to accept that her darling daughter has buggered off and simply not bothered to get in touch.'

'She thinks Genevieve was seeing someone else,' I said.

'What?'

I nodded. 'Honestly, she does. She thinks Alexander flipped when she told him she was leaving him for another man.'

'That's ridiculous,' Bill said. He shook his head. 'That's just crazy.'

I smiled at him gratefully.

'Although if she was in love with someone else and wanted to be with him, it would explain why she just upped and left like she did,' I said.

'I suppose.'

'Don't tell Claudia about any of this, will you, Bill?'

'Of course not.' Bill tapped his fingers on the steering wheel. 'You still look awfully worried, Sarah. Was there something else?'

'No.'

'Are you sure?'

'Oh, it's just . . . Virginia told me some things about Alexander that I didn't want to know. Things he'd said and done . . .'

Bill sighed and stretched his arms against the steering wheel.

'Try not to worry about it,' he said. 'Virginia always had trouble seeing anything beyond Genevieve. She's never been able to understand the bigger picture.'

Through the window glass I saw two crows settle in the field. We were quiet for a few moments and then I remembered something that had slipped my mind.

'Bill, have you still got your stalker?'

'He seems to have moved on,' Bill said. 'The police have been pretty good. They're sending a patrol car round every so often, but they haven't seen anyone. And we've had another alarm fitted.'

'I think I know who it was,' I said. 'I should have said before. I think it might have been Claudia's brother.'

'Damian?'

'He was here, in the village, a little while back. I saw him. He seemed a bit—'

'Damian was here? In Burrington Stoke? Are you sure?' Now Bill sat up straight and tensed.

I nodded.

'Why didn't you tell us? Oh, Sarah, why in God's name didn't you say anything?'

I moved closer to the window. I hadn't expected such a strong reaction.

'I thought Claudia would be hurt that he hadn't been to see her. And he was only here a day or two – at least that's what I thought. He seemed harmless.'

Bill exhaled and stared straight ahead.

'He's poison,' he said. 'If you see him again, call me. Don't say anything to Claudia but call me straight away.'

'OK.' I nodded. 'Sorry.' I felt close to tears again. 'I didn't realize it was such a big deal,' I said miserably.

'Don't worry about it,' Bill said, but there was no genuine reassurance in his voice. His mind was on something else. 'That man's dangerous. He's bad news, Sarah.'

He dropped me off at the end of the track and I walked the last quarter mile or so to Avalon beneath the trees, the shopping bumping against my calves. Every now and then the wind rustled the trees and a leaf would spin to the ground just ahead of me. May used to tell me it was lucky to catch a falling leaf, but none of them stuck to my hair or my clothes. I kicked some of the loose leaves up in front of me. I felt I could use a little luck.

I had learned so much that morning, and nothing I had learned was good.

If Alexander wanted me to be on his side, shouldn't he have trusted me with his skeletons? Of course he should. Unless the secrets he kept hidden were so terrible that he couldn't risk sharing them.

I kicked open the gate with my foot and put my shopping down on the path while I searched in my bag for the key to the door to Avalon.

Alexander was a good man. He *was* a good man. He was my lover, my man. If we could not trust one another, if we were to lose our faith in each other, then we had nothing.

I unlocked the door and picked up the post. There was a brown envelope from the Inland Revenue and two equestrian auction catalogues and a postcard for Genevieve. I put them on the counter and heaved the shopping through the outer room and into the kitchen.

I plugged in the kettle and sat down on the settee with my head in my hands.

Virginia had handed me a poisoned apple, and I had bitten into it. I must not let her infect me with her insinuations. I wouldn't.

CHAPTER TWENTY-SEVEN

I didn't tell Alexander about meeting Virginia. I *would* tell him, but only when I'd decided, in my mind, how to broach the subject. There was no point trying to have a rational and objective conversation when I was feeling so upset and wrong-footed. He would want to know what she had said and I would not be able to lie to him. I was a terrible liar. As soon as the truth was out, he would have to endure the humiliation of knowing that I knew things about him he hadn't wanted me to know.

So I kept quiet.

He was working very hard on a major commission, the restoration of some important historical building in Sherborne, often not coming home until Jamie was in bed, and his hair would be grey with dust. The skin on his hands was thick and calloused and muscle and sinew was carved out of his arms and chest. He was not a heavy man, but years of lifting, moving and cutting stone had made him very strong. I was aware of his physical strength. When we made love, he lifted and moved me as if I were a doll. In bed, his strength was part of his attraction. I enjoyed my powerlessness, his complete domination. Knowing I was entirely in his hands made me feel feminine and sexy and I knew that part of the thrill was the danger. Laurie, with his soft, desk-job body, had always been a courteous, polite lover, committed to my comfort and pleasure. He used oils, candles and music. He even warmed his hands. Alexander's roughness, in contrast, was breathtaking. Sex was a rollercoaster and I was scared and exhilarated in equal measure.

Sometimes, when I looked at Alexander, I saw a gentle, good man who had been damaged by circumstance. Other times, his reluctance to talk about himself and his introspection were beginning to make me feel uneasy. I started to have nightmares, terrors that left me drenched in sweat and my jaw aching from clenching and grinding my teeth. And when I woke from those dreams, alone in my bed in the eaves, the house scared me. I was afraid to creep into the bathroom; going downstairs to make tea was unthinkable. I had a small stash of sleeping pills as well as the hoarded antidepressants. I had not liked the hangover they gave me, nor the dulling of my feelings and responses. Now I took to experimenting with them, taking a quarter or a third of a pill each night, making cocktails until I knew the exact quantity of drug that would send me to sleep soundly enough not to be disturbed by the house's creaks and sighs but not so deeply that I would not wake up if I needed to.

I could have left Avalon. I was certain Alexander

would not try to stop me if I told him I wanted to go. But I didn't want to leave Alexander and I couldn't bear the thought of leaving Jamie.

I hadn't meant to, but every day I grew closer to the child. What had begun as an awkward, difficult relationship was changing into something deep and sincere. I never said the words out loud, but what I was feeling for Jamie was more than simple affection. I loved him.

We had fun when we were alone together. Jamie taught me to play racing games on the Wii, but I was rubbish. I taught him to play card games and he was good. We both liked drawing and often would sit companionably at the kitchen table, Jamie, with the tip of his tongue sticking out of the corner of his mouth, drawing people shooting one another and me drawing Jamie. I tried time and time again to make a half-decent image of him, but found it impossible to do him justice. His face was small and precise, but that wasn't the problem – it was the fact that it was so alive, and that vitality was difficult to capture in two dimensions. I thought if I could make a good drawing of Jamie, I would give it to Alexander for Christmas, but I could never translate the essence of his son on to paper.

As the leaves fell that autumn, Jamie and I went down to the trees and stood beneath them, waiting for a gust of wind, and when the wind came we rushed to catch the leaves for luck, and we saved the ones we did catch and I bound them together with cotton and hung them around the house. I hoped they would protect me. I prayed for them to take away the nightmares, and the fears that stalked me during the day.

I wished Genevieve would come back to prove to me, and to everyone else, that Alexander had done nothing to harm her. I prayed she would not come back to take her son away.

CHAPTER TWENTY-EIGHT

Jamie invited Christopher, his best friend from school, to stay over at Avalon for his birthday. We were going to have a bonfire and fireworks in the back garden because, although Jamie's birthday was a few days after bonfire night, those two treats were what he loved best in the world. Christopher was to sleep in a put-me-up bed in Jamie's room, but the room was a tip. That morning, I asked Jamie if he'd mind if I gave it a proper tidy round, and he said it would be all right.

'Is there anything you want to tidy away first?' I asked him.

Through a mouthful of bacon-and-bean sandwich, he assured me there wasn't.

'It's OK,' he said. 'I don't mind if you want to play with any of my things.'

Alexander, behind him, peeling a banana, winked at me and smiled.

'Thanks, Jamie,' I said.

I was nervy. The date felt significant. I thought if Genevieve was going to make contact, if she was going to return, it would, most likely, be on her only child's birthday. She wouldn't want to miss it; no mother would.

While Alexander washed upstairs, I straightened the collar of Jamie's polo shirt and helped pull the sweat-shirt over his head, feeling the small, solid muscles of his back and the ridge of his spine. Jamie's shaved hair had grown out now. Its true colour was pale brown, like honey, although the ends were still bleached from his time in Sicily. He had the bone structure of his mother; his eyes were shaped like hers, although the colour was different, and I imagined, from what I'd heard of her, that he had inherited his vivacity and charm from Genevieve. It was difficult to find anything of Alexander in Jamie's face, although he had definitely inherited some of Alexander's mannerisms and much of his stubbornness and preference for using no words when a few would have been helpful.

I smiled at the child, passed him his lunch box and his bag, and told him to have a good day at school.

That morning was truly beautiful, the air chill and the grass wet where the frost was melting, and dew-jewelled spiderwebs hung like decorations amongst the twigs of the shrubs. The swallows were long gone and the cows had been moved to different pastures, but the rooks still flew over the roof of Avalon and blue tits argued on the feeders.

In daylight, the house felt better now. It was lighter and less suspicious, less creepy. Still, I disliked being on my own, particularly upstairs. Usually I found reasons not to be there, but on this occasion I had an imperative to make Jamie's room welcoming for his friend. I carried out a number of diversionary and procrastinatory tactics. I hung the wet washing on the line, then I sorted out some of the mess in the rosette room next to the kitchen. Behind the horse paraphernalia was a black plastic bin bag, tied at the top. I tore the plastic open with my fingers and they sank into the soft fabric of clothing.

I put my hand through the tear of the bag and took hold of the softest, silkiest material I could find. It slipped through the torn plastic like water. I shook it out and held it up to the light. It was a shift dress, just a plain shift dress, nothing fancy, but it was beautiful. I felt the quality of the fabric between my fingers, the slip and rub of it. I had never owned anything like it. I had never been, and doubted I ever would be, able to afford a garment of such quality. I slid it over my head, pulling it down over the top of my jeans and sweater. It was emerald green, deeply cut at the front with tiny, fabric-covered buttons running down the back. It was made of the most exquisite material, so fine that I could have pulled the whole dress through the ring on my finger. I turned this way and that, watching a dark reflection of myself in the door-glass. It was a beautiful dress, far too good to be put in a recycling bin – and it fitted me.

I kept the dress, screwed it up like a guilty secret, re-bagged the rest, and took it to the end of the drive, where I left it with the paper, plastic and glass beside the cattle grid, ready for collection.

After that, I set to work in Jamie's room. It took a

while to sort out all the toys into their proper boxes and bins, and to make up the beds, and it was only when I was polishing the desk where Jamie sat and did his homework that I found the letter, still in its envelope, sticking out from between the pages of the atlas that Jamie always kept there.

The envelope was addressed to Jamie, just the five letters of his name written in blue felt pen. It was covered in stickers of smiling ladybirds, spiders and beetles.

My first response was surprise. I'd tidied Jamie's bedroom often and I'd never seen the letter before. I picked the envelope up, and held it to my lips. Then I put it down. What it contained was private, not for my eyes. I put new bedding in the hamster cage and topped up the water bottle. I lined Jamie's collection of Transformers on the window ledge. I'd opened the windows to air the room, and a late wasp buzzed confusedly in and flew a few spirals before disappearing outdoors again. The envelope lay on the desk. I opened it and took out the paper folded in half inside.

Only a few words were written on the paper, words that Jamie would, I knew, understand. They were: 'Blue teddy is for Jamie. I love you, from Mummy.'

Beneath were three simple little pictures. The first was of a little boy with sticking-out ears: Jamie, looking glum – well, his mouth was an inverted smile at least. The second was an outline of the blue bear, also looking unhappy. The third was of the boy cuddling the bear, and both were smiling. It was done so tenderly, these instructions to the child to pick up the bear when he was feeling sad, that I felt my eyes grow hot and prickly. It wasn't much, but it was as much as Jamie could take in and understand on his own, without help from another adult. It was enough. Genevieve would have known that when she left the letter for her son.

I lay back on the bed and closed my eyes. I felt overwhelmed with sadness, the feeling so strong that it seemed to be in my bloodstream, like a drug. The weight of it held me down. The sadness came from nowhere, it filled me up, and for one strange, nightmarish moment it occurred to me that it was Genevieve's sadness I was feeling. She was punishing me somehow for taking her place, or else she was trying to show me how it was to be her and how much she missed Jamie. Then I heard the Land Rover pulling up on the drive and the feeling slipped away, although I still felt odd, dizzy and not quite myself.

I crossed to the window and looked out. Alexander climbed out of the car and walked towards the house. I folded the letter carefully and put it back in the envelope. I slipped the envelope back between the pages of the atlas, and put several different books on top so that Jamie would not know I'd seen it. I ran downstairs and met Alexander in the kitchen. He held out his arms to me and kissed me full on the lips. He smelled of outdoors.

'The pump's broken at the yard. I had nothing to do so I thought I'd come home early. Is the coast clear?' he whispered into my hair.

I nodded.

He said: 'Thank God!' and his mouth was on my ear

and his hands slid down the back of my body, one on my waist, the other fingers working down the waistband of my jeans. He turned me on, oh God, he turned me on, but although my body was Alexander's my mind was full of Genevieve.

Jamie's letter had made her more real to me, that's what it was. It was easy to think of her as a bad mother, a heartless woman who had walked away from her family without a second thought. Now I knew how much she cared and I felt guilty. I felt as if I should not be there, about to make love with Genevieve's husband in the house that belonged to her, on her son's birthday, when I was certain, wherever she was, she was wishing she was with Jamie.

'What is it?' Alexander asked, holding my chin in his fingers so that I had to look into his eyes. 'What's wrong, Sarah?'

'Nothing,' I said. 'Everything's fine.'

'Hey,' he said gently, 'you are still with me, aren't you?'

'Of course I am.'

'Are you sure?'

'Yes,' I said. 'Yes, I'm sure.'

CHAPTER TWENTY-NINE

We made love and, this time, for the first time, I let go, because I felt as if I had already seen the end and I had nothing left to lose. Whatever happened, whatever Genevieve did next, whether she returned or she did not, was out of my control. It was nothing to do with me and everybody knew about Alexander and me now so what was the point of pretending? I abandoned myself to Alexander. He was inside me and on me and over me and under me like a poem. I was rubbed raw, I was slippery as silk and strong as pearl. Alexander's mouth, his hands, the scar beneath his ribcage – he was everywhere and I was nothing but an exhaled breath between lips kissed sore. I was found and at the same time I was lost.

Afterwards, we went to the Quarrymen's Arms. It was Alexander's idea. We walked to the pub, which was about halfway between Avalon and Jamie's school, and Alexander went to the bar and ordered a pint and a large glass of red wine. I sat on a bench with my hands clasped between my knees and my hair all messed up, trying to look like I hadn't just been doing what I had just been doing. But I must have had it written all over me.

Alexander came back with the drinks and people were staring because everybody knew about us now. Phoebe's whispers had established themselves as facts and had, most likely, been exaggerated. The regulars were wondering if we were deliberately flaunting ourselves. I could feel their angry, disgruntled thoughts knocking about the pub's walls and its low ceiling.

Alexander put our drinks on the table, sat down on the bench beside me, took my hand and held it between his knees. The other people in the pub didn't hide their distaste for us. I felt uncomfortable. The clientele was mostly elderly, mostly men, mostly tenants of Virginia and Philip's, decent country people with their dogs and their preconceptions watching as Genevieve's husband and his housekeeper sat, love-flushed, drinking alcohol in the middle of the afternoon.

A scruffy Jack Russell came up to our table, begging for crisps.

'Come away,' its owner called. 'I don't want you mixing with their sort.'

There was a murmur of approval around the bar.

'We shouldn't have come,' I said quietly. 'Can we go?'

'We've as much right to be here as the next person,' Alexander said.

'Please, Alex . . .'

I half-stood but he shook his head and pulled me down again, almost roughly.

'Let them think what they like,' he said, a little too loudly. 'They're the ones with the dirty minds.'

A heavily built man at the bar snorted.

'Where is she then?' he asked. 'Where is your wife?'

'I don't know,' Alexander said.

'Convenient, though, isn't it, that she's out of the way so you can carry on with your fancy piece?'

Alexander picked up his glass and swallowed slowly.

I had not touched my wine. I did not want it now.

'Please, Alexander . . .'

'We've done nothing to be ashamed of,' Alexander said in a low voice. Something about his tone made the hairs on my arms stand on end. One of the group at the bar whispered something and there was a chuckle of cynical laughter.

Alexander stood up and pushed back his chair. I made a grab for his arm but he shook my hand off and walked the few steps back to the bar. His posture was relaxed but determined. The men held their drinks defensively in front of their chests. Their faces were set firm, but they backed off a little.

'If any of you has something to say, I'd appreciate it if you'd say it to my face,' he said pleasantly.

'I'll say something,' said a small, elderly woman I hadn't even noticed. She was perched on a stool that was half-hidden from my view by a wooden-backed chair. 'Don't you have a heart, Alexander Westwood? Don't you even care that our Genevieve's missing and nobody knows where she is, or if she's alive or dead?'

'She's not missing, Mrs Spencer,' said Alexander. 'She left because she wanted to leave.'

'And why was that? What had you done to her?'

The men stepped forwards now with a bristle of indignation, and the landlord intervened.

'Maybe it's best you went home,' he said to Alexander. 'We don't want any trouble.'

'I'm not causing any trouble,' said Alexander. He glanced back at me. 'And Sarah certainly isn't. We just want a quiet drink.'

'Bastard!' said a young, heavyset man. 'You bastard! We know how you treated Genevieve! We know what you did to that girl! We don't want your sort in here, not you or your little tramp of a girlfriend.'

Alexander turned – he was so quick – and he grabbed hold of the young man's collar and raised his fist.

'Alex!' I screamed, and the scream distracted him, and as he turned to me the young man hit him and he stumbled and fell backwards, hitting his head on the corner of the fireplace.

I clambered out of my seat, and got to him before the young man did. The landlord and a couple of others were holding him back, but he was fighting to get at Alexander, spitting swear-words from between his fat lips. He was pale with rage and I could feel his aggression, I could smell it in the air. He wanted to kill Alexander and I was terrified.

I helped Alexander to his feet. There was blood on the back of his head, sticky and warm on my fingers, and his eyes were rolling like somebody drunk.

'Get out!' the landlord said quietly to me, and there was not a flicker of compassion or pity in his eyes. 'Get out and don't come back.'

The barmaid passed me our coats as we hobbled to the door, with Alexander leaning heavily against me. I was whispering to him like a mantra: 'Don't worry, we'll be OK, we'll be all right.'

All the eyes in the pub were on us and it was awful; it was humiliating. I felt ashamed and I felt dirty and I was sick with anxiety about Alexander's head wound.

I took him home and bathed the back of his skull; it was thick with hair matted with blood. It wasn't so bad: his scalp had sliced cleanly and the skin was already beginning to knit over the cut. I made him promise to rest but stay awake, then I drove back to the school to meet Jamie and Christopher. Word of the fight hadn't reached the school gate; nobody looked at me any differently from normal, although I was shaky and nervous. Betsy tried to tell me a story about her eldest, but I couldn't listen. As soon as the boys came down the path, I bundled them into the car and took them straight back to Avalon.

Alexander had showered. He had a towel wrapped around his head and, though his skin was grey, he didn't let on to the boys that anything was wrong. He put his energy into making sure they had a brilliant time, setting up the fireworks, preparing the bonfire and even making a guy. Both children were so busy and happy, their shouts and laughter ringing out across the fields, that I think Alexander was distracted, too. As I prepared the dinner, I watched them in the back garden throwing sticks on to the fire, the boys dancing around in their wellingtons and hats with flaps over their ears and Alexander, huddled into his coat, allowing them a thrilling degree of access to the flames. I felt a surge of affection for him.

There were plenty of other pubs in Somerset. We didn't have to go to the Quarrymen's Arms. I told myself that I didn't care. I would not let people who knew nothing of the real nature of Alexander and Genevieve's relationship dictate how we lived our lives.

No, I didn't care then. Only, later that night, after the fireworks had been set off and the bonfire had been reduced to a pile of hot ash, while Alexander was downstairs locking up and I was in the bathroom brushing my teeth, I had a very strong sensation of being watched. The connection to the bulb in the light was bad; the light flickered constantly. Alexander had told me it was because the squirrels had gnawed at the wire, but the flickering was spooking me. I spat out into the basin, rinsed my mouth and felt a draught about my bare legs.

I switched off the electric toothbrush and put it in its holder. I cleaned the basin with my fingers and turned quickly, catching sight of myself on and off in the stammering light in the mirrored door of the bathroom cabinet. Something drew me to it. I squinted and drew closer to the mirror.

Then I realized it wasn't my face reflected back at me but Genevieve's. There was panic in her eyes, absolute fear, and I knew she was pleading with me for help.

I was terrified.

In my room, I swallowed half a sleeping pill and one of the others, and still my night was racked with nightmares of the worst kind.

CHAPTER THIRTY

The next day, I called Betsy.

'It's me,' I said.

'I thought it would be,' Betsy said in a weary voice.

'Are you OK?'

'The baby's teething. She had me up all night.'

'Poor you. I'll come over and take her out in the buggy. You can have a rest.'

'No, you're all right,' said Betsy.

That's when I knew something was wrong. Betsy never turned down the offer of free childcare.

'What have you heard?' I asked.

'That you and Alexander were in the pub and Dale Vowles gave Alexander the seeing-to he's been asking for.'

'It wasn't like that at all.'

'Maybe not. But I think you and Mr Westwood should exercise a little more discretion,' she said in a matter-of-fact voice.

'All we did was go for a drink.'

'It's a tabloid world out there, hon,' Betsy said. 'You

know that. A missing young woman, especially a pretty one, is always going to be the victim, and a well-built husband with a temper on him is always going to be the villain, particularly when he shows no remorse and starts flaunting his bimbo. I'm sorry, but that's how they see you.'

I leaned my head against the wall.

'Bimbo . . .' I sighed.

'And the rest.'

'Can I come over to yours for a bit?' I asked.

'It's not a good idea right now.'

'You don't want to be seen drinking coffee with a bimbo?'

'Dale's cousins live over the road. They might give you some grief.'

'Could we meet in the village then?'

'I'd stay away from the village for a couple of days if I was you.'

'Betsy, what am I going to do?'

'Oh, don't start with the dramatics. I'll come up to yours.'

'Thank you,' I said.

I could not have been more grateful. I don't think I'd ever needed a friend so much in my whole life.

CHAPTER THIRTY-ONE

One crisis passed and another arrived. They were like waves coming closer and closer together. It was Claudia who came round to warn me on the morning the posters went up, but she was too late: I had already seen them when I was taking Jamie to school. Genevieve's face was smiling out from every lamp post, every telegraph pole and wall. Scores of laminated A4 posters had been stuck up in Burrington Stoke with the word 'MISSING' above a colour photograph of Genevieve. There was an appeal for information and the offer of a 'substantial' reward to any person who could tell the police where Genevieve was, or give information as to her whereabouts.

The posters were obviously a direct response to Alexander and I going to the pub. It would have taken no time at all for word to get back to Virginia, and for her suspicions about Alexander and me to be raised another notch or two.

'Why is Mummy's picture on the lamp posts?' Jamie asked. 'Is it because she's famous?'

'Yes,' I said, grateful that he had come up with his own rationale. 'Your mummy's one of the best horse-riders in England.'

'In the whole wide world,' Jamie said. He spelled out the letters of the word above her head. 'Why does it say "Missing"?'

I sighed. 'Because for the moment we don't know where your mummy is.'

Jamie nodded. 'I wish she would tell us,' he said.

I squeezed his shoulder. 'So do I, Jamie.'

Genevieve was already in my life so much, and now she was in it more. She was everywhere. That morning, after I'd dropped Jamie at the school, I carried on walking towards the village with my head held high, because to turn back would have been the action of a coward, and a person with something to hide. The first people I met were an elderly couple who ran a bed-and-breakfast business from their cottage behind the Spar. Normally, we exchanged pleasantries, but on this occasion, when they saw me they crossed the road and pretended to be so involved in their own conversation that they had not noticed me.

Then I met Roseanne, a very pretty girl a few years younger than me who worked as a nanny for a couple who had a second home in Somerset. I often spoke to her at the school gates. She pulled a sympathetic face when she saw me.

'Looks like the shit's about to hit the fan,' she said. 'Those pictures are all over the place and Mrs Churchill was on the radio this morning talking about a reward.'

'Oh no.'

'And Midge told me there'd already been a newspaper reporter in the shop asking about Genevieve and what she was like and what people thought might have happened to her.'

I swallowed and looked past Roseanne up the road. I half-expected to see a pack of paparazzi hurtling towards me, but there was only a tractor trundling along.

'Are you all right?' she asked. Her breath smelled of peppermint chewing gum.

'Yes, I'm fine.'

'You sure?'

'Actually, I think I will go back to Avalon.'

I looked at Roseanne. I was going to ask her to come with me, but I realized it wouldn't be fair.

'I'll see you later,' I said.

CHAPTER THIRTY-TWO

Autumn was dying around us, pulling in its reds and golds, its berries and its dampness. On the moors, the bracken browned and collapsed. Seedheads were everywhere, tiny silver parachutes like fairies swarming over the walls and clinging to our clothes.

The posters were outside the house, in the village, even on the lamp posts outside the school gates. There was no avoiding them, so as much as possible, I stayed inside, where I was not obliged to look at the image of Genevieve's smiling face, and where people could not look at me with mistrust and fear in their eyes.

For Jamie it was a game. He counted the pictures of Mummy in the village. Some days he counted twenty; some days he told me he'd counted to more than a thousand. The other children talked about the posters for a few days, but they soon became part of the landscape of the village, and were no longer remarkable. Even Jamie stopped looking.

It must have been terrible for Alexander, but he would not talk about his feelings. He went to work as usual, and came back and said nothing. Once, he was door-stepped at the yard by a photographer and a journalist; they tried to get him to talk, to 'put the record straight' by giving his side of the story, but he wouldn't. He didn't even mention it to me. I only knew because Betsy, whose sister worked in Castle Cary, told me at school the next day.

The prank calls increased in number and regularity. Sometimes the phone would ring thirty times in succession and, each time I answered, there was nobody there. Sometimes I didn't say anything when I picked up the receiver, I just held it to my ear and held my breath, trying to hear the breathing of the person at the other end, but there was nothing. I tried dialling 1471 to retrieve the caller's number, but always it had been withheld. When I told Alexander, he said it was obviously an automated cold-call system trying to connect. This was the only sensible explanation, but it never happened if Alexander or Jamie answered the phone. When they picked up the receiver there was always a perfectly normal human being on the other end of the line.

At first I suspected the silent calls were part of a campaign of disapproval by the villagers. Maybe somebody was watching the house to see who picked up the telephone and muting the call if it was me. Then, one evening, when all the curtains were drawn, the phone rang again. Nobody looking at the house from outside would know who was going to answer. I held my breath, picked up the receiver and held it to the side of my face.

Again, there was nothing. Only, it felt like more than

nothing; there were whispers in the low-level static buzz down the line. A chill went through me. The fingers on the hand that was holding the phone began to tingle. I dropped it and the handset swung stupidly on its cord, to and fro, between the legs of the dining-room table. I jabbed at the button on the base to cut off the call, but it didn't cut off; I could still hear the buzz that hid the silence. Only the caller could terminate the call. I picked up the handset and banged it back into its cradle.

'Stop it!' I told the telephone. 'Please stop it!'

I steadied myself against the table and told myself not to be stupid. It was an inanimate object, that was all. It didn't have feelings, it was incapable of malice.

Still, I didn't dare pick up the handset again, because I knew perfectly well that, if I did, that ghostly static would still be there.

When the telephone rang the next time, I disconnected the cable at the wall socket.

A few evenings later, I was standing at the kitchen sink peeling carrots. The potatoes were already cooking in a big pan of boiling water on the hob, and the room was warm and steamy. I put the carrots into the colander and crossed to the window, to open the skylight to let out the steam. The panes were hazy. I reached up to the skylight latch and, clear as anything, saw two words written in the condensation on the window, as if someone had spelled them out with a hasty, shaky finger. HELP ME.

I dropped the colander. Alex came in to see what had happened and made me sit down.

'Are you OK?' he asked, and I nodded.

'I just came over a bit faint,' I said. He put the kettle on and, when I dared to look, the window had steamed over again and the words were gone. I must have imagined them.

Eventually, I casually suggested to Alex that Genevieve might possibly be behind the silent phone calls. They were coming so often now, usually when I was alone, that I felt as if I could not stand them any longer. It had reached the point where I was becoming afraid to pick up the phone even to call May.

'Of course it's not Genevieve,' Alexander said. 'Don't be ridiculous.'

'How can you be so sure?'

'Because it isn't! It can't be!'

I gazed at Alexander.

'Because,' he repeated, 'if Genevieve had something to say, she would come out and say it. She wouldn't do some freakish heavy-breathing act down the line. That wasn't her style.'

'There isn't any breathing,' I said miserably.

Alexander took my hands in his and squeezed.

'Look,' he said, 'if the calls are bothering you that much, just keep the line unplugged.'

That could have been a solution, but I didn't like keeping the line unconnected when I was at Avalon on my own, because it was the only sure means of communicating with the outside world. As a compromise, Alexander and I worked out a system. When he called he did a two-ring code first, and I asked Betsy and May to do the same. I told May it was because we were being bothered by salespeople. We stopped subscribing to the answerphone service and, if I didn't hear the code, I didn't pick up the phone.

Neil left a message on my mobile asking what was going on. He called from work, obviously not wanting May to hear what he had to say. He said he'd seen a background feature about Genevieve's childhood that was being touted round the papers by a south-west news agency 'ready for when the big story broke', together with photographs. The news desk at NWM was collating information about the Churchills. He asked me to call him urgently. I didn't. In my increasing paranoia I was worried that he might betray me, or that I would somehow betray Alexander.

I watched Alexander, and he moved around me, sometimes warming me with his smile and his touch, sometimes, more frequently now, even when Jamie was in Avalon, coming into my bed secretively like a night-creature hard and sinewy and masculine; a wolf. He possessed me silently and I allowed it because our love-making overrode all other thoughts, all anxieties. I knew he was thinking, as I was, that we had nothing left to lose.

At other times, he was oblivious to me. I may as well not have existed. He was so wrapped up in his thoughts that he ignored Jamie too. Then I made an extra effort with the child, to compensate. The two of us established a rapport that was independent of Alexander, and it was something that we both fell back on when he was in one of his uncommunicative moods. I was terrified Jamie would pick up some cruel insinuation in the playground and that he would come home one day full of renewed mistrust of me, but so far that had not happened. He was young enough, and his friends were young and innocent enough, to be largely oblivious to the gossip and the rumours and the suspicions.

Jamie was the only person in my life with whom I could relax completely. He did not judge me, or doubt my motives; he accepted me as I was. I loved sitting on the settee beside him as he, forgetting himself, cuddled into me, putting his hot feet on to my lap, leaning his head against my chest to be soothed by my heartbeat. I knew him so well by then: I knew every tiny part of his body, I worried over every bruise and scab, I delighted in his strong bones, his perfect skin, his eyelashes. He came home one day with a note about head lice and, sure enough, when I combed his hair I found a tiny creature caught in the tines of the comb. He sat patiently in the bath while I washed his hair and doused it with medicated shampoo, and I told him a made-up story about a family of dinosaurs who lived in a cave in the quarry while I went over his scalp with a metal nit-comb and wiped the resultant debris on a pad of toilet tissue.

'That was a good story,' Jamie said sleepily, over the thumb that was in his mouth, as I rinsed his deloused hair with warm water. 'Can we do that again tomorrow?'

I tried not to let thoughts of Genevieve spoil my time with Jamie. I tried not to let her come between us. I told myself that it wasn't my fault I was growing so close to her son. She was the one who had chosen to go away and leave him. She was the one who had created the hole in his life and, if somebody had to fill it, then why not me?

I wondered if Genevieve had any idea what was going on in the village. She must, surely, be in contact with somebody. There must be a spy, somewhere, who was letting her know that Jamie was OK. Or did she trust Alexander enough to know that he would never let the boy suffer?

The next time the phone rang, I counted one, two, three rings and then I picked it up. All I could hear was the faint static rustle.

'Genevieve,' I said, but my voice caught on the word and it came out faint and strange. 'Genevieve, if that's you, please would you let your family know you're all right because everyone's so worried; nobody knows where you are. Please, Genevieve . . .'

I heard something down the line. Something changed: the static became more high pitched, so high and frantic that it hurt the inside of my head, like fingernails on a blackboard.

'Genevieve?' I asked, and the handset leapt out of my hand, wrenching back my wrist, and threw itself against the dining-room wall. The casing shattered and shards of plastic flew everywhere. I was too shocked to scream. I ran in my socks out into the garden and I huddled in the hay in the old horse trailer until it was time to meet Jamie from school.

Everyone stared at me. I had no coat, even though it was cold and the nights were drawing in, and I was wearing a pair of filthy old wellingtons that I'd found in the trailer.

'Are you all right?' Betsy asked.

'Yes, fine.'

'Only' – she took my elbow and moved me away from the other women – 'no offence, Sarah, but you look a bit freaked out.'

I sat with Jamie in the library, counting the minutes until I knew Alexander would be back at Avalon.

We bought fish and chips for supper because I had nothing else prepared, and I warmed them up in the oven and waited for Alexander to find the broken telephone.

'What happened?' he asked, coming into the kitchen and carrying the shattered appliance in both hands as if it were an injured bird. Bits of wire and metal stuck out of the casing and the wire trailed behind him. 'Somebody must have really upset you.'

'It wasn't me,' I said, keeping my eyes fixed on the mushy peas I was heating in a pan on the hob.

Alexander laughed. 'Who was it then?'

I looked up at him. His expression was a combination of amusement and confusion.

I opened my mouth, and then I closed it again.

'It was an accident,' I said. 'It must have been an electrical surge.'

Alexander looked at me, trying to work out if I was joking or not. When I didn't respond, he sighed, and threw the whole telephone into the kitchen bin.

He thought I was acting oddly, I knew he did, but I wasn't the cause of our troubles. It wasn't me, it was Genevieve or, more precisely, Genevieve gone away.

Her absence was at the centre of everything.

* * *

Alexander came home the next day with two shiny new cordless telephone handsets in a box, one for upstairs, one for downstairs. He spent a while charging their batteries and making them work. They smelled fresh, of chemicals and polythene.

I made more of an effort to stay in touch with my family back home. I recognized the pattern between Genevieve and me, how both of us had fled a situation for our various reasons, and how difficult that was for the people who loved us, and who we'd left behind. It was easy for me to keep the lines of communication open, and I made sure I did.

'Do people ask about me?' I asked May the next time we spoke.

'Of course they do,' she said. 'They wonder if you're all right and when you're coming home.'

'What do you tell them?'

'I tell them you're no more screwed up than usual and that we expect to see you when you run out of money.'

'Thanks for your support.'

'That's OK. Sarah . . .'

'Mmmm?'

'Laurie called round the other day. He wanted to know . . . God, this is difficult . . .'

'Just tell me.'

'He wanted to know if it would be all right to give your pushchair to his sister. She's pregnant again.'

I looked up at the ceiling. Suddenly I felt furious. I was angry with Laurie for even asking. Why couldn't he just make a decision by himself? And also I was angry with May for passing on the message and reminding me that my son was dead and that life was moving on, and most of all I was angry with myself for feeling so upset. *Now* I wanted to smash the phone against the wall.

'Tell him to do whatever he wants,' I said coldly. 'Like he normally does.'

CHAPTER THIRTY-THREE

By mid-November I began to feel as if I were a prisoner in Avalon. The nights were closing right in, and the weather was cold and wet. I only normally left the house to fetch Jamie from school. Once a week Alexander drove me to the supermarket on the outskirts of Glastonbury to shop for the week's groceries so there was no need to keep going to and from the Spar. I didn't like being in the village any more. If I was compelled to go on some urgent errand, I wrapped myself up and huddled along, with my chin tucked into my collar and the hair blowing across my face, hoping nobody would notice me.

There didn't seem to be a problem with the new telephones. They rang infrequently, but when they did ring, there was always somebody there. I convinced myself that there must have been a fault with the old one. That would explain the silent calls and its violent self-destruction.

Because I spent so much time in the house, I had a lot of time for drawing. I'd always enjoyed it and it was one of the few activities that demanded my full concentration and stopped me thinking about Genevieve.

Alexander was not a man for compliments, but he said my pictures were good. He said I should take them into Wells and tout them around the art shops. I couldn't imagine that anyone would pay money for anything I'd drawn but he said I should give it a go, because otherwise I'd never know. He said it would get me out of the house and give me something to take my mind off things.

So I picked out the best drawings and caught the bus into Wells with my portfolio under my arm.

There were several small art shops in the city. It took me a long time to pluck up the courage to go in, and the lady in the first shop was polite but unenthusiastic about my pictures. The owner of the very next shop, a willowy woman who wore a long cardigan and spectacles on a chain around her neck, could not have been kinder. She wasn't so interested in the sketches of Jamie but liked the pencil drawings of flowers. She said they were intimate and sensual. Even more than the flowers, she liked my coloured drawings of apples, not beautiful, perfect apples but the damaged, misshapen ones, the windfalls that looked so ugly but whose flesh tasted so divine.

We drank ginger tea sweetened with honey and ate the thinnest cinnamon biscuits, and then the gallery owner chose four pictures to frame. Two were apple studies and two were drawings of fading roses. The woman said they were subtly erotic, but honestly I don't know how she came to that conclusion. We agreed to share the framing costs and she would do her best to sell them. I felt so happy I practically skipped out of the gallery. I longed to call Alexander to tell him the good news, but I knew he didn't like being disturbed at work.

The art shop was huddled cosily amongst a number of very nice upmarket chi-chi little shops that were already preparing for Christmas. I spent a while wandering up and down the street looking in the windows, and bought a few bits and pieces.

It was only Wells, the smallest city in England if you don't count the City of London, but it had traffic and shoppers and people talking into their mobile phones. It had a pub that used to be the town gaol, pretty almshouses, a moated bishop's palace and a cosy archway leading into the cathedral gardens. It did not have suspicious glances and posters of Genevieve and women who looked me up and down. That day, Wells could have been a million miles from Burrington Stoke. It felt deliciously cosmopolitan. I had a few errands to run. I went to the post office and to the bank, and dropped an envelope full of invoices off at the office of Alexander's accountant.

After that, feeling more cheerful and normal than I had for a while, I went into a coffee shop and treated myself to a proper coffee, a panini and a magazine. I found a seat by a sunny window that overlooked the quaint cobbled streets and was eating my lunch while reading a magazine about celebrities that Laurie would have thoroughly disapproved of when a voice at my shoulder said: 'Hello, it's Sarah, isn't it?'

I turned and looked into the face of a smiling man

who was attractive in that rugged, confident way some older men are. He was holding out a hand in greeting and balancing a mug of coffee and a pastry in the other.

'Sorry,' I said, putting what was left of my panini back on the plate and wiping my fingers on a paper napkin. 'I know we've met but I . . .'

'DI Twyford,' he said. 'My colleague and I interrupted your dinner to talk to Mr Westwood a few weeks back.'

'Oh yes, of course.'

I half-stood and took his hand. His grip was firm and assertive; his skin warm and dry. He held my hand for a moment longer than was strictly necessary.

'Should I call you Inspector?'

'I'm Ian, to my friends,' he said.

I hesitated.

'And acquaintances.'

'OK. Hello, Ian.'

I smiled into his smile. My heart was thumping like I had something to hide. 'Would you like to join me?' I asked.

'If you don't mind. There's not much room here.'

I glanced around quickly. That wasn't true. There were several free tables, albeit at the edges of the room and not by the window, in the sunshine, like mine. Had he looked in and seen me sitting there by the window as he walked past? Was he following me? I felt panicky and held my breath to calm myself.

The detective put his coffee on the table, beside mine. Some white froth had spilled over the lip and into the saucer. He pulled a couple of paper napkins from the dispenser and used them to soak up the spill. He seemed relaxed. I told myself to stop being paranoid. Wells was so small that any two people who were there at the same time were bound to bump into one another.

'So what brings you into the city. Errands?' he asked, stirring rather a lot of sugar into his latte.

My shopping bag was leaning against the window, and so was my portfolio.

'Your powers of deduction are impressive,' I said.

He laughed.

I smiled too. 'And you? Are you based in Wells or are you just visiting?"

'I'm off duty. Here on errands, like you.'

I sipped my coffee. I had no appetite left for the remains of the panini.

'So how are you getting on in Burrington Stoke?' he asked, emptying another twist of sugar into his cup. 'You're from Manchester, aren't you? Isn't village life a little provincial for a city girl like you?'

'It's a beautiful village,' I said. 'Everyone's very nice.'

He tapped his spoon against the side of the cup.

'Did you ever see that film *American Werewolf*? That scene in the pub called the Slaughtered Lamb when the strangers walk in and all the locals stop talking and stare at them? They filmed it in the Quarrymen's Arms because they didn't need actors there.'

I smiled hesitantly, although I was certain the pub hadn't come into the conversation by accident. DI Twyford knew about the fight. He probably knew everything there was to know.

'Burrington Stoke is an old-fashioned place,' I said carefully. 'I guess they don't really like seeing new faces.'

He shook his head. 'This isn't the Middle Ages, Sarah. It's not you per se that worries them. It's what you represent.'

'What do you mean?'

'You being there, with Alexander, makes them think that Genevieve's never coming back.'

Here she was again.

'I'm sure Genevieve is absolutely fine,' I said. 'Wherever she is, she's probably having the time of her life.'

The inspector, Ian, stirred his coffee and said: 'Oh yes?'

I told him about Genevieve's letter to Jamie, and the teddy bear. I told the inspector that she could only have organized those things if she were planning to leave of her own accord. I even offered to show him the letter and the bear if he doubted my story.

He didn't seem particularly interested in what I told him. All he said was: 'That was convenient.'

'What do you mean?' I asked.

He shrugged. 'You finding the letter that corroborated what you'd been told about Genevieve leaving.'

'Yes,' I said. 'It was convenient. But it happened.'

The inspector didn't respond. He gazed out of the window for a moment. Then he asked if I got on well with Jamie, and I told him that I did.

'You haven't known him long,' he said.

'A few months. We met in the summer, in Sicily, a couple of weeks after Genevieve left. I'm sure Alexander told you that.'

The inspector nodded.

'Why are you even asking me these questions?' I asked. 'You said you weren't working.'

'It's a conversation, not an interrogation.'

'It feels like one.'

The inspector raised his hands and made a face as if to say: 'Guilty.'

'It's the job,' he said. 'It takes over sometimes.'

'Why does everyone think there's something suspicious about Genevieve being gone?' I asked. 'She left letters. She prepared her son. Don't you think . . .?' I paused – I wasn't sure if I should say what I was about to say – and then I thought, why not? 'Don't you think it's possible she was having an affair and that she's gone away with another man?'

'It's possible,' said the inspector.

'What do you think has happened to her?'

'It would be unprofessional and unethical to comment.'

'Theoretically, then.'

He shrugged and sipped his coffee. 'People leave home all the time,' he said. 'They walk out of their old lives and don't look back. You'd be surprised how often it happens, and most of the time there's no foul play involved.'

I made the inspector hold my gaze.

'So what's the problem?'

'The problem is people like Genevieve don't disappear unless they have a very compelling reason to do so.'

'Wouldn't a lover be a compelling enough reason?'

'Even if that is the case, why the silence? Why hasn't she been in touch?'

'Perhaps she's waiting for the dust to settle.'

He shook his head. 'The dust's never going to settle. And Genevieve might not have been a model wife, but she definitely loved her family and the kid. You never saw them together, of course.'

A cold feeling came over me.

'You knew her? *Know* her, I mean?'

'Oh yes. Virginia taught my daughter dressage. As often as not, Genevieve would be up at the yard. She used to lean on the gate and watch the lesson with me or she'd be riding too, demonstrating. She could make those horses dance; she was incredible. Sometimes Jamie was with her. She was always laughing and messing around with him, swinging him round, chasing him, tickling him. If you'd asked me, I'd have said Genevieve would let nothing come between her and her son. Nothing.'

I felt utterly helpless and as if I were terribly in the wrong. I shouldn't have told the inspector that Jamie and I were close. I shouldn't have spoken so carelessly of Genevieve. My mouth was dry as dust. I looked out into the street. People were passing by; to them it was an ordinary day – a bright, autumn day in a beautiful city – and all they had to worry about was what they were going to eat for supper, and there I was, trapped in the corner of a café by a man who knew so much more than I did.

Neither of us spoke for a long time. The inspector finished his coffee.

'You seem like a nice girl,' he said eventually, more gently. 'I'm guessing you wouldn't still be in Somerset if you had any concerns about Alexander.'

I blinked and continued to stare through the window glass. A very young woman in a red puffa jacket and hooped earrings went past, leaning forward to push a twin buggy uphill.

'Somebody like you,' he said, 'would be in the best place to notice any irregularities.'

The make-up bag didn't mean anything. Genevieve could have had a thousand reasons for leaving her pills behind. Maybe those had been spares and she had a stash with her. Maybe she wanted to get pregnant.

'I haven't noticed anything,' I said.

He was watching me.

'Are you sure?'

'Yes.'

The detective paused for a moment. Then he said: 'Genevieve had a laptop. A white MacBook. Mr Westwood told us he hadn't seen it since she left. Is it in the house?'

'No.' I shook my head. 'I've cleaned everywhere and I haven't seen it. Is it important?'

'She used it all the time, took it everywhere . . .'

'Then she'll have taken it with her.'

There was another pause.

The detective drained his coffee in one go, put a few coins on the table and stood up.

'Listen, Sarah, if you ever want a chat, you know, if you think of anything, give me a call.'

He passed me a card.

'Thank you,' I said. 'I will.'

CHAPTER THIRTY-FOUR

We were working in the garden, the three of us, raking up the leaves. It was an enjoyable task, and we worked well together. Alexander's mood was lighter and more buoyant than it had been. I held open a sack for him to load with freshly fallen debris, the smell of smoke and leaf mould and autumn in my head, and he leaned forward and kissed me.

It was a gesture of such sweetness and spontaneity that my heart softened. I looked around the garden, but there was no sign of Genevieve watching, no unexplained shadows, nothing sinister at all. I smiled up into Alexander's face, his eyes, his lips, and for the thousandth time I was bowled over by his beauty. I had to look away. I could not believe I was actually with a man like him.

I carried the sack over to the bonfire we were building in the far corner of the garden and turned it upside down, shaking it by the corners to empty it. Something trapped beneath the now bare branches of a large old rambling rose caught my eye. I leaned down to pick it up; it was a dog chew, a plastic ball fastened to a rope. The rope was almost rotted through, and the squeak had gone from the ball, which was punctured with teeth marks and tears. I bounced it in my hand and walked back to Alexander.

'Look what I found,' I said.

Jamie came running over.

'It's Pete's ball!' he cried, jumping up and down for the toy. 'He lost it ages ago!'

'Who's Pete?' I asked Jamie, tossing the ball to him.

'Our dog.'

I remembered the dog bed and bowls stacked in the rosette room. I glanced towards Alexander. He had turned away and was raking furiously; despite the coolness of the air his shirt was dark with sweat down the back, at the neck and beneath the arms. I could tell from the shape of his shoulders and the rhythm of his movements that he was angry again.

I returned to the bonfire pile and began to tidy it, throwing sticks and debris on to the top of the heap. Jamie came with me.

'What happened to Pete?' I asked, quietly.

Jamie looked up and me and shrugged. 'He had to go and live somewhere else.'

'Was someone allergic to him?'

Jamie shook his head.

'Jamie?'

'I don't know why he had to go away!' he cried. 'Shut up fucking talking about him!'

Jamie lifted the ball high, swung it by its rope and let it go. It flew into the heart of the huge old daphne bush at the centre of the far shrub bed. We both watched it disappear into the leaves. Jamie wiped his nose with his hand.

'Sorry, Jamie, I didn't mean to upset you,' I said quietly.

'Then why do you keep asking me about things I don't want to talk about?' Jamie said in a quiet, furious voice. 'Why do you keep doing that? Where's my mummy? Why are you here and she isn't?'

'OK,' I said, briskly. 'OK, never mind. Do you think it's time for a cup of tea and a piece of cake?'

Jamie looked up at me with his beautiful eyes, clear and blue as the day. He made a sneer with his lips.

'You're a bitch,' he said, and he ran down to the swing and sat on it, pushing himself backwards and forwards with the toes of his blue plastic wellington boots.

CHAPTER THIRTY-FIVE

A bleak cloud of bad temper and introspection settled over Avalon for the rest of the day. For a while I tried to cajole Alexander and Jamie out of their moods, to placate them with food and humour and kindness, but they were intractable, the father and son so alike in their stubbornness it was infuriating. They shared the same ploy of retreating into themselves whenever something happened they didn't like.

It wasn't my fault. I hadn't known there was a problem with the dog; nobody had so much as mentioned its name before. It was Alexander's fault. If he didn't want me to keep putting my foot right bang in the middle of these sensitive subjects then he ought to bloody well warn me.

I left Alexander and Jamie to the garden, each at either end of it, one raking, one swinging, both sulking, and I went into the kitchen to clean the last of the vegetables. I also had a colander of tomatoes from the greenhouse. I washed the fruit, halved them and laid them on trays, drizzled them with olive oil and sprinkled them with salt and garden herbs to heat in the Rayburn's hot oven and then to roast overnight in the cool one. I was in the middle of these enjoyable culinary tasks and feeling a bit better when Claudia phoned to ask if I'd like to stand in for one of their regulars on the pub quiz team who had fallen sick. They'd thought of me, she said, because they were desperate and also because it would annoy Virginia no end, and she wanted to annoy her because she was so sick and tired of Virginia refusing her access to her father, who was ill again, and confined to bed.

I sympathized with Claudia for a few moments and then asked where the quiz was.

'It's in Sherborne. Don't worry, the Quarrymen's Arms won't be sending a team.'

'OK,' I said. 'Hold on.'

I stepped out into the garden and called Alexander to ask if it would be all right with him. He told me to do what I liked. So I thought: fine, I will.

'Yes, I'd love to do it, Claudia,' I said into the mouthpiece.

She said: 'Great. I'll pick you up at seven thirty.'

I hadn't had a proper evening out since I'd been at Avalon and that afternoon I was so edgy and irritated I thought it would do me good to be somewhere different.

I prepared a great dish of buttered mashed potatoes for tea and served it with the cassoulet I'd put in the oven earlier. We ate it with home-grown green beans and sweetcorn from the freezer. Alexander and Jamie ate well enough – in fact, they had two helpings each – but they were both monosyllabic during dinner. I put forward several potential topics of conversation and had a sarcastic talk with myself – 'What do you think of the dinner, Sarah? Oh, it's lovely, thank you. Do you like the beans? Mmm, they're delicious!' – but they took no notice so I gave up. We ate in silence. A late, black fly banged itself against the window glass and then became trapped in a dusty cobweb in the corner of the frame. I went to rescue it but Alexander waved me away.

'It's a filthy fly,' he said. 'Leave it.'

So we listened to the fly's increasingly frantic buzzing and were all, I think, relieved when it was at last rendered silent by the spider that lived in the latch.

After dinner, I stacked the dishes in the machine and gave the kitchen a wipe-round. Alexander was poring over some papers in his office and Jamie was lying on the settee watching television in the living room. I banged the pots a little to let them know I was upset by their behaviour but still neither of them took the slightest notice. So I opened a bottle of wine, poured myself a large glass and I took both the glass and the bottle upstairs to my bedroom and stood in front of the chest of drawers that was my wardrobe.

It was only a pub quiz. There was nobody to dress up for but that night I wanted to look my best. I hadn't realized until that evening how much I craved the stuff of females: make-up, jewellery, perfume, high heels and fabrics that felt good against the skin. I couldn't even remember the last time I'd been out with a group of girlfriends with the single intention of having fun; it must have been well over two years, before I was pregnant, before Laurie and I had even started trying for the baby. I had stopped drinking well in advance and taken vitamins and folic acid, all the things you're supposed to do in order to end up with a perfectly healthy baby.

I knew the pub we were going to was not going to be a party pub, but it was somewhere different at least and that was something to celebrate.

I wondered if Genevieve had felt suffocated by the countryside; by its mud and its tractors, its masculinity and its relentless inevitability? Was this one of the reasons she had so wanted to get away from Burrington Stoke? But she'd been born into this life, she'd never known any different.

I told myself to stop thinking about Genevieve and concentrate on going out.

I took off the long-sleeved T-shirt, jeans and socks that had become my uniform, gulped a mouthful of wine and danced in my underwear with my arms above my head in front of the spotted old mirror that was perched on the chest of drawers. I hummed to myself, drank some more wine, refilled the glass from the bottle, rummaged in my bag and found a pair of black leggings. They had been a little tight when I left Manchester, but I must have lost some weight because now they fitted perfectly. I put a long-sleeved purple dress over the top and fastened it at the waist with a black belt with a gilt buckle. I sat on the bed and wiggled my feet into my long black velvet boots. Then I put on my make-up: eye-liner, dark eyeshadow, dusky lipstick and thick black mascara. I straightened my hair, licked my lips. I narrowed my eyes and blew kisses at myself in the mirror. I looked young and juicy and dangerous.

In that different life of mine, the happy old Manchester life, I used to go out once a week with a group of girlfriends, Rosita among them. We used to dress ourselves up to the nines and go clubbing. We'd dance and talk and drink and laugh. I couldn't remember what it was that was so funny, but I used to feel as if nothing could hurt me.

I lay back on the bed and stared out of the window. It was dark but there was a good moon lighting up the orchard, the grass and trees, painting them pale blue and casting beautiful shadows. What had started, earlier, as a quiet ache had developed into a full-blown heartfelt missing of Manchester. I missed it with a kind of desperation. If there had been any way for me to get back there, that evening, I would have gone. I'd have hooked up with some girlfriends, drunk vodka shots and danced my socks off.

The view from this window must have been the same, give or take the odd cow, since the house had been built four hundred years ago. A person can, I thought, have too much serenity. I finished my wine, filled the glass again; now the glass was fuller than the bottle. I hoped Claudia wasn't relying on me too much for the quiz. I trotted downstairs. The clock on the mantelpiece above the fire in the dining room said it was quarter past seven. I went into the office and stood behind Alexander, one hand resting lightly on his shoulder. He was staring into his laptop. On the screen was an Excel page, a mass of figures as incomprehensible as Latin to me. I was hoping he would turn to look at me, and admire me, as Laurie would have done. Laurie was always appreciative; that was one of the good things about him. He made everyone feel special. Oh lord, I thought, are things so bad between Alexander and me that I'm seriously beginning to miss Laurie?

I let my fingers play with the ends of Alexander's hair; it was slightly greasy. I started to make a little plait. Alexander didn't seem to notice I was there. I leaned down so that he would feel the warmth of my skin, and smell my perfume. If he looked, he would be able to see my cleavage, the lace of my bra. I knew I was looking good. I wished he would notice; I wished he'd pay a little more attention to me.

'What are you doing?' I asked huskily. I wobbled ever so slightly on the heels of my boots.

'Accounts. I'm trying to make the books balance.'

'Is there a problem?'

He nodded. 'I've always been shit with numbers. I'm dyslexic and numbers are worse than words. They look like they're dancing across the page. Before Genevieve left she . . .'

'Oh, her again.'

I took my hand from his shoulder and turned away. For a moment he did not move, then he put his pen down and slowly turned to face me. He exhaled.

'What? What is it?'

'Nothing.'

'Oh come on, Sarah.'

I sucked at my lower lip and twirled a skein of hair

around my finger. I looked into his beautiful, beautiful face. He was already in a bad mood. I did not want to criticize or hurt him. But I had to say something.

'It's just that everything – every conversation, everything we do, everything – always revolves around Genevieve.'

'Yes.' He nodded in agreement.

I almost stamped my foot in frustration. 'But Alexander, she's not here!'

'I know.'

'She's gone!'

'A-ha.'

'So why is she still the centre of the universe?'

He was confused. It was written on his face. He did not understand why we were even having this conversation because, to him, it was obvious.

'You knew the situation,' he said. 'I warned you it would be difficult.'

'I know, but she's like a black hole,' I said, warming to the astronomical analogy. 'You can't see her but she influences everything.'

'Yes, she does.'

'But I can't stand it! It's not fair! She's *not here*!'

Alexander pushed his chair back and stood up. I caught my breath at the beauty of him. I loved the grace and manliness of him. I loved the shape of him, the scruffiness, the bagginess of his clothes, the way his shirt hung over his trousers, his beautiful eyes, his mouth, his chin. Still I withdrew a little. No matter how I was drawn to him, I could not get round this thing between us. Genevieve gone.

'Hey,' he said, holding out his hands in a conciliatory manner. 'Come on, Sarah. I'm sorry, but Genevieve . . .'

I was on the point of conceding. If he had not said her name, I would have let it go. But he said 'Genevieve' and I was tired of that pretty French name, tired of protecting Alexander from the things I knew about her, about him, about them. I had had enough of Genevieve.

'I'll see you later,' I said, and I picked up my jacket and went outside.

I waited for Claudia at the bottom of the drive, hopping from foot to foot, and was shivering by the time the car pulled up. I should really have worn a coat, but couldn't bear to go back inside once I'd flounced out. I slipped into the passenger seat and reached for her handbag.

'Do you mind if I have a cigarette?' I asked.

'Help yourself,' she said.

There was a ten-pack of Silk Cut in her bag. I shook one out, lit it, wound down the window and inhaled.

'Trouble in paradise?' Claudia asked. I snorted.

She accelerated the car down the lane. It was pitch black between the tall hedges on either side of the road. I thought: Heaven help us if we meet anything coming at our speed the other way.

'What's the matter?' Claudia asked.

'It's Genevieve,' I said quietly.

Claudia held out her fingers for a draw on the cigarette.

'It's not her fault,' she said. 'You can't blame her for any of this.'

I turned to look at her profile. She was driving but I could see her face lit by the headlights of oncoming cars. There was a shine to her eyes and I was ashamed of myself.

'No, of course not,' I said. 'I'm sorry.'

Our quiz team was called, with irony, 'The Trophy Wives'. It consisted of me, Claudia and two of Claudia's book-group friends, Bess and Libby, both of whom were, like Claudia, well bred and scruffy and rather horsey, and they both had daughters at the same school as the twins. Neither, fortunately, lived in Burrington Stoke. I was an unlikely member of the foursome, and had not realized how competitive the event would be. The other teams were predominantly male, and mostly older than us. They lined up their real ales on the sticky tabletops and we lined up our plastic mini-bottles of Merlot and Chardonnay, and the landlord, who was known as John the Steak because he used to be a butcher, handed out the sheets and read the questions over a microphone.

Within a very few moments I realized that my only helpful role that evening was likely to be in making up the numbers. While the other women answered the questions, I drank one drink, and then another. When the quiz was over, while the answers were being collated, I moved into the snug with Libby. We ordered more drinks and sat at the only available table and, at the bar, a man waved at me. It was Tom, Betsy's partner. I beckoned him to come and join us.

We talked of the children, of this and that, but sooner or later, inevitably, the conversation came back to the fight in the pub. I tried to explain to Tom how humiliating it was to have everyone in the village pointing fingers at me. He nodded and sipped his cider.

'It's not you they're really interested in,' he said. 'It's her. People have been talking about Genevieve all her life. They can't get enough of her.'

I took a drink of wine.

'There's always been some drama going on around her,' said Tom. 'My mum remembers the scandal when Philip swapped his first wife for Virginia and Genevieve came along six months after the wedding, if you get my drift. Same day as . . . well, you know. People used to say that she was bound to have bad luck after a start like that. They said she'd be cursed, but she turned it round. She was such a good rider she was winning trophies almost as soon as she could walk. Then . . .'

'What?'

'She was sweet on a lad from the village, Robbie Innes. They used to ride together. He was the only one who could match her cross country. And you know what happened to him?'

I shook my head.

'He drowned in the old quarry.'

'Oh!' I looked up. 'The boy who died was Genevieve's boyfriend?'

Tom nodded.

'God, poor Genevieve.'

I was beginning to feel very tired and emotional.

'Tombstoning, they call it,' Tom said. 'Jumping off the cliffs into the water and never mind what's below. Everyone used to do it, all the young lads. I went up there myself a few times. Everyone knew that old quarry was an accident waiting to happen. To give them their due, the Churchills put up signs warning of the danger and fenced the area off. They tried to keep the kids out but they didn't take any notice. Boys never do.'

'That's terrible,' I said. I wiped my nose with the back of my hand. 'That's so sad.'

'Genevieve was there when it happened, her and her brother. People say that's what tipped Damian right over the edge, no pun intended. She never got over it either,' said Tom.

'She got over it enough to marry Alexander.'

'Yeah, but . . .'

'What?'

He shrugged. 'After Robbie died, everyone thought she'd end up with Luke.'

'Who's Luke?'

'Robbie's brother.'

'So where is Luke now?'

'Fuck knows.'

'Maybe it's him!' I said.

'What's him?'

'Maybe he came back to Burrington Stoke and met up with Genevieve and she realized she still loved him. Maybe she decided she should have been with him all along and that's why she went away.'

Tom sighed and tipped his head back to drain his glass. There was a stubbly patch on his throat that he'd missed with the razor.

'Or maybe not,' he said.

Somewhere along the line, Tom and Libby swapped places. She was having an animated conversation with someone else, which I was too drunk and tired to listen to. Tom seemed to have run out of things to say and was staring morosely into his glass. I rested my head on his shoulder. It was wide and hard with muscle. He smelled of deodorant, something strong and spicy. I didn't mean anything by it. It was just somewhere to put my head. It was heavy and sleepy and already beginning to ache a little.

'I'm glad you're with Betsy. I think you're very nice,' I said to Tom, holding out my glass for a top-up.

'I think you're very nice too,' he said. 'Only move your head.'

'Why?'

'You're involved with Alexander Westwood and the Churchill family,' he said. 'You should be careful.'

'Why should I be careful?'

He leaned forward so that I had to sit up straight.

'You'll see,' he said.

I don't remember the exact sequence of events but some time later, when Alexander came into the pub, I was asleep, curled up on the bench with my head pillowed by Libby's jacket.

Claudia helped me to my feet and passed me to

Alexander. I stumbled into his arms. He apologized to Claudia for me and half-dragged, half-carried me into the cold outside air beneath a starlit night and a blue moon, and helped me into the Land Rover. He didn't say a word to me. Nothing.

We drove home in silence. I was determined not to make excuses for my behaviour. I felt sullen and resentful of Alexander. Everyone else seemed happy to talk to me; other people seemed to like me. What was wrong with him that he couldn't open his heart to me? Was he *still* so in love with Genevieve? My forehead bumped on the car window. Alexander drove with one hand on the wheel. He rested the elbow of the other arm on the door, and rubbed his forefinger along his lips.

At Avalon, Alexander ran up to check on Jamie, who had been left unattended, then he helped me up the stairs and lay me down on my bed. Several times I insisted I was all right, but I wasn't.

'I'll bring you a cup of mint tea,' he said, easing my boots off my feet.

'Yes, because that'll put everything right,' I said miserably. Now I felt sorry for myself and tearful.

'It's supposed to prevent hangovers.'

'Like I said.'

'Sarah . . .'

'What?'

I rolled over on to my side, facing the window with my back to him. I could see my face, in duplicate, reflected in the panes. My mascara was smudged around my eyes and my face was pale. I looked like a zombie, a living dead person.

I felt the weight of him as he sat down behind me on the bed, and my body moved along the depression of the mattress towards him. His back was reflected in the window glass. He had his head in his hands.

'What's the matter, Sarah?' he said. 'Why did you have to go and do that?'

I felt my eyes fill with tears of self-pity. There was a salty taste in my mouth.

'It's you,' I said.

'What did I do?'

'It's what you don't do. You don't let me into your life. You won't let me help you. Most of you is closed off from me. I feel like a stranger.'

His reflection shook its head. It put the heels of its hands into its eye sockets and rubbed ferociously.

'You live in my house, Sarah, you look after my son, we eat together and sleep together and spend most of our free time together. I've done things with you I've never done with anybody else. You *are* my life.'

I shook my head.

'There are too many secrets. You don't trust me.'

'I wouldn't have brought you here if I didn't.'

'Then why don't you tell me anything?'

'I tell you everything.'

'No.'

I turned over to look at Alexander. His eyes were red where he had rubbed them, his hair stuck up. He looked unkempt, tramp-like and vulnerable.

'You don't tell me about anything important,' I said. 'You don't tell me about why Genevieve really left, or Pete, or' – I took a deep breath – 'or why you were in prison.'

'Oh.'

I sighed.

I saw the tiny muscles in his face tense. I could feel him closing himself up.

'That was always the deal, wasn't it, Sarah? We took one another on trust because we believed in each other.'

'But it's all one way,' I said. 'If you asked me a question, any question, I would answer it honestly.'

'I don't want to know. I don't care about your life before I met you.'

I thought of my baby wrapped in a cotton hospital blanket, blue for a boy. I recalled his tiny fingers and how warm and sweet and solid he was in my arms; the perfectly peaceful expression on his face. I remembered how I put the tip of my little finger between his lips – they were dry and slightly purple – and felt the fading heat of the inside of his mouth. I put the smallest amount of pressure on his gum and pleaded in my heart for a miracle, for what nearly all babies do instinctively and naturally; I willed him to suck. My lips were on his forehead. I tried to make a deal with God, I begged Him to let me see my baby take just one breath. It was such a small thing to ask for: a single breath, a tiny movement of his ribcage. Nothing happened. My whole body ached with the exhaustion of childbirth and with tenderness for my son. He was the best thing that had ever happened to me. Did he not matter now because he was in the past? Didn't he count?

'Don't say that,' I said. 'There are things I'd like to tell you, things you ought to know. If you cared about me . . .'

'I didn't say I don't care about you,' said Alexander. 'But what happened to you before I met you is irrelevant to us now.'

It wasn't! What happened to me before I met him was the reason I had been in Sicily in the first place. If it hadn't happened we would never even have set eyes upon one another . . . but I was too drunk to rationalize my frustration or to put it into words.

'I've never lied to you,' he said.

That wasn't the point. I hadn't accused him of lying but of being evasive. I struggled, in my fug of misery, for a cohesive response.

'Then tell me why you went to prison. What did you do?'

His face was tired and closed.

'It doesn't matter. It was nothing.'

'Most people, Alex, would think being sent to prison was quite a big thing.'

'I thought you were different from most people.'

He looked so disconsolate, so disappointed, that I was ashamed of myself.

I wanted to throw my arms around him and assure him that I was, indeed, different. I wanted to apologize so that we could have some kind of happy ending to that miserable day; kisses and tears and apologies, sex and reconciliation. But I was angry and hurt and jealous. I shuddered and curled myself a little tighter.

I had the feeling he was waiting for me to speak, but I said nothing.

'It's over,' he said at last. He stood up and left the room, pulling the door shut behind him.

I didn't know what he meant. Did he mean the past was over, or the evening, or that we were over?

Ordinarily, I'd have tried to sort it out there and then, but I was in no fit state to do anything that night.

I heard him banging about downstairs even as my headache began to kick in.

I pulled the duvet over me and hid beneath it. I wasn't exactly comfortable. I was still wearing the dress, belt and leggings, and there were clips in my hair, but I thought I'd wait until Alexander was in bed before I went to the bathroom.

I didn't mean to sleep, but I must have dropped off almost at once because the next thing I remembered was waking in daylight, dry-mouthed and achey, to see Alexander standing at the open door to my room. He was rubbing the knuckles of one hand with the palm of the other.

He nodded towards the chest of drawers and said: 'I brought you a cup of tea.'

'Thank you.'

I did my best to smile, but the smile did not last long because Alexander said: 'This was a mistake. Us, I mean. It was a stupid idea you coming here. I think it would be best if you left.'

CHAPTER THIRTY-SIX

I stayed in my room until Alexander and Jamie had left for school, then I crept into the bathroom and sat on the toilet, peeing for an eternity. I rested my forehead on the cold tiles, which were damp with condensation, and wondered what I should do.

I could just pack and go. I could call a taxi to take me into Wells, or Shepton Mallet, and catch a train to Bristol and pick up a Midlands connection there. Nobody back in Manchester apart from my immediate family knew anything about Alexander and Genevieve. Nobody knew and nobody cared. It wasn't as if anyone would accuse me of having failed. I could slip seamlessly back into my old world. It would feel like death to me, but to everyone else it would be a small, insignificant death. It was possible. I could leave.

But I didn't want to go. I would not leave the two people I cared for now more than anyone else in the world – not unless Alexander really wanted me out of his life, and in my heart I doubted that. I was almost certain he'd told me to go because he did not want me to know the truth about his past, not because he wanted shot of me. In his own, awkward way he had come to depend on me. What he needed was for me to be completely on his side. He had believed in me. I had not granted him the same respect.

I was at a crossroads. Now was the time to commit to Alexander completely, or to throw in the towel and walk away. Really, there was no decision to be made.

CHAPTER THIRTY-SEVEN

I had a hot shower and dressed, then I did what I always did first thing in the morning: I prepared supper for that evening. I made Jamie's favourite pasta bake, covered it with grated cheese, wrapped the whole thing in tin foil, and put it in the fridge.

The weather had turned lately; it was significantly colder. My eyes were drawn outside, to the back garden separated from the orchard by its barbed-wire fence. It was small, disorganized and hidden behind the house. I had hardly been out there, but Alex used it as a place to dump stuff, and for bonfires. We'd spent all our time and energy working in the front, with its lawn and flower beds, trees and vegetable patch.

That morning, I decided to do what I could to clear the back; it might be my last chance. Then I'd pack my bag and, if Alex's mind was still set when he came home, I'd make him promise I could visit Jamie every now and then, and I'd leave.

I wrapped up warm and went outside. The back garden was overrun with brambles and dead and dying nettles. It was so cold that my breath clouded around me, but I was ruthless with the secateurs, and soon a pile of cut-back material big enough for a bonfire was heaped in the corner. I tugged at a bunch of twiggy dead wood with my gloved hands, and as it came away I saw the shape of something solid beneath it.

Curious, I pushed at the overgrowth until I had revealed the object. It was an unfinished statue of a woman, cut into a piece of stone.

The stone was whitish, hardly weather-worn. The woman's head had been sculpted to look out across the orchard. I took off one of my gloves and felt the cold stone icy beneath my palm, the shape of Genevieve's face.

I knew Alexander had made the statue.

The sad feeling rushed over me again and tears came to my eyes and ran down my face. I knew that no matter how hard I tried, I would never be beautiful and I would never be Genevieve, and Alexander would never love me enough to carve my face out of stone.

I don't know how long I sat there by that statue; long enough to run out of tears and to begin to ache with cold. The sky above was pewter-coloured, streaked with cloud. If I stayed there long enough maybe I would turn to stone. I was lost in self-pity when I heard the crunch of car tyres on the gravel at the top of the drive. I stood up, brushing soil from the knees of my jeans, and, hobbling on cold feet prickling with pins and needles, went to the gate.

It was DI Twyford. He had parked his car and now

was speaking into his phone, looking towards the open door at the front of the house. He was laughing at something the person at the other end of the line had said.

His timing was spectacularly bad.

For a few moments I toyed with the idea of hiding. I could creep behind the pile of cuttings I'd just made. Or climb over the wire fence and hide in the orchard; I could lie down in the long, wet grass and make myself disappear. He'd probably wait a while but eventually he'd go away.

But then . . . The rosette-room door was open.

It would look odd, the door being open and nobody there. I didn't want to raise any more suspicions. I didn't want to draw more attention to myself and Alexander, or behave in a way that might look strange. Hiding and running away were not options. I would have to face the inspector. I put on a cheery smile, and opened the gate just as he stepped out of his car.

He smiled when he saw me, but then his smile changed to a frown of concern.

'Are you all right?'

'Hay fever,' I said.

'In November?'

'I'm very sensitive.'

'To what? Frost?'

'Actually, I had a bit too much to drink last night.'

'Oh,' he said. 'I see.'

Now he thinks I'm a dipso, I thought. Or else he thinks the pressure's getting to me or that I'm drinking to numb my guilt.

He took off his sunglasses and squinted. 'Alexander

not around?' he asked. It was a ridiculous question. It was 11 a.m. on a weekday. Of course Alexander was not there. I narrowed my eyes and gave the inspector a cynical look.

'He's at work.'

'Of course,' he said. 'Listen, I just happened to be passing . . .'

I toed a pebble with my boot and tucked my hair behind my ear.

'This was going to be my last call of the day,' he said. 'I was hoping to have a quick word with Mr Westwood but, as he's not here and I'm more or less off duty, would you like to join me for lunch?'

My hungover mind turned slowly. Was he allowed to ask me out for lunch? Was he asking in a professional capacity, or was he flirting with me? If I refused, what would he think? That I was being unhelpful, possibly, or that I was afraid or had something to hide. Even if he was just playing with me, would it put his back up if I refused? I owed it to Alexander to deal with this situation, especially after what had happened the previous night.

So I said: 'OK. That would be nice. I just need to . . .'

'Slip into something more comfortable?' Oh lord, he *was* flirting.

'Wash my hands.'

'Oh well . . .'

For a middle-aged man, he was remarkably confident of his attractiveness.

'Are you married?' I asked.

'In the middle of a divorce,' he said. 'So I'm open to offers.'

When I came back outside again, changed, made up and holding my handbag, Detective Inspector Ian Twyford was waiting, leaning on the bonnet of his car and enjoying the winter sun. He wore his shades and a dark coat that strained slightly at the belly. He smiled when he saw me and opened the passenger door with a little theatrical bow. I thanked him, and stepped lady-like inside. I put on my dark glasses and waited for him to take us out of Burrington Stoke, the hangover rubbing away at my right optic nerve like a carpenter with a plane.

'Where are we going?' I asked.

'Rather nice country pub I know called the Pony and Trap,' he said. 'Good ale, good food, good views.'

'I don't mean to sound ungrateful, but could we go somewhere a bit urban? Somewhere where there'll be loads of people and nobody will stare at us?'

He chuckled.

'Going a bit stir crazy in the sticks, are we?'

'More than a bit.'

'OK. Whatever you want.'

He smiled at me. I thought it would hurt my head to return the smile so I closed my eyes behind the sunglasses and actually managed a little doze before we reached our destination.

We went to Wells, and the city was busy, heaving with the pre-Christmas rush. We walked through crowds of people and went into a nice little pub.

'Two pubs in two days. People will start talking about me,' I said as he helped me, graciously, into a seat beside an agreeably hot and welcoming log fire. I snuggled into the chair and felt better.

'Like they're not talking about you already,' he said. He jingled the change in his trouser pockets. 'Do you need a hair of the dog?'

I shook my head.

'You look like you do.'

I knew I looked fine. I'd put on make-up before we left.

'How about something to eat?'

'OK.'

While he stood at the bar, which was all gilt and mirrors and retro-optics, I picked at a beer mat. Then he sat down on a stool opposite me and passed me a glass of what looked like iced tomato juice. A swizzle-stick protruded from the viscous red liquid.

'Drink it,' he said. 'It'll make you feel better.'

He ripped open a packet of cheese and onion crisps with his teeth and placed it on the table between us.

'Got to be cheese and onion,' he said, 'if you want to cure a hangover.'

'Is that official?'

He nodded and took a drink of his pint.

'Why did you want to see Alexander?' I asked.

'I can't tell you. Besides, I'm off duty now. I don't want to talk about work.'

I eyed him with suspicion. Either he really did fancy his chances with me, or he was lying – or maybe both.

A few minutes later, a harassed-looking teenage girl

in a white apron interrupted us to put a plate of cheese and chutney sandwiches and a bowl of chips on the table. My stomach rolled with pleasure at the hot, oily tang.

'Those look fantastic.'

I took a sip of the tomato juice cocktail. It was savoury and it had a fabulous kick. There must have been at least a double shot of vodka in there.

'This is how people become alcoholics, you know,' I said. 'By being given drinks that taste like pure vitamin C when they're feeling awful.'

'So have you found any more letters in Avalon?' he asked, completely wrong-footing me. 'Have you found Genevieve's laptop?'

'No, no, I haven't.'

'What about emails? Have you had a look on Alexander's computer?'

'No,' I said. 'He keeps it in his office and I don't go in there.'

'So you haven't had a chance to look?'

'I don't need to. I trust him.'

'What about his mobile phone? Have you checked to see if Genevieve's number is still on there?'

I had and it was, but all the messages, both sent and received, had been deleted.

'No.'

The inspector smiled. 'I don't believe you. Everyone spies on their partner's texts.'

'I'm not his partner, I'm his housekeeper.'

'That's not what I've heard, my lovely.'

DI Twyford brushed the crumbs from his lips with a

paper napkin and took a drink from his glass. The whites of his eyes were ever so slightly pink, and his eyebrows were dark and bushy. I couldn't work out if he was my friend or not.

I thought I would give him something to make him like me. I'd give him some information.

'I found something out last night,' I said. 'I think I know who Genevieve was seeing, who she might have gone away with.'

The inspector raised an eyebrow.

'Go on.'

'I heard she was in love with the boy who died in the quarry. And that after he drowned, everyone thought she'd marry his brother.'

'Luke Innes.'

'You know about him?'

'His name has come up a few times.'

'Then shouldn't you be looking for him?'

'We do want to speak to Mr Innes, yes.'

'Do you know where he is?'

The inspector shook his head.

I felt a twinge of frustration.

'If he's missing too . . .'

'We don't know that he's *missing*, we just don't know where he is. We're trying to track him down, but he pretty much disappeared off the radar after university. He went to the same one as Genevieve, at the same time. Did you know that?'

'No.'

'He was brilliant, by all accounts, and devoted to her but something happened. He dropped out in his second year and spent a while with a group of eco-activists trying to sabotage the Churchills' quarrying business. He must have blamed them for his brother's death.'

'He and Damian would have been soul mates,' I said quietly.

'They were in it together.'

'And after that?'

'Nobody knows, or at least nobody's saying. According to Damian, Luke went off travelling on his own. He may have settled abroad somewhere. He certainly doesn't appear to have returned to Somerset.'

'He might have stayed in touch with Genevieve.'

'It's possible.'

'You don't seem to think much of the idea.'

The inspector puffed out his cheeks and shook his head.

'It seems, to me, highly improbable that Luke Innes and Genevieve Churchill would have had anything to do with one another after he left university. I don't know what it was, but something came between them – most likely their families. Luke teaming up with Damian would have seemed like the ultimate betrayal to Genevieve, don't you think?'

'Perhaps. But if they really cared for one another . . .'

DI Twyford gave a little shrug.

'You don't think Genevieve had a lover, do you?' I asked.

'I'm keeping an open mind. The point is, Sarah, that no man, married or otherwise, vanished from the area at the same time as Genevieve disappeared from Burrington Stoke. There's been so much publicity we'd have expected someone to come forward and give us a name if there were any likely candidates, either locally or further afield. We've talked to a lot of people and nobody – not one single person – has said anything about Genevieve having an affair. She didn't mention a lover in the letter to her parents, either.'

'Perhaps she thought they wouldn't approve.'

'Perhaps. Let me get you another drink,' he said.

He did and I drank it. The pub had filled up. It was packed with a mixture of shoppers and young, attractive professional people. I felt something of a country bumpkin in my seat in the corner, getting quietly sozzled with an older man.

'Is something wrong?' the inspector asked. 'You've been very quiet.'

'I might go home,' I said. 'Back to Manchester, I mean. I'm not sure yet.'

He raised an eyebrow but did not seem unduly surprised.

'Things not working out?'

I shrugged.

'Oh come on,' said the inspector. 'Did you really expect an easy ride with a man like Alexander Westwood? In his situation?'

I sighed and looked up at the ceiling so that the tears would run into my throat and not down my cheeks.

'I didn't take you for the sort of girl who'd give up at the first hurdle.'

'Genevieve is a very big hurdle,' I said. 'Please don't look at me like that. It's not that I don't want to be with Alex, only he won't let me . . .'

'What?'

'Get close to him.'

The inspector passed me a paper napkin. I took it and dabbed at my eyes. There were mascara smears on the paper and probably also on my lower eyelids and cheeks.

'Maybe he's trying to protect you, Sarah.'

'From what?'

'I don't know,' he said, but I knew what he meant to say was: 'The truth.' I heard the words so clearly in my mind that I did not doubt them.

'He shuts me out all the time, from everything,' I said. 'I don't think he trusts me.'

The inspector smiled at me kindly. 'One thing I know for sure is that Alexander Westwood has made some fuck-awful decisions in his life. Something tells me you're not one of them.'

I was flattered and reassured by the compliment. I screwed up the napkin and tucked it under the rim of my plate. 'So have you found out anything else about Genevieve?' I asked. 'Anything at all?'

He shook his head. 'We've increased our efforts in trying to track her down, poured in a load of resources. We've interviewed dozens of people, we've liaised with our colleagues nationally and internationally, we've put our computers to work and we haven't found a trace of her. Nothing. Nada, nix, zilch.'

'Oh.'

I picked up the empty crisp packet and folded it very small. There was a banging sound in my ears. The detective turned his glass round in his hand.

'The world's a big place,' I said. 'It must be hard to find someone, especially if they don't want to be found. I mean, look at Luke Innes.'

'Let's just say a few things are giving us cause for concern.'

'What do you mean?' I asked in a small voice.

He shuffled in his chair and pulled at his tie.

'In Genevieve's letter to her parents, she said she was going abroad, but there's no record of her leaving the country. If she went, she didn't go by plane or via any port. She didn't use her passport.'

'Aren't there other ways?'

'There are, but why complicate things?'

The barman came over to put another log on the fire. He poked at it and a rush of hot air scorched my ankles. The headache had started to throb again.

'And,' the detective continued, 'none of her various credit cards, nor her mobile phone, has been used since the day she left.'

'She could've bought a new phone. And maybe her lover, if there is one, is paying for everything. He might be wealthy. They might be using different names. That's why there's no trail.'

DI Twyford swirled the pint slowly in his hands. He didn't say anything. He didn't have to.

I knew then that he believed Genevieve was dead. I realized that the lunch, the whole thing, had been a set-up. He must have known Alexander wasn't at Avalon. He must have known he'd catch me there alone. And there must have been a reason for him wanting to talk to me.

CHAPTER THIRTY-EIGHT

DI Twyford drove me back to Burrington Stoke. I asked him to drop me at the crossroads. I felt like I needed the walk back to Avalon to clear my mind. A mizzle had settled in the cold air and the dull afternoon suited my mood. The lunch and the city and the alcohol had picked me up temporarily, but now the anxiety about Genevieve was back again, several times worse than before. She was a missing person. I was certain the police believed some kind of crime had been committed, and although none, so far, had been specified, crimes against missing people were always terrible, weren't they?

Was Alexander a suspect? Was I?

I kicked at leaves on the pavement, swung my bag and turned these thoughts over in my mind, and as I did so a car pulled up beside me. I looked up. It was the Land Rover. Alexander leaned across and opened the door. He didn't say anything, so I climbed in.

He drove past Avalon and out through country lanes until we reached a narrow road with a cattle grid at the end that wound up through a steep gorge. White goats stood precariously on the sides of the grey cliffs as if they were paper cut-outs that had been pinned there.

'Where are we going?' I asked.

'For a walk,' he said.

'My shoes . . .'

'Your boots are in the back.'

'What about Jamie?'

'Claudia's giving him tea.'

He parked close to the top of the hill and I changed into my walking boots. He passed me one of his old waxed jackets.

'Thanks,' I said, as he helped me into it and its weight settled on my shoulders.

I followed him over the road, up a stony path that led to the side of a huge hill, moorland really, fashioned into a beautiful big curve like the hip of a sleeping woman. The hillside was covered in purple-brown, dead bracken, and the ground underfoot was damp.

'This way,' he said.

We walked for several miles, heading around the side of the hill, and we didn't say anything. I followed his back, and every now and then we stopped to look at the view. He paused to help me cross a galloping stream. He held my eye for a second and then turned and set off again.

It was a steep tramp up a wet, rocky path between flanks of heather and scrubby little wind-blown trees. Several times I had to stop to catch my breath, but Alexander ploughed on. He took off his jacket and tied it by the sleeves around his waist. There were sweat patches under each arm, in the centre of his back and at the neck of his shirt. I saw a deer leaping through the bracken and we startled some noisy hen-pheasants. I wanted to tell Alexander to slow down, but I couldn't. I didn't. I pushed myself to keep up with him.

At the top of the hill, he made me turn.

'Look,' he said.

I looked.

Beyond the black, pointed treetops of a managed evergreen woodland was the Severn Estuary, spread out breathtakingly wide and reflecting the silver sun, with the distant hills of North Devon and South Wales stretching indistinguishably beneath an immense white sky made of sunlight.

'It's beautiful,' I said.

Alexander reached out and took my hand and led me a little further, to a benchmark monument.

'This is Beacon Batch. It's the highest point of the Mendips,' he said. 'It's the best place to watch the sun go down.'

'Alexander, I . . .'

'No,' he said. 'Don't say anything.'

He cleared his throat and he said very softly: 'I went back to Avalon and you weren't there. I thought you'd gone.'

We sat down side by side on the mound with our backs against the monument.

He picked up my hand and turned it over so it rested, palm upwards, in his larger one, cradled.

'Don't go,' he said.

I glanced at his face. Alexander gently bent each of my fingers forward and examined each fingernail carefully as if it were something precious.

'I mean,' he said, 'I can't be without you.'

I leaned my head back against the monument and gazed out. I could see for miles, hundreds of miles probably. The sun sank behind a low cloud and, as it dropped behind the Welsh mountains, the temperature fell with it. Sunlight slipped away from the hills like sand through a timer.

'I found the statue of Genevieve in the back garden,' I said.

'I know.'

'You should have been a sculptor.'

He shook his head. 'No chance.'

'What happened to Pete?' I asked.

He behaved as if he had not heard. I took my hand away from his.

'You have to tell me, Alexander. You can't keep not telling me. Your secrets are what's driving us apart. They're poisoning everything.'

'It's better you don't know.'

'If you trusted me, you'd tell me.'

'But you won't like it.'

Alexander looked out across the countryside. The sun was gone now – only its reflection remained, and its glorious colours were fading inevitably on the underside of the clouds.

He said: 'Genevieve and I had a fight.'

'Because she was leaving?'

'No, no. I knew she was going. I had resigned myself to

that. It was because she was going to take Jamie with her.'

'Oh.'

'I told her . . . I said she could do what she liked with her life but if she tried to take him from me, I would . . . oh Christ, Sarah, I said that I would kill her.'

I was less shocked by this than I might have been, because Virginia had already told me about the argument.

Alex's hand was inside his shirt, under his rib, scratching at the place where the scar was, and his face was a picture of pain and something else, something ugly. It was anger.

'But you didn't mean it,' I said.

'I did at the time. I told her I would kill her. I was shouting . . . We were in the kitchen and the knife was on the counter . . .'

'She stabbed you?'

'She didn't mean to. She was frightened; she thought I was going to hurt her and she grabbed it, it just happened, but I was bleeding, doubled over, and she was screaming at me and . . .'

I wanted him to stop. I wanted to put my hands over my ears. He had been right, it was better I didn't know, but now Alexander was telling me the cruel truth it became part of me, in my mind for ever.

He shook his head and his voice changed. 'Pete was the gentlest dog. He caught rabbits and rats but he'd never hurt a person,' he said. 'But he was my dog, and his instinct was to protect me. He went for Genevieve.'

I held my breath. The cadence of his voice was falling now; anger was replaced by sadness and resignation.

'I had to pull him off her. After that Pete wasn't the same. He'd been badly treated before I had him and all his old aggression came back. I couldn't trust him round people.'

'Genevieve, you mean?'

'And Jamie. Jamie was so little, and he was rough with Pete . . . The dog never hurt him, he growled and tried to back off, but Jamie was too young to read the warning signs. He kept jumping at him and I knew that sooner or later . . .'

I rested my head back against the monument.

'So Pete couldn't stay with you?'

'No.'

I waited, but Alexander didn't say any more. A couple of cheerful, loud Australian men, spattered from head to toe in mud, came by on their mountain bikes and stopped for a few moments. In their dirty Lycra shorts they made the world seem more normal again.

'Where did Pete go?' I asked.

'To a colleague of Bill's in Bristol. He'd just lost his dog and wanted a replacement.'

'Oh, good.'

Alexander swallowed. 'But Pete wouldn't settle. He kept running away, escaping out of the garden . . .'

I could tell by Alexander's voice that this story was not going to have a happy ending.

'Don't tell me any more,' I said. I covered my face with my hands.

'I'm sorry,' Alexander said quietly. 'This is what I was afraid of.'

I leaned over and I kissed him. I kissed him

insistently, persistently, until he responded and kissed me back. I pulled away a little then, and licked my lips. It was a promise, a pledge.

'You won't go back to Manchester?' he asked. Or perhaps it wasn't a question.

'No,' I said. 'I won't go anywhere.'

'It's going to get worse,' he said. 'I mean, about Genevieve.'

'I know,' I said, feeling like I didn't care. Only back then I had no idea how bad it would become.

CHAPTER THIRTY-NINE

For a short while after that Alexander was exquisitely tender with me. He was gentle and careful in his words and actions and, together, in this newfound atmosphere of calm and trust, he and I communicated our feelings for one another through our mutual affection for Jamie. We were proud of every small achievement; we delighted in his chatter, his energy and his humour. Even his naughtiness – playful now rather than angry and foul-mouthed – charmed us, because we took it to mean he was recovering. If ever there was a time when we ran out of conversation, we talked about Jamie. Jamie was the light in our lives. In the middle of the police activity, and the family pressures, and the increasing burden of not knowing where Genevieve was, Jamie was something pure and innocent and untainted.

The search for Genevieve had been ramped up a gear, and being in the village was intolerable to me now. Outside the school gate, I stood alone, isolated from the other women. Only Betsy talked to me, but her loyalty was making things more difficult for her, so if she was already with another group when I arrived I didn't do anything to attract her attention.

At Avalon, I sat with Jamie for hours making Lego models or drawing while we waited for Alexander to come home, which was the time when we could lock the doors and draw the curtains and be safe, together. The three of us – Alexander, Jamie and I – encased ourselves in a private bubble where we could simply be; untouched by the outside world.

But the status quo couldn't last. There were almost daily appeals for information about what had happened to Genevieve, and rumours were flying about with so many different theories. On the rare occasions I went down to the village, I would see a police car parked outside a particular house, or one would be pulling out of the lane that led past the quarry up to Eleonora House. Journalists from the local weekly papers were hanging around asking questions and collecting photographs. Genevieve's disappearance was exciting to them. They didn't care how Jamie felt when 'friends who asked not to be named' were quoted on the pages of their publication, speaking about frictions between Genevieve and her husband or how she used to turn up at the school gates looking as if she'd been crying and complaining about his moodiness. I had no idea how much of what they reported was true. I didn't know if the unnamed friends were exaggerating or elaborating because they enjoyed the attention, or if these things really had taken place.

Sometimes I dreamed of how it would be if

Genevieve returned. I imagined her walking through the village like the heroine in the last scene in a film – ideally with Luke Innes walking beside her, holding her hand. Alexander and I would be exonerated, and the villagers would be sorry for all their unkind speculation and snide comments.

And sometimes, as I watched Jamie beside me on the settee, curled up with his thumb in his mouth, stroking his nose with a finger, I prayed that if my dream came true, Genevieve would carry on walking out of our lives again, leaving her boy with his father, and with me.

I could not talk about my fears with Alexander but at last I understood his reluctance to discuss the past. I didn't want to talk about it either.

CHAPTER FORTY

One of the knock-on effects of the media interest in Genevieve's disappearance was that everyone in the village wanted to be involved in some way. There was never any shortage of people volunteering to talk to journalists; everyone had an opinion and a theory and, as speculation mounted, so did suspicion. I was used to conversations stopping when people saw me coming but it was becoming worse.

It took me a while to realize that some of the village women were jealous of my relationship with Alexander. I was an outsider and he belonged to the village. If he were to take up with anyone, it should have been a local girl.

By this time a small but increasingly outspoken group was complaining about the disruption caused by the media intrusion. They said it cast Burrington Stoke in a bad light. They were afraid it would become one of those places that is synonymous with tragedy or scandal. They didn't blame the police or

Virginia, of course; they blamed Alexander and me.

I was grateful that Christopher's mother, Karen, who was a teacher, had been resolute in her support for our little family. It was she, I knew, who protected Jamie from the worst of the gossip and made sure he was not picked on in the playground. One afternoon she called me at home to warn me there was a gaggle of reporters waiting outside the school. She suspected the police had issued some kind of news release concerning Genevieve, and suggested she take Jamie back to her house that night to save me having to face the barrage of cameras and journalists. I thought I ought to get Alexander's permission first, but his phone was switched off. I couldn't bear the thought of facing the journalists so I called the school back, thanked Karen and said I'd be grateful if she would look after Jamie. Then I switched on the television and waited for the news. It turned out that a man in his thirties had gone to an unnamed police station to answer questions about events leading up to the disappearance of Genevieve Churchill-Westwood. He had not been arrested and had attended the station voluntarily. Unconfirmed reports were that the man was Alexander Westwood, Mrs Churchill-Westwood's husband. There was a lovely picture of Genevieve in her show-jumping gear, looking her most glamorous and laughing as if she didn't have a care in the world, followed by a snatch-shot of Alexander going into the police station; he was frowning, unshaven, unkempt, his shoulders hunched, his hands in his pockets, gaunt and haunted.

I turned off the television.

The phone rang. It rang until it rang out, and then it started ringing again. It had to be journalists. What if it was the police? What if it was Alexander? What if it was the silence? What if it was Karen and something was wrong with Jamie? I picked the receiver up and held it to my ear.

'Hello!' said an excited female voice at the other end. 'Is that Sarah?'

I knew it was a journalist. Neil said they always tried to sound really open and friendly when they were cold-calling for quotes. I replaced the receiver and immediately it rang again. I didn't know what to do. If I pulled the plug out of the socket, Alexander would have no sure way of contacting me. Something distracted me. Through the window, I thought I saw somebody in the garden. The photographers and journalists weren't allowed on private land; they shouldn't be in the garden. Neil said that didn't always stop them though. If the stakes were high enough they'd do anything for the money shot. I ran round the house, breathless with panic, drawing the curtains. The phone kept ringing. It was driving me mad. I begged it to shut up and put my hands over my ears, but it rang again and again and again. In the end I unplugged it, and then the silence was almost worse than the bell. I turned on the television, the volume up loud, and watched some *Coronation Street*. May and I used to be addicted to soap operas, but I hadn't watched much TV since I'd come to live at Avalon and I didn't recognize half the characters. I tried to concentrate, but it was useless. It was just noise and it didn't shut out the noise in my head.

A cramp seized hold of the toes of my left foot. It was painful, the big toe splaying stiff at an awkward angle to its neighbour. I pulled the toes back towards my ankle, as Laurie had taught me, but it didn't help. Nervy and cramped, I hobbled into the kitchen, filled a glass with ice and poured over a double helping of Southern Comfort. I took a good drink and felt the alcohol warm and anaesthetize me. I licked the sweetness from my lips. Then I opened the oven door to check the chicken I'd put in to roast. There was no rush of hot air, no warmth around my knees. The chicken, beneath its foil, was lukewarm, uncooked, its poor naked skin still flaccid, but ever so slightly yellowed.

'Fuck,' I said. Even the Rayburn was against me.

My toes were still cramped.

I slid open the hatch that gave access to the wicks and furnace of the Rayburn and, although there was a strong smell of kerosene, that was cool too. It didn't make sense. How could the flame have gone out while the door was shut? I felt uneasy. I went over to the door that opened into the rosette room and checked, but it was closed. I locked the door. I should have locked it before. Why had I not thought to do that? What if someone had come in while I'd had the TV turned up loud? What if someone was hiding in the house?

'Don't be an arsehole,' I said to myself. It was a phrase that Jamie had recently picked up and, although I told him off every time he said it, he knew it made me laugh. 'Don't be an arsehole, Sarah!' I said out loud. 'Don't be such a pathetic little arsehole.'

I needed the spills to relight the wicks in the oven

heater but I didn't know where Alexander kept them.

I rummaged through the cupboard under the sink to no avail, and emptied the kitchen drawers, but they weren't there either. Then I remembered the little oil heater in Alexander's office. He must use the spills to light that. I hardly ever went into that room, partly because I was afraid of disturbing the paperwork that was spread about the desk and floor in a system that only Alexander could possibly understand, but mainly because Alexander had expressly asked me not to go into the room when he wasn't there. Jamie was also forbidden from going into the office, because it was where everything dangerous was kept, including Alexander's gun, in a secure, steel cabinet. The door to the office, which was at the far end of the house, at the back, was always locked, but I knew Alexander kept the key on top of the frame. I stood on tiptoe and patted my fingers through the dust until I felt the cold metal. I slipped the key down, unlocked the door and pushed it open carefully. I did not switch on the light until I had drawn the curtains.

The office was horribly cold and it smelled of the damp that was seeping through the ancient walls. The room was chaotic. Files were stacked upon files, papers spilled out of envelopes and plastic bags, and the computer printer was balanced precariously on twin piles of CDs. The locked cabinet was behind the desk, at the far end of the room. I could see the spill-box on top of it.

I stepped carefully across the paperwork on the floor but, as I did so, my foot slipped. I reached out to steady myself and knocked over a sheaf of papers heaped on the table. I went down on my hands and knees to pick them up. They were pictures printed from the computer. I sat back on my heels and turned one over.

It was a picture of Genevieve, just her head and shoulders and a hand holding the hair out of her eyes. Alexander must have zoomed in from a bigger picture, because the image was grainy. Even in black and white, even in poor resolution, Genevieve looked so alive.

I turned another sheet of paper. It was the same image but zoomed in even further so that Genevieve's face covered the paper. Her eyes were distorted so far as to be almost abstract, but they stared out, dark and clear, with the window of light in the pupil magnified until it was almost large enough to see into her soul.

I looked at the next image. And the next. And the next. I spread the images around me until the floor was carpeted in them. It became a kind of compulsion to look at Genevieve and examine her in such close detail. She had the kind of face and eyes that held your attention. She was so lovely. But the images, so many pictures, were deeply unsettling. I knew Alexander's heart and mind were still full of Genevieve, but he must have spent hours looking at her face on the screen, zooming into her eyes, looking at her, making new images from existing ones, printing them out, all those scores of pictures.

I thought I knew why he'd done it. It was because he wanted to see her face again, like he used to see it. She wasn't there, but he needed to see her in detail, as he did when she lay beside him in bed, as she was in the mornings, in the evenings, when she was at Avalon, when he was hers and she was his wife. Yes, I understood what had driven Alexander: still the images struck me as sinister. They made me angry; they scared me.

And I was jealous. Alex would never want to look at me in close-up. He had never taken a picture of me, not even on his mobile phone. If I were to go out of his life, there would be nothing at all to prove I'd ever been in it.

Furiously, I put the photographs back, face down in a pile, left the spills where they were so Alexander wouldn't know that I'd been there, retreated out of the room, and locked the door.

By the time Alexander came in my fingertips were burned and there was a pile of matches, charred and curled like the lashes of some mythical creature, on the lino on the floor. The chicken was inedible, the potatoes, carrots and parsnips uncooked and greasy.

I had been almost sobbing with frustration but when he stood in the kitchen I composed myself. He looked terrible. I had never seen him so drained. He was crumpled, messed up, and the fronts of his jeans were soaked and mud-spattered.

'Are you all right?' I asked. 'What happened? What did the police say?'

'Just more of the same,' he said. 'Is there anything to eat?'

I looked towards the Rayburn.

'The pilot light went out,' I said.

Alexander shrugged.

'Where's Jamie?'

'At Christopher's. I thought he'd be safer there. Are there photographers outside?'

He nodded. 'I left the Land Rover at the bottom of the lane and came in on foot through the orchard.'

He went to the fridge and took out a beer.

'I'm going up for a shower.'

'Do you want a sandwich or something?'

'Not now.'

He went upstairs, and I heard footsteps on the landing and the creaking of the boards in the bathroom. I rubbed my elbows with the opposite hands and waited. From upstairs, he called me, as I had known he would.

He stood in my bedroom. His clothes were heaped in a pile by the door and I could smell the sweat and heat of him.

My room was lit by candles. Not in a romantic, cosy way but darkly, so the flickering light seemed threatening. I looked at Alexander naked and it was obvious that he wanted sex, but I wasn't sure if he wanted me or just the comfort of another person.

Despite the pictures I'd found in his office, despite everything, even then, I was drawn to him irresistibly like the tide to the shore. I stepped forward and touched him and there it was again, that heat between us, a compulsion that seemed to be growing in intensity, something that frightened and obsessed me and that could not be denied, not then; not ever.

Afterwards we lay side by side amongst bed linen twisted and churned, and the cooling room smelled of candle smoke. Alexander held me very close. I was exhausted; I had been shameless – a harlot, a hussy, a whore – and I didn't care. I would do anything to please him, to ease him, to make him forget.

He stroked my head.

'Oh, Sarah,' he said. It was all he said.

CHAPTER FORTY-ONE

After Alexander's visit to the police station, media activity in Burrington Stoke increased incrementally. Betsy reported that there was a kind of war mentality gripping the village. Everyone, even the journalist-haters, was excited and unified by the drama and the shared desire to find Genevieve and 'bring her home'. That's what they all said. They were committed to bringing their girl home. I think most people knew, in their hearts, by then that the odds of her being brought home alive were diminishing, but the phrase was rousing and ambiguous enough to cover any eventuality. There were rumours that the police were going to start searching the surrounding countryside.

The newspapers were having a field day. The *Daily Mail* paid Dale Vowles a five-figure sum to give them an exclusive on the tragedy of Robbie Innes. Betsy told me somebody had told her that he'd been offered the same again to talk about the day he fought Alexander Westwood and won, should it transpire that Alexander had had anything to do with Genevieve's disappearance. As well as the story, Dale gave them a photograph taken at a Young Farmers' fund-raising event the autumn before Robbie died. I stared at the face in the newspaper. Robbie was an attractive, fair-haired, ruddy-faced young man, not at all like Alexander. There was an accompanying image of Genevieve, aged seventeen, sitting on a gate, holding tight to the top bar with her hands. She had long hair and was wearing jeans and wellingtons, and she was laughing. I'd hardly seen a photograph of Genevieve where she wasn't laughing.

Somebody had seen a woman who looked a lot like Genevieve Churchill-Westwood in a travel agency in Axbridge a couple of weeks before she disappeared. 'Confirmed' sightings were reported from the South Welsh seaside resort of Tenby, where Genevieve had, apparently, bought a 'love nest' or a 'bolt hole', depending on which paper you read, under the name of Juliet Bravo, 'her favourite horse'. The words 'Missing', 'Beauty' and 'Heiress' featured predominantly in the headlines and those in the accompanying write-ups were full of poignancy and implied that whoever was responsible for her disappearance may have had some financial motivation. A national television news crew did a piece to camera from outside the entrance to Eleonora House. I didn't see it, but Betsy told me the presenter banged on about how wealthy the family was. Alexander told me that when he was at the station, the police had asked him about Genevieve's life insurance. He did not tell me what his answers had been.

I called my family to reassure them that I was OK and

that things weren't as bad as they possibly thought they were, but they'd seen the news coverage and read the papers. Neil hadn't let on how serious the situation was, although he knew how big the story might become. Still, they knew what was going on. My mother wept and said I was breaking my father's heart. My father told me that my mother was going mad with worry. May pleaded with me to get away while I still could.

'I can't leave Alexander now,' I said. 'I just can't.'

'Come back for a while,' May begged. 'For a few weeks, until all this is over. Neil thinks – *we* think – things are going to be difficult for a while, but it won't last for ever and, once Genevieve's turned up, we'll stand by you whatever you decide to do, I promise. Only come home now, please.'

Jamie was holding my hand, swinging on my arm as we walked home from school. He was kicking a pebble and singing under his breath. Genevieve's face, sun-faded and rain-damaged, looked down from the posters. They were curling at the edges.

'I'm needed here,' I told May.

The wheedling went out of May's voice and was replaced with frustration.

'Sarah, that man doesn't need you. He could manage perfectly well without you. He's got you exactly where he wants you, with no thought of what's best for you. If he cared for you even the tiniest bit he'd tell you to get out.'

In the distance the siren call of the quarry rose up. Jamie looked up at me, wide-eyed with mock horror. We had made up a game that whenever we heard the sirens it meant that the dinosaurs who lived in the quarry were on the loose and we had to run home as fast as possible.

'May, I have to go,' I said as Jamie tugged at my arm. 'I have to get Jamie his tea.'

'Just think about what I said about coming home . . .'

'This is my home now.'

'Oh, for goodness' sake!'

The only good news was a call from the owner of the art gallery in Wells. My pictures had sold and she wanted more. It was pin money, hardly anything, but still I was profoundly proud. Betsy said I should start selling pictures over the internet, because there was always a demand for original art, but I didn't know how to do that. I mentioned it to Alexander and he said that we should set up an eBay account.

We didn't, though. We never got round to it.

CHAPTER FORTY-TWO

And then, while all this was going on, while the village was in mayhem and the police were searching an area around Tenby, having found forensic evidence linking Genevieve to the love nest/bolt hole, we received, through the post, an invitation in an envelope addressed to both Alexander and me. We were invited to Eleonora House to a party to celebrate Philip's eightieth birthday.

I had known the invitation was coming; Claudia had told me. She had been round to Avalon several times seeking refuge because she was finding the situation in the village as difficult as I was. The journalists hadn't bothered her and Bill, but they had been hanging around the entrance to Eleonora House, alarming Philip when he'd spotted them as Virginia drove him to the hospital to have his leg looked at. He'd become very agitated and Claudia realized what Virginia hadn't: the last time journalists had been clamouring to speak to him had been when his first wife killed herself. Virginia had been confined inside the big house with baby

Genevieve. From there, she wouldn't have been able to see the entrance to the drive and Philip must have done his best to protect her, as well as the children from his first marriage, from the mayhem. Now all those awful, conflicting memories had come back to trouble him. Only Claudia was able to comfort the old man. She told me that, ironically, it was because she reminded him of her mother. She had to keep telling him that he was not to blame, that none of this was his fault. The situation was so terribly difficult for her and, like me, every time she went out she had to bear the staring and the whispering. When she came round to see me, she offloaded, talking for thirty minutes or more at a time, hardly pausing for breath, sometimes dropping her head into her hands and saying: 'I wish it were all over. I wish it would just stop. I wish *I* could go away!' Then she'd apologize for talking too much. She couldn't do this with her 'circle'. With them, she had to maintain the decorous façade, she had to be brave; she couldn't let them see how much it was getting to her. I sympathized, made tea, put biscuits on a plate and understood.

Now Philip's milestone birthday was imminent, the whole family agreed that the right thing to do was to proceed with the celebrations that had been in the planning since well before Genevieve went away. It wasn't just because she would have wanted the party to go ahead, no matter where she was, but also because not to hold the event would send out the wrong messages to their friends, relatives, acquaintances and neighbours. It would imply that they were assuming the worst. The caterers had been booked in April, the entertainment in May, and Genevieve herself had commissioned the decorations in June. Besides which, it would take Philip's mind off everything and give him at least a few hours of pleasure.

When Claudia told me that Alexander and a 'plus one' were to be invited, I was surprised, but not shocked. She'd kept talking about the event and I knew the family's primary aim was that it should be exactly the kind of party that everybody was expecting, and to give nobody any further reason to worry, gossip or speculate.

Claudia had told me many times that Philip regarded Alexander with affection – he was more of a son than a son-in-law to him – and that he always stuck up for Alexander, no matter how Virginia criticized and blamed. She said Philip admired his skill and craftsmanship. He had always respected that kind of talent and had been pleased to encourage it. He believed Alexander had been a good influence on Genevieve, and he loved him for that too. It was Philip's birthday and he would want Alexander to be there, and because Virginia would do anything to make her husband happy, Alexander was invited. She knew he wouldn't go without me, so I had been grudgingly asked along as his 'guest'.

It felt more than a little humiliating.

'Philip's muddled,' Claudia said. 'He keeps confusing the past and the present, and the strangest things upset him. He's told me we should all be grateful to Alexander, but when we ask why he can't tell us. Or he won't. Half the time I have absolutely no idea what he's rambling on about! Poor soul.'

Later, when Alexander and I were alone together, watching television, he rubbing my feet, which were on his lap, I turned the invitation over in my hands. It was good-quality card, printed in gold ink with a gold ribbon running along the edge. 'This feels all wrong,' I said.

'Philip's very ill,' said Alexander. 'It's his swan song.'

'I don't think we should go.'

Alexander shrugged. 'I owe it to Philip to be there. The old man's been good to me.'

'Claudia said he keeps saying something about him being grateful to you.'

Alexander didn't flinch. He massaged the ball of my left foot.

'What does he mean?' I persisted. 'What did you do for him?'

'Nothing.'

'So why did he lend you the money to set up your own business?'

Alexander pushed my feet off his lap, stood up and walked out of the room.

'I was married to his daughter. Why wouldn't he?'

A couple of days later, Claudia called to take me shopping at the Christmas market in Wells. I was amazed to see that nobody was waiting at the bottom of the drive to try to grab a photograph through the car window.

'Where has the press gone?' I asked Claudia.

'Don't you watch the news? The local MP's been caught *in flagrante* with his brother-in-law. Your fan club is sitting outside his house right now.'

'Thank God for political scandal,' I sighed.

Claudia and I were giddy with freedom in Wells, where nobody knew us. We picked our way amongst the stalls, shouldering through the crowds of cold shoppers, trying to avoid the freezing rain and filling our bags with candles, satsumas and intricate Christmas decorations.

'You are coming to Philip's party, aren't you?' Claudia asked as we queued at a stall selling exquisite ceramic candle-burners shaped like trees.

'Yes.' I picked up one of the burners and weighed it in my hand. 'Alex said he'd never let your father down.'

'Alex is good like that,' she said.

We stacked our purchases in the back of her Volvo and went for lunch in a crowded little café. I ate a cheese and onion pasty and chips while Claudia picked at a green salad and a miserable piece of cold chicken. She wanted to lose weight before the party because Virginia, despite being racked with worry about Genevieve and Philip, still found the time to make derogatory comments about her stepdaughter's size. I made an effort to look as if I wasn't enjoying my deliciously hot salty food as much as I was.

'I ought to get a present for your father while I'm here,' I said. 'Do you have any ideas?'

Claudia shrugged. 'Oh, I don't know, anything – a Dick Francis, a bottle of port.' Her voice was catching.

'Claudia?' I reached my hand out across the table and covered hers. It was hot and clammy.

She shook her head and her eyes glistened. 'Poor Philip,' she whispered. 'Poor old man. He ought to be enjoying a peaceful retirement but this whole Genevieve thing is killing him. God, I wish she would come back!'

I had no idea what somebody like me was supposed to wear to a black-tie event at a place like Eleonora House and, even if I had known, I certainly didn't have anything remotely right with me. I asked Betsy for her advice and she told me to choose something simple and classy.

'You won't go wrong with black,' she said. 'Only go for the best black you can afford.'

The next time Alexander was out pricing a job, I asked if I could borrow the laptop. I took it upstairs, into Jamie's bedroom, which was the only room in the house where, by some architectural inconsistency, an internet connection was achievable. It also meant I could hear, and see, anyone who came to the house, because the window overlooked the drive.

I sat with my back against the door with the laptop balanced against my legs. Although the connection was painfully slow, I found the websites Betsy had recommended and ordered a couple of demure black dresses, a lovely velvet trouser suit and an expensive but very pretty pair of shoes.

Sunlight moved across the room. Jamie's hamster stirred in its cage. I went over to the window and crouched down to watch it. The hamster with its dear little black-bead eyes picked a sunflower seed between its tiny paws and gnawed at it. I smelled the hamster smell, and it reminded me of my own childhood; sawdust and must.

I put my finger through the bars and stroked the hamster's back, but it didn't like the intrusion. It scuffled away and hid in its tube.

I went back to the computer. With a racing heart and a dry mouth, I Googled the name Genevieve Churchill-Westwood. Page after page of hits came up. Many were articles about promising riders or lists of the winners of eventing and dressage competitions but also, now, Genevieve and what had happened to her were popular topics on a number of forums. The most popular was hosted by somebody called Slumdog, who had not only given a brief biography of Genevieve and other family members – biographies that were scathing and vituperative, but never quite crossed into the territories of libel or slander – but had also included photographs of Burrington Stoke and even an aerial photograph of the village with Eleonora House, Avalon and the Quarrymen's Arms marked with red circles. I studied the image myself for a long time. From above, I could see how the two quarries bit into the hillside. Masses of woodland had disappeared to be replaced by open rock-face. The new quarry was many times bigger than the older, disused one. In the picture, the blue sky was reflected in the water that filled the old quarry pit. Bushes and trees had grown right to the edge, and it seemed as if nature was soothing the damage caused by machinery and explosives. The new quarry, from above, was a moonscape, desolate; an act of destructive vandalism on a huge scale. Slumdog agreed. He said it was a perfect example of the exploitation of nature for commercial benefit.

It dawned on me that Slumdog was probably Damian. I Googled Damian Churchill and found he had his own website. It was impressive; up to date, beautifully presented, and emotive but well written. His next public 'event' was a protest at the greenfield site of a proposed new shopping centre in the Midlands. He had friends in high places. Some were travelling to America to lobby a high-profile construction industry conference. I wondered where they got their money from; wealthy sponsors, I supposed.

I didn't read any more. Instead I Googled Alexander Westwood. His name came up in relation to Genevieve's disappearance, and I discovered he had won a couple of industry awards for his work on major restoration projects, but there were no results prior to the last four years. If there had been newspaper reports about his trial, they were no longer online. I sighed and turned to look at the montage of photographs hung on a frame over Jamie's bed. Genevieve must have made it for her son. I'd seen it many times but never really looked at it before. There were pictures of Jamie as a baby, and as a boy, in his school uniform, dressed as a shepherd in a nativity play, walking with a sandy bottom along a beach. There were pictures of Jamie and Genevieve, their faces close together, he with his arms around her neck, the two of them sharing an ice-cream. I searched for Alexander's face. Where was he? I found him at last in one single picture. Jamie and his cousins were sitting on a roundabout in a park. Genevieve must have been holding the camera. Standing behind the children were Alexander, Claudia and Bill. One of the Labradors was walking out of the frame; you could just see its back legs and its tail.

I smiled and reached out my fingers to touch Alexander's face. He was smiling at the camera, smiling at Genevieve. He looked happier, and more settled, than I had ever known him. He looked younger.

There was a creak behind me, on the landing, and I turned but it was nothing. I scolded myself for jumping.

Still, I whispered: 'Genevieve?'

And then I gasped in horror as the two new telephones, one upstairs on the landing, the other downstairs in the dining room, rang in unison – only it wasn't the normal ringtone, it was a constant screeching peel like the sound somebody would make if they were in agony; an awful, desperate sound.

I put my hands over my ears and stumbled back against the door, and the latch clicked shut but the ringing seemed to increase in volume and I was engulfed by something powerful, much stronger than anything I'd felt before. It was like the heat that precedes nausea. I felt I was on the edge of falling. I experienced a horrendous dizziness, an awful influx of terror. I was spinning, I couldn't breathe, there was nothing to hold on to, nothing to stop me.

I fell against the door. I grabbed on to the handle and tried to lift it but I had no strength in my muscles, no coordination between my fingers and my brain. The door seemed to be locked and beyond was the howl of the telephones. I thought I was dying; what I was going through had to be something massively traumatic, a heart attack or an aneurysm, something cataclysmic.

I slid down the door and curled against it, like a foetus, sobbing dry-eyed, remembering the picture of myself as the gold-digger-hole-digger, and all I could hear was the insidious screaming of the two phones and I thought: This is Genevieve! She's here!

Some time passed, I don't know how many minutes went by, but eventually the terror subsided. I opened my eyes. Sunlight filled the room. It was a child's room, that was all. It was bright and cluttered and cosy. The hamster wheel rattled as it spun on its bracket. The little green 'on' light winked at me from the side of the discarded laptop. I picked it up and held it tight as I scrambled through the door and ran down the stairs, out of Avalon into the cold air beyond.

I went down to the lane, where there was a signal for my mobile, and I called May as I walked along, putting as much distance as I could between myself and the house.

'What is it?' she said. 'You sound terrible.'

'I'm all right,' I said. 'I'm OK. May, if I tell you something, will you promise not to worry or overreact?'

'I promise.'

'It's just . . . I don't know how to say this without sounding like I've completely lost it, but I think . . .'

'What?'

'I think Genevieve's haunting me.'

May laughed. I didn't say anything and her laughter gradually subsided.

'Don't tell Neil,' I begged. Already I was beginning to feel embarrassed and awkward.

'What exactly has happened?' May asked gently.

'I don't know. I just . . . oh, a couple of times now I've felt as if Genevieve was inside me . . . only for a few moments, but I've felt like I was feeling what she was feeling. As if she was trying to make me understand something . . . As if I was her.'

'As if you were Genevieve . . .'

'Yes! No! No, I don't mean I think I am her, or anything like that, I just . . . I don't know . . . and there've been words, a couple of times I've heard things in my head and I don't know where they're coming from. They're in my mind but they didn't come from my mind, do you understand?'

'Not really, honey.'

'You think I'm mad, don't you? This sounds so stupid, doesn't it? It doesn't make any sense. I'm not making any sense. Oh, May, I don't know what to do! I'm so scared! I'm so tired of all this!'

'Shh, shh,' May said down the line. I wished I was with her. I wished I could put my head on her shoulder and let her stroke my back. 'Listen, Sarah, will you listen to me? Find somewhere to sit down and breathe slowly and listen.'

I looked around, went over to the bus shelter, and perched on the bench.

'Now listen,' May said. 'You are not losing your mind, you are not going mad and you are not being haunted. OK?'

'Yes.' I nodded and pressed the phone as close as I

could to my ear. A car drove past from the village and I saw the woman in the passenger side stare at me intently.

'You're under a lot of stress,' said May, 'and you're tired, and I think you've let yourself become a tiny bit obsessed with Genevieve.'

'Yes.'

'I've noticed and Neil's noticed that you seem to talk about her all the time, and you're obviously thinking about her a lot, and all that's happening now is that your brain has got a bit overloaded and it's finding a way to release the tension. Like a stress valve.'

I swallowed. 'Yes, you're right.'

I heard May exhale deeply at the other end of the line.

'You're going to tell me to come home, aren't you?' I asked.

'You need to get away from there. You need a break. But right now, what you really need is rest.'

'Yes.'

'What time do you have to pick Jamie up?'

'Quarter past three.'

'So there's time for a couple of hours in bed. I want you to go back to Avalon, make yourself a warm milky drink and a hot-water bottle, and sleep. Or if you can't sleep, lie quietly and think about . . . think about kittens.'

'Kittens?' In spite of everything, I laughed.

'They're the least stressful thing I could think of,' May explained.

* * *

I did as she said. I went back to Avalon and I realized May was right. It wasn't haunted, it wasn't hostile or sinister, it was an old house, that was all. Still, I disconnected the phones before I took myself and my hot-water bottle up to bed, and when I was there, I snuggled right down and I held on to the spare pillow as if it were a life jacket and I was drowning.

CHAPTER FORTY-THREE

Over the next couple of days packages of clothes arrived through the post for me. The postman, who had always been pleasant to me, asked each day what was in the parcel and I'd tell him and he'd raise his eyebrows.

'You all right, my love?' he asked. 'You're looking a bit peaky.'

'I'm fine,' I said.

'Looks like you haven't had a decent night's sleep in a while.'

'Oh, you know.' I laughed. 'It's worrying about what to wear.'

Dave rolled his eyes.

'You'd look good in a plastic bag,' he said kindly. 'Well, you would if you looked after yourself a bit better.'

I thanked him and took the parcel, and closed the door.

I had another visitor. The local doctor. I had never met him before, but he turned up one morning unannounced and said he had been passing by and wanted to introduce himself.

I made coffee and I also made a huge effort to be normal and charming and not to let him see how exhausted I felt.

'My sister called you, didn't she?' I asked as we sat in the living room, him nibbling a gingernut and my mouth aching with smiling.

He nodded. 'She asked me to look in on you.'

'She's such a worrier,' I said. 'Really, I am absolutely fine. I've never felt better.'

'I am surprised you didn't register with the surgery when you came here,' the doctor said. He made it into a question with his tone.

'I haven't needed to. I haven't been ill.'

'Hmm.' He put the last part of the biscuit into his mouth and dabbed his lips with a handkerchief that had been ferociously ironed. 'Your sister told me you've had a couple of funny turns recently.'

'I was overtired.'

'All right.' He took a notepad out of his briefcase and flicked through the pages until he arrived at where he wanted to be. He scanned through some handwritten notes. 'She told me you thought you were Genevieve.' He looked at me then, straight at me. I felt myself blush.

'She misunderstood,' I said.

'What did she misunderstand?'

'I don't know. I can't remember exactly what I said. I was so tired, I was in a bit of a state, that's all.'

The doctor nodded, but said nothing.

'All this speculation about Genevieve, all this worry, it

got to me. I'm sorry. I shouldn't have said anything to May.'

There was another silence. This time I was determined not to fill it. It went on so long that the atmosphere between us became uncomfortable. I was hugely relieved when the doorbell rang and I had an excuse to leave the room.

It was a man with a parcel.

'Delivery for Mrs Churchill-Westwood,' he said. 'Is that you?'

I smiled and took the package. 'Yes,' I said. 'Thank you.'

CHAPTER FORTY-FOUR

The trouble was, none of the clothes were right. One of the black dresses was too tight; it made me look pornographic. The other was deeply unflattering; I felt bulky, frumpy and too old in it. The trouser suit was gorgeous and, although I decided to keep it, Claudia said trousers just wouldn't do for a party at Eleonora House, I would have to wear a dress.

By now it was Friday. There was still time to catch the bus into Bristol, but my plans were scuppered when I received a call from Karen asking me to go and fetch Jamie from school because he'd been sick. I found him, pale and hot, swinging his legs on an orange plastic chair outside the secretary's office. He was wearing his coat and held a plastic bowl on his lap. His eyes were watery and red-rimmed. My heart melted.

'Look at you,' I said, forgetting about myself and leaning down to kiss his forehead. His skin burned my lips. 'Oh, Jamie, what's the matter?'

'I feel bad, Sarah,' he whispered. I took the bowl from him and he fell into my arms. I could feel his hot breath beneath my ear. He smelled over-sweet, of infection and temperature.

I carried him piggyback all the way home, telling him stories about the dinosaurs who lived in the quarry. Back at Avalon, I made him a bed on the settee, and left him with a cup of chicken soup and the television remote whilst I went upstairs to try the dresses on again. Neither was right.

I ran downstairs to check, but Jamie had fallen asleep. I pulled the duvet from him to let his skin cool, then I had a bath, dried my hair in front of the mirror and fastened it into a French plait. I put on my best underwear and a silky slip and then I made up my face, more subtly than usual. I used the palest pink lipstick, a touch of green eye-shadow and a hint of black mascara. Then I picked up Genevieve's emerald dress, the one that had been hidden in my bag, and I slipped it over my head.

I'd forgotten how beautiful the dress was. The fabric was exquisite, it changed in the light: one moment the colour was almost turquoise, the next it was midnight blue. And it moved with my body, it floated with me; it was so light, so easy to wear, it was absolutely perfect. I stood on tiptoe to make myself taller, and the effect was even better.

My heart was pounding with excitement. I had never worn a dress like this before – I could never have afforded anything like it – and even though Genevieve was so much smaller than me, it fitted beautifully. On her, the hem would have fallen mid-calf. On me, it just skimmed my knees. I reached under the bed for my shoes, slipped them on, and stood tall in the dress. It felt just right. I felt perfect.

I was so engrossed in my reflection I never heard the sound of the Land Rover tyres crushing the gravel as it came up the drive. I didn't hear Alexander come up the stairs.

The door to my bedroom was open. I didn't see him come in. I was leaning over the bed, searching for some silver earrings in my bag. Alex came up behind and put his hand on my shoulder, and he must have said: 'Sarah . . .' but what I heard was: 'Genny . . .'

And I turned and for a second I saw sadness in his eyes, and then the sadness dissolved into a kind of horror. I reached up my arms to hold him but he pushed me away so hard that I stumbled and had to hold on to the top of the chest to stop myself from falling.

'What are you doing?'

'I was just trying on the dress.'

'Genevieve told me she'd got rid of it.'

'It was in a bag of rubbish. It can't have meant anything to her. And it's hardly been worn.'

'It was worn once.'

I felt hurt and humiliated and betrayed.

He had told me on numerous occasions that he had not loved Genevieve for a long time. Yet here we were again: Alexander angry with me for trespassing on his wife's territory.

'I don't mean to upset you, Alex, but if she only wore it once,' I said hesitantly, 'does it matter so much that I tried it on?'

'For Christ's sake, Sarah!'

He let out his breath. His fists were clenched and he was trembling. I took a small step backwards.

'That's the dress Genevieve wore when we married,' he said.

'It's not a wedding dress.'

'No. It's a maternity dress.'

'Oh.'

Alexander turned away. He unwound his fists, swept aside the cosmetics, hair pins and other clutter on the top of the chest of drawers, put both hands flat on its surface and dropped his head between his shoulders.

'I didn't know,' I said. 'I thought . . .'

'You're obsessed with her,' Alexander said. 'You can't leave her alone, can you? You can't just let her be.'

'It's not me!' I cried. 'It's you! You're the one who can't stop talking about her – all the time it's Genevieve this and Genevieve that and . . .'

'No,' Alexander said. 'I'm just trying to get on with my life. Of course Gen's name is going to come up in conversation now and then. It's no big deal to me, *you're* the one who thinks it's so relevant.'

'Why did you print out her picture a million times then?'

He looked confused.

'I saw the pictures you'd printed out in your office. Hundreds of them. Like you couldn't stop looking at her, you couldn't get enough of her, you—'

'I didn't print those pictures out.'

'Nobody else goes in your office.'

Alexander shook his head. 'Gen did them. She was

designing some T-shirts for somebody . . . Her eventing sponsors . . . They were introducing a line of clothes. She needed close-ups of her face.'

'Oh . . .' I dropped my hands to my side.

'I didn't want to throw them away . . .'

'No.'

The fabric of the dress, which had, just a few moments before, seemed so beautiful and light, now felt constricting and tight. I glanced down at myself in utter dismay, and the colour, even the colour was no longer lovely, it was a muddy green, like the slime in old water; everything was wrong, it was awful and wrong.

'Alexander, I'm sorry,' I said. 'I'm so sorry. I shouldn't have touched the dress, I . . .'

'Take it off!' he said, turning away. 'Just take it off! Get rid of it!'

I heard him galloping down the stairs, and then I heard the sound of the door opening and closing. I heard the Land Rover engine start up. I put one hand over my mouth and tried to contain a sob.

'Sarah?'

Jamie stood barefoot in the entrance to my room, his poorly white face all pinched and anxious.

'What's wrong?' he said. 'Why did Dad go out again?'

'Nothing's wrong, darling,' I said as calmly as I could. I bent down and smoothed his face with my fingers. He was burning hot. There were two circles of red on his cheeks, like on a doll's. I blew on his forehead.

'Daddy was cross.'

'Yes,' I said, 'but it was my fault, not yours.'

Jamie wiped his nose with the back of his hand and

left a glistening trail across his cheek leading all the way to his ear.

'Are *you* going to go away?' he asked. 'Is that why Daddy was shouting?'

I kissed the top of his head. He tasted salty and sweaty.

'No, Jamie,' I said. 'I'm not going anywhere.'

'Definitely?'

'One hundred per cent.'

Jamie nodded. He reached up and took hold of my hand, and his lower lip was swollen and trembling.

'Oh, sweetheart, Jamie!'

I took the little boy in my arms and when I picked him up he wrapped his legs around my waist and snuggled his head into my neck.

'You are a darling, beautiful boy,' I told him. 'I will never leave you, ever, no matter what.'

I stroked his back and held him tight while he cried with all his body, great big cathartic sobs, and I knew he was crying for his mother and, although I would never be Genevieve, I promised him that I would be there for him whenever he needed me.

I promised.

CHAPTER FORTY-FIVE

The next morning, the morning of the party, Virginia came to Avalon.

I did not hear her car on the drive, or the banging of the gate, or her footsteps on the path because I was fresh out of the shower and preparing to dry my hair. I heard the outer door opening and I ran to see who was there and it was Virginia, standing in the rosette room. She looked up at me. The hairdryer was in my left hand. My hair was wrapped in a towel.

'Hello,' I said.

I held out my free hand but, for the second time, she ignored it. She stepped up into the kitchen. She was wearing baggy old trousers, a polo-necked sweater, a quilted body-warmer, and her hair was tightly tied back.

'I came straight from the stables,' she said, crossing to the sink to wash her hands. 'I didn't have time to make myself presentable and I didn't have the chance to call to tell you I was coming.'

'It doesn't matter,' I said. 'You're always welcome.'

She looked around for something to dry her hands

on. I passed her the kitchen roll. She tore off several pieces.

'The police came to Eleonora House yesterday,' she said, rubbing at her palms. 'Did you know?'

'No.'

'Claudia was with me. We were decorating the hall for the party. They came and they made us sit down in the living room.'

'Oh no!' I steadied myself on the back of a chair. My towel came loose and fell across my face. I pulled it away and let it fall across my shoulders. 'What's happened?'

'You don't know?'

I shook my head.

'Human remains have been found,' she said, and her voice was calm and clipped but I could sense the fear beneath it and I realized how bleak those words were. They were cold words to describe something that had once been a warm and vital person, somebody's child; perhaps somebody's parent.

'Yes,' she said. 'The police came and they were very professional. It was a family friend, Detective Inspector Twyford, and a family liaison officer. I . . .'

I watched her quietly as she tried to find the right words. Her stoicism was humbling.

'I felt like an actor who didn't know his lines,' she said. 'I didn't know what one is supposed to say in those circumstances. Nothing prepares you.'

'I'm so sorry,' I said, but I didn't know what to say after that. Was she telling me Genevieve was dead? I stared at her stupidly.

'The remains were found in a shallow grave in the

sand dunes at Tenby. Hidden. Dumped. That's the word they'll use on the television.'

Her voice was faltering.

'I'm so sorry . . .' I said again.

'My husband was resting when they came. I haven't told him.'

'No.'

'You see,' she said, pulling out a chair and sitting down, 'the police don't know anything themselves. All they have are bones and . . . and hair. They could belong to anyone. What is the point of distressing him if it turns out to be somebody else?'

I could tell that her mouth was dry. I filled a glass with water from the tap and passed it to her. She took it and drank. A trickle of water ran down the line from the corner of her lips to the edge of her chin. It made her look terribly vulnerable.

'I keep praying, God forgive me, that it is somebody else,' she said. 'Anybody. I don't care who it is, so long as it's not Genevieve.'

I nodded. I wanted to reach out to Virginia, but did not know how.

'And the worst thing, Sarah, the worst of it is that it was I who pressured them into searching the area once we knew she had connections there. I thought I wanted to know the truth, but I don't. If that is Genevieve they've found, I don't want to know. I'd rather go back to knowing nothing.'

'I'd feel the same.'

'But surely Alexander told you about this? They spoke to him yesterday too.'

I opened my mouth to tell her she must be mistaken, and then I remembered how Alexander had come straight upstairs the previous evening, still in his boots, and found me wearing Genevieve's dress, and the shock on his face and how he had gone straight out again. He had not returned until I was in bed. We had not spoken since. I died a little inwardly. The police had told him they'd found bones that most likely were Genevieve's and he'd come upon me all dolled up in my make-up and her wedding dress. What had I done to him?

Virginia wasn't looking at me. She stared through the window, into the distance. 'It's Philip's birthday,' she said. 'It's his birthday today. He is hoping Genevieve will surprise him at his party. That's what he's hoping. So how can I tell him about the bones? How can I do that to him on his birthday?'

'It's not Genevieve,' I said, and as soon as the words were out my hand flew to my mouth as if to stop any more emerging.

Virginia looked at me.

'How do you know?'

I shook my head. I didn't know where those words had come from but I was certain they were true.

'Do you know where my daughter is?' she asked, fixing me with her eyes. I moved my fingers from my lips.

'No,' I said, 'I don't, but I'm sure she's not in South Wales.'

There was a very long silence. I heard Virginia's stomach rumble. She had almost certainly been up all night.

'That was a very strange thing to say,' she said at last.

'I just had a feeling,' I said, but it had been more than a feeling. I *knew*.

Virginia continued to stare at me.

'Do you often have "feelings"?'

I realized how I must look to her, how stupid and how insensitive. I said nothing.

'You don't have any children, do you?' she said eventually.

I thought of my baby boy. I remembered the feel of his little heel pressing against my swollen belly the week before he was born. I remembered the angle of his elbow, how utterly charming I used to find his foetal hiccups and how, when he slept curled inside me, I could feel the shape of his back, even the little buttons of his spine beneath my skin. How I used to balance a mug on my stomach and how touched and endeared Laurie and I were when the baby made it wobble and shake with his movements.

I remembered the stillness of him deep as an ocean.

I looked up to Virginia.

'No,' I said. 'No, I don't have any children.'

'Then you can't possibly understand how it feels to lose one,' she said.

'Genevieve's missing,' I said quietly. 'She's not lost yet.'

CHAPTER FORTY-SIX

Some hours later, Alexander came home. He looked exhausted. I went to him and kissed him gently, careful not to crowd him.

'Virginia's been here,' I said. 'She told me they've found—'

'It's not Genevieve,' Alexander said, echoing my words earlier. Was it him I had heard, somehow? He went to the sink and turned on the taps.

'Is it certain?'

'Watch the news,' he said.

I switched on the television and flicked through the channels. The bones belonged to a young girl who had gone missing from Swansea several years earlier. She had a drug problem that she fed with the proceeds of prostitution. She had a boyfriend who kept her on the streets. There was a picture of her. She was fair-haired and chubby, pulling a face at the camera. She looked very young, sweet, naïve.

I stopped feeling sad and started feeling angry. I went out into the garden and said the dead girl's name over and over; I pictured her smile. At the end of the drive, down below on the lane, I saw the news crews drive past. I heard the crackling of their radios and phones, their laughter. I knew why they were laughing.

They knew about the bones. They had been poised to start door-stepping in Burrington Stoke, asking vulnerable people, stricken with grief, how they felt now that Genevieve's body had been found.

Now that task would have gone to a crew in Swansea instead. The journalists and the camera people were as relieved as everyone else that the Tenby bones were not Genevieve's. They had been let off the hook, at least for now. That was why they were laughing. They could go home and enjoy the rest of the weekend.

CHAPTER FORTY-SEVEN

In the end, I wore the ill-fitting black dress to Philip's birthday party. No matter what I did with my hair and my face, I felt ugly and plain. Alexander didn't notice, as usual, or if he did he didn't say anything. I tiptoed round him, keeping quiet, being gentle. Jamie was still poorly. I was worried about leaving him, but Alexander said he'd be fine with Claudia and Bill's sitter.

So later that evening, we bundled Jamie up in thick socks and his duvet and I held him on my knee while Alexander drove us to the Barn. There we kissed Jamie goodnight and left him in the adoring hands of his twin cousins, who were committed to attending to his every need, and Claudia's sitter, a capable woman in her forties who looked as if she would brook no nonsense. I huddled my chin into my coat collar and we drove the short distance from the Barn up to Eleonora House.

It was an icy-cold night and the moon was so bright that the trees, all but leafless now, cast spiky shadows across the fields. Alexander had the heater turned up high and hot air billowed against my knees and blew back my hair. The day before I had wanted to look beautiful so that Alexander would be proud of me and I wouldn't be unfavourably compared to Genevieve. Now I wanted to look unremarkable. I wanted to simply fade into the background so nobody could say anything bad about me; at least, the worst they could say would be that I was plain, and quiet.

Alexander smiled at me as he pulled through the huge metal gates that led to Eleonora House. I thought it was as much to reassure himself as me. I could see the lights of the house up ahead, the big windows glowing yellow, their light spilling on to the patios and gardens, and Christmassy lightbulbs had also been strung along the drive. The effect was supposed to be festive and welcoming but so much artificial brightness made me feel intimidated. It was all too big, too bright, too noisy.

Genevieve had arranged the decorations for the party, I remembered. This was her work.

Inside an entrance hall that gleamed with polished wood on the walls and tiles on the floor, a maid took our coats and showed us where to put Philip's cards and presents, and another maid offered us a glass of Buck's Fizz. We took one each and followed the noise into Eleonora House hall.

It was a huge room. I couldn't take it all in at once but the impression was of wood panelling, a springy floor designed for dancing, rugs and mismatched worn but elegant chairs, heavy brocade curtains, old paintings in enormous, ornate frames; everything green, red, gold and sparkling, a great crackling fire in the marble fireplace, girls in black skirts and aprons wielding canapé trays, the largest, most opulently dressed Christmas tree I'd ever seen and people; many people.

There were probably a hundred guests, most of them at least one generation older than we were. It was noisy in the room, a combination of music, laughter and the high-pitched, excitable tune of people flirting and flattering and showing off. It was a more relaxed, jollier atmosphere than I'd envisaged and I realized that everyone was relieved because every single guest had spent most of the day worrying about the Tenby bones. They had been half-expecting the party to turn into a wake.

I spotted Claudia in a long floaty cream and pink dress which flattered her colouring. With her hair newly dyed and piled on top of her head, she looked classically beautiful, like a woman in an Old Master painting. She was standing with two elderly women, listening to them, smiling and nodding, and as her head moved diamonds twinkled in her earlobes and at her neck. Bill stood nearby. He was also being talked at, and he was half-listening, but his sleepy, loving eyes were on Claudia. Across the room she caught my eye and she smiled and held up her hand in greeting. I smiled back.

I glanced at the face of the ornate clock that stood handsomely on a magnificent sideboard. How long, I wondered, before we could decently leave?

Alexander took my elbow.

'Let's say hello to Philip,' he said.

We walked through the throng until we found the old man standing with his back to the fireplace, supporting himself on a silver-headed mahogany stick. His head was a little too big for his body, and silver hair, still bushy, stuck up from the age-spotted skin of his skull. He was a tall man; he must have been imposing not so long ago, before illness and anxiety brought him down. Although he feigned an interest in the conversation around him and his free hand still held a glass, there was something of death about his eyes. Looking at him made me feel sad.

We waited on the periphery of the group until he saw us. His face changed when his eyes lit upon Alexander. He smiled and beckoned and we stepped forward.

'Good to see you, young man!' Philip said in a croaky voice. The two shook hands, and at the same time Philip pulled Alexander close and embraced him. I stood back.

'And this is your housekeeper. I'm sorry, I've forgotten your name.'

'Sarah,' said Alexander, his hand in the small of my back.

I stepped forward with my hand outstretched. I had an almost irresistible urge to curtsy.

'Sarah. Good evening.'

'Happy birthday, Mr Churchill,' I said.

He and Alexander started talking, their heads close together, so I was excluded. I pretended to be fascinated by a picture on the wall beside the fireplace. It was a portrait, no doubt of a family member, a sad-looking, dark-eyed young man with a large moustache, in military uniform and incongruously holding a little dog in his arms. I wondered what had happened to him. Was he Philip's father? I tried to make my drink last. I ate several canapés and moved on to the next picture.

I wished I had the confidence to go and speak to somebody, introduce myself, but I didn't. I kept my back to the room.

Then a friendly and familiar voice at my shoulder said: 'Hello, hello, hello!'

I turned with a smile.

'DI Twyford, I presume.'

'What's a nice girl like you doing in a place like this? And what on earth are you wearing?'

'I didn't know you had an interest in fashion.'

'I wouldn't call that fashion, Sarah – it makes you look twice your age.'

'Flattery will get you nowhere.'

He chuckled, took my empty glass from my hand and replaced it seamlessly with a full one. He leaned towards me to tell me something, but at the same time I felt Alexander's hand on my waist.

He said: 'Philip and I are going into the study. We have a little business to attend to.'

'At a party?'

'It won't take long.'

'OK.'

'You'll be all right?'

'I'll be fine.'

'I'll keep an eye on her,' said the detective.

'As long as that's all you do,' said Alexander.

DI Twyford held his hands up submissively.

'No offence intended,' he said quietly.

'None taken,' Alexander said.

'Alexander . . .' I said.

He shook his head. 'That man's not your friend,' he

told me, loud enough for DI Twyford to hear. Then he turned and took hold of Philip's arm and helped the old man from the room.

When they were through the door, and even their shadows were gone, I turned to the detective and I said: 'Sorry.'

He shrugged. 'It's par for the course. You're a lovely girl. Of course he's possessive.'

'He's not usually like that,' I said, trying not to give away how pleased I was by the adjective he'd chosen to describe me.

'To lose one woman is unfortunate. To lose two would be classed as careless.'

'I'm no literary expert but that didn't sound at all accurate.'

'Don't be pedantic. We're supposed to be having fun.'

'Have you found Luke Innes yet?'

'We're working on it.'

'I don't mean to be rude, but you don't seem particularly good at finding people.'

'Luke Innes is a tricky one. He's changed his name at least twice and has a penchant for foreign travel. Enough of him. Tell me, what's new in your life. Any developments?'

'Nothing new,' I said.

'Nothing at all?'

'Ummm . . .' I looked up at the ceiling. The lights from the chandeliers played prettily on the plaster. I considered my new information, turned it over in my mind and thought there was no reason to withhold it. I could see no harm in sharing it.

'Well, there's one thing. I found out that Genevieve was pregnant when she married Alexander.'

The detective shook his head. 'No, she can't have been.'

I thought one of us had misheard the other. I smiled at a waitress who was proffering a tray of tiny mozzarella balls smeared with pesto. I popped one into my mouth. The cheese was sour and milky on my tongue.

'She definitely was,' I said. 'I found her wedding dress – it was a maternity dress. She must have been more than a little bit pregnant because all her other clothes are way too small for me but . . .'

The detective was looking at me in a curious way.

'What?' I asked.

'You do know that Alexander spent some time in prison?'

I nodded.

'What exactly do you know, Sarah?'

'Just that he was locked up for a while. I don't know what he did or anything.'

'Then you wouldn't know. Alexander and Genevieve married almost as soon as he was released.'

'So?'

The inspector leaned forward and spoke quietly, but distinctly, into my ear.

'If Genevieve was pregnant with Alexander's child when they married, she couldn't have been more than a couple of weeks gone. She wouldn't have needed a maternity dress. All told, he was inside for the best part of a year.'

The penny dropped. The inspector steadied my arm and turned me away from the crowd so they would not see the shock on my face. My legs were shaky.

'So Jamie isn't Alexander's son? I mean, not his blood son?' I asked in a whisper.

'If what you told me is true, he can't be,' he said. 'And Alexander must know that.'

I remembered what Alexander had told me about the fight that led to Genevieve stabbing him.

I remembered how worried Alexander had been about the Churchills taking Jamie from him.

I thought of the way Alexander looked at Jamie; the way his eyes softened with love when he saw the boy.

'Oh God,' I sighed, as the full implications rolled over me, one after the other. 'Oh no.'

CHAPTER FORTY-EIGHT

There was a breeze at my arm and the scent of Chanel and hairspray, and I turned to see Virginia all wafty and out of character in a dress and high-ish heels.

She said: 'Hello, Sarah, how are you?' in a tone of voice that made it clear she didn't much care one way or the other, and then she said: 'I'm afraid I must stop you monopolizing one of the few eligible bachelors in the room,' and led DI Twyford away. He looked over his shoulder and jerked one hand upwards to mimic a hanging motion. I smiled and took another sip of wine. I felt a little sick. I had the strongest urge to be with Jamie, to sit beside him and hold his hand and make sure no harm came to him.

I hadn't been able to protect my own son, but I could protect Jamie.

I decided to slip out, pick the boy up from Claudia's and take him back to Avalon. I would not exactly be lying if I said I was feeling unwell. I could take Jamie into my bed, sleep with my arms around him so that nobody could take him from me. In the morning we could work something out, Alexander and I, some way of guaranteeing Jamie would always be with us. I could ask Neil for advice. That was what I would do. I'd call him first thing. I was halfway across the room, on the way to the exit, when I sensed, rather than saw, Alexander return. I could tell by his stride and the set of his shoulders that something good had happened. He came straight across the floor to me, took hold of my hand and leaned down to kiss my cheek gently.

'Come on,' he said. 'Let's go and get another drink.'

'Alexander, I think we ought to fetch Jamie and go back to Avalon,' I said.

'Why?'

'Something's wrong.'

'He's fine. I've had my mobile on. Claudia's sitter hasn't called.'

'She doesn't know him very well. She wouldn't be able to tell if he was getting worse.'

'Sarah, he's perfectly all right.'

'But what if this is all a set-up? What if the Churchills set this up so they could take Jamie away from us?'

Alexander pulled a face and took a step back from me.

'What's put all this into your head?'

I stared at him. He looked like a film star. He stood tall and confident with his shoulders straight and his head held high. For the first time since I'd known him he looked proud – not in a defiant way, but in a heroic way.

'Sarah? What happened? Did that bastard Twyford say something to you?'

'No, no. I'm just worried. I've got a bad feeling about Jamie. I'm scared something awful's going to happen. Alexander, please . . .'

'OK,' he said. 'OK. We'll call the sitter. We'll speak to Jamie. Will that help?'

I nodded miserably.

Alexander led me to the far end of the hall, through a narrow drawing room, beautifully decorated and lined with chairs, and into a kind of anteroom, where bottles of red wine were breathing and Sancerre chilled in buckets on tables covered with white linen cloths. Sparkling crystal glasses were lined in ranks. The waiting staff had been re-stocking their serving trays from the room, but it was empty when we went in. They were busy preparing the dining room for the sit-down supper.

Alexander took out his mobile phone and called Claudia's number. He switched the phone to loud-speaker so that I could hear.

The sitter answered.

'Hello, Mr Westwood.'

'Hello, Sue. I'm sorry to bother you, but we just wanted to check that Jamie was OK.'

'He's fine. He's been good as gold and his temperature had gone right down last time I checked.'

Alexander raised his eyebrows at me. I chewed at my thumbnail and shook my head. That wasn't good enough.

'Would you mind passing the phone to him? We need a word.'

'You want me to wake him?'

Now Alexander pulled an exasperated face at me. I reached over and took the phone from him.

'I'm sorry, I know it's hassle for you, but I need to hear Jamie,' I said. 'Otherwise we're coming back now.'

The woman sighed. We heard her pushing herself to her feet. We heard her footsteps as she crossed the hall and went up the stairs. We heard the creak of a bedroom door being pushed open. We heard her say: 'Petra and Allegra Lefarge, why aren't you in bed, you naughty girls?', and we heard the twins giggling.

'We're looking after Jamie,' one of them said.

'Is he still awake? Are you awake, pet?'

We heard Jamie sigh.

It was definitely Jamie – I recognized that sleepy little voice, and my body responded with a surge of tenderness.

'Your daddy wants a word with you.'

'Daddy?'

'Just wanted to say night night,' Alexander said.

'Night,' Jamie sighed.

'Sleep tight, pet,' the sitter said. There were some muffled sounds as she tucked Jamie in, and then we heard the footsteps retreating.

'All right?' the sitter asked.

'Fine now, thank you,' I said.

'You're welcome,' the woman replied frostily.

'OK?' Alexander asked. He put the phone back in his pocket.

I nodded.

He took hold of a bottle of red wine, filled two glasses and passed one to me.

'What are we celebrating?' I asked tentatively.

Alexander beamed. 'I've now, officially, repaid Philip Churchill every penny of the money I owed him.'

He leaned down and kissed me hard, full on the lips. One of those kisses that made me thrill to the core because it was a kiss for me and nothing at all to do with Genevieve.

'It means we're free,' he whispered. His hand was in my hair, the heat of his breath was in my ear.

'Free from what?' I asked, all low and soft because he'd said: 'We're free'; he was including me in his future.

'Avalon, Philip, Genevieve, this family. We don't owe them anything any more. They have no hold over us. I've paid off my debt.'

'You mean we can leave? We can take Jamie and leave? We can go somewhere else? Somewhere far from here?'

'We can do whatever we want,' said Alexander.

'Let's go now,' I said. 'Let's go tonight.'

But we didn't. The night wore on and the clock turned slowly. After an exhausting dinner of curried soup, game pie and roast potatoes and plum pudding, during which I struggled to make conversation with the two elderly gentlemen between whom I was sitting, a four-piece band struck up. They were playing old dance music, tunes I recognized but did not know well.

I didn't care about the music. All I wanted was to be with Alexander and Jamie, somewhere, anywhere, that wasn't Burrington Stoke.

Philip and Virginia were first to the dance floor and

the spotlight was on them, and it was touching. Together, the disparity in their age was obvious. She looked almost a child in his arms. He hobbled, supported by his stick and his wife. They gazed at one another like the young people they once were, with unconditional adoration. I felt sorry for them. Virginia and Philip looked into one another's eyes, but I supposed neither was seeing the other; each would be looking at Genevieve.

CHAPTER FORTY-NINE

The next morning there was no opportunity to talk about leaving because we had invited Claudia, Bill and the girls to Avalon for lunch. I got up early to ramp up the heat in the Rayburn's oven and to lay the table in the dining room. In my mind I was severe with myself. It was imperative I acted normally, not like somebody who was making plans to escape. I had to be charming, cheerful – a good hostess.

It was the first time, and now I knew it would also be the last, that Alexander and I entertained anyone at Avalon. I wanted to make it special to thank Claudia for her friendship and loyalty over the past months. She was not to know, but I intended it to be my farewell gift to her; something pleasant to remember me by when we were gone.

I put down a clean cloth, and the mats I'd found in the old dresser, and I laid out the best cutlery and glassware. I filled a vase with mistletoe and I put my homemade horseradish sauce into a little silver pot I'd found at the back of a cupboard. Jamie had a cough, but was better than he had been. He sloped around helping me. Alexander, who was hungover, lay in.

The Lefarge family arrived punctually at 12 o'clock. I guessed that they had come straight from church, only stopping to pick up the dogs and their wellingtons.

As I worked in the kitchen, I heard the other adults in the living room talking about this and that, and soon enough the conversation turned to the fact that Alexander had paid off his debt to Philip, and their voices dropped, as if this was not a subject that should be discussed within earshot of me.

No, I was being paranoid. It was the children who must not hear. Jamie and the girls were running about upstairs playing some convoluted daylight version of Murder in the Dark. I heard their thrilled squeals and giggles while I stirred the roux for the leek sauce.

I was proud of the way the table looked when we sat down to eat, although I had to move the mistletoe after Claudia told me it signified bad luck at the table. The last thing Alexander and I needed then was ill fortune. It was only a small glitch. I was proud of the food, too, which turned out fine, but mostly I was proud of Alexander and Jamie. I looked across at them both, and I remembered how they were when I first came to Avalon, and it was not my imagination, things were better now, despite all that had happened. Some of the introspection and some of the hurt was gone.

We managed to go through the whole meal without anyone mentioning Genevieve. It was a record.

I knew we were making the most of the fact that there

was, as yet, no conclusive proof that anything bad had happened to Genevieve. For those few hours, everything was all right. We had no reason not to be in a good mood. It was nearly Christmas. Nothing terrible ever happened at Christmas.

After we had finished the lemon meringue pie, Alexander raised his glass to me and said: 'Thank you for everything, Sarah.'

The whole family followed suit and I had to look down at my plate.

'I mean it,' Alexander said quietly. 'Thank you for putting up with us.'

'Hear, hear!' said Bill, and he winked at me.

And that's when the dizziness came over me, just as it had done before, in Jamie's bedroom. This time, the nausea overwhelmed me so fast that I had to cover my mouth with my hand. I stumbled from the room, and ran upstairs to the bathroom, where I was terribly sick. When I finally stood up to wash my face, my eyes were red and swollen and my skin was deathly pale and somebody was standing behind me. I saw a movement in the mirror and I felt breath on my neck but, when I turned, nobody was there.

'Please, Genevieve,' I whispered. 'Please leave me alone. I didn't do anything to hurt you, I'm only trying to make things better.'

I didn't hear anything, but words came into my mind, just as they had before, as if someone had whispered into my ear. The words that were there, but which I did not hear, were: 'You next.'

* * *

'You OK?' Alexander asked when I went back downstairs.

I nodded. 'Fine.'

He looked at me quizzically. 'Are you sure?'

'It's nothing.'

I saw him and Claudia exchange glances.

'*Nothing*,' I said tetchily.

When the dishwasher was loaded and was sloshing away in its loyal, reliable fashion, we put on our boots and jackets, called the dogs in and put them on their leads ready for a walk.

'Where are we going?' asked Allegra.

'What about walking up to the old quarry? We haven't been there for ages.'

'I don't think we should take the dogs there,' said Alexander. 'What if they were to chase a rabbit over the edge?'

'Mendips then?'

'OK.'

So that's where we went. Alexander, Claudia and the twins went in the Land Rover and Bill drove Jamie, me and the dogs in the Volvo.

It was a lovely drive and Jamie was talkative. He was very fond of the dogs and maintained a running commentary with them. I, on the other hand, was silent. I turned the words I had heard over and over in my mind. Why was I going to be next? What did that mean? Next to do what? Disappear? Die? I sat, quietly terrified, pretending to listen to Bill's operatic music on CD. We soon pulled on to the airport road and headed west towards Crook Peak, and I tried to work out what the warning meant, because it was a warning, I was sure of that.

I gazed out of the window. The trees were black and bare now, skeleton trees, their bony branches stark against a pale, wintry sky, and the grass was a winter green. Twiggy black hedges lined the fields and smoke curled from the chimneys of the farmhouses that sat square and grey in the landscape. The music seemed a fitting soundtrack to the bleak countryside.

You next.

Not if I got away from Burrington Stoke first. Alexander and I had to leave, as soon as we could. That's what we had to do.

In the car, I lost myself in imagining how it would feel to be driving away from Burrington Stoke for ever. I wondered if this would be the road we'd take. Would tomorrow be too late? When was I going to be next? How long did I have?

When Bill spoke, it took me a few moments to bring myself back into the present.

'I know you've had a rough time but, if it's any consolation, I think you've done a great job with Alexander,' he said, turning to smile at me. 'He's like a different person now.'

'Oh, thank you,' I said.

I looked over my shoulder. Jamie was entirely engrossed in his game with the dogs.

'Maybe he's starting to get over Genevieve,' I said quietly. 'At last.'

'Let's hope so,' said Bill. 'He was in a bloody awful state when she left.'

We drove on a little longer and then were stuck at traffic lights.

Bill shook his head.

'Poor bugger, she put him through hell,' he said.

'Are we nearly there?' asked Jamie, leaning forward.

'Nearly,' said Bill. He was staring straight ahead now. The lights changed and he put the car into gear.

'Don't blame Alexander,' he said.

'What do you mean? Don't blame him for what?'

Bill turned slightly and gave me a strange look.

'Being the man he is,' he said.

Jamie was leaning on the headrest, his breath was hot in my ear, and I did not have the opportunity to pursue the subject any further.

CHAPTER FIFTY

We had a lovely walk, although Blue had to be kept on the lead after he bounded after a child with a football and knocked him flying and then punctured the ball. Bill gave the boy's parents a ten-pound note and a long-winded apology to compensate for the dog's bad behaviour. Afterwards everyone came back to Avalon for tea and cake and we laughed at Blue's inability to repent his sins.

'Do you know, the only person he ever listened to was Genevieve,' said Claudia.

I tensed a little.

'That's right, isn't it?' she asked Bill. 'Gen never even had to raise her voice; she only had to look at him and he'd behave. She was so good with animals!'

Bill smiled indulgently, but I had the feeling he thought Claudia was remembering things differently. I felt sorry for them both. And it felt odd that even Claudia was talking about Genevieve in the past tense now.

It was evening before I had a chance to speak to

Alexander alone. As soon as the Lefarge family left, I told him I wanted us to leave Burrington Stoke immediately, straight away, now.

'Hey,' he said, stroking my back. 'Don't get in a state about it.'

'We have to go. It's really important we go,' I said. 'You don't understand.'

'What don't I understand?'

'I think if we don't go now, something really awful's going to happen,' I said.

He laughed. Then he stopped laughing and took hold of my hands.

'What do you mean? Has somebody said something to you? Have you been threatened?'

'No, not exactly. I don't know, I've just got a feeling.'

'Oh, Sarah, come on,' he said. 'It's been a tough week, that's all.'

I shook my head. 'No. I mean it, Alexander. We have to get away.'

He took me seriously enough to go upstairs and do some internet searches, and after a while he came back downstairs with the laptop tucked under his elbow.

He was smiling, looking pleased with himself.

'There's a yard up for rent in Fowey. It was being used by a memorial mason but he's retired. It's got the space and the kit I'd need. We could move the business down there. What do you think?'

'Fowey in Cornwall?'

'Didn't you say you liked Cornwall?'

I did like Cornwall, and Fowey in particular was

beautiful. Laurie took me there for a long weekend once. I remembered the church tucked away in a hollow at the bottom of the hill; sea water splashing against the wall beneath the restaurant where we ate scampi and chips; a boat trip along the green estuary that took us all the way along to Daphne du Maurier's house: we saw its gardens rolling down to the water, cold and clear like glass. I had thought it one of the loveliest places I'd ever been. I'd always thought of Cornwall as somewhere to visit, not somewhere to live. How small-minded I used to be. I thought the civilized world began and ended in Lancashire.

'It sounds perfect,' I said.

'Then we'll do it. We'll go.'

'What about your work here?'

Alex shrugged. 'I'll have to give a month's notice on the yard. Everything else we can take with us.'

I leaned back and breathed. It seemed as if, at last, everything was being made easy for us. Everything was going our way.

'How quickly can we leave?' I asked.

'As quickly as we like.'

He put his hand on my shoulder, leaned down and kissed my head. He wound his hand in my hair and the vegetables I was stirring in the pan sizzled and the rain tapped and spattered against the window panes.

'What about this place?'

'We'll send Philip a letter. With Genevieve gone the house belongs to him.'

'The Churchills won't want Jamie to leave Burrington Stoke. Do you think they'll try to stop us?'

'Probably. It'd be best if you didn't say anything to anyone, not even Jamie. We'll leave quietly and after a couple of weeks we'll let them know where we are and that we're OK.'

I felt a frisson run through me. Wasn't that almost exactly what Genevieve had said in the letter to her parents? Had she had this exact same conversation with somebody?

'It seems a bit cruel on Philip and Virginia,' I said. 'First Genevieve, then Jamie.'

'If you want a quick getaway without any fuss,' said Alexander, 'that's how it's going to have to be.'

CHAPTER FIFTY-ONE

Alexander spoke to the agent on the phone the next day and arranged an appointment in Fowey. He was going to stay overnight and come back the following evening. When Jamie was asleep, we sat at the door to his room and looked at properties for rent there on the internet and saw a couple of cottages just a stone's throw from the sea. In the gloom of the mid-winter, I imagined summers to come, sitting bare-legged in a tiny courtyard garden, surrounded by pots of lavender, and drawing. I thought of Jamie, tanned and healthy, growing his hair, turning into a surfer-boy, and the three of us on the beach, barefoot, cooking fish over a driftwood fire and watching the sun set over the green and white waves. The picture was so appealing I wanted to leave there and then. I felt as if I could hardly bear another moment in Avalon. I wanted to feel the sand beneath my feet.

I cooked a full English breakfast the morning before Alexander left. We had told Jamie his father was going to price some work a long way away; still, Jamie was whiney and anxious. I hoped fried bread, sausage and beans would help, but they didn't. None of the usual distraction techniques had any effect.

'We'll go and choose a Christmas tree when I get back,' Alexander said. 'Father Christmas won't come if we don't have a tree.'

Jamie put on his challenging face. 'Father Christmas isn't real,' he said.

'Oh?'

'Allegra told me. She said he's just a made-up person to make children go to bed early so the adults can put the presents out.'

Alexander raised an eyebrow. 'Are you sure about that?'

Jamie looked at his father.

'That's what Allegra said.'

'Did she also tell you that he only comes to children who believe in him?'

Jamie looked from Alexander's face to mine.

'How does he know the difference if you're asleep?' he asked carefully.

'He just does.'

Jamie swung his legs. 'All right, but I'm going to ask for a dog for Christmas and, if I don't get one, I won't believe in Father Christmas any more.'

I laughed. Alexander wagged his fork at Jamie. 'Don't push your luck, son.'

'Sarah, do *you* think we should have a dog?'

'Yes,' I said. 'Yes, I do. But not for Christmas. Wait and see what happens in the New Year, eh?'

* * *

Alexander hurried Jamie along and soon had him strapped in the Land Rover ready to drop off at school on his way down to the motorway. It was so cold outside that our breath steamed. A thick frost had lain down on the garden and the roofs of the old barn and the loose boxes, the trees were white and freezing mist swirled picturesquely above the course of the stream. The countryside did look particularly beautiful that morning, but already my heart was in Cornwall.

I passed Jamie his lunchbox and stood shivering at the side of the vehicle, waiting to wave them off. Alexander wound down his window. Close up, in the bright sunlight, I could see how tired he was, how much the past months had taken from him.

He reached out and touched my cheek with his hand.

'We'll be all right,' he said. 'I promise.'

That morning, I caught the bus into Castle Cary and then the train into Bristol. I planned to do as much Christmas shopping as possible. We were going to be so busy over the next few days, packing and clearing out, that there simply wouldn't be time if I left it any later. Jamie was going for tea at Karen's after school, so it didn't matter if I was late back. I had been looking forward to this day, a day to myself, shopping in the city, for a while.

Bristol didn't disappoint. I felt like a child in a sweetshop. Everything delighted me: I didn't know what to look at first, which shop to go into. After the quiet of Burrington Stoke and those few, same, suspicious faces,

I felt at home amongst all the thousands of people. I was a city girl. I belonged.

I was queuing up to try on an armful of clothes in Debenhams when my phone beeped. A text message had come through. I took the phone out of my pocket and checked. It was from DI Twyford.

My finger hovered over the button. I could just switch the phone off and read the message later. Or I could put the phone back in my pocket and ignore it. Or I could delete it without reading it, and deny I ever received it.

Only, in my heart, I would know it was there. Not knowing what it said would eat away at me. It would spoil my day.

The day was tainted already.

The woman in front of me stepped forward. I opened the message. It said: *Need to talk asap.*

'How many items?' asked the young girl who was looking after the changing rooms.

'Sorry,' I said. 'I have to go.'

I went back outside the shop and called the detective's mobile phone. It was switched off. I rummaged in my bag until I found his card and called the landline, but the man who answered said the DI was in a meeting, and asked if I wanted to leave a message. I said I didn't, switched the phone off and put it back in my bag.

There was still plenty of time for shopping but, now, the crowds no longer seemed jolly and exciting, they seemed overwhelming. I had to get out, away from all the people.

I went past a newsagent's. The board outside said: MISSING HEIRESS LATEST. I went inside and read the front page of the *Bristol Evening Post*.

There was a photograph of Damian, with a police officer on either side of him. One of the arms of his coat hung loose at his side. The headline read: SECRET LIFE OF GEN'S HALF-BRO.

Damian had been arrested for some crane-climbing stunt and it turned out his fingerprints matched those found at the Tenby flat. What were they intimating? That Genevieve and Damian were in a relationship? Or that he was stalking her? I put down the paper and saw the girl at the counter watching me. I bought a packet of mints.

I followed my feet. I didn't know where I was going. I left the centre and the shops, crossed a busy road and found myself walking beside the cathedral. It was much quieter there, and the old stone of the building calmed me. I walked beside it and past it and found myself at the door to Bristol's Central Library.

I had not intended to seek out the library, I had not even known where it was, but now I stood outside it, looking in through the window in the door.

I realized I was at a crossroads. If I went in, if I searched for the records of Alexander's trial and read them, then I would never be able to undo the knowledge. It would be inside me, part of me, always.

If I walked away, I might never know what Alexander had done. I would go with him, wherever it was we ended up going, and I would be innocent, but the not knowing would constantly be between us, like a wall. I did not really have a choice. I pushed open the door and went in.

I went to the help desk and asked if I could go through back copies of the *Western Daily Press*. I didn't know where Alexander's trial had been held but figured that, even if it was London, the paper would have covered the story of a local man.

The librarian was very helpful. She asked when Alexander had been convicted. I worked it out to within a few months by counting backwards from the date of Jamie's birth. When I'd given her the information she requested, she disappeared for five minutes and returned with a stack of boxes of microfiche coils.

'These are copies of the papers covering that three-month period. We haven't had the time to put all these online yet,' she said apologetically. 'This way: I'll show you where the machines are.'

It took an age to go through the records. The film, which was inches wide, springy and hard to manage, had to be fed through spools at either side of the projector and then wound on manually until the pages showed up on the screen in front of me, and I had to adjust the focus constantly. After a while, I learned where, in each paper, to look for the court reports, each time half-hoping that I would see Alexander's name and half-hoping I wouldn't.

It took a couple of hours – but eventually I found it. Not in the court report section towards the back of the papers, but on the front page.

The headline was: GUILTY! And the strapline said: SHAME OF MAN WHO STOLE FROM FRIEND.

There was a photograph of Alexander – a younger, desperately handsome Alexander – wearing a dark suit, shielding his face with a newspaper as he went into court. A few steps behind him was an older, suited man – his lawyer? And a short-haired pixie-like girl in a chic dark-coloured dress with a wide, white belt: Genevieve. Inset was a smaller picture of another young man, his face haggard and hard set. A dark-haired, plump young woman wearing sunglasses had her arm around the man: the friend and his wife, I assumed.

The headline and the images disturbed me and my eyes were burning from looking at the screen for so long. I switched off the machine and sat for a few moments rubbing my temples with my forefingers. Perhaps I should leave it there. Perhaps that was enough. So Alexander was a thief. At least he hadn't murdered anyone.

I rummaged in my bag and found the mints. I prised one loose with my thumbnail and put it in my mouth. Its sweetness made me feel slightly less nauseous.

Shame of man who stole from friend. There was little space for misinterpretation of those words.

I felt terribly tired.

I had come this far. I might as well know the whole truth.

I flicked the switch to power up the projector and, as the screen came into focus, took a deep breath and began to read:

> A man who pleaded guilty to stealing more than £100,000 from his best friend and business partner

has been sentenced to 18 months in prison.

Alexander Westwood, aged 29, of Wells, Somerset, dramatically changed his plea after just one day in court, admitting to taking money from the reclamation and masonry recycling company established by Matt Bryant. Westwood had also been accused of tampering with the accounts to hide the theft.

Judge Hilary Enright described Westwood's actions as 'despicable'. 'What you did to Mr Bryant and his family goes beyond theft. You sacrificed a lifelong friendship to satisfy your greed,' she said. 'You deceived and lied to a good man, a man who had worked hard to build up his business and who believed it was in safe hands; a man who trusted you. Because of your actions, Mr Bryant's company is on the brink of bankruptcy. His health and relationships have suffered. He is facing repossession of his home. I have no qualms about sentencing you to the maximum gaol term possible in these circumstances.'

Westwood, wearing a black suit, a white shirt and a dark tie, remained expressionless throughout.

The court had earlier heard how Westwood and Bryant had been friends since school.

Westwood had served an apprenticeship as a mason and spotted the potential in restoring damaged stoneware for Bryant's reclamation business, which had been set up with the help of a loan from Bryant's father. The Worcester-based business recently won a national sustainability award and was attracting major contracts.

> Until today, Westwood had denied any involvement in the theft, despite records proving that the money was moved through a number of private accounts to which only he had access. He has consistently refused to say what he did with the cash.

There were a couple more paragraphs, but I stopped reading there.

It was pretty conclusive. I could see no mitigation, no possible vindication or excuse for what Alexander had done.

He was a thief and a cheat and he'd deceived his best friend. Morally, Alexander's actions were unjustifiable. And if he were capable of such disloyalty to his best friend, somebody who had, as I understood from the report, helped Alexander, then could anyone truly trust him again?

Yet still . . . I found it difficult to believe what I had read.

I'd only known him a few months, but Alexander seemed to be one of the least materialistic people I had ever come across. He had no interest in cars or holidays, designer labels or investments. He worked hard, but that was because he was a hard worker, not because he wanted to be wealthy. Or, at least, he'd never expressed that ambition to me. He was not a gambler; he did not use drugs, or drink excessively. And I had always believed him; he had told me some unpalatable truths but I had been utterly convinced he was not a liar.

But he had lied. I'd heard him lie to Virginia about

him and me. And first he said he hadn't and then he admitted that he had stolen the money from Matt Bryant. He stood up in court and said he was guilty. He had accepted the humiliation of prison without protest; he hadn't gone down arguing his innocence, like innocent people generally do.

Even if I accepted Alexander's guilt, there were more questions than answers. Where had the money gone? If Alexander was penniless when he came out of prison and married Genevieve, if he had to borrow more money from Philip to set himself up in business, then what had he done with all that cash?

I had been tired before. Now, I was exhausted and I felt terribly lonely. There was nobody I could talk to about this; not a single person. My friends and family would be outraged and horrified to find out yet another damning chapter in Alexander's history, and to raise the subject in Burrington Stoke, given the current mood against Alexander and myself, would be stupid and perhaps even dangerous.

And what about Jamie? Alexander had a criminal record. I was almost certain that people who'd been in prison weren't allowed to look after small children. If he'd been Jamie's biological father then it would be nothing to worry about, but he wasn't, and that made his position – our position – even more tenuous.

We had to get away.

I switched off the machine and wound the microfiche back into its coil. I put the coil in the box and carried it, with the others I'd collected, back to the desk. I thanked the librarian. I was wondering if there was anywhere in the library I could lie down and sleep for a couple of hours, some dark corner where nobody would notice me. It was so nice and quiet in there with just the books and the readers, the soothing rustle of paper, the warm air pumping from the radiators and the occasional hum of the photocopier. Even the phone bells were muted.

'Are you feeling all right, my love?' asked the librarian.

'Yes, I'm just a bit tired.'

'Did you find what you wanted?'

'Yes,' I said, although the truth was the exact opposite.

I went back outside. The cold air was shocking.

Already the morning was over and the short, winter afternoon had begun. I had no appetite for shopping. I walked through cobbled streets to the waterfront, ordered a coffee and sat at a bench-table that looked out over the river. The sun was low in the sky and there was a bitter chill in the air. The narrowboats and houseboats moored in the harbour were strung with fairy lights that reflected in the black water. It was a lovely view but I was not in the mood.

Trust, I thought. With Alexander, everything always seemed to come down to trust.

I had broken his trust by looking up the history he wanted to keep secret from me; but my betrayal was nothing compared to what he had done to Matt Bryant.

CHAPTER FIFTY-TWO

When Alexander called that evening, I found it difficult to speak to him, knowing what I now knew. I encouraged Jamie to spend as much time talking to his father as possible, and when it was my turn I struggled to keep my emotions under control. I asked questions, listening but not hearing as Alexander described his day and enthused about the Cornish mason's yard.

'Are you all right, Sarah?' he asked. 'You're very quiet.' He was in a pub; I could hear people laughing behind him. It made me feel very lonely out in the big house, in the middle of nowhere, with the child I loved and who wasn't Alexander's son. A light snow was falling beyond the window and the old oil burner was struggling to keep the radiators warm.

'Yes, of course, I'm fine,' I said, but I wasn't. My world felt increasingly shaky around me, as if it were about to collapse. Everything was precarious. I felt as if I were on the brink of losing the man I thought I loved most in the world, and the child I knew I did. My mind was full of things I wished I didn't know. I couldn't say that to Alexander, so I told him I was tired.

'Busy day shopping?' asked Alexander, with the hint of a tease in his voice. The implication that I'd spent a frivolous day doing nothing much but spending money that I had legitimately earned angered me.

'I have to go,' I said. 'Something's burning in the oven.'

Later, I sat beside Jamie on the living-room settee, and my arm was around him. I held him as close as I could, smiling at his chatter. I had promised Jamie I would never leave him, and I had made a vow with myself that I would protect the child, no matter what. I would not let him be hurt any more, in any way, by anyone. So there were no decisions to be made. Where Jamie was, I was too; always. I might not like what Alexander had done to Matt Bryant. I didn't like the fact that he was an ex-convict or that he'd told me what he'd done to go to prison was not a big deal, but, as he was always saying, the past was over. It didn't matter; it was not relevant to us now. Perhaps in time I'd be able to convince myself of that.

Jamie fell asleep beside me on the settee. The hands on the clock went round, but I didn't move. I couldn't bring myself to carry him upstairs. I was afraid of what might happen up there, beneath the eaves of that big, dark house. I had a feeling something was lurking, waiting. I looked at the television but was not concentrating on the narrative of the programme. My mind was full of two little words that filled me with terror: *You next*. They went round and round my brain on a loop. If I didn't know what had become of Genevieve, how would I know when the same thing was about to happen to me?

I fetched the chenille throw from the kitchen and Alexander's big coat and made a makeshift bed for the two of us on the settee. I left the lamps on in the living room and unplugged the telephone. I tried to think pleasant, soothing thoughts but, every time I was about to drift off, the words came back and tapped me on the shoulder before they whispered in my ear: *You next.*

I had to get away.

I couldn't leave Jamie.

'Genevieve, help me,' I pleaded. 'Tell me what's going to happen.'

I must have fallen asleep because I dreamed that she came home.

It didn't begin as a nightmare; no, to start with it was a calm, surreal dream, like watching a sequence in a film that appealed to me but in which I had no emotional involvement.

In the dream, I woke in my bed and slipped out of the covers, went through the door on to the landing and drew back the curtains at the window. Outside, everywhere was covered in virgin snow. The garden and the fields, the walls and trees all glowed white in the moonlight. I leaned closer to the glass and my breath clouded the window. I felt very tired. It was difficult to keep my eyes open but the scene was so beautiful. Walking up the drive was a young woman, and I knew at once she was Genevieve. She was barefoot in the snow, wearing a dress that seemed to be made of water. The dress flowed around her and her hair was wet; it stuck to her cheeks and her skull. She stopped to stroke the faces of the horses in the stables. Then she looked up to the window, and saw me and waved, and, tired as I was, I held up my hand and waved back.

In my dream, I wanted to go back to bed but I knew if I took my eyes off Genevieve she would disappear and I'd lose her for ever. Her feet must be cold, I thought. She had to step high through the deep snow. She was smiling. She beckoned me down, but when I went out into the garden, she was gone. Her footprints stopped halfway up the drive and the woman was no longer there; only an oval of ice, like a mirror, lay in the snow. I leaned down to look into the ice, and I saw not my face reflected back but Genevieve's, and then as I looked she reached out to me, through the ice, and grabbed hold of my shoulders and pulled me towards her. I screamed as I fell, gasped for breath as I plunged into the ice, and once again I had the sensation of falling into an abyss. That was what woke me.

After that, I could not get back to sleep.

The next morning, after I'd dropped Jamie at school, I tried to divert myself from my worries by clearing out and packing up some of the stuff at Avalon. Alexander had told me to get rid of as much as I could, but to do it surreptitiously so as not to raise any suspicions about our plans. If I bagged and boxed everything that could be given away, he'd drive it to charity shops somewhere where people didn't know us. We'd burn what we couldn't recycle or take it to the tip. I found the disposal exercise surprisingly cathartic. Alexander and Genevieve's history was tied up with the things in the house. It would be better when they were gone.

I started with Genevieve's dressing room, reasoning that Jamie wouldn't notice anything that disappeared from there. I folded and packed the clothes carefully and neatly. The wind was gusting around the eaves of Avalon, little sneaky draughts blowing icy through the gaps in the window frames, rattling at the glass like something demanding to be let in. I tried to keep calm and worked as quickly as I could, singing to myself for reassurance. I thought we should leave the clothes behind for Claudia or Virginia to find and look after. Then if Genevieve ever did come back, she'd have plenty of nice things to wear and, if she didn't, Allegra and Petra would probably find a use for them.

The excess bed linen, towels and other bits and pieces I bagged for recycling. After that I went down to the kitchen and set to clearing out the cupboards. I started with the cutlery drawer. It needed a good clean; there were crumbs in the plastic tray and the knives, forks and spoons were muddled together. Under the tray, face down, was a photograph. I peeled it from the bottom of the drawer. It was a faded picture of the statue at the entrance to the drive at Eleonora. The stone statue of the poor dead girl was standing as it always stood, one hand touching its breast, the other outstretched and inclined towards the entrance. I could not work out, at first, what was wrong with the image.

Then I remembered.

Last time I saw it, Genevieve had been in the picture too. She'd been standing beside the statue, imitating its pose.

No, she couldn't have been.

But she was: I remembered how, at the time, I had found the picture disturbing.

I screwed it up and threw it into the rubbish bag.

It must have got damp, face down as it was in the drawer. The damp must have erased Genevieve out of the picture. That was all.

It was important to me that we left Avalon in order, but sorting out the house was a mammoth task. I didn't want to leave a mess. I could imagine Virginia complaining about our slovenliness. So I stacked dusty old crockery and pans and utensils on the floor, washed them, and then everything that didn't look as if it could possibly be useful to us in our Cornish cottage I put into boxes. As much again went into bags to be thrown away.

I'd been working for hours when I heard car tyres scrunching on the drive. I glanced out of the window. Through the wild swaying of the empty branches of the apple trees, I saw a police car and remembered I still hadn't spoken to DI Twyford in response to his message the day before. I looked round the kitchen hopelessly and pushed a couple of the boxes under the table, but there wasn't the time to tidy up. Somehow, I would have to front it out.

I forced myself to breathe slowly, went through the kitchen door and opened the rosette-room door. A gust of wind caught it and slammed it wide open against the wall beyond, cracking the glass in its window.

'Seven years' bad luck,' said the inspector.

'That only applies to mirrors,' I said.

He shrugged. 'Still not a good omen.'

He almost pushed past me to go into the kitchen, followed this time by another middle-aged male officer in plain clothes. DI Twyford looked around and raised an eyebrow at the mess.

'I'm having a clear-out before Christmas,' I said briskly, dusting my hands on the thighs of my jeans.

'Looks to me like you're planning on going away,' he replied in a matter-of-fact tone of voice.

Immediately, my neck and cheeks burned hot.

'You wouldn't even think of leaving without talking to me first, would you?' he asked.

'I'm just sorting out this junk,' I said, which wasn't exactly a lie.

'Right. Why didn't you call me back yesterday?' he asked.

'I did. You were busy. If it was that urgent I thought you'd find a way to reach me.'

'We came round to the house twice yesterday. You weren't in.'

'I was Christmas shopping in Bristol.'

'Oh, right.'

He let his eyes wander, very obviously, over the boxes and the bags, the old plates wrapped in newspaper.

'What is it you want?' I asked briskly.

'Where's Mr Westwood? We called at the yard yesterday, and they told us he's taken a couple of days off to look after you. Apparently, you had suspected appendicitis. I'm glad to see you've made such an excellent recovery. Now I know you were shopping, but where's Alexander gone? And why did he lie to his colleagues?'

'I'm not sure exactly.'

DI Twyford picked up a blue ceramic jug decorated with daisies and turned it over in his hands. There was a chip in the rim. I had not decided whether to take it or box it.

'Where is he, Sarah? What's he doing?'

I pulled the sleeve of my jumper down over my hands and stood with my back against the Rayburn.

'He's gone to quote for a business opportunity.'

'What does that mean?'

I looked up at the ceiling. 'I don't know.'

'That's helpful.'

There was a silence. The inspector put the jug back on the table and stared at me.

'If that's all he's doing, why didn't he just say as much at work?'

'I don't know.'

'You don't know much, do you, Sarah?'

'He'll be back tonight,' I said. 'Is there a message? Should I get him to call you?'

'No, no. We'll find him.'

'Has something else happened?' I asked.

'No, nothing has happened. But we're going to start searching the Burrington Stoke area tomorrow. That includes this house and its grounds. It'll take a few days but we'll be as thorough as possible.'

'Why?' I whispered. My stomach had turned to liquid; my head felt light and dizzy.

'Oh, come on, Sarah, why do you think?' he replied. All the friendliness, all the flirtatiousness was gone from his voice. He'd been playing with me all along.

'It's nearly Christmas,' I whispered.

He gave me a withering look.

'We'll be as quick as we can. In the meantime, I'd appreciate it if you wouldn't throw anything away.'

I chewed at a hangnail.

'While I'm here,' said DI Twyford, 'I'd like to take the letter that Genevieve left for Jamie.'

'Don't you need a search warrant or something?'

He shrugged. I did not like or trust this new, hard-faced man.

'They're preparing a handful of warrants back at the station. We can come back in an hour or so and start our search with this house, or you could run upstairs and fetch me the letter now. We'll give you a receipt.'

I hesitated. To take the precious letter from Jamie's room and give it to a police officer seemed like a terribly disloyal thing to do.

'I don't think I . . .'

'The letter's important. If it is genuine, it might help exonerate Alexander if it turns out some harm has come to Genevieve. And if it's not, we'll know that somebody round here has been lying.'

I swallowed. 'But . . .'

'We've been keeping an eye on both you and Mr Westwood over the last couple of weeks,' the inspector said calmly. 'Alexander, probably assisted by you, has been disposing of certain personal items belonging to his wife, items that could be construed as evidence.'

Had they been going through our bins?

I thought of the green dress. And the make-up bag, the contraceptive pills that I'd shoved into a bag full of rubbish; the myriad, printed images of Genevieve's face that had gone in the bottom of the recycling box. Inwardly, I groaned. I felt my stomach slide to my feet. I held out my hand to steady myself against the kitchen table. DI Twyford was watching me. He knew I knew what he meant.

'Come on,' he said. 'Let's get the letter.'

All three of us went up to Jamie's room. The curtains were still drawn and the room was as untidy as usual. The hamster rattled in its cage. I crossed the floor to draw back the curtains and the room filled with a milky light. Outside, the trees were swaying madly in the wind and the flock of rooks cawed in the sky.

'Where is it?'

'Over there,' I said. 'On the desk.'

The desk was strewn with toys, clothes and books. The inspector moved them carefully, respectfully.

'Was it in a special place?' he asked.

'Inside the pages of the atlas.'

The inspector had put on gloves. He leafed through the pages of the book. Then he held it up by its spine and shook it. Nothing fell out.

I pulled the duvet up to the top of Jamie's bed and went to the corner to help search. The letter wasn't in the atlas, or on the desk, nor was it underneath it.

'It's been there every time I've tidied the room,' I said.

'He could have moved it somewhere.'

'Under the bed?' I kneeled down to look, but the letter was not amongst the jumble of toys there either.

Over the next thirty minutes or so we searched every inch of the room and, with every second that went by, I felt more frantic. What had Jamie done with the letter? He never moved it. Surely he wouldn't have taken it out of the bedroom.

'Maybe he took it to school,' DI Twyford said.

'No, he didn't, he wouldn't have. And I always check his bag to make sure he's got everything he needs each morning. It wasn't in there.'

'Could it be anywhere else in the house?'

'It could be,' I said, but I knew it wasn't.

'OK,' said the inspector. 'It's gone.' He put his hands in his pockets and jingled his change.

'This isn't a coincidence,' he said. 'Somebody has taken that letter because they didn't want us looking at it too closely.'

I laughed. It was a false, brittle laugh.

'Why would they do that?'

'Because it wasn't written by Genevieve.'

'Why would anyone forge a letter to Jamie?' I asked.

'To reassure the kid. To put his mind at rest. So that he could tell everyone Mummy had left him a note, because everybody knows Genevieve wouldn't have left without saying anything to him.' He paused. 'When did you last see it?'

It had been in the atlas on the desk, with the blue teddy sitting on top of it, a few days earlier.

I glanced around the room. Where was the teddy?

'Sarah?'

I lifted the edge of the duvet, pretended to straighten it: the teddy wasn't beneath it. Had Jamie brought it downstairs the previous evening? I tried to remember.

'A couple of days ago,' I said.

DI Twyford rubbed his cheek with the palm of his hands.

'Something's wrong here,' he said. 'This whole thing stinks.'

'It's a letter,' I said. 'It's not as if anything of value has gone missing.'

He gave a sarcastic laugh. 'Only Genevieve,' he said.

CHAPTER FIFTY-THREE

I was waiting outside the school gate when Jamie came out that afternoon. I stood towards the back of the crowd of women, my hair wrapped in a scarf that also covered my face, but it was all right. The political scandal was still in full swing and no journalists were there. Jamie was amongst a tumble of boys who came noisily out of the classrooms and down the path at 3.15, their shirts hanging out and their coats and scarves flying behind them, skidding on the icy path. When Jamie saw me standing apart from the other parents and carers, he came running over, threw his rucksack at me and carried on with the game. I waited until there was a pause and then beckoned him over.

'Come on,' I said. 'I thought we'd go to the shop and get you a hot pasty as a treat.'

Jamie beamed and swung on my arm, scuffing his shoes on the pavement. The wind was blowing up and the naked, black branches of the trees were bending and dipping.

'Is Dad coming home tonight?'

'Yes, he is.'

'Will he bring me a present?'

'I don't know.'

'Is he definitely coming home tonight?'

'Yes, darling boy.'

We went into the Spar, and Jamie chose a traditional Cornish pasty and a bottle of fizzy lemonade. Midge microwaved the pasty. I bought a coffee in a cardboard cup and we went to the village green, a small triangle of land where the war memorial stood, faded poppy wreaths from November still stacked against its base.

It was bitterly cold. I warmed my fingers around my cup. Jamie sat on the bench beside me and swung his legs. He was holding the pasty in two hands and taking big bites then letting the steam escape through his lips.

I licked my finger to remove a crumb of pastry from his cheek.

'Jamie,' I asked, 'when your mummy went away, she left you a letter, didn't she?' I almost had to shout to be heard over the wind.

He shrugged and took another big bite of the pasty.

'Only I was tidying your bedroom today and I noticed it wasn't on your desk, where it usually is.'

'Sarah, do you support Arsenal or Man U?'

'I'm a Manchester City girl, but, Jamie, this is important. When was the last time you looked at Mummy's letter?'

'Dad said he'd take me to a football match one day.'

'Jamie, listen to me.'

I took the pasty from him and turned his chin gently with my fingers so that he had to look into my face. 'I need to know where the letter is.'

'I don't know where it is,' he said. 'It's gone. I put it on the fire.'

'You put your mummy's letter on the fire?'

'Uh-huh.'

He looked at me with the old expression of defiance. I did not know if he was lying or not; either way, he knew he was risking trouble. I dropped my hand and pulled my coat a little tighter.

'What about your teddy?' I asked. 'Where's your blue teddy?'

'He went on the fire too.'

'Jamie, you know you shouldn't tell lies. You know that's naughty. You wouldn't put blue teddy on the fire, you love him!'

'He's in the fire, he's in the fire, he's in the fire!' Jamie sang. 'And he got burned to pieces, burned to death and he's gone for ever!'

CHAPTER FIFTY-FOUR

Back at Avalon, I phoned the detective to tell him what Jamie had said. He sounded harassed and distracted. He thanked me for my call but didn't prolong the conversation.

I put the phone down and wandered around the house. Maybe there was a perfectly straightforward explanation. Maybe destroying the letter and the toy were Jamie's way of finally accepting that his mother was gone; a child's way of finding closure. But surely children didn't put their teddies on the fire? Not normal children anyway.

I took vegetables out of the larder and started to prepare a cauliflower for dinner, but the knife slipped and sliced my finger. It bled awfully. I made a tourniquet out of a handkerchief and managed to staunch the blood, but it seemed like another bad omen. Jamie was behaving oddly – he was being rude and difficult – and the storm was growing fiercer outside. I sent Jamie upstairs to change while the dinner was cooking and I reinforced the cracked pane of glass in the outer door with Sellotape. I'd just finished that task and was praying for nothing else to go wrong when the power went down, throwing the house into a noisy darkness, draughts whistling through the black like bullets. At first I thought it was a power cut, but when I drew back the curtains I could see the distant lights along the quarry road at the bottom of the hill. The electricity had tripped again. This usually happened when a squirrel gnawed through a cable in the loft. I felt close to tears. Not only were we in the dark but there was another poor dead squirrel in the roof.

I knew where the fuse box was – it was in the cellar – but I'd never had to deal with it on my own before. Always, in the past, Alexander had been there to mend the fuses. I had never even been down to the cellar, partly because I hadn't needed to and mainly because it was cold and dark and cramped and creepy. Now I wished I had carried out a practice run in daylight, while Alexander was with me.

'Sarah! It's dark – where are you?' Jamie wailed from upstairs.

'It's OK, love, it's just the electricity gone again,' I called. 'Don't try to come down, you might fall. Just stay where you are, I'll sort it out.'

I patted my way along the kitchen walls to the cellar door, and found the key on the hook beside it. It was cobwebby; I felt something run across my hand and cried out in alarm and dropped the key.

'Shit!' I said, half-sobbing, shaking my hand. 'Shit, arsehole, shit.'

I dropped to the floor and fingered along the tiles,

fearful of squashing the spider or whatever it was. The key had worked its way half under the skirting board. I managed to free it, then I rose to my feet again. The wind was howling now, making a truly terrible noise, and the windows were rattling in their frames. I found the handle to the cellar door, and held it tight while I worked the key into the hole, and turned it.

'Sarah!' Jamie yelled from a distance.

'OK,' I called. 'It's OK, Jamie, I'm going down into the cellar to fix the fuse. Stay there!'

I pulled the door open. I knew there was a flight of steps in front of me, with the wall to my left. I knew the ceiling was low; there was not room to stand upright. There was a torch on the ledge to my right. Gingerly I reached out and felt through the air, black as pitch, until my hand found the cold plastic casing of the torch. I picked it up carefully and held it close to my chest. I felt for the switch, and when the light went on, its beam sweeping madly around the cellar walls, I was weak with relief.

'Jamie,' I called, 'I've found the torch. I'm going to get the fuse then I'll come upstairs and get you. Stay there, don't move.'

I pointed the torch down the cellar steps.

I hated enclosed spaces almost as much as I hated heights.

My heart was already thumping as if it wanted to escape my chest, and my knees were flimsy.

I turned to make sure there was no way the door could close behind me. It was wide open, pushed back as far as it would go. I tested it with my hand. It was all right. It was not sprung. It would not move by itself.

Slowly, I put one foot on the first step.

It was a concrete step. It was icy cold but solid as rock beneath my socked foot. I flashed the torch down into the cellar and in the dark I saw cardboard boxes, an old rucksack, a broken chair, a couple of suitcases: the usual junk. I took another step down; and another.

The cellar roof was lower than I'd expected; there was only about four feet between the floor and the ceiling, and the underground room was airless: what oxygen there was tasted of fungus and soil. I crouched in the space and let the torch swing its beam. It was a large area, pipes and cladding crawling over the walls. I sucked my bottom lip and tried to calm my heart and suppress my imagination. I had to concentrate on the job in hand. I found the fuse box with the torch and crept forward.

When I reached the wall, feeling panicky in the low space, I balanced the torch on a cardboard box, within easy reach. The beam of light now ran parallel with the fusebox wall, pointing to where the logs for the fire were stacked. Because the torch was casting its beam at such a strange angle, I could see there was an empty space behind the log stack. A passage? Or an alcove? I could have been into the cellar a thousand times and never realized it was there.

Why had Alexander stacked the logs in front of the alcove, blocking it off, when he could have put them anywhere? What were they hiding?

I picked up the torch and hobbled, hunchbacked, over to the wood stack.

By holding the torch at an angle, I could direct the light behind the logs. Behind was an opening about five feet square. At its base was a large wooden lid the size of a manhole cover.

Carefully, breathing hard, I moved a few of the top logs so I could get a better look. They were heavy and awkward and scratched at my skin but I didn't stop. I knew Jamie was in the house alone and scared, but I had to know what this was and why Alexander had kept it hidden.

When I had made space for my arm to fit through, I reached over and tugged at the rope handle looped through an iron ring hammered into the wooden lid. I couldn't shift it with one hand. So I put the torch down carefully, on the floor beside my foot, and, using both hands, I managed to work the lid free. I moved it enough to be able to see down inside the hole that it had covered. I picked up the torch and directed it into the area beneath the lid. A narrow hole had been chiselled out of the stone beneath the house. It seemed to go on down for some distance.

I wriggled my head and shoulders through the gap in the logs to get a better look. Now, I could direct the light downwards, and I realized that what I was looking into was a well. It must have been dug out beneath the house centuries ago. No doubt it had been walled in behind the wood stack so there was no danger of Jamie ever finding it and falling in.

I smiled to myself, feeling silly. I didn't know what I'd been expecting to find, but I was giddy with relief. The hole probably didn't even go down that far. I leaned over as far as I could and pointed the torch so the light went vertically down the well. The distance between the upper rim and the water was probably about seven feet, and the well's diameter was big enough for an old-fashioned pail, nothing larger than that.

But there was something in the well, something smooth and modern and shiny. It took me a moment or two to recognize what it was. It was stuck between the wall and the well-bottom at an awkward angle, as if it had been dropped; it was something that shouldn't have been there.

I could distinctly see the logo of an apple with a bite missing on the shiny white surface of the exposed part. It was an Apple MacBook.

It had to be Genevieve's.

'Oh Christ,' I muttered under my breath. 'Oh Jesus Christ, no!'

There was only one possible explanation: Alexander had hidden the computer in the well, and then he'd hidden the well. It couldn't have been anyone else.

I backed away, put down the torch and began piling up the logs I'd removed. Alexander had some kind of system, but I had trouble making them fit and balance; it didn't matter, I told myself: just put them back. I was sobbing with fear and frustration as I rammed them on top of each other, swearing and cursing under my breath like a madwoman. When I'd more or less replaced them, something on the shelf at the edge of the stack caught my eye. It was a small ceramic pot full of screws and nails and bolts. Underneath the pot was a pad of pale-blue writing paper.

My hands trembled as I hobbled across the cellar, moved the pot and picked up the pad. It was the same paper that had been used for Genevieve's letter to Jamie, with the same daisy pattern around the edge. Several sheets were missing, but on the top piece of paper were doodles and drawings, practice drawings for the cartoon of Jamie holding blue teddy.

I licked my lips to moisten my mouth. My knees felt very weak. I flicked over the paper to the next page and I realized the truth.

On the page was writing. It started off in the rounded feminine hand that I'd come to recognize as Genevieve's and deteriorated into Alexander's untidy scrawl. He had scribbled over the lettering, but it was quite clearly his.

Alexander was dyslexic. He found handwriting difficult. He had practised a dozen times to make the letter plausible. There was no doubt at all: it was Alexander who had composed and written Genevieve's goodbye letter to her son.

From way away, up in the house, I heard Jamie's terrified screaming. I felt as if I'd been in the cellar for hours, but it couldn't have been more than a few minutes – still too long to leave a seven-year-old alone in the dark. I put the pad back and reached for the pot, but in my haste I knocked it over. Nuts and bolts scattered and bounced all over the cellar floor and the pot shattered.

'Shit, shit . . .'

I fumbled and scrabbled, but the little pieces of metal had rolled away into the dark. Gasping with panic and frustration, treading on bits of china, I picked up what I could.

'Sarah!' Jamie screamed. He was closer; he must have made his way downstairs in the dark. He mustn't come into the cellar.

I told myself to calm down. I took a breath and held it.

Lights first, I told myself. Sort out the lights then you can go to Jamie and come back to tidy the mess later.

Still clutching the torch, I opened the fuse box, but I didn't know what to do. The switches were the old-fashioned slot-in ones. They weren't numbered or named, and they all looked exactly the same. I didn't know which had tripped. I didn't know what to look for. My fingers moved over the switches, searching for the one I needed.

'Please,' I said again. 'Oh please God, help me . . .'

And then the cellar door crashed shut. There was a rush of air so strong it nearly knocked me off my feet and I dropped the torch. I heard the crack of the casing and the rattling of the batteries as they spilled across the floor. The dark was relentless. I could see nothing. I scrabbled for the steps but was disoriented. I didn't know which direction I was facing. Cold sweat chilled my skin and I fought for breath; panic engulfed me like a wave. I tried to scream but no noise came. It was a waking nightmare, a terror, a kind of death.

The last thing I was aware of was a pain on the top of my head so intense that it was almost divine.

CHAPTER FIFTY-FIVE

I drifted in and out of consciousness.

When I came round properly, I was lying on the settee in the living room. A log fire was crackling in the grate and the electricity was back on. I was reclining on a nest of pillows, covered over with my own duvet. I felt warm and sleepy and comfortable, and it was only when I tried to move that the pain in my head reminded me what had happened. I put a hand to my face. My nose and upper lip were terribly sore.

'Jamie?' I called. 'Jamie?'

'Hey you!'

Alexander appeared beside me. The firelight cast shadows behind him, devilish, frightening, spiky figures that danced on the walls. His face was strangely shadowed by the firelight too. I retreated a little into the duvet.

Alexander smiled and leaned over, smoothed my forehead. His fingers were cool and dry.

'You OK?'

'Yes.'

'Headache?'

'Mmm.'

'You knocked yourself out, you idiot!'

I curled and withdrew into myself.

'You banged your head on the floor joist in the cellar and then you hit your face on the shelf as you went down. You're going to have a shiner in the morning.'

'I was trying to fix the fuse.'

'I know.'

'The door slammed shut.'

'It must have been the draught from when I opened the outside door. I'm sorry it made you jump, but it was lucky I got there when I did. Jamie was in a right old state.'

'Is he OK now?'

'He's fine. In bed fast asleep.'

I felt the top of my head tentatively with my finger-tips. There was a huge egg. It was very sore.

'Did it bleed?'

Alexander shook his head.

'I think you'll survive.' He had a glass in his hand. He was drinking beer. 'Do you want a drink? Glass of water?'

'Tea,' I said. 'Please. I'm dying for a cup of tea.'

I had to think. I needed time to think. I wanted Alexander to go away and leave me alone so that I could remember what had happened.

The storm was still raging outside. Every now and then the flames in the grate shrank and cowered beneath the onslaught of rain being blown down the chimney. Any movement was painful and awkward. It wasn't just my head and face; my neck ached terribly too.

I tried to remember.

Had the door blown shut, or had somebody slammed it?

Had I banged my head, or did somebody hit me?

Had Alexander seen the cellar door open, come down the steps and found me reading his practice letters to Jamie by torchlight? Had he hit me in anger, or desperation?

No, of course he hadn't. When the door slammed and I panicked, I'd forgotten how low the ceiling was and stood up quickly. That was all. I'd knocked myself out.

Alexander came back into the room with a glass of water and two tablets in the palm of his hand.

'Take these,' he said. 'They'll help with the pain. I've put the kettle on.'

I tried to remember what they tell you in Accident and Emergency about head injury but I couldn't recall the exact advice. Something about being sick, losing consciousness . . .

'I think I should see a doctor,' I said.

'It would be madness to go out in this weather,' Alexander said. 'There are trees down and flash floods all over the place. The Glastonbury road's under two feet of water. I wouldn't have got back at all if it weren't for the Land Rover.'

'But I must have been unconscious for a while.'

'It wasn't that long,' Alexander said. 'Only a few moments. You walked out of the cellar on your own two feet. We were talking. Don't you remember?'

'No.'

'You told me you were very tired so I made up the bed on the settee so you could have a sleep.'

I was thinking that was impossible. I had no memory of any conversation at all.

'What else did I say?'

'Not much. You were a bit confused.'

He smiled at me fondly, like a parent might smile at a sick child.

'I think mainly you just need a good, long rest,' said Alexander.

'But my head . . .'

'You're going to be fine. I'm going to watch over you tonight to make sure.'

He leaned down and kissed me very gently, just above my left eye.

'Ow,' I said.

'Is that sore? You poor thing. Rest now. Nothing's going to happen to you. I'm going to watch you like a hawk.'

CHAPTER FIFTY-SIX

Alexander had been right. I was tired to my bones, but still I had trouble sleeping that night. I drifted off from time to time and, whenever I awoke, he was there beside me, holding on to me. When I tried to go to the bathroom for a glass of water, he sat up at once and insisted on fetching it for me.

'Don't move,' he said. 'Stay there and let me look after you properly for a change.'

I was resigned to the situation. I had no means of getting away from Avalon, even if that was what I wanted to do, and it wasn't, or at least I didn't think it was. I was so confused. I did not know what was right and what was wrong any longer, or what was true and what was a lie. I wanted to keep faith in Alexander. I had waited for months for him to tell me that he would look after me and that he would let nothing come between us, and now he'd said those words and they weren't making me happy.

I lay in bed, facing the window with my eyes closed. Rain lashed against the pane like thousands of tiny fists knocking on the glass, and then the wind changed direction for a while and all I could hear was the howling in the eaves. I hoped none of the trees would come down on to the house. I imagined huge branches tearing into the fabric of Avalon, ripping it apart and bringing everything pounding to the ground, the three of us crushed inside like berries. Several times I heard the awful grating of a tile coming loose from the roof and then the crash as it fell to the ground. Water would be tumbling over itself to find a way through the gaps left behind. We would lose the power again. The house would smell of wet wood, plaster and carpet in the morning and we'd have to go round finding the leaks and putting pans and buckets beneath them. I thought of all the practical things that would need to be done and that stopped me thinking about what I'd found in the cellar.

When I couldn't put off thinking about Genevieve's laptop any longer, I asked myself if anything had changed by my finding it. Nothing, was the answer. It was one more hidden thing, one more secret, that was all.

The only new fact I could be certain of was that Alexander *had* written the letter that was purportedly from Genevieve, to convince Jamie that his mummy was fine and was thinking of him. His original motivation could only have been to reassure and console Jamie when his mother left. But if Genevieve had left voluntarily, why hadn't she written to Jamie herself? Wouldn't she have at least talked to him about her plans? Everyone agreed that she was devoted to the child; it made no sense her going away and leaving him without a word.

I took a mental step back. I was trying to think logically. I didn't know why Genevieve hadn't left a letter of her own for Jamie. I did know that Alexander had made sure I found and read his letter to convince me he was telling the truth. His plan had worked. I had believed it was conclusive evidence that Genevieve had left her home and her life because that was what she wanted to do and that she intended, at some point, to return. Now I knew that wasn't the case. And now the police were closing in, preparing to search Avalon. Now that they wanted to see the letter, the letter was gone.

Of course it was. If the police found it they would know Alexander had written it and they would wonder what other, greater deceptions he may have carried out.

Why had Alexander kept the writing pad, I wondered. Had he intended to send further letters from Genevieve?

My head hurt inside and out; it was full to bursting with too many thoughts and too many questions.

Outside, the storm raged and banged and, beside me, Alexander breathed deeply and peacefully, his arm around my waist, holding me tight to him so that my back was hot with the heat he emitted from his front. I imagined how the well in the cellar would fill up as the new surface water seeped its way down through the rock. I wondered if the laptop would rise with the water or if it would stay at the bottom of the well. It might have been down there for months. The water would have killed it. Laurie once comprehensively fucked up a laptop by spilling a can of Vimto over the keyboard.

Genevieve's computer's memory would have been destroyed long ago. Whatever secrets it held would stay secret and whoever put it in the well must have known that.

The storm blew itself out overnight and I opened my eyes to a sunny December day. Beyond the window pane, clouds floated across an optimistic blue sky. The rooks wheeled and cawed and danced. Over the sound of the wind and the birds, I heard the low wailing of the quarry siren. It sounded like an animal desperate, in pain. The dinosaurs were loose again, I thought; running rampage through the valley. Jamie never tired of inventing bad deeds for the dinosaurs to do. One day, I'd told him, we'd put the stories into a book. We'd already made a start on the illustrations. I smiled at the thought and then I heard a noise behind me and turned to see Alexander opening the bedroom door with his elbow and putting a tray of coffee, toast and orange juice on the chest of drawers.

'Hello, you,' he said, leaning down to kiss me. My neck was stiff and my head was sore but I reached up to receive his lips. He kissed me on the side of my face that wasn't hurt.

Alexander held my chin in his hand and examined my injuries. He had been right about my eye: I could barely see out of it, it was so swollen. I could feel that my lip was huge too, and there was blood on the pillow.

'You look a bit of a mess,' he said. 'I'd hate to see the other fella.'

'Ha ha.'

'You had me worried last night, Sarah. You weren't yourself at all.'

'Of course I wasn't. I'd banged my head.'

'It wasn't just that. Did something happen while I was away?'

'Nothing much,' I said.

He sat beside me and passed me my coffee.

'Don't you want to know how I got on in Fowey?'

'Fowey . . .' I said, and the word sounded strange and unfamiliar. The last time we'd talked about Fowey had been in a different life, another era. 'Yes, of course. How was it?'

'It's perfect,' he said. 'Just a small yard; the rent's cheap. I don't think there'd be a huge amount of business locally, but it's close to the main road with good access to the motorway.'

'Oh, good,' I said.

'And there are loads of places to rent to live in, nice places. You'd love it, Sarah. You could do your art. We could live quietly there. We'd be safe.'

'That's great.'

'I spoke to a few people. I had a look at a flat in the town centre. It's furnished, a bit shabby, but the views are lovely and it's cosy, and we could manage there, for a while. Until we found something better, at least. I thought maybe we could go straight after Christmas – Boxing Day even. We'll be all right until then, won't we? That's only a few days away. The landlord's desperate to have it occupied. Sarah?'

'Mmm?'

Alexander pushed back my hair and held my

undamaged cheek in his rough hand. He looked at me intently. I had to return his gaze. I noticed how dark his eyes were and their intensity.

I was certain he could see into my doubting soul. I blinked.

'You would tell me if something was wrong?'

I found a smile from somewhere.

'Of course I would.'

I must have sounded convincing because he exhaled and leaned down to kiss my forehead.

'You're lovely,' he said. 'You're so good for me.'

But I'm not Genevieve, I thought. You say I'm lovely, but you have never said that you love me. You say you trust me but you keep your secrets from me. I am so lost now that I don't know which way to turn.

I thought maybe I had been wrong all the time about Alexander. Maybe I had been out of my mind when I met him in Sicily. I'd so wanted a hero to take me away from Laurie and Manchester and all the things that had gone wrong, maybe I'd just invented one and turned Alexander into that person.

But it had felt so real. It had all felt so right. And all along, right up until I'd seen the laptop in the well, I had believed Alexander. I was trying so hard to believe in him now.

I raised my eyes to look at him and then the door swung back and Jamie ran into the room in his pyjamas and bounced up on to the bed. The movement jarred and hurt my face but I could not help but smile and relax. At least my feelings for Jamie were unambiguous.

'Are you better now?' he asked me, putting his face

very close to mine and staring at me with his father's intensity but with paler, blue eyes. I smelled that honey and hay smell of newly woken child.

I put my arm around him and pulled him close. He elbowed his way into my side, fidgeted under the covers.

'I'm absolutely fine.'

'Your eye looks like yuk and there's a big scab here.' He pointed to the space between his nose and his top lip.

'Thanks, Jamie.'

'That's all right. Daddy promised we'd get the Christmas tree today. You did, didn't you? You said it's time to do the decorations!'

Alexander looked at his wrist. He wasn't wearing a watch.

'You know what?' he said to me. 'The boy's right!'

'Brilliant,' I said.

Jamie regarded me suspiciously.

'Don't you *want* to put up the tree, Sarah?'

I smiled. 'Yes, yes, of course I do.'

'Daddy said I can choose it *and* help cut it down.'

'Too right,' said Alexander, and Jamie used my thighs as a springboard to launch himself at Alexander, who hugged the child roughly, half-play-fighting with him. As the mattress bounced, my coffee slopped out of the cup and over the edge of the saucer, staining the coverlet pale brown. I didn't resist, I let the stain take its course while I rested back against the pillows and watched the father and his son.

While Jamie was downstairs eating breakfast, I went back upstairs and opened the bathroom door.

Alexander was standing at the basin clipping his beard, wearing just a towel around his waist.

'Hi,' he said, watching me through the mirror. My face looked awful, like I really had been in a fight.

I came up behind him, flicked both parts of the lavatory seat down and sat on it.

'The police came round yesterday,' I said quietly. 'They're going to start searching the area around Burrington Stoke.'

There was a pause, because we knew what they would be searching for.

'It was bound to happen sooner or later,' Alexander said.

'It seems horrible timing what with Christmas and everything but . . .'

'What?'

He moved the shaver carefully around his neck, holding the skin taut with his free hand.

'Well, they're going to search Avalon too.'

Alexander switched off the shaver and nodded.

'I suppose that's inevitable.'

'The thing is, I think they're watching us. I think they've been looking at the stuff we've thrown away and . . .'

'They wouldn't be doing their job if they weren't.'

'No, but I'm worried there might still be things here, in the house, I mean, that it might be better if they didn't find. You know.'

Alexander smiled at me.

'You worry too much,' he said.

This time I nodded. I held my wrists between my

knees. I was feeling quietly desperate. If Alexander was perturbed by the news, he wasn't showing it. He turned on the hot tap and rubbed soap between the palms of his hands, working up a lather.

'Did they say when they'd be coming?' he asked casually.

'I can't remember exactly. Soon. Maybe not today though. Maybe not for a few days.'

'It'll be OK, Sarah. We'll probably have left by the time they get round to Avalon.'

'You don't think they'll want to start here? It was the last place Genevieve . . . The last place we know she was.'

'It's possible. But there's no point worrying about it until it happens. Pass me the towel, would you? You never know, there might be some new development that'll make them change their plans.'

I could not understand why Alexander was so relaxed when we were having such a terrible conversation. Didn't he realize the implications?

He turned round and kissed the top of my head.

'Don't look so worried,' he whispered. 'It might never happen.'

After breakfast, Alexander went up to the attic and fetched down the Christmas decorations. He was in such an upbeat mood that it was difficult not to be infected. I had never heard him whistle before but that's what he did as he spread the boxes and bags out on the living-room floor. There were hundreds of lights and ornaments and baubles, all meticulously wrapped in tissue paper. It made me feel a little sad and a little jealous to know that the last hand that had touched the decorations had been Genevieve's. Jamie didn't make the connection; he was far too excited. As I uncovered each new treasure, he exclaimed in delight – 'Oh, the Santa in the sledge! The bird with the real feathers! The jingle bells – listen, they really chime!' He ran in and out of the living room like a whirlwind, taking his favourite Christmas ornaments up to his bedroom and distributing the rest where he thought they ought to be.

I had a tiny pang of homesickness. This would have been my baby's first Christmas. I had looked forward to it so much. The previous year, I had been pregnant during the holiday. The foetus was four months old and I had already begun to feel him kick. At four months he was six inches long, almost perfectly formed, and the soul had been breathed into him, according to Rosita. Laurie and I, flushed with the imminence of parenthood, shopped that year with different priorities. For my Christmas present, Laurie bought me and the baby a Mamas and Papas Pramette that cost as much, Laurie told me, as a small family saloon. My mother shook her head, partly at the extravagance, but mainly at our foolishness. She said we were tempting fate. She said we shouldn't buy anything until at least the seventh month. We giggled about her primitive superstitions behind her back, bought more decorations and spoke of how they would become our child's heritage. I wondered if Laurie was unpacking those carefully chosen things now. I wondered if he was thinking of what might have been.

I had to be strict with myself to put those thoughts from my mind, and then I joined in with Jamie, helping him thread differently coloured baubles on to ribbons to hang over the fireplace in the dining room and making a big fuss of the handmade glitter and cotton-wool snowmen he'd made at school. I loved being with Jamie and doing these enjoyable jobs with him, but still I felt as if I were acting. Together we unravelled the fairy lights and plugged them in to make sure they all worked. Then, with the tangle of wires and tiny coloured bulbs heaped up and twinkling on the carpet, we moved back the furniture to clear a space in the corner of the living room for the tree.

'That's where it always goes,' Jamie said solemnly. 'Mummy says it's the best place.'

He looked up at me in surprise, realizing what he had said and that he was without his mother at Christmastime.

'She's right,' I said. I squeezed Jamie's shoulder. He had put his thumb in his mouth and was staring at the dusty space on the carpet.

'Come on, Jamie!' Alexander called. 'I need you to help me put the lights up outside.'

I made sure Jamie was wrapped up warm enough to go outside, then, while he and Alexander attended to their task, I filled the vegetable bowl with water, peeled some potatoes and cut them into chips. I was frying mushrooms to go in an omelette when Alexander opened the door, letting in a rush of cold air. Beyond, in the garden, I could hear Jamie loudly singing: *Jingle bells, Batman smells . . .*

Alexander was wearing his big boots, a jacket, gloves, and in his hand was an axe.

'Jamie and I are going up to the farm to cut down a Christmas tree,' he said.

Robin's flown away . . .

'Are you coming?'

I shook my head. Alexander weighed the axe-head in the palm of his right hand.

Uncle Billy lost his willy . . .

'I need to get lunch on.'

'OK.'

On the M4 motorway.

Still, he paused.

'Are you all right?' he asked.

'Please stop asking me. I told you there's nothing wrong. I've just got a terrible headache is all. And my face looks like shit.'

Jingle drums . . .

Alexander frowned. 'You've been distant. You've had a look in your eyes like you'd rather be somewhere else.'

Batman bums . . .

'Oh, for goodness' sake, where's Jamie got that from?' I asked. 'He shouldn't be using that kind of language.'

'It's never bothered you before. Sarah, what is it?'

'For the thousandth time, I had a bang on the head!'

'No,' he said. 'It's not that.'

Robin did a smelly poo.

'And the police came. I've been worrying about the search – I mean, about what they might find. I've had a horrible couple of days. Stop fussing,' I said. I turned back to the counter, picked up a chilli and began to slice it.

Mr Whippy's got a stiffy . . .

'Go and fetch the tree,' I said in a light voice. 'I'll get everything ready here. What do you normally put it in? A bucket?'

'There's a stand somewhere,' said Alexander. 'It's biggish, red, it's got three legs, made of wrought iron. I haven't seen it since last year.'

And the penguin's got one too.

'I'll have a look,' I said.

Alexander bounced the head of the axe up and down in his gloved hand. He pulled a comedy face.

'Do me a favour, Sarah – if you come across anything incriminating, perhaps you could find a really good place to hide it.'

'Ha ha,' I said. 'How about down the well?'

There was a pause between us. A heartbeat. Jamie appeared behind his father, his eyes bright, wanting to know without asking if we'd heard his song and if we were amused or annoyed. For once, Alexander and I took no notice.

'What do you mean?' Alexander asked.

'I looked down the well yesterday. I saw what's down there.'

'The well in the cellar? You can't have done.'

'I did.'

'Sarah, the cover's padlocked, and I don't know where Genevieve kept the key. It hasn't been opened in years.'

I shook my head.

'I moved the cover myself.'

'That's impossible.' Alexander frowned. 'It must have

been the knock on the head that's confused you. There's no way you could have moved it.'

I swallowed and looked at my fingers. I felt tearful. I *knew* what I'd seen. Why was he lying to me? Was he trying to make me feel as if I was losing my mind?

'Hey,' said Alexander. 'Come on, it's dark down there, creepy; it's easy to think you've seen something that isn't there.'

He stepped forward and kissed my cheek.

'You will be here when we come back, won't you?' he asked me.

'Of course,' I said. 'Where else would I be?'

As soon as the Land Rover had pulled out of the drive, I unlocked the cellar door, propped it open with a box of ready-to-recycle crockery and then, to be doubly sure, taped over the latch so it could not possibly close by itself. I switched on the light, picked up the torch, just in case I should need it, and went down the concrete steps for the second time.

The cellar wasn't nearly so oppressive in daytime. A naked bulb at the foot of the staircase illuminated the area brightly. As well as that, light from the door filtered down, and daylight also shone around the edges of a hatch that I hadn't noticed in the dark. It obviously opened to allow wood, coal or other bulky essentials to be delivered directly to the cellar. The floor was damp, though, and slippery in places. Shiny slug and snail trails criss-crossed the walls like graffiti.

I looked around to orientate myself. There was the fuse box on the far wall and beneath it was the cardboard box where I'd rested the torch the previous evening. I followed the line of the wall over to the wood pile and realized at once that something was different. The stack was the wrong shape. The logs I'd moved then tried to replace had tumbled down in the night so there was a V-shaped gap in the stack. The alcove and the well cover were entirely visible. I looked over the logs down on to the well lid. Metal plates had been bolted on to either side of it, and these were set into the floor. The bolts were huge. They were solid. The metal plates were held together at the centre of the cover with a large, closed padlock.

Alexander must have put the bolts and the padlock there in the night, I decided. But how could he have done that without my noticing? I was certain he had been with me the whole time. I'd slept so fitfully, and every time I'd woken he'd been there, and it would have taken ages to move all the wood to get the access he would have needed. The storm had been raging and it was possible he could have drilled into the wood, and the floor, without me hearing but . . . How could he have?

Was I just looking at it from a different angle? Had the dark been playing tricks on my eyes when the lights went out the previous evening? Maybe the bolts had worked themselves loose or something. Maybe they'd rusted and rotted away and that was how I'd managed to lift the cover. Crouching, and taking care not to knock my head, I tugged at the rope handle.

The cover wouldn't budge.

My heart began to race. Had I imagined the whole scenario?

Alexander had told me I was obsessed with Genevieve, and maybe he was right. Perhaps my subconscious had given me what I wanted, showing me a place where the laptop, which I'd been looking for for weeks, could have been hidden?

Or maybe my mind wasn't quite right. I knew that sometimes what was in my head wasn't quite how things were outside it.

After the baby was stillborn, I had remembered some events wrongly, muddling sequences and recalling thoughts as facts and imagined conversations as having taken place. The doctors told me that my confusion wasn't unusual. It was one of the symptoms people experience when they've had a bad shock. It didn't mean I was losing my mind; quite the opposite, it showed that my mind was trying to find a way to manage. I'd been so tied up in my feelings, and my sense of loss, it had been so consuming that I'd misinterpreted some of what real life was all about. Was that happening to me now?

Only, I was *so* certain of what I'd seen.

The lump on the back of my head was real. I reached up to touch it. My face had been smashed by the fall. That was real too. I stared down at the well cover.

It was obvious that the only way to open the well would be to take off the padlock that held the plates together.

I went back up the cellar steps, switched off the light, put the torch in its place and locked the door behind me. Then I called May. I desperately wanted to talk to her, but there was no answer on her landline or her mobile phone. Neil's mobile went straight to answerphone too. I left messages asking them to call me, made myself a coffee and sat at the kitchen table, jiggling my legs and waiting to hear their voices. I wanted to hear familiar, normal people talking to me as if the world was a happy, straightforward place.

I wanted to feel like myself again, because I was so out of sorts now, so confused.

The phone didn't ring.

They were probably out shopping. May always left her Christmas shopping until the last week; she said it put her in the festive spirit. They'd call when they returned.

I remembered the Christmas-tree stand. I'd promised I'd find it.

I knew it wasn't in the house, and if it had been in the cellar I would have noticed it. I gazed out towards the dilapidated outbuildings. If I were looking for a place to store a largish item that I wouldn't need for eleven and a half months, that's where I would put it – out of the way.

I put on my boots and went outside. The winter sky was reflected in the puddles on the drive. Twigs and branches had been torn from trees during the night and littered the garden and the orchard and the drive. I walked around them, followed by a tiny robin. All the ramshackle barns and stables were open to the elements except the largest and oldest, at the bottom of the drive. I checked inside the trailer, peered through the overgrown ivy and brambles into the hay store, but I knew the Christmas-tree stand wasn't there. If I had been

Genevieve, I'd have put it in the big barn, where it would be protected from the weather. I paused beside its big old wooden door, the green paint peeling from its surface in wide curls revealing older, white-grey paint beneath.

I had never been inside the barn. I'd had no need to go there. I hesitated. Then I took a deep breath, pulled back the heavy iron bolt and the door swung open of its own accord.

The interior was not pitch dark. There were holes in the roof and walls which the birds and bats used for access, and patches of light fell in random places. An old tractor filled most of the space, and around and behind it were various pieces of ancient agricultural equipment and sacks of animal feed splitting at the seams, spilling their contents on to the floor.

There was a smell of damp, of bird-shit and of rodents. Dirty cobwebs billowed from the rafters.

I took a step forward. To the side of the tractor was an old fridge, and behind that was a dusty old wardrobe, the mirrors still on its door. There were piles of newspapers, their edges chewed to shreds for mice bedding. Behind, I could see more modern junk. I took a deep breath of clean, outside air and squeezed through the gap between the tractor and the furniture.

The barn went back a long way. Behind the tractor were all manner of abandoned items: bits of carpets, a roll of chicken wire, fence posts, plastic buckets. Sticking out from amongst the clutter was the shiny, ornate, red metal leg of what could only be the Christmas-tree stand.

I felt a rush of relief. I leaned down and pulled at the leg. The stand was stuck beneath a pile of things that had been thrown on top of it. I put my back against the wardrobe door and my feet against the huge rear tyre of the tractor, braced myself and tugged again. It took several goes, but gradually the stand became looser and freed itself. The release was so unexpected that I was pressed back against the wardrobe and I felt the lock snap as the door caved in behind my back. I lifted the stand over the tractor's enormous hubcap and, as I squeezed myself back towards the open barn door, the wardrobe door silently opened.

I turned to push it shut but something caught my eye.

Inside was a bag. A pretty, pale-blue and brown, Animal-brand travelling bag.

I knew what it was – there was only one thing it could be and only one person to whom it could have belonged.

It was Genevieve's.

I didn't stop to think what I was doing.

I tugged it out of the wardrobe, hauled it over the tractor's bonnet and into the daylight. I kicked the Christmas-tree stand aside, knelt down and pulled open the zip on the bag.

The clothes inside had been neatly packed, not in haste, but with thought. In one of the side pockets, toothpaste, shampoo, conditioner and various cosmetic creams had been wrapped in a towel that still smelled of washing powder. There was a pouch of jewellery.

In the front pocket was a purse full of euros and a folded piece of paper that, when I opened it, had the details of a flight scrawled on it. The flight booked was to Sicily. It was a 9 p.m. flight from Heathrow and the date was 24 July. The day Genevieve had disappeared.

The only other item in the pocket was a passport. I picked it up and opened it.

It was hers.

'Oh sweet Jesus Christ,' I whispered. 'Oh God!' There was no doubt then.

Genevieve had not gone away. She had never left. And that being the case, she must still be here, somewhere.

A car drove past on the lane beyond and I jumped. Alexander would be back soon, he'd be back any minute. If he came up the drive and saw me there, with Genevieve's bag . . .

I picked up the bag and its contents, threw them back into the barn and pushed the door shut. It wouldn't latch. I tried to lift it high enough for me to push the bolt back into its collar, but it was too heavy. Sobbing, I searched for a stone to hold it in place, found one, kicked it to make it stay, and then I ran back to the house. I didn't have a plan, I just wanted to find my phone so I could get out of Avalon and, when I was somewhere else, I'd call for help. I didn't know who I'd call but . . .

No, I couldn't do that. I couldn't leave without Jamie.

Either way, I needed the phone. I searched frantically, pulling open drawers, tipping piles of paper on to the floor and going through the pockets on the coats hung in the hall, but it was nowhere. Maybe I'd dropped it in the barn. Breathless with fear and frustration, I called

May again from the landline. I tried both numbers and, both times, it went through to answerphone. The only other number I could remember off the top of my head was Claudia's. I dialled and was so relieved when Petra answered that I could hardly speak.

'Petra, it's me, Sarah. Listen, I need to speak to your mummy now, it's urgent. I . . .'

'She can't talk,' Petra said, and despite my own distress I could hear the anxiety in her voice.

I held my breath to try to stop the panicked breathing and asked as calmly as I could: 'What's the matter, honey?'

'Mummy has to go to Grandma's house and . . .'

I heard Allegra's voice in the background and Petra must have put her hand over the receiver because everything went muffled for a while and then I heard a wail from one of the girls.

'Hello?' I called. 'Petra, are you all right? Petra?'

She dropped the receiver and I heard frantic voices and, at the very point when I was about to cut off the call and dial 999, Bill picked up the phone and said: 'Hi, Sarah.'

'What's the matter?' I cried. 'What's going on?'

'Where are you?' Bill asked.

'At Avalon.'

'What about Alexander and Jamie?'

'They've gone to get a Christmas tree.'

I heard another muffled conversation, Claudia's voice, strained and more highly pitched than normal, and then a bustle of activity, then the slam of a door. Bill came back on the phone.

'Sarah, I'm going to come and pick you up. Wait outside for me.'

'Why? What's happened? Has there been an accident?'

Bill sighed. I could imagine him taking off his spectacles and rubbing the bridge of his nose.

'The police searched the old quarry this morning,' he said, and he sounded as if he had the weight of the world on his shoulders.

'And . . . ?' I asked in a voice so quiet it was barely even a whisper.

'They found a body.'

CHAPTER FIFTY-SEVEN

I didn't stop to pack a case. I picked up my coat and ran out of the door. I heard the garden gate bang shut behind me as I ran down the puddled drive.

I reached the barn and saw, to my horror, that its door had swung open again. Genevieve's clothes had come out of the bag where I had thrown it and were weirdly stuck to the front of the tractor; it looked as if there had been a road accident. As I heaved my shoulder against the door, I heard the sound of tyres on the drive.

Thank God, I thought, pushing the door with both hands; it was so heavy, it resisted and the car came into view, and it was not the Volvo or Bill's big off-roader but the Land Rover, spattered in mud up to its windows with the back of a Christmas tree jutting out from its tailgate.

Alexander tooted the horn and, from the passenger seat, Jamie waved frantically through the window. I tried to put a smile on my face but I honestly couldn't remember how to do it. Time slowed until there were several seconds between every heartbeat. The muscles in my face were retracting cautiously; I closed my eyes for a moment and felt the top lashes spring as they met the lower ones.

'Hi,' Alexander said, leaning out of the window. 'What are you doing?'

He was smiling but there was concern in his eyes. I kept one hand on the door, holding it shut, blocking the inside of the barn from his view.

'I found the Christmas-tree stand,' I said, and my voice was like a record played at the wrong speed, like a sound effect in a horror film. I pointed at the object with the toe of my boot.

'We got a great big tree, Sarah!' Jamie called. 'And I helped put it in the tube to get wrapped.'

'What's the matter?' Alexander asked. He turned off the engine of the Land Rover.

'Nothing.'

The car door opened and Alexander stepped down. His face was pale.

'Are you all right? What's happened?'

'Nothing.'

The barn door was heavy behind my back. He took a step towards me. I pressed back against the door. Dry old paint crackled and crumbled to dust behind my fingers.

'Come on, Dad, I want to put the tree inside!' Jamie called. He was struggling to unfasten his seatbelt. Stay in the car, Jamie, I thought. Please, please, please stay in the car.

'Sarah?'

Alexander stood in front of me.

Now the smile that wouldn't come before twanged on to my mouth like the smile of a puppet.

'Why don't you go in and put the kettle on?' I said in a voice that had speeded up so far as to sound like it belonged to a cartoon character. I felt myself sway on my feet. I mustn't faint, I couldn't afford to faint now.

'Let me see,' he said in a quiet voice.

I shook my head. 'No.'

He put one hand on the barn door, above my head.

I didn't have a plan but, as he did this, I ducked under his arm, ran round him and jumped into the driver's seat of the Land Rover. Alexander, confused, turned from the door, but I was too quick. I started the engine and, sliding forward in the seat to reach the pedals, put the vehicle into reverse.

'What are you doing, Sarah?' Jamie asked. He was still strapped into the passenger seat. He did not look at all worried, just a little confused. The gear grated.

'We're going . . .'

'Where?'

'I don't know.'

I put the gear stick back into neutral and tried again.

'But Sarah, we have to put the Christmas tree up!' Jamie tried to open his door.

'No, Jamie, don't!' I leaned over to grab his hand.

'What are you *doing*?'

Alexander had let the barn door swing open but had not looked inside. He was walking down the drive towards us as I fought the pedals, trying to coordinate the gear and the clutch and the accelerator. His hands were at his sides, the palms turned up like the hands of Jesus in those pictures where he is beseeching God. Behind him was the tractor, strewn with Genevieve's clothes and her upturned bag. He put one hand on the Land Rover's bonnet.

'Sarah . . .?'

And suddenly the gear took hold and I felt the wheels move backwards.

'Sarah!'

Alexander thumped the bonnet with the flat of his hand and he had an awful expression on his face, but I wouldn't look, I wouldn't feel sorry for him. I turned my head to look over my shoulder to navigate the bend in the drive and immediately realized what was going to happen. I slammed on the brakes, but not quickly enough to avoid the awful crunch as the back of the Land Rover collided with the front of the police car that was coming the other way.

CHAPTER FIFTY-EIGHT

If I'd only had myself to think about, I would have gone straight home, back to Manchester, but I could not leave Jamie behind and I could not take him with me. Genevieve's family would not have contemplated that option for a single moment and the police family-liaison officer said it would be best for him to be in familiar surroundings, with people he knew, during what she called 'this difficult time'. Jamie and I could not stay in the familiar surroundings of Avalon, because the police had closed the house off – literally taped over the entrance and stationed a guard by the gate – so they could conduct a fingertip search. We went to stay with Claudia's family at the Barn. All I had with me was my coat, purse and the phone, which I'd found on the Land Rover's dashboard. I don't know how it got there. Poor Jamie had nothing but the clothes he had worn to the farm to cut down the tree.

The atmosphere in the Barn was awful, a mixture of grief and anger. Cutting through it were pure streaks of innocence that were the twins and Jamie. They knew somebody had fallen into the quarry but they didn't know that the person was dead, or that it was almost certainly Genevieve. They didn't know that everybody thought Alexander had killed her. They didn't seem to realize the horror of the situation. They were excited about Christmas. I supposed they were used to the irrationalities of adults, their seemingly pointless changes of mood, and could not differentiate between the various levels of despair.

Claudia could hardly bear to look at me, and it was nothing to do with my face, which had become more bruised and swollen as the day wore on. I knew what she was thinking. She was thinking I was the woman who had slept with the man who had killed her sister. I'd slept with him when he was already a murderer. His murderous hands had been all over me. She thought I must have known something, I must have had my suspicions yet I never mentioned them to her. She was right. I'd had to decide where my loyalties lay and I had chosen Alexander, every time. If it was true that I had chosen wrongly, then I was almost as guilty as he was.

If it was him.

If he was a murderer.

My heart and the voice in my head still insisted that Alexander had not and never would have done anything to hurt Genevieve. At the same time, I didn't know if I could trust my head any more. Knowing how strongly my heart beat for Jamie, I could even empathize, to an extent, if Alexander *had* killed his wife. I understood how the urge to protect and keep Jamie might have become overriding in Alexander knowing that if Genevieve took the child, he would, quite possibly, never see him again. I could understand how emotion could overcome all rational thought in those circumstances.

Something else was eating away at me.

The police hadn't wasted any time when they came to Avalon. They had been friendly and brisk with Jamie, keeping him occupied so he hadn't seen the officer go over to his father, and he hadn't seen Alexander's face when he heard what the policeman had to say. But I had.

I'd seen Alexander's face, the horror on it, and then Alexander had raised his eyes and looked over to me.

He didn't say anything, he just looked, and what he was looking for was reassurance that I was still with him.

I couldn't hold his eyes. I'd had to look away. In the moment when he'd most needed me to be there for him, I had let him know I doubted him.

At the Barn, I went into the kitchen to make a snack for Jamie. Claudia was washing up at the sink furiously, as if she could vent her despair on the innocent china. Many mugs had been soiled, because Claudia had been making drinks for the police who kept coming and going.

'Hi,' I said tentatively. 'Is it OK if I make a sandwich for Jamie?'

Claudia turned and frowned at me. Then she threw

the dishcloth into the bowl, sending suds flying into the air, and stripped off her rubber gloves.

'I tried to help you!' she said in a voice that was spiky with anger. It was awkward for Claudia because she was naturally so calm and gentle. Her eyes looked sore and red and her hair, showing an inch of grey at the roots, hung unflatteringly around her heavy face. 'I showed you the ropes, I befriended you, I even gave you a second chance when I found out you'd been lying to me about . . . about *him*.'

I tried to interject but Claudia held up her hand to stop me.

'I thought we were friends!' she said in a desperate voice.

'Oh, Claudia, we are!'

'Really? So it's not true that you were planning to run away with Alexander? The police didn't come across you packing boxes ready to go?'

'They did, but—'

'You knew they were going to start searching the area! You knew they were going to find my sister! So you thought you'd get away before they closed in on you, didn't you?'

'No, no, it wasn't like that . . . Claudia, I didn't know about Genevieve. I didn't know anything!'

Claudia's eyes narrowed. She jabbed a finger towards me.

'You didn't say anything to me! I have been so loyal to you, Sarah, and you didn't say anything about leaving!'

I tried to remember how it was, but the last few weeks

were a blur to me. I couldn't pick out any mitigation at all.

'And worst of all, you were going to take Jamie away from his grandparents when he was all they had left! At Christmas! How could you do that to them?'

'They still have you, Claudia. They have our daughters,' a voice said quietly. Bill had come into the room behind me. He stepped forward and took Claudia in his arms, and she collapsed into him and began to sob. He stroked her hair. She was crying like a child, her shoulders heaving, and Bill pushed his glasses up on to his forehead and soothed her, cradling her like a baby.

'Shhh,' he whispered. 'It's all right.'

I turned and left the kitchen. I went into the garden, even though I had no coat and it was freezing cold. Blue, who had been sniffing around the shrubs at the far end, turned delightedly when he saw me, and bounded over. I had my arms wrapped around myself and I turned my back to him, but still he jumped up at my side, causing me to stumble and fall. Because I was at his level, he could reach my face, and he started to lick and nuzzle me roughly. I pushed him away, and climbed to my feet. I went to stand at the garden's edge, where I was hidden from the house, and I looked out across the winter countryside, so colourless it was almost entirely black and white and shades of grey, and I thought: It's over. Genevieve is found and everything between Alexander and me is lost. I had always known that when Genevieve returned, there would be no place for me with Alexander. I just hadn't expected it to end this way.

* * *

A little later, Jamie came out to find me.

'Sarah, I'm still hungry,' he said patiently. 'I told you I was hungry ages ago and I'm only going to keep being more hungry until you get me something.'

'I know, sweetheart,' I said.

'Aren't you cold?'

'Yes.'

Jamie looked at me strangely.

'I am very starving,' he said.

We went back into the kitchen. Claudia now was sitting at the table, her hands cupped round a steaming mug of tea. Bill was taking the packaging off frozen pizzas and heating them in the oven.

'Ah, Jimbo!' he exclaimed. 'Just the man. I need you to help me move the furniture around in the den so you guys can eat in front of the TV.'

He shut the oven door and he and Jamie disappeared.

I wanted to comfort Claudia and make her feel better but I did not know how. I wanted to explain myself, but could think of no way to do that either.

She sighed heavily, like an old woman.

'Sarah . . .'

'Yes.'

'I know you didn't know about Genevieve. I shouldn't have said that.'

'It's all right,' I said. 'I understand. I just wish—'

'I'm going up for a bath.'

'Would you like me to make you another drink?'

'No.' Claudia shook her head. 'I don't want you to do anything for me.'

She heaved herself to her feet, and hobbled towards the stairs as if her back and her hips hurt.

I hated myself for betraying Claudia. I could have told her we were planning to leave Burrington Stoke: she would have kept our secret; she would have understood why we had to go. Only Alexander had made me swear I wouldn't tell a soul, and I hadn't. It was too late to change things now. I knew Claudia would never want me near her again. She had, that day, discovered her sister was dead. At the time when she most needed a friend, I had let her down. Again.

I went into the living room and switched on the TV with the sound muted. I saw the exterior of Avalon on the screen. It was so odd to see somewhere I knew so well on the television. I was compelled to watch. Everything was the same but it looked different. The Land Rover was being manoeuvred on to the back of a truck to be taken away for forensic examination and the Christmas tree lay on its side by the wall, still encased in its plastic netting. The police had taken Alexander away. He had been arrested, but not charged at that point. I imagined him sitting hunched and humiliated in some small, tiled room, the police despising him, thinking him a murderer, asking questions, and my stomach clenched with sadness like a pain.

I'd tried so hard to trust him.

I'd tried.

'Turn it off,' said Bill, coming in behind me. 'For goodness' sake, turn it off before the children see.'

* * *

The first television crew turned up at the entrance to the old quarry before dark. From the bathroom window of Claudia's house, I could see the lights of outside broadcast vans stretched down the lane. The police had strung crime-scene tape across the entrance to the quarry and a respectfully serious-faced officer was standing guard in case anyone tried to sneak in. All the news reports I'd ever watched over the years about murders or suspicious deaths, all of them featured artificially illuminated streets or forests, a burly policeman cross-armed by the tape and earnest journalists doing pieces to camera, gesticulating with their arms, wires trailing around them. I had, I supposed, always thought they were acting out roles. It was a circus, and everyone knew what was coming next.

Now I realized those people weren't acting – it was their job – and what I saw on television was exactly how it was in real life.

Genevieve's body wasn't there, in the quarry, any more.

They had taken her away, zipped up in a body-bag in the back of a blacked-out estate car. The vehicle had sped through the Somerset lanes. Of course, the body was not, officially, Genevieve's – it had not been identified – but we all knew it was her. The police divers had pulled her out of the water and now a tent marked the place where they'd cleared the undergrowth to lie her body down and examine her.

I couldn't bear to think of it but I couldn't stop imagining how it was. In my mind Genevieve was like a mermaid, pale green and bleached white like fishbone, shimmering as she dried in the winter sunlight.

The children ate their pizzas on their laps in front of the TV screen in the den. Bill had disconnected the aerial so they could not watch live programmes, only DVDs. He had set them up with a stack of films. Then he'd gone up to Eleonora House to manage the media and host calls from friends and relatives who had seen or heard the news reports. He told Claudia that Genevieve's face was all over the television channels; her charismatic face. He said, with bitterness in his voice, that they loved her – the journalists, editors and TV presenters. She was perfect material: a beautiful, talented heiress, unlucky in love, a young mother whose husband had threatened to kill her if she left him. She had been ready to leave and now she was dead, found broken at the bottom of the quarry that had been mined to exhaustion to make her family's fortune. Stories didn't come any more romantic or satisfying than that. That's what Bill told Claudia. Nobody was talking to me. I was the thorn in their side and they didn't want me there. I didn't blame them. They'd tried to persuade me to go to Betsy's, or to a hotel – there was a Travelodge on the airport road and Bill offered to drive me there – and I said thanks, but my place was with Jamie. Bill rolled his eyes at Claudia and I saw her tighten her lips.

They didn't want me there and I didn't want to be there, but what could I do? I could not leave Jamie. I would not. Claudia and Bill must have had some inkling that it would cause more trouble for them if I went, that night, than if I stayed. They could have insisted I go, but they didn't. Probably they thought Jamie would be upset if he were separated from me as well as Alexander, all in the space of a few hours, and they simply did not have the capacity to deal with any more trauma. So I stayed in the Barn and I crept through it, like a bad smell or an infection. I only went into spaces that were already empty in that beautiful, family home; I learned how to make myself and my injured face completely invisible.

There was a drinks cabinet in the living room. Carefully, making sure it didn't chink its neighbours, I removed a large tumbler and mixed myself a small gin and tonic. I just wanted a little pick-me-up. I sipped my drink and I thought of Alexander lying on a thin mattress in a police cell somewhere. He would cope with prison, he'd been there before and survived – but he'd had less to lose then.

It would destroy him to be separated from Jamie, knowing that he was going to lose him for ever.

Jamie and I were to sleep in Claudia and Bill's spare room that night. The bed was already made up for visitors because Claudia had invited her maternal cousins over for the holiday period and they had been due to arrive the following morning. The room was lovely; huge soft towels on the heater and red flowers in a vase on the window ledge. Jamie was over-wound and over-excited. At midnight, I took him out of the snug and, upstairs, we changed into borrowed nightclothes together. He stood beside me, peeing into a spotlessly clean toilet bowl in a comradely fashion even though he was wearing a Barbie nightie, while I brushed my teeth in a voluminous pair of men's pyjamas.

I looked down at Jamie and he grinned up at me, a gappy grin, and I thought how strange it was that there was nothing of Alexander in the child, no genetic bond at all, and yet he was so irrefutably Alexander's son.

'I like this house better than ours,' Jamie said. 'It's warmer.'

'Yes,' I said noncommittally. 'It's nice.'

'Where's Daddy?'

'He's busy.'

'Why?'

I stared at my reflection in the mirror above the basin, a white froth of toothpaste on my chin.

'I don't know exactly. He has things he has to do.'

Jamie looked at me. 'What things?'

'Jamie,' I said calmly, 'why did you get rid of the blue teddy and your mummy's letter?'

He shrugged and looked a little sheepish.

'I don't care why,' I said. 'It really doesn't matter but I just want to know is all.'

'Mummy told me to,' he said.

I leaned down to fill my mouth with cold water from the tap. I cleaned my mouth and spat out and then rubbed at the chalky residue in the basin with my finger.

'Did she tell you in a dream?' I asked.

He shrugged. 'I don't know. She just did.'

'Did Daddy tell you to say that?'

Jamie pulled the face he used when accused of

something he had not done or even known about.

'No!'

I felt a rush of relief in my bones and, at the same time, it became perfectly clear to me what I should do.

I needed to get Jamie away from Burrington Stoke and take him somewhere safe where I could look after him and protect him.

If he stayed, what would happen would be this.

In the morning, probably, Genevieve's body would be formally identified by poor Claudia or her mother and somebody would have to tell Jamie that his mummy was dead. The man he had always believed to be his father was not there to protect him. He would, no doubt, learn soon enough that everyone believed his father was responsible for his mother's death. There would be a media frenzy. It would be impossible to keep it all from him. His fragile world would come crashing down and his life would never be the same again. For ever after, he would carry the burden of having a mother who died when he was very young and wear the stigma of a father who had, at best, failed to protect the family and, at worst, destroyed it. He would be a different child, and would grow into a different man. He might struggle with relationships. He might become clingy because he was so afraid of loss, or he might reject intimacy, knowing it could lead to pain.

He grinned gappily up at me and I smiled down at him as if nothing at all was wrong. To have to face so much sadness and shame seemed so unfair on Jamie. If he stayed here, then this was his last night of innocence.

His whole future would have been decided and mapped out by other people.

If I took him away, all this could be avoided.

'Go on, you,' I said. 'Into bed.'

In bed we sang 'Rudolph the Red-nosed Reindeer' about a thousand times. Jamie's feet were pressed against my thighs. I was trying to put meat on the bones of my plan, but I couldn't think beyond the next hour or so, especially not with Jamie nagging me all the time to keep singing. What I was thinking was that, if we could somehow get to Manchester before morning, we would be all right. I'd be able to keep Jamie safe. I knew the city well enough to know where we could rent a place where nobody would ask questions. All we had to do was travel a few hundred miles through the night. After that, I wasn't sure. I'd wait and see what happened to Alexander and, in the meantime, I would look after Jamie just as I had been looking after him. We'd manage somehow, and Jamie would be happy. That was the most important thing.

'Sarah!' he said crossly.

'What?'

'You're not concentrating!'

'Sorry,' I said. 'I'm so sorry, Jamie.'

He fell asleep eventually. I left the lamp casting a gentle yellow glow over the face of the child, and climbed carefully out of the bed. I crept downstairs. The clock over the fireplace showed 2.10 a.m. The only light still on was in the kitchen. Gently, I pushed open the kitchen door. Bill was sitting at the table, in the same place where Claudia had sat earlier, with a whisky bottle and a glass in front of him. He was dishevelled and his head was cradled in his arms, his mouth slightly open. From the whistling of his nostrils, I was sure he was asleep. Blue, in his basket by the back door, looked up at me and thumped his tail on the floor. I held my finger to my lips, and carefully pulled the door to.

CHAPTER FIFTY-NINE

I dressed Jamie as he slept, wrapped him up all warm again, and then I put my clothes back on, and I took a blanket from the wardrobe and threw it out of the window and closed the window carefully. I scooped the child from his warm hollow in the bed. He stirred a little, and put his arms around my neck and his legs around my waist, helping me lift him.

'We're going for a little walk,' I told him, and he murmured and snuggled down into me.

I didn't feel afraid as I carried him down the stairs. I think it was because I knew I had no choice. I had to take him away, for his sake, no matter what the risks. At the kitchen door, Blue raised his huge square head to look at us.

'Quiet, Blue,' I whispered. He heard me and tilted his head to one side. 'You stay here,' I said. 'Stay!' He put his chin back on his paws. 'Good boy,' I said.

I knew the front door would probably be locked or alarmed. Instead, I went through the living room and gently slid open one of the French windows.

Outside, the night was bright, but shockingly cold. Already Jamie was becoming a weight in my arms. I wondered if I could make some kind of sling out of the blanket, but it was difficult on my own. So instead I wrapped it around Jamie, making him into a big, cosy bundle and, talking to him for my own reassurance, we set off. I'd forgotten about the electric gates at the entrance to the drive, but fortunately they were still open. With a sigh of gratitude, I set off down the lane.

All the way, I told Jamie a story about a dinosaur who was fed up with living in the quarry and wanted to make a better life for himself so he decided to run away. Jamie was sleeping, but I hoped he'd hear the words subliminally and that they would help him understand what was happening to him when he woke.

At first we were fine going down the hill. I walked in the middle of the lane, following the frozen, muddy grass that grew in a long, narrow strip where car wheels never rolled, but when we reached the entrance to the old quarry I saw the shape of a police car parked outside the gates. There was no other way round so I hugged my precious bundle to me tight and crept through the shadows as best I could. I couldn't see inside the car, I didn't know if there was even anyone in it, but I couldn't take the chance of being spotted. I huddled over Jamie, like an old woman, and hoped the steam-cloud of my breath would not give us away.

The car made me worry. What if journalists or camera crews were lurking in the lane on the off-chance of snatching a shot of one of us? It was all right, though. The rest of that remote road was quiet. In the trees I heard owls calling, and little, secretive animals rustled in the frozen hedgerows, but that was all. Nothing dangerous. The moon rolled slowly across the sky and the stars twinkled in the black and it was beautiful.

We made it all the way down to the bottom of the lane without any trouble, but by then my shoulders were aching and I knew we wouldn't be able to go much further on our own. I sat down, for a moment, at the village bus stop, but as soon as the movement stopped Jamie stirred, so I stood again and lost myself in the rhythm of my footsteps. It was only a couple of miles to the main road, where we'd be able to catch an early bus to Bristol or Wells. It was unlikely anyone at the Barn would notice we were missing until the morning. I'd turned off the lamp and scrunched up the duvet to make it look as if we were huddled beneath, just in case Bill awoke and put his head around the spare bedroom door before he went to bed. So, I thought, so long as we were safely onboard a train travelling north before anyone started looking for us, we'd be all right.

I didn't know what time it was. I guessed it was approaching 4 a.m.

During the walk from the bottom of the hill to the main road, we were only passed by two vehicles coming from the direction of the village. Each time, I turned my back to the road so that nobody would see I was carrying a child, something which was bound to attract attention in the middle of the night, in the freezing cold. I don't think either of the drivers noticed me; neither slowed their vehicle down.

At the junction to the main road, I stopped,

considering which would be the best direction to travel. All the time I'd been walking I'd been planning on Manchester, but that would be the obvious place for me to go and that's where people would start looking. If I went south instead of north, I'd have more time to sort us out with accommodation and a story. Nobody would ever think we'd go to Fowey, for example. Why would they? We hadn't told a soul about our plans. Alexander said there were plenty of places to rent in the town. I could probably find the apartment he'd spoken of, and he'd said the landlord was 'desperate' to have it filled. It wouldn't even look odd. I could just turn up and say that we were Alexander's family and we'd come early, in time for Christmas. They wouldn't know anything about what was going on here in Fowey, surely. The pictures in the papers would be of Genevieve, not me. Jamie would love it by the seaside. That was a good plan, a better plan. That's what I'd do.

A vehicle's headlights were approaching along the main road. I stepped back, into the shadows, but the car indicated left and, as it turned into the Burrington Stoke road, I felt the full glare of its headlights. I squinted and turned away, but I was too late. I had been spotted. The car came slowly to a halt and the driver door opened. A tallish, slight man stepped out and walked calmly across the road towards me. He was wearing a dark-blue beanie. He leaned down to look at my face in the light of a street lamp.

'Are you all right?' he asked very gently.

I nodded.

'You must be frozen.'

'No, I'm fine.'

The man held out his arms.

'Let me take him now,' he said. 'You can sit in the car and have a bit of a rest.'

'I couldn't leave him,' I said. 'I promised I'd look after him. I couldn't leave him to face everything on his own.'

'Of course you couldn't,' said Neil. 'But you don't have to worry because we're here now. We're here to help.'

CHAPTER SIXTY

We sat in the car for a while, in silence. May rubbed my chilled hands between her warm ones and we listened to Christmas music on the radio. Then Neil said. 'We'll have to take you back, Sarah, or else you'll be in all kinds of trouble. You know that, don't you?'

'Oh, please don't . . .'

'Sweetheart, think about it,' said May. 'I know you want what's best for Jamie, but you setting off a nation-wide manhunt the day after Alexander's been arrested isn't the best way of guaranteeing a happy ending for the little lad. If you want to be with him, you'll have to show that you're responsible and go through the proper channels.'

'But they'll never let him come to me,' I said. 'The family will close ranks round him and they'll tell him lies about Alexander and he'll end up never knowing how it really was.'

May sighed. 'He'll know in his heart,' she said.

'They'll change him,' I said. 'He won't know anything of the truth.'

'Perhaps that would be for the best.'

'Oh, May, don't say that!'

I was cradling the sleeping child on my lap. Most of him was hidden by blanket and clothes, but I could see his eyelashes and the lids of his eyes in their perfect little hollows. I leaned over him and touched my lips to his forehead. He tasted so dear, so familiar. His skin was so warm.

The car windows had steamed up. The engine was idling to keep the heater working. Outside, the night had darkened as the moon disappeared behind the hill.

'What happened to your face?' May asked.

'I fell over in the dark last night.' Was it only last night? It felt like a million years ago.

May and Neil exchanged glances.

'You look like you've gone a couple of rounds with Mike Tyson,' Neil said gently.

'No,' I said, but I was feeling hopelessly tired again. No matter how much I protested, they wouldn't believe that Alexander hadn't hit me. If they truly thought he was capable of murdering Genevieve, then what was a little domestic abuse? I yawned and, at the same time, Neil must have made a signal to May, because she nodded and said: 'Come on, let's just do it.'

I didn't bother fighting them. I was exhausted, and everything seemed inevitable. They coached me on what we would say when we got back to the Barn to cover my tracks but, as it turned out, I didn't have to say anything, because nobody had noticed we were missing and the French window was still slightly open. I went in that way with Jamie and Neil, while May rang the doorbell. Blue went mad barking in the kitchen and when Bill came out to investigate, May kept him distracted at the door. Bill was half asleep and fuddled with alcohol and didn't notice Neil and me creeping back in. Jamie was undressed and back in bed before he, or anyone else, realized he had ever been out of it. Neil insisted I lie down too, although I knew I would not sleep. I lay with my arms around Jamie listening to the muted conversation downstairs, May's cheeping voice explaining that they had got here as quickly as they could when they picked up all the messages, and it was all so terrible, and she couldn't even begin to imagine what it was like for the family, and Bill listening to her and making polite noises every now and then. Neil sat with me for a while, stroking my hair as if I were a child.

'Go and be with May,' I whispered.

'You're going to be fine, you know,' Neil said. 'And Jamie will be all right too. Life has a way of sorting everything out, you know.'

After a while he went out of the room. I lay there, feeling the seconds peel away, and each second that went hurt a little more than the one before and I thought that when I reached the last one, the one where I had to leave Jamie, I might die of hurt.

I heard Bill fetching blankets for May and Neil so they could snatch a couple of hours' sleep on the sofas downstairs, and then his footsteps coming up the stairs, the sound of a toilet flushing somewhere, and then everything went quiet. I could not sleep. I didn't want to. I wanted to be wide awake for every precious moment I had with Jamie.

The rest of the night passed very quickly.

A while after the birds had started their singing, I heard the household stirring. I lay still, and Jamie, thankfully, slept on. He had been very late to bed the night before and maybe the fresh air in the night had also tired him.

There were breakfast noises in the kitchen, the sound of Claudia and May talking, May flustered and apologetic, Claudia at her most posh, her most brusque, sounding like her stepmother. I heard the police arrive. They were complaining about the barrage of press that was rolling up along the lane. Some of their vehicles were so large the police were having difficulty making their way through. The police voices were deep and business-like. I heard the female family-liaison officer ask how Jamie was. Then a door closed and all the talking became muffled and hushed and I knew they were talking about me and planning how to persuade me to leave Jamie behind.

He murmured and stretched beside me. I felt his ribcage expand beneath the palm of my hand and his feet worked their way down my legs. The nightie had tangled itself around him. He yawned and rubbed his eyes.

'Hello, Sarah,' he said.

'Hello, Jamie.'

'Can we go home and put the Christmas tree up today?'

'I don't know,' I said. 'I wish we could.'

* * *

May came into the bedroom with tea and juice and toast. She told Jamie to run along and find his cousins, and when he'd gone she sat on the edge of the bed and I knew she had been elected to break the bad news.

'Sarah . . .' she began, and I shook my head.

'I know,' I said. 'Please don't say what you were going to say. I know.'

'It's for the best, my love. What that poor little lad needs now is to be with his family.'

'I promised I'd look after him.'

'And you have,' May said. 'You've looked after him very well. But now it's time for you to let him go.'

The downstairs of the Barn was crowded and it smelled of cold air and aftershave. Plain clothes police officers were drinking tea in the living room with Virginia and Claudia and several people I did not recognize. Somebody had switched on the Christmas lights. They sparkled and twinkled and the room looked cosy – anyone looking in through the window who did not know what was happening would not have guessed the truth. They'd have thought it was some kind of social event. I noticed the footprints on the carpet around the French windows and I thought it was only a few hours ago that I'd gone out into the night with Jamie. I'd tried to do the best for him. I'd tried to protect him and I'd fallen at the first hurdle. God knows what was going to happen to him now.

The previous day I had been numb. That morning the shock hit me physically. I sat hunched at the periphery of the room while arrangements were made, and all the time I ached for Jamie and for Alexander. If Alexander was here, I thought, he would look after us all. He'd know what to do.

May wrote down addresses and telephone numbers for the police and agreed to various conditions on my behalf. An officer explained that I would need to be formally interviewed at some stage and that I should not, under any circumstances, have any contact with Alexander. He was due to be charged that morning, and I would be a key witness. I nodded to show I understood.

The police wanted to photograph the injuries on my face, but I wouldn't let them do that.

'Come on, Sarah,' Neil said as soon as the police officer had finished. 'Come on, love, it's time to get going.'

'I need to say goodbye to Jamie.'

'No,' said Claudia. 'Don't you go near him.'

'I have to, Claudia. I have to explain.'

Bill stepped forward and put his arm around Claudia's shoulders. She reached up and took hold of his hand.

'Children are resilient,' he said. 'Jamie will be fine. We'll take care of him now.'

'Please . . .'

'You'll only upset him. Is that what you want?'

'Hold on,' said May, who could never bear to see me thwarted. She stood beside me and took my hand. 'Sarah's not going to *upset* the lad, she loves him.'

'She's only known him five minutes. And she doesn't know the first thing about love.'

Neil joined the two of us.

'Let's just go,' he said. 'Come on, Sarah. I'm sure you'll be able to see Jamie again when things are different.'

He took my other hand and his hand was cool and made me feel safe. May squeezed my fingers. I let the two of them guide me into the hall. The front door was open. The dogs were sniffing about on the lawn. We were on the drive, our heads held low against the stinging flash of lights from the photographers grouped behind the gates, when I heard the cry.

'Sarah!'

I turned my head and there was Jamie, hurtling towards the front door, holding his arms out to me.

Bill caught Jamie under the arms at the door, and pulled him back. He wasn't properly dressed. His skinny bare legs were flailing.

'Sarah!' he screamed. 'Where are you going?' There was a barrage of lights.

'You can't snap the kid!' May shouted, dropping my hand and heading towards the assembled press. They immediately turned their lenses towards her.

'Leave her alone!' Neil shouted.

'Let me go to him!' I pleaded to Neil. 'Let me just have a word!'

'Get in the car, Sarah,' said a voice at my shoulder. It was Detective Inspector Twyford.

Jamie was screaming: 'Let me go, let me go, let me go! Sarah!'

'Oh God,' I cried, trying to pull my hand away from Neil's. 'Please let me go to him!'

'You bastards!' May yelled at the cameramen.

DI Twyford gripped my arm and spoke in an authoritative voice.

'Turn to Jamie,' he said. 'If he sees you panicking, he'll be even more scared. Smile like nothing's wrong and wave and say you'll see him soon.'

I turned and I saw the little boy reaching both arms out to me and screaming to come to me.

Bill was trying to close the door but Jamie had his fingers gripped around the edge. He was going to get his fingers trapped. I knew he wouldn't let go.

'Why are you going away?' he screamed. 'Where's my Daddy? When are we going home? *Where's my Mummy? Don't go!*'

I opened my mouth but could not speak.

'Go on,' said the inspector. 'Smile. Reassure him. I'm going to get your sister before there's trouble.'

I turned and caught Jamie's eye, and he was so distressed it was terrible to see.

'I'm going to get Daddy. I'm going to bring him home,' I said, and I said it so quietly that I could not be sure I'd actually spoken the words, but may have just held them in my mind.

Jamie did not hear of course. He couldn't possibly have heard. He screamed and held out his arms to me: 'Sarah! Sarah! *Don't leave me!* You promised you wouldn't go! You *promised*!'

'Get in the car,' May cried, shaking the detective away. 'Please get in the car, I can't bear this! It's horrible.'

Bill prised Jamie's fingers from the frame. He closed the door. I climbed into the back seat of Neil's car and put my head in my hands, and I wept.

CHAPTER SIXTY-ONE

I went back into the bed in May and Neil's spare room and I stayed there for a while – days, a week, longer. The bruises on my face turned black and then yellow. The scabs started to heal. May took me back to see my old GP and I was scolded, gently, for not even having bothered to register with a doctor in Somerset.

'Still,' said Dr Rooney, 'saves us having to start all over again, eh?'

I closed my eyes. I didn't want to be there, I wanted to be back in bed, warm under the duvet.

'You'd been through a lot last time we spoke,' said the doctor, 'and now you've been through a whole lot more. Can you tell me how you're feeling?'

'I'm not feeling anything,' I said, which was the truth.

I was prescribed some tablets and I went back to bed.

I didn't read, I didn't think, I didn't sleep, I didn't dream, I didn't talk, I didn't eat or drink or remember or laugh or cry or anything. I was like a non-person. I didn't wash my hair. Every so often May ran a bath and filled it with nice-smelling bubbles and while I soaked she straightened the sheets on the bed, gave the room a clean, took away whatever it was I'd been wearing and replaced it with something soft and folded. Poor May. It must have been awful for her, and she was so patient and so kind.

Betsy called. I saw her number come up on the phone, but I didn't answer. I was too tired. May must have called her back because a parcel arrived from Burrington Stoke with some of my things in it.

'They must be letting people back into the house,' May said, holding a jumper up to her nose and sniffing, before tossing it into the laundry basket.

'Does that mean I can go back?' I asked.

May shook her head. 'Oh, I don't think so,' she said. 'I don't think that would be a good idea.'

In the evenings Neil came into my room and he sat beside me and read me articles from his collection of film magazines. Neil's visits became the only thing I looked forward to. I listened to him and I became interested in what he had to say.

He never tried to persuade me out of the room or the bed or even out of my head. He never passed any comment on the situation. May, of course, was the opposite, it was her nature, but Neil's complete acceptance of how things were was good for me. Then, one evening, he came in as usual but he didn't sit down. He stood at the door and said: 'Sarah, this isn't doing any good, you know. It's not helping Jamie or Alexander.'

'How can I help either of them?'

'You could find out the truth about what happened to Genevieve.'

I propped myself up on one elbow.

'How?'

'It's been quiet at work lately,' said Neil. 'It always is this time of year. I've been reading a lot of stuff about your man and his wife and the family. I think there's more to this than meets the eye.'

'What have you found out?'

Neil smiled. 'Sarah, I can't take you seriously while you're lying in bed looking like a child. Get up, get dressed and we'll go out somewhere grown-up and I'll tell you.'

I went into the bathroom and splashed my face with hot water. I cleaned my teeth with May's electric toothbrush. Then I dried myself with a towel and smoothed May's moisturizing cream into my damaged, uncared-for skin. It made me smell a bit better. I went back into the bedroom.

'What day is it?' I asked Neil.

'December the twenty-ninth.'

May and Neil had completely foregone Christmas to protect me from myself. Their selflessness moved me. I had not felt anything for days, but I felt something then. It was a combination of gratitude and sorrow.

'Are the pubs open?'

'Of course.'

'Let's go for a drink then,' I said.

So we went to the Lion, which was a big old Manchester estate pub. Lately it had been done over by a chain and now it had old-fashioned prints on the walls and catered for people looking for good-value food and widescreen-TV sport.

While Neil ordered the drinks I picked at a beer mat and remembered that the last time I'd been in a pub had been in a life about three times removed, with DI Twyford. I recalled the kindness of the inspector as he'd ushered me into Neil's car outside the Barn, how he'd coaxed me into reassuring Jamie that everything would be all right. That thought led me to how I had failed the child, and I couldn't bear that. I felt the shutters in my mind beginning to slide together and, just as they were about to lock, Neil returned with a pint of beer and a large glass of Merlot and a small pink raffle ticket.

'Chips and curry sauce,' he said, putting the ticket in the centre of the table, and my dry, withered-up stomach uncurled itself and stretched with pleasure at the prospect of its favourite Lancashire supper.

For a while, Neil asked questions about Alexander and me, filling in the gaps in what he knew about our relationship. The food came and I realized I was ravenously hungry and the wine was making me relax.

My top lip was still a bit sore, but I ate through the pain. The scab was gone and, when I pressed the scar with the tip of my finger, I could feel it was healing.

'When you met Alexander, was there anything about him that made you feel uncomfortable?' asked Neil. 'Did your instincts tell you anything was wrong? Did you have any inkling that he might be capable of violence?'

I tried to think back to how it had been in Sicily. It was so hard to remember, but I did recall the pull there had been between Alexander and me, and I didn't think

I would have felt so strongly if his feelings for me had not been completely open.

'No,' I said. 'And in all the time I've known him he's always been gentle with Jamie and me.'

'He started a fight in the local pub.'

'Oh that . . . God!' I put my head in my hands. 'I was there. It wasn't his fault.'

'That's not what the locals are saying.'

'They're wrong. They're just talking everything up to make it dramatic.' I ate another chip. 'Anyway, how do you even know about that?'

'It's been in all the papers, Sarah. They're not so interested in you, but Alexander and Genevieve are big, big news. At this time of year, when there's nothing much going on, the broadsheets love a nice, juicy scandal to fill up the feature pages, especially if it involves proto-aristocracy.'

He paused a moment and swirled his pint around his glass. Then he said: 'The thing is, the thing that struck me, is that everyone, even the police, are assuming that Alexander is guilty. Everything is clear-cut. He has a criminal record and a strong motive, he's clearly taken steps to cover up the truth and he's made well-documented threats to kill his wife. He's admitted they had violent rows. He hasn't acted like a man whose beloved has left him; he moved in his new girlfriend, you, barely a month later; he's destroyed evidence and has done nothing to co-operate with attempts to trace Genevieve. He also made you complicit in his plans to do a bunk.'

'I know.'

'It's almost too . . .' Neil paused. 'It's too neat. Life is messier than this.'

'Isn't the most obvious answer usually the right one?'

'That's what they say. But just because everything points to Alexander being guilty, it doesn't make him a murderer.'

I felt a flicker of excitement in my belly. I put down my glass and waited for Neil to carry on.

'What if he isn't guilty?' he asked me, and this time my heart missed a beat and then it began to beat strong and fast.

'What if,' said Neil, 'Alexander has been telling the truth all along? What if he had nothing at all to do with Genevieve's death?'

I opened my mouth and closed it again. So many questions and ideas were crowding together in my mind I couldn't pick them apart.

'What if,' said Neil, 'everyone is so busy building up the case against him that the truth never has a chance to come out?'

The implications of what he was saying were so immense my mind could hardly process them. After so many days of complete despair, now it seemed as if a ray of light so bright I could barely look at it was piercing the darkness. I was overwhelmed with joy and relief. At last, something positive was happening.

Neil took my hand and squeezed.

'Sarah, don't get your hopes up. As it stands, it's looking pretty bad for Alexander. I don't know if he's innocent or guilty. I don't know anything. I just thought you and I could maybe do a little research and see if we can find some new information that might help.'

I nodded.

'I can't promise anything.'

'I know.'

'But we'll give it our best shot, eh?'

'Yes.'

Neil told me what he already knew about Alexander. He hadn't had the best start in life. His mother was a chronic alcoholic with severe mental-health problems and he never knew his father. When he was a child, he was in foster care on and off, and he was often in trouble.

'Basically,' said Neil, 'he gave out all the usual signals that he'd turn out a bad'un.'

I thought of Jamie and how Alexander tried so hard to be a good father to the boy, and my eyes grew hot.

'He's not bad,' I said.

Neil shook his head. 'Sarah, if we're going to get to the bottom of this, you're going to have to behave as if you're not involved. You must not let your feelings or your perspective on things influence what we're doing. From now on, your opinion isn't relevant. We're looking at the facts here. Try to be objective.'

'OK. Sorry.'

'Alexander may or may not have suffered abuse as a child. He was certainly neglected. His relationship, or lack of relationship, with his mother may have affected his ability to connect with other women.'

I winced.

Neil pretended not to notice.

'Genevieve had told her mother that she was afraid of Alexander, that he'd already come close to killing her and she thought that, next time, he might go through with it.'

'No, that's not true,' I said. 'She was the one who hurt him! He didn't lay a finger on her.'

'Genevieve told other people she thought her life was in danger. That's all that's important right now. That's a *fact*. She reiterated her concerns and Alexander's threat in the "goodbye" letter to her parents. That's another fact. She was spelling out her reasons for leaving him. As it's the last documented communication from Genevieve, it makes pretty compelling evidence.'

'It also proves she definitely was planning to leave that morning.'

'Yep. If it weren't for the letter, her parents would have reported her missing much sooner. She was quite specific that she wouldn't be in touch for a few weeks and that they shouldn't worry.'

'She didn't mention anyone else in the letter, did she?'

Neil shook his head.

'Only' – I paused for a moment – 'her mother let on to me that she might have had a lover.'

'She was right.'

I felt another frisson.

'How do you know?'

'NWM has had someone on the case for weeks. Genevieve used to travel to different horse events all the time and, according to various sources, never socialized with the other competitors in the evenings. She'd always slip away. Somebody using the name Juliet Bravo – we're certain it was her – booked into hotels all over the place. Nice hotels – quiet, expensive country places; discreet. She was always accompanied. Always a double room, always champagne on ice and dinner served in the room, so none of the staff ever clocked the lover.'

'Don't we have his name?'

'Romeo Delta.'

I smiled. It seemed a sad little joke. I felt sorry for Genevieve, sorry for Alexander. He must have had some inkling that he was being cuckolded while Genevieve was away with her horses and he was at home looking after Jamie. He must have known and yet he never said anything. Was it pride, or shame, that kept him quiet? Or simply hope that the relationship would blow over and the Alexander–Genevieve–Jamie family unit would remain intact?

I wondered if Genevieve had mentioned 'Romeo' in her last letter to Alexander and if that was the real reason why he had destroyed it.

'Do *you* have any idea who he might be?' Neil asked.

'Genevieve used to go out with someone called Luke Innes. An old friend. The police have been looking for him but haven't found him.'

'She knew Luke before she knew Alexander?'

'Yes. They were boyfriend and girlfriend in Burrington Stoke before she went to university and for a while afterwards.'

Neil ate a chip pensively.

Then he said: 'These are the facts we know. Someone

– let's assume it was Genevieve – pushed the "farewell" letter to her parents into the letterbox at the end of their drive the morning of the day she left. She wanted to be certain they opened it that morning, which is why she hadn't risked posting it. Philip had an appointment at the hospital, and Virginia had gone with him. Genevieve must have known they'd be out. You'd know the geography better than I do, but the police think she walked up the hill, probably to say goodbye to her horses before she left.'

That would be about right.

Neil took a drink and then continued: 'According to Alexander, he left for work that morning as usual and dropped Jamie off at school. It was the end of term, the last day before the holidays. Normally, Genevieve would have taken Jamie to school, but she'd decided to take a bath – probably didn't want to have to look Alexander in the face. He says he found his letter propped up on the kitchen table when he came home from work that afternoon. He was earlier than usual because the school had called him when Genevieve didn't turn up to meet Jamie.'

'But that letter doesn't exist any more.'

'No. Alexander says he burned it.' Neil drained his glass. 'And then there's the matter of Genevieve's letter to Jamie, which has also gone missing but which, logically, should not have existed.'

'It didn't,' I said. 'Alexander wrote it.'

'Why would he do that?'

'To put Jamie's mind at ease because Genevieve hadn't thought to say goodbye to her son.'

Neil rubbed his chin. 'That's because she didn't think she had to.'

'Why not?'

'Because she always intended to take him with her. You found the bag she'd packed for herself, but there was another one, full of Jamie's things. Jamie's passport was kept in Alexander's office. Genevieve wouldn't have wanted to move it until she was ready to go in case Alexander got wind of what she was up to. It's likely she planned to wait until she was sure he was at Castle Cary, then she'd get everything ready, deliver her letter to her parents and pick Jamie up from school on her way out.'

'Neil, how on earth do you know all this?'

He smiled.

'Excellent contacts in the police. Expensive ones.'

'Do you know that Alexander isn't Jamie's genetic father?'

'I do. And, this is assumption, but if Genevieve *was* seeing someone she'd known for some time – let's say it was this Luke Innes – there's a definite possibility that *he* was Jamie's real father, especially if she was seeing him before she met Alexander. If they *were* planning to take Jamie abroad, Alexander wouldn't have had a proverbial cat's chance of getting him back.'

'It's a pretty strong motive for Alexander stopping Genevieve leaving,' I said. 'It makes him more likely to be guilty.'

'Agreed. But if Alexander is the guilty party, why hasn't the lover come forward?'

'Because he feels guilty. Because he was indirectly

responsible for Genevieve's death. Because maybe he doesn't want anyone to know he was involved with her. Because he's too distressed. Because he's married.'

'Or maybe it's because he was the one who killed her,' Neil said.

I exhaled shakily.

'There's one more thing,' Neil said. 'Genevieve's inheritance. It's substantial.'

'Alexander wouldn't have cared about that,' I said. 'He's not interested in money.'

'Everyone's interested in money,' said Neil, 'if there's enough of it at stake.'

CHAPTER SIXTY-TWO

When we were back in the flat, for the first time since I'd returned to Manchester I didn't want to go straight to bed. My head was fizzing with thoughts and ideas. I would have liked to start researching Alexander and Genevieve's history right there and then. Neil had a laptop, and I thought perhaps I could spend an hour or so on the internet, but May was using it to chat with her Facebook friends and she'd been so patient and put up with so much from me that I couldn't ask her to move. Instead I went into the kitchen and made hot chocolate for the three of us, and then I sat on the sofa snuggled up next to May and watched television beside her. She moved the laptop, put her arm round me and squeezed me tight.

'Better?' she asked.

'Yes. Thanks to you and your lovely husband.'

May smiled.

I reached up to my sister and kissed her cheek. She was warm and smelled of shampoo.

'Thank you,' I said. 'For everything.'

'That's what I'm here for,' she said.

CHAPTER SIXTY-THREE

By seven thirty the next morning I had showered, washed and dried my hair, dressed in a tweed skirt, oyster-silk blouse and green coat that May was, one day, hoping to slim into and was walking with Neil towards the staff entrance of the NWM building. It was good to be back in the city with its wide streets and lights and buses. I felt optimistic. I felt positive. I was proud to be doing something to try to prove that Alexander was an innocent man, even if it turned out to be wasted time. I wished I had some way of letting him know I was back on track, fighting for us all.

Neil signed me into the building as a visitor and we took the lift to the massive newsroom, where he found me a spare computer. It was hushed in there: people worked quietly, TV monitors were turned to silent, even the phones were muted. About half the desks were empty. Neil said there'd been some redundancies before Christmas and, of those staff who remained, several were on holiday. I wasn't going to be in anyone's way. I hung my coat and scarf over the back of the chair and ramped the seat up to a comfortable position. Neil perched on the edge of the desk and scratched his head.

'I think we should start with Matt Bryant,' he said. 'He's the chap Alexander embezzled from. Do you know the story?'

I nodded. 'I read a newspaper report of the trial.'

'It's the furthest back we can go right now. Alexander and Genevieve married as soon as he'd finished his gaol sentence, right?'

'Yes.'

'So they must have been close before he went into prison. All the reports suggest he and Bryant were good friends before then, so Bryant can probably tell us more about his relationship with Genevieve.'

'Right.'

'If Bryant's business is still going, you might be able to find it on the internet,' Neil said. 'Are you OK with that?'

I nodded. I felt like a child on her first day at school. I was literally itching to get started.

'While you're doing that, I'll see what I can find out about Genevieve. Is there anything important I don't know about? Do you have any leads for me?'

'Only Luke Innes,' I said.

'OK. I'll get on to him. I'll be over there by the news desk. You'll be all right?'

'I'll be fine,' I said. I wanted him to go away and let me get on with the job.

In the event, it took about two minutes to find what I was looking for. By eight o'clock I was already familiar with Bryant's Reclamation and Restoration, having found the business website and looked at all the pages. It wasn't a particularly fancy site, but it was clear that, far from folding, the business was thriving and had expanded into selling garden furniture and stoneware. I showed Neil and asked him what I should do next, and he looked at me as if I was a complete idiot and told me to call the contact number and ask to speak to Matt Bryant.

'What should I say?'

'Ask him about Alexander.'

'But he must hate Alex, after what he did. Why should he help me?'

'You're not asking for help, you're asking for information.'

'What should I do if he doesn't want to talk to me?'

Neil pulled a face. 'Be charming. Flirt. I don't know, you'll think of something.'

It took me several minutes to compose myself enough to dial the contact number. It wasn't even half past eight and I thought it was unlikely there would be anyone there. I expected to be put through to an answer-phone and was planning the message I'd leave when a gruff voice at the end of the line said: 'Hello, Bryant's Reclamation.'

As it turned out, I had got straight through to the right person. Matt Bryant was not exactly unfriendly, but he was suspicious. He'd heard the news about Alexander and Genevieve and had already been contacted by several national publications wanting to sign him up for an exclusive story about how he knew the murderer when he was only a thief. They wouldn't be able to publish any of this before the trial because it was *sub judice*, but they'd be able to run a bumper supplement when . . . *if* Alexander was found guilty.

'Can't stand the vultures,' Matt said. 'I had quite enough of them last time round, but they won't bloody leave me alone. I told them to piss off, I'm not speaking to anyone.'

'But I'm not a journalist,' I said quickly.

I told him who I was and explained my relationship with Alexander. I did my best to convince him that my intentions were honourable but he said he'd been 'stitched up' too often in the past and refused to speak to me over the phone.

'If you want to talk, we'll do it face to face,' he said. 'But I'm not promising anything.'

He put the phone down. I sat for a moment, trying to work out what to do. I crossed to Neil's desk.

'What now?' he asked.

'He won't talk to me on the phone.'

'Well, go and see him then.'

'He's in Worcester.'

'It's not that far.'

Neil put his hand in his pocket and pulled out a set of keys.

'You know which car it is,' he said. 'Go on. Off you go.'

I listened to Radio 4 as I drove back down the M5, and by lunchtime I was sitting in the café that faced the reclamation yard, eating a cheese and tomato toastie. Matt Bryant sat opposite tucking into a hot meat pie and chips. When I'd arrived, he had recognized me from a newspaper photograph taken the day I left Burrington

Stoke. He'd put a hand on my shoulder and squeezed and said: 'It *is* you. I had to be sure. Might have been somebody pretending to be you. It's a terrible bloody business. Let's get something to eat.'

I liked him. He was a chatty, friendly man with a strong chin and an even stronger country accent. He was proud of his business, his family and his success. He wore an expensive watch and overalls. His boots had steel toecaps yet he smelled of Calvin Klein and his car had a personalized plate. I could imagine him being Alexander's friend, but in a different world from the one in which I knew Alexander. The café was busy, hot and steamy, decorated with tinsel and battery-operated Santas who tinkled and chimed in competition with the end-of-year songs playing on the radio.

Matt shook his head as I told him my version of the story.

'I knew it would end in disaster,' he said. 'I bloody knew it.'

'What would end in disaster?' I asked.

'Alex and Genevieve. We all warned him, but he wouldn't listen.'

'It wasn't exactly her fault how it ended,' I said quietly.

'Listen,' Matt said, waving his fork at me. 'She sucked Alex up and we knew she'd spit him out when she'd had enough.'

'How did they meet?' I asked.

'She was a friend of my sister's. They'd been at university together.'

'Oh, right.'

'We all used to hang around in a crowd. All the girls

liked Alex but he only had eyes for Gen. He thought they were fated to be together. He was one of those people who was always trying to make things right. I expect you know what he's like.'

I felt a pang of missing Alexander. Up to that point, I hadn't met anyone who knew him before Genevieve. If things had been different, I thought, if I had known him then, when we were younger, before any of these bad things happened . . . But he wouldn't have been interested in me. He would still have chosen Genevieve, of course.

Matt took a drink of tea and swallowed.

'No matter what the mess was, he'd try to clean it up. It was the way he was, probably because of his useless bloody mother. And Genevieve, for all her fancy education and her horses and her looks, she was a mess.'

I had never heard her described like that before. It contradicted everything I knew about her.

'How was she a mess?' I asked.

Matt rolled his eyes.

'She was involved with an older man. He was married but had promised to leave his wife – usual story – then the wife went and fell pregnant and so he had to stay with her for the sake of the kid, and that's why Genevieve came to live with us for a while. She was in a right old state, crying all the time, threatening to do all sorts. One minute she was going to front it out with the wife, the next she was going to kill herself. She said she couldn't bear to be at home trying to put a brave face on it with her mother asking questions all the time.'

The man couldn't have been Luke Innes, because

Luke wasn't older and he hadn't been married. I felt a twinge of frustration. I could imagine Virginia interrogating Genevieve, trying to get to the bottom of her daughter's unhappiness, and Genevieve being unable to tell her mother anything for fear of the repercussions. I could understand why she needed to get away.

'Did she ever go on!' Matt said. 'She was a class-A victim, the world's greatest drama queen. Any normal person would have thought "silly cow" for getting involved with a married man. But Alex took her side completely. He blamed the bloke, thought she'd been used and abused, and wanted to make her happy again.'

I nodded encouragingly.

'He loved the girl,' Matt said. 'He worshipped the ground she walked on. He would have done anything for her, anything.'

He picked up a piece of buttered bread and wiped his plate. I gazed out of the window for a moment while I composed myself. I was furiously jealous of Genevieve and furious with Alexander for being so good to her.

'I didn't think you'd be defending Alexander,' I said. 'Not after what he did to you.'

Matt paused with the bread between his fingers. He looked right into my eyes. Then he looked away again and put the bread into his mouth. I waited while he chewed. He washed it down with a drink of tea, and took a long time swallowing. He replaced the cup in its saucer slowly.

'You don't know the half of it,' he said.

'I know he stole a lot of money and brought you to the brink of bankruptcy.'

Matt nodded. 'That's what it said in the papers, yes.'

'Isn't it true?'

'Alex confessed. He pleaded guilty. That much is true.'

'I don't know what you're trying to say,' I said.

Matt leaned forward and spoke quietly.

'You don't know what happened after the trial, do you?'

I shook my head.

'As soon as Alex changed his plea to guilty, magically all the missing money reappeared in the company accounts.'

'All of it?'

'Every penny.'

Matt sat back up straight again. He folded his arms across his chest. I put the crust of the toastie back on the plate and wiped my fingers on a paper napkin.

'I don't understand. Are you saying the money was never stolen?'

'No, it was stolen all right. Only, once Alex took the rap, somebody gave it back with a note to our accountant that it was an anonymous donation from a well-wisher.'

'Why would anyone do that?'

'I figured that somebody told Alex that, if he changed his plea, they'd bail the business out. So he put his neck on the line to save mine.'

'My God.'

'Of course he was also protecting whoever did take the money.'

The breathless, excited feeling was creeping back under my skin. My mouth was dry. I took a sip of tea. I felt a surge of affection for Alexander. I held the next question in my mouth for a second or two before I asked, because the answer was so important to me.

'You're certain it wasn't Alexander? He's not the thief?'

Matt snorted.

'How long have you known him? He can't do numbers, he can barely manage email. He counted as special needs in school, his dyslexia was so bad. No way he could have pulled off a stunt like that and covered his tracks.'

'If it wasn't him . . . ?'

'Oh, come on, it's not rocket science! Who had a rich, besotted father willing to do anything to keep his baby out of trouble? The same person whom Alex wouldn't have thought twice about going to gaol for? The poor sod probably thought she'd see it as proof of his devotion.'

'Genevieve?'

'Who else?'

I had to look down in case Matt saw the jealousy in my eyes. I was ashamed of myself. Poor Genevieve was dead, she was lying ice-cold in a mortuary drawer somewhere, she would never see Alexander's face or hold her son again, and still I was jealous. Still that nasty little worm of resentment burrowed away at me.

'But her father's rich as Croesus,' I said to Matt. 'Why would she need to steal money?'

'I don't know, but I'd wager it was something to do with the married lover. Maybe he'd told her he couldn't afford to leave his missus now they had a kid. Maybe she wanted to buy a love nest. She could hardly go asking Daddy for money for that.'

I remembered the flat in Tenby.

'So you don't think it was over between Genevieve and this man even though he'd told her he wasn't going to leave his wife?'

Matt shrugged. 'She didn't get pregnant by herself, did she?'

'No, no she didn't.'

'I'm sorry the girl's dead,' said Matt. 'She didn't deserve that, but there was never going to be a happy ending for those two. Genny was eight months pregnant when they let Alex out of prison, and still he believed her when she told him he was the one she'd wanted all along.'

We chatted for a little longer. I asked Matt if Genevieve had stayed in touch with his sister, and he said he didn't know. Charlene had married and gone to work for a bank in Hong Kong. She had a couple of kids and was settled there; he hadn't seen her for several years. I came to the impression they weren't close.

When I stood to say goodbye, he stood too, and he shook my hand and clasped my shoulder.

'I hope it's all going to turn out all right for you and Alex,' he said. 'He's a lucky man to have you fighting his corner for him.'

I shook my head. 'I lost the faith for a while.'

'You're all right, love,' he said. 'You're doing fine. And when you see Alex, when you get him out of the clink, give him my regards. Tell him I could do with an extra pair of hands round here if he's at a loose end.'

'Thank you,' I said. 'I will.'

Alexander is innocent, I thought, as I left Worcester and headed back towards the motorway. He was definitely innocent of the theft and he was probably innocent of murder. The things he'd told me about his relationship with Genevieve – that she had been in love with somebody else when they married, that he had tried to make her happy but couldn't – had all been confirmed by what Matt had told me. Everything was complicated and hidden behind secrets and lies, put in place to protect darker secrets and lies. The story was the same, it just depended which way you told it.

I told myself that I'd known Alexander was a good man in my heart all along but now I knew it in my head too. I wished there was some way I could wind back the clock to the day Alexander and Jamie went to fetch the Christmas tree. I wished that, instead of running away from Alexander, I'd gone to stand at his side and taken his hand and had the courage to tell the police officers that he was incapable of dishonesty or worse.

But I hadn't.

I'd believed he was a thief. I'd suspected him of hiding Genevieve's laptop in the well and deliberately making me doubt my own mind. When I'd looked at him, I'd remembered the words *You next*, and I'd wondered what he was going to do to me.

Alexander had loved Genevieve unconditionally, until she made it impossible for him to love her any more. I began to understand why she had acted as she had, why she had stabbed him. His devotion must have frustrated her. She must have felt trapped by it. Perhaps she had wanted to make him understand that she would never reciprocate his feelings for her. She wanted to set him free.

But she'd also wanted to keep her child.

Alexander had done nothing but look after me and put his trust in me. He didn't love me like he loved Genevieve, but maybe that sort of passion only comes once in a person's life. I could hardly blame him for that.

Alexander was innocent, but I was guilty of the worst disloyalty. I didn't know if he'd ever be able to forgive me. I knew I would never forgive myself.

CHAPTER SIXTY-FOUR

It was late by the time I arrived back in Manchester. The Christmas lights were still lit but the sales had started and there were leaflets and posters defacing the shop windows and the streets seemed to be full of sodden litter. Everywhere was quiet. It was the calm before the chaos of the New Year's Eve celebrations. The eyes of a fox gleamed in the headlights and then the creature turned and trotted into the darkness. I watched the city pass me by and I wondered where Alexander was and what he was thinking; if he had any inkling that I was doing my best for him or if he had given up on me as he believed I had given up on him.

When I got back to the flat, Neil opened the door to me, and we hugged enthusiastically.

'Through here,' May called. 'I've made kebabs.'

'I just need to wash my hands!'

I went through to the bathroom and freshened up, then I went into the spare room – my room – and crossed to the window to draw the curtains. I gazed out. I couldn't see much in the dark, only the lighted windows of the houses that backed on to May and Neil's street. For a moment I felt the weight of a baby on my shoulder. I had imagined broken nights standing at a window like this, patting my baby's back, singing him to sleep as he nuzzled his hot little head into my neck, and the little snuffling noises he would make. I had imagined that scenario so many times it was almost as if I was remembering something real. Almost.

I pulled the curtain across.

We sat in the living room. May had made a buffet supper and laid it out on the table. She and Neil sat on the settee, and I sat on the floor opposite. The room was cosy. I felt safe and hungry and normal, like my old self.

'Look at you!' said May, passing me a glass of wine. 'All bright-eyed and bushy-tailed! You're dying to tell us what you found out, aren't you?'

I shuffled about a bit.

'Go on,' said Neil, gesturing with his hand.

'Well,' I began, like a child about to recite a poem in front of the class, 'the main thing is that Alexander didn't steal a single penny from Matt Bryant's business.'

I beamed at May and Neil. They nodded at me encouragingly.

'In fact it was quite the opposite. Matt thinks Alex made a deal to save it. He thinks Alex agreed to plead guilty because he knew, if he did, the missing money would be paid back to Matt.'

Neil pulled a face.

'That may be the case, but it doesn't rule out

Alexander from being the person who took it in the first place,' he said.

'Matt's theory is if the trial had progressed Alex would have been proved innocent and the identity of the true culprit would have been obvious. That's why it was imperative he changed his plea when he did.'

'Goodness!' May raised her eyebrows. Her eyes were wide. We exchanged smiles.

'Matt thinks Genevieve took the money,' I said.

'What do you think?'

'I think he's probably right.'

'How did she do it?'

'I don't know.'

'I think I might!' said Neil.

May and I gazed at him expectantly.

'Hold on,' said Neil. 'Let me start from the beginning.'

He told us he'd tracked down the last of Genevieve's old schools easily enough through the internet and spoken to her long-suffering house mistress. Genevieve had been a 'wilful' girl, according to the woman, who didn't go into details but implied that Genevieve, having successfully contrived to get herself expelled from two boarding schools, had spent most of her time at the third endeavouring to achieve a hat trick.

'She told me that everyone was surprised when Genevieve announced that she wanted to go to university,' said Neil, 'because she wasn't at all academic and had shown no inclination to study. All she wanted to do was ride. Everyone assumed that, if she bothered with further education at all, she'd go to the agricultural college in Cirencester, but one day she decided that university was what she wanted to do, and that's what she did.'

'She must've done OK at school to get in,' said May.

Neil shook his head. 'She did terribly. The school suspects strings were pulled. The family must have had friends on the staff.'

'It's all right for some,' May said. She wiped her fingers on a sheet of kitchen paper and then sat back into the settee.

'Genevieve was at university with Matt Bryant's sister,' I said.

Neil nodded. 'That's where she and Charlene Bryant met and became friends. And that lad you mentioned, Sarah, Luke Innes, he was in the year above her and they all shared a flat for a while.'

'Ahhh . . .' said May. 'That's why she wanted to go to university. Her boyfriend was there.'

'You could well be right,' said Neil. 'Only if it was love's young dream, it didn't last long. Luke dropped out in the second term of his second year when he found out Genevieve had been seeing someone else.'

A thrill of excitement ran all the way through me, like an electric shock. Everything was falling into place. I put up my hand to interject.

'Matt said she was involved with somebody who was married.'

'Blimey,' said May, wide-eyed.

'That's right,' said Neil.

He put his plate on the carpet and leaned forward, resting his arms on his knees. 'The fourth person in the university flat-share was a woman called Isabel Gerard.

She thinks Genevieve may have been seeing somebody she'd met on the eventing circuit. He'd promised to leave his wife . . .'

'But then the wife fell pregnant and that changed everything,' I said, thrilled that our two separate lines of investigation were marrying. 'Matt made it sound as if Genevieve had some kind of breakdown. She couldn't cope with being at home, because Virginia wouldn't leave her alone, so she went to stay with Matt's sister and the family. That's how she met Alexander.'

'So if she was living with Matt's family, and was friendly with Alexander, she would have known all about how the business was doing,' May said.

'Exactly. And she must have known Alexander had trouble with numbers, so she probably offered to help out with the accounts or something. That's how she stole the money.'

'We don't actually know this,' I said. I was looking for reassurance or confirmation, because I desperately wanted it to be the truth.

'It all fits,' said Neil.

'You didn't find out the name of this married man?' I asked Neil. He shook his head.

'Isabel wasn't even sure he was a rider, only that somebody from Genevieve's horse-riding life would be the most likely candidate, and that does tie in with what we know about her more recent activities – assuming it's the same bloke. She said Genevieve was very protective about him so she thought he must be somebody important, perhaps someone famous, maybe somebody titled even. The family rubbed shoulders with the gentry. It's feasible.'

'We can rule out Luke Innes if it was Genevieve's new relationship that drove him away.'

'It could have been anyone,' said Neil. 'If it was somebody rich and famous, and if whoever-he-is is still married, he certainly won't want to be identified. Especially not now.'

'Isn't there anything you can go on?' May asked.

Neil shrugged. 'Isabel said that, once, and only once, she overheard Genevieve talking on the phone. She was upset and drunk and she was pleading with someone called Lee. Does that ring a bell with you, Sarah?'

'No.'

'Bollocks.'

We sat up a while longer, talking, but soon I was overwhelmed with tiredness. I kissed May and Neil goodnight, washed and changed, and snuggled down into my bed with the electric blanket turned up high, but I couldn't sleep. My mind was full of Alexander and Jamie and the secrets between us, keeping us apart.

CHAPTER SIXTY-FIVE

The next morning, Neil had to do an interview on his way to work, so he left his laptop with me and told me to make a written record of everything we'd found out so far. May worked as a volunteer teaching assistant at a school for autistic children three days a week and, before she left that morning, she asked me to shop for the evening's dinner. I had plenty to keep me occupied, but there were other things I needed to do first.

I watched the television news while I drank my coffee. The newsreader had a kind, authoritative face. He was wearing a dark suit and tie. Behind him was a photograph of Genevieve. It wasn't a horsey one: she was wearing a pink ballgown and jewels sparkled at her earlobes and around her throat. Her hair was exquisitely styled. She looked like a princess.

The newsreader spoke slowly and precisely.

The body in the quarry had been identified as Genevieve's a week ago, while I was curled up depressed in bed. Now, preliminary results of the post mortem indicated that she had died from a single wound to the head. There was no doubt it had been deliberately inflicted. She had been murdered.

I closed my eyes. It didn't really matter *how* she had died; still, each new detail made me sad. It made the image in my mind worse. Every time I found out something new, the desire to be with Jamie and to look after him and to protect him increased. I ached for Jamie. I wondered what he was doing and who was caring for him. And in the next heartbeat my mind jumped to Alexander. I wondered if he knew yet how Genevieve had died. I doubted the news would have been broken to him gently; it would most likely have been used as a whip to beat him with. Was he alone? Was his heart breaking? I closed my eyes and tried to imagine myself inside Alexander's head, and his body, and when I did I had a dry taste in my mouth and a numb coldness in my head like death.

As far as Alexander knew, not a single person in the world was on his side.

I opened Neil's notebook, found a few empty pages and began to write.

Dear Alex

I held the pen over the next line but I didn't know how to condense everything I was feeling into few enough words to fit on the narrow sheet of paper. I didn't know how to explain what had been happening or what I was doing to help put things right or why it had taken me so long to get in touch.

I wrote:

I don't know everything, but I know some of the truth about Genevieve.

Then I crossed the words out. They sounded melodramatic. Alex would think I was obsessing about Genevieve again. He wouldn't understand, from those words, what I meant. I started a new piece of paper.

Dear Alex
I think about you every moment of every day and I hope you are . . .

I stopped again. I hoped he was what? Bearing up? Keeping well? Thinking about me?

I tore out the paper and screwed it up.

Dear Alex
I am sure you're worrying about Jamie and I wanted to let you know that he's . . .

I didn't know how Jamie was. I didn't know where he was or who was looking after him. I put the pad down, muted the television and, without giving myself time to fret about it, I called Claudia's number. Bill answered.

'Hi Bill, it's Sarah,' I said.

'Hello,' he said, and his voice was cold and defensive. He didn't ask how I was. He didn't say anything apart from that one word.

'I saw the news,' I said. 'I'm so sorry, Bill.'

'Thank you.'

'How's Claudia?' I asked. Bill sighed at the inanity of the question and didn't bother to answer.

'And Jamie?' I asked. 'Has anyone spoken to Jamie yet? Does he know about Genevieve?'

'He knows she's dead,' said Bill. I flinched at the way he said this, the brutality of it.

'What did you tell him?'

'Sarah, I don't really think it's appropriate that I—'

'Is he there?'

'No.'

'Then where . . . ?'

'He's with his grandparents.'

I thought of Jamie, prickly, difficult Jamie, how he pulled the hem of his sweatshirt or his pyjama top up over his nose to hide the fact that he was sucking his thumb, how he tried so hard not to care. I imagined Virginia exhorting him to be brave, to be a strong little man. I imagined her subtly, oh so subtly, feeding him poison about Alexander. My eyes felt hot.

'Is he all right?'

'As all right as he can be. We're doing our best to protect him from the truth.'

'Nobody knows what the truth is yet,' I said.

'Well, listen,' said Bill, 'I'd love to chat but . . .'

'Would you just tell Claudia she's never far from my thoughts? And also tell her that Neil, my brother-in-law, he's a journalist, he's looking into everything and—'

'Sarah . . .'

'I know. I'm sorry. You've got more pressing matters on your mind. Just tell Claudia that we're almost certain Alexander didn't hurt Genevieve. Would you tell her that?'

'I won't because it will upset her. We know all about your weird little obsession with Genevieve and, quite frankly, Sarah, what you're doing now is sick.'

I shook my head. This conversation was going all wrong.

'Bill, maybe I was a bit obsessed but . . .'

'Let her go, Sarah. Let go of us all. Stop your stalking. It's over.'

I held the receiver close to my face.

'I'm sorry, I just . . . Bill, when you see Jamie, please tell him that I'm missing him and that I'll see him soon.'

But the line was dead. I don't think Bill heard any of my last words at all.

CHAPTER SIXTY-SIX

I had a shower and dressed up warm, then spent an hour on the internet and telephone tracking Alexander from the police station in Castle Cary via the local court to Bristol prison. I called the prison and asked if it would be possible to speak to him, but it wasn't. The officer was brisk, but not unkind.

'Could you give him a message?' I asked. 'Please tell him . . .' Again I searched for the right words.

'Why don't I just tell him that you're missing him?' he suggested.

'Yes,' I said. 'Thank you. And tell him not to worry about Jamie. Tell him everything's going to be fine.'

I spent another hour or so typing everything I knew and had been told about Genevieve and Alexander into a document on Neil's computer. I was careful to date and reference everything, then I emailed the document to Neil at work.

After that, I put on my coat and boots and walked down to the small supermarket at the end of the road. I passed a small group of revellers already in fancy dress, laughing and waving football rattles. I smiled at them and we all wished each other a Happy New Year. A large man dressed as Top Cat kissed me full on the lips.

The last newspapers of the year were stacked inside the shop. They were full of round-ups and lists. I couldn't see any new Genevieve headlines.

I bought the ingredients to make a spaghetti carbonara, and had just reached the check-out when my phone rang.

I wriggled the phone out of the pocket of my jeans and checked the display: it was Neil. Before I could say a word he said: 'Sarah, there's something I need you to see. Where are you?'

'In the Co-Op.'

'Get a cab, will you? Come to the office as quickly as you can.'

'What is it?'

'Just hurry. You'll see.'

He met me at the staff entrance, grabbed my hand and pulled me into the stairwell.

'The lifts are broken,' he said. 'We'll have to climb.'

'Tell me what you've found!' I was struggling to keep up. Neil had longer legs than me and was taking the stairs two at a time.

'Proof that we're on the right lines,' he said. His voice was euphoric and proud.

My heart was thumping as I followed him along a corridor, through some swing doors and back into the newsroom.

Neil indicated that I should sit on a wheeled chair in

front of his desk while he rebooted his computer. He logged in, his fingers working deftly and quickly, and within moments a screen full of emails appeared.

'What is it?' I asked.

He leaned over my shoulder. 'Look.'

The account belonged to someone called Charlene Ho.

'Matt's sister?' I asked Laurie. He nodded. And he pointed to the screen.

On 21 July, there had been a message from Genny C.

I looked up at Neil.

'Open it,' he said.

'This is a private account. How did you get into it?'

'Doesn't matter.'

'Is it legal?'

'Just read the email.'

I clicked on the envelope icon and the email filled the screen.

Genevieve had written:

```
All set for Friday. I'm SOOOO nervous!
I can't believe it's really happening,
but this time it is – definitely!!!
```

'Is she talking about leaving?'

Neil nodded. I read on.

```
You understand, don't you, Charlie,
this is the ONLY way we can be together,
honestly, and we are both sick of the
lies and deception. It just gets worse
```

the longer it drags on. It'll be better for everyone this way in the long run. Hope all's well in Hong Kong. Write soon, I'm going to miss your emails while we're in Sicily. All love, Gen xxx

I closed my eyes for a moment. Genevieve wrote how I had imagined she would talk, with her emphatic capital letters and her dramatic exclamation marks. She had been apprehensive and excited when she wrote that message, believing that her elopement was imminent and that all her problems would soon be over. It was almost unbearably intimate, and knowing that all her plans had come to nothing made me feel terribly sad.

She had written another email on the same date, just before midnight.

Charlie, I'm worried. Alex has been watching me tonight, I'm sure he suspects something. I'm having to write this from the bathroom(!) it's the only place I can get any privacy. I wish I could leave right now. I don't think I can stand another day of this scrutiny. I know I won't be able to sleep and he'll know I'm not sleeping and then he'll be wanting to know what's wrong etc. I'll be so glad when this is over. Gxxx

I looked up at Neil. 'I don't like the sound of this.'

'There are more,' he said.

Charlene and Genevieve had continued to write to one another until well into the early hours of that morning, Genevieve sounding increasingly tired and fraught and Charlene reassuring her and urging her to rest.

Finally, at 4.30 a.m., Genevieve had written:

> Oh, Christ, it's getting light. I can FEEL the dawn coming. It's too late to sleep now. I'm looking at my face in the bathroom mirror and I look like a ghost. If L saw me like this he'd change his mind for sure. I'm off to see the horses. Thanks for keeping me company, C, you are SUCH a lovely friend, love Gxxx

'What's the time difference between here and Hong Kong?' I asked.

'They're seven hours ahead,' said Neil. 'Genevieve's sleepless night would have been Charlene's morning.'

There was nothing from Genevieve for the next ten hours, but the following afternoon she'd written:

> Managed to snatch some time with L. We went to our place, he calmed me down a bit. Says it will be fine. Says not to worry. I don't know how he can be so RELAXED. I made him promise me that this time it will really really happen

`and he says this time it really really will. Am so tired. Gx`

'This is the day before she died?' I asked Neil. He nodded. He had made a steeple with his fingers and was resting his chin on its point.

I swallowed. 'It feels wrong,' I said, 'reading this. It's too . . . intimate. It feels like spying. Like stalking.'

'Genevieve's dead,' said Neil. 'It won't hurt her. Think of Alexander. Think of the child.'

'I know but . . .'

Neil squeezed my shoulder.

'This is important,' he said.

Later that day Genevieve had written:

`J's been playing up since school. I showed him pictures of the house in Sicily. Told him a 'story' about a boy who lived on the beach with his mummy and his daddy etc. He's going to miss Alex. Am not proud of myself. Gx`

I exhaled slowly. At 6 p.m. she'd sent another email.

`You're right. It WILL be better when everything's out in the open. I guess the family will forgive me one day!!! Alex thinks I'm ill. Made me come up here for a lie-down. I called L just now, he promised me he's going to tell the family he's leaving tonight. It's` going to be awfully hard for him but he promised this time he will do it. Christ, Charlene, you must be SICK of hearing this same story over and over. I don't know how you can bear to be my friend but I'm so glad you are. Gxxx

At 11 p.m. there was another brief message:

Haven't heard anything. Have called L a dozen times. His phone's switched off. Do you think that means he's told them? Why didn't he text? He said he was going to text to let me know that he'd done it, but he hasn't.

11.05 p.m.:

You're so wise! Of course he can't text – either they'll be fighting or talking. Poor him. Poor them. Gxxx

11.45 p.m.:

I couldn't bear it any longer. I called the landline. He answered. He said he couldn't talk but he said it in a way that made me think he was in the middle of something deep. He HAS told her. I know he has.

2 a.m.:

I STILL haven't heard anything but, like you say, no news is good news. Just think, Charlie, in less than 12 hours we're going to be together, me, him and Jamie – first time we'll have been a proper family, out of the closet so to speak!!! Can't wait!

Wish me luck, Charlie! Don't expect to hear from me for a while. It's going to take ages to sort out broad-band etc in Sicily. I'll be back in touch when I can. But I promise I'll be fine. I've never been so happy in my WHOLE LIFE!!!

Love you loads, Genny xxx

I read the series of emails three times. Neil perched on the corner of the desk and passed me a corrugated-cardboard beaker full of coffee.

'Are you all right?'

I nodded. Then I shook my head.

'Poor Genevieve,' I said. 'That last sentence . . .'

'It sounds as if Lee's been leading her right up the garden path,' Neil said. 'But it doesn't tell us any more about who he is.'

He peeled the lid off his coffee and blew at the steam.

'The trouble is, none of these emails proves Alexander didn't kill his wife. Genevieve says he's watching her, that he suspects something, that she's nervous. One could argue that all this points to the possibility of her deciding to front it out with Alexander that morning and him losing his rag and doing her in. Or him finding out, somehow, that she was planning to take Jamie away.'

'But it does confirm that she was due to meet this L – Lee, it's got to be Lee – on the morning of the twenty-fourth and that they were planning to go to Sicily with Jamie.'

I imagined Genevieve's excitement that morning, her anxiety and how she'd be thinking about her little house by the sea, and of being a family with her son and her lover. I'd had exactly the same fantasy, only I'd pictured Jamie, Alexander and me in Cornwall. I remembered how I had enjoyed that imaginary scenario, how I'd played the tape forward until Jamie was a long-haired, broad-shouldered teenager and Alexander and I had lines on our faces from laughing so often, and so well. No doubt Genevieve had done the same. Was there anything I had done that she had not done first? Even in my mind?

'Did you read Genevieve's earlier emails?'

Neil nodded.

'What do they say?'

'Much the same. She was getting increasingly frustrated by her lover's procrastination. Scroll down a bit to 19 June. Yes, that's the one.'

`I told him today that if he won't tell her, I WILL!!!`

'She's threatening to tell his wife about their relationship?'

'Yep. She says she doesn't care about the consequences any more.'

I pulled a face at Neil. 'So how did Lee react to that?'

'Look at the next email.'

```
He showed me pictures of the house in
Sicily. He says we can rent it for six
months while we sort ourselves out.
It's beautiful and remote and it will
give us the time and space we need to
become a proper family.
```

'It sounds as if he's trying to buy time,' I said.

Neil nodded.

'There's something, somewhere, about the brother, Damian, too.'

Neil leaned across me and flicked through some of the messages.

'Here.'

Genevieve had written:

```
Sicily is going to be our new start. And
once everyone knows, I'll finally get my
evil half-brother off my back!!!
```

'What do you think that means?' I asked.

'Well' – Neil tapped his teeth with the end of his pen – 'this is just a guess, but you told me Damian hated Genevieve, didn't you?'

'He was just a little kid when . . .'

I stopped speaking as I realized that Damian had been almost exactly the same age as Jamie was now when his mother died. Damian had been brought up by Philip and Virginia Churchill and never been loved as he should have been. I knew how damaged he was. I could not, would not, let the same thing happen to Jamie. I felt a rush of anger inside me and it made me feel stronger.

'Yes,' I said. 'Yes, he hated Genevieve. He blamed her for everything.'

'Well, let's suppose he found out about her affair. Damian was estranged from his family, he needed money to finance his campaigns and causes, he didn't have a job but he needed somewhere to live . . .'

'You think he was blackmailing Genevieve?'

'Yep,' Neil nodded. 'I think he was. I think the original hundred thousand that was taken from the Bryant account was to keep him quiet when lover-boy's wife was pregnant. Probably it was an agreed one-off, and it would have lasted him a while, but what if he'd been getting greedy again? That would have put Genevieve under a huge amount of stress and would have been another compelling reason for her to come out, as she puts it, and get everything into the open.'

'And it would explain why Damian came back to Burrington Stoke when he heard she was missing. He'd need to know if what he'd heard was true. Do you think he'd tell us, or the police, who Genevieve was seeing?'

'He'd have to admit to blackmail. I don't know the man, Sarah, but there could be any number of reasons why he wouldn't want to get involved. Possibly he now regards the lover as an even more reliable source of funds.'

We were both silent for a few moments.

Then Neil said: 'There's something we haven't considered yet. Remember when we first met Alexander in Sicily, he said he was there "on business", or something like that.'

'Mmm.' I nodded.

'And that night we had dinner with him, Jamie was complaining that he'd spent ages talking to some man.'

'Yes.'

'Do you know who this man was?'

I shook my head. 'I got the impression that Alexander was paying him for something.'

'Private detective, maybe?'

'It's possible.'

'Alex had obviously got wind of the fact they were planning to go to Sicily.'

I took a sharp intake of breath.

'Neil, if he and Jamie were in Sicily looking for Genevieve, then he *can't* have known she was dead.'

'You're right,' said Neil. 'Think, *think* who this man could have been. We need to speak to him.'

I racked my brains.

'Rowl,' I said. 'Or Rowell perhaps. Alex probably spelled it wrong, but someone he called Rowl was trying to call Alex in Sicily. I saw the name on the phone.'

Neil wrote the name down.

'I'll see what I can do,' he said.

* * *

I went to the canteen to buy us some sandwiches. When I returned, Neil was sitting in a chair, leaning back, talking on the telephone. He had fastened a mini-recorder to the set, to keep a copy of the conversation. When he saw me, he beamed and gave me the thumbs-up.

'Bingo!' he mouthed.

I put our lunch down and sat at the desk, my hands between my knees, while I waited. Neil kept saying things like 'Yes, I know,' and 'I completely understand,' and 'Right, OK.'

It seemed to take for ever.

At last, he thanked whoever was on the other end of the line profusely, switched off the phone, scooted his chair right up to mine and kissed my forehead.

'Not Rowell but Raul. Sam Raul. He's a private detective based in Catania who specializes in gathering evidence in transnational child-custody cases.'

'Were you speaking to him?'

'No, to his assistant. The general gist was she couldn't discuss individual cases but could confirm that a Mr Westwood had been to their office. And she remembered Jamie.'

'So what you're saying is . . . Alex had gone to Sicily to prepare himself to fight Genevieve for custody of Jamie?'

'Yep. He must have assumed she was going to come back for him. He had an idea she was in Sicily so he wanted to find a local expert who understood the law and how the system worked.'

'And that's why he needed me,' I said quietly. 'Somebody who wasn't a Churchill to keep a close eye on Jamie in case Genevieve came back to take him.'

'Maybe that's part of the reason.'

Neil took my hand and squeezed.

'Sarah, this is the evidence we need to clear Alex's name,' he said. 'It doesn't matter that we haven't identified this Lee person. That's a job for the police now.'

I hardly dared believe what he was saying.

'What do we do next?' I asked.

'I'll put the facts into order to present to the police. Then I'll tip off some of the nationals that we've got a cracking story about to break. That'll put pressure on the police to hurry things along and get your man out of gaol fast. You don't mind us going big on this?'

'Can you keep Jamie out of it?'

'I'll do my best.'

'What about me?' I asked. 'What should I do?'

Neil reached over and hugged me.

'Get yourself back down to Somerset and start picking up the pieces.'

'You don't think it's too late?'

'It's never too late,' he said.

CHAPTER SIXTY-SEVEN

I stopped on the way back to May and Neil's flat to buy a postcard with a picture of Manchester By Night on the front. The streets were busy now, packed with taxis and people dressed up to the nines. I enjoyed the bustle and the atmosphere. I wrote the postcard in the shop: *We know what happened. You'll soon be out of there.* I didn't know how I should sign it, so I just wrote my name underneath. The shopkeeper gave me an envelope and I addressed it to HMP Bristol. I posted it first class.

At the flat, I checked the train times back to Bristol. Then I called DI Twyford, but he didn't pick up his phone. I tried police headquarters but they wouldn't tell me anything or let me explain why I was calling. I didn't know who Alexander's solicitor was. I called Claudia's number but there was no answer there either so I recorded a message on the answerphone saying that I would be returning to Burrington Stoke first thing in the morning.

I ran myself a bath, and I lay in the hot water with my

eyes closed. I was exhausted, but also excited. Alexander was innocent of everything except love, misplaced loyalty and a ridiculous pride that could have cost him everything. He was a hero in my eyes. I was ashamed and sorry ever to have doubted him. I wished he'd trusted me enough to explain the past to me and, at the same time, I understood why he didn't want to return to it. Maybe he regretted sacrificing so much for Genevieve. Perhaps he thought the best way to protect Jamie was to bury painful truths as deeply as he could and hide them behind more palatable lies. Either way, he thought those times were behind him, but they weren't. He was the same as everyone else: he carried his past inside him. There was no escape from it, he could not shut a door and close it away.

No matter how hard you push it down, the truth always comes to the surface – that's what Betsy had said.

When my bones were warm, I climbed out of the bath, wrapped myself in warm towels from the airing cupboard and sat on the bed drying my hair.

I looked at the picture of Alexander and Jamie on my phone: Jamie with his wide grin and his sticking-out ears, his blue, blue eyes with the darker outline of the iris; Jamie who was not going to turn into another Damian, not while I had breath in my lungs.

'I'm coming to get you,' I whispered, and I held the phone to my lips.

The city was noisy and joyful. The pubs were full and people were singing. I knew May and Neil would have been invited out, but both, separately, told me they'd used me as an excuse to stay at home. They didn't feel like going out, they said.

'I'm perfectly all right now,' I said. 'Honestly, I'm fine!'

May looked at me, searchingly, and a little smile came on to her face, and she beckoned me with her finger and I followed her into her bedroom. She opened the top drawer of her dressing table and took out a narrow plastic wand.

There were two lines down the centre of the wand.

We stood together and stared at it as if it were a miracle, which, in a way, it was.

'Oh, May,' I whispered. 'I'm so happy for you!'

'You won't tell a soul, will you?' she asked, and I shook my head. I'd learned my lesson about tempting fate. I would never do that again.

I had trouble sleeping that night and it was nothing to do with the fireworks going off around Manchester, although the dawning of a new year did feel significant in a positive, 'line drawn' way. I was tired but I was buzzing; my mind was busy, overloaded with thoughts about how the next few days would pan out. I didn't know the order in which things would happen. I supposed that, when the police were presented with Neil's new evidence, they would release Alex and then he'd be free to go and fetch Jamie – as long as the Churchills were willing to give him up. I knew there was a very strong possibility that they wouldn't. Virginia must have known that Alex wasn't Jamie's blood father. If she decided to fight Alex for Jamie, I didn't know who would have the stronger claim on the child, the genetic grandparents or the man Jamie had known as Dad since the day he was born.

Even if, by some miracle, Virginia was happy to reunite Jamie with Alexander, I still wasn't sure where that left me.

I didn't know how Alex would be.

I knew he would want to be with his son, but I couldn't be sure that he would still want to be with me.

In the next moment I thought of poor Genevieve and how her whole life had been manipulated by her lover, the cruel, cowardly lover who strung her along and allowed her to suffer for their mutual mistakes; who failed her at every step. Stealing the Bryants' money was a terrible thing to do, but she did it to protect him. And then she fell pregnant and must have felt considerable pressure to marry, to provide a father for the baby, and once again Alexander's willingness to take care of her and Jamie let the real father off the hook. At the very end, when she finally believed that everything could be made open and honest, her lover let her down again.

So many times I had felt angry with Genevieve, jealous, bitter and frustrated.

That evening, all I felt was sympathy.

In my half-sleep I whispered: 'Genevieve, what should I do?'

And in the next breath, I half-dreamed she whispered back to me: 'Don't close the gates.'

Then I drifted away.

CHAPTER SIXTY-EIGHT

For a second time, I caught the train south and alighted at Bristol Temple Meads, but this time there was nobody there to meet me.

It was a dark day; the first day of the new year, but the rain was relentless. The station was deserted; almost empty. Only a handful of hungover or desperate people had turned up for the limited-service trains that would run that day.

My boots clicked along the wet platform. I went under the tunnel then out through the barrier. I didn't even have to queue for the taxi outside and it took me all the way to Burrington Stoke. A tiny Christmas tree stood on the dashboard, its lights plugged into the cigarette lighter.

The driver was full of the story of Genevieve's murder. It was all anyone in that part of the country was talking about, he told me. He asked if I was anything to do with the Churchill family, and I answered honestly that I was not, and he said it was the poor little lad he felt sorry for. What had that kid done to deserve to have a mother who went and got herself killed by his father? I was on the point of correcting him – Alexander had *not* killed Genevieve – but I remembered the truth about Jamie's parentage and realized the taxi driver was possibly right. So I kept quiet and, eventually, the taxi driver turned the stereo to Radio Two and we listened to New Year songs interspersed with news bulletins that all led with the Genevieve Churchill story. Her husband, Alexander, was due in court the very next day.

The taxi dropped me off at the Burrington Stoke Spar and I stood there, for a moment, looking around me. I hadn't been gone very long but nothing was familiar any more. The village was so quiet compared with Manchester. A few dim Christmas lights glowed in the windows of the line of council houses and the hotel, but beyond was a gloomy darkness; the January countryside bleak as midwinter, the fallen leaves now blackened and slippery, the stone wet, the gardens empty and the hills lonely, their dull greenness broken only by the mud of footpaths and farm-tracks, a spattering of heavy young cattle up to their hocks in water and slush.

Inside my coat pocket, my mobile phone beeped. There was a text from Neil. It read:

`Can't get hold of Twyford. Be careful what you say.`

I switched the phone off to save the battery and put it back in my pocket, and I turned and began the long walk to the lane that led uphill past the old quarry, and to Eleonora House.

This would almost certainly be the last time I ever came to Burrington Stoke. I could not imagine returning voluntarily again. I'd stay in touch with Betsy, of course, and a couple of other people, but if we were to meet, it would have to be somewhere neutral. Maybe we could all go out for a celebratory lunch, with the children, when Alexander was freed. Except we couldn't really celebrate, could we, not when we remembered what had happened to poor Genevieve.

My feet followed one another up the hill. I grew warm and my breath was cloudy.

At the top of the lane, the news crews were gone – I supposed they would all be camped outside the court now – but they had left a terrible mess. The turf had been churned up and ruined, there were dents and ridges left by heavy vehicles everywhere and the lane was slippery with half-frozen mud. Discarded cardboard coffee beakers and fast-food wrappers littered the hedgerows like cynical Christmas-tree decorations. Police crime-scene tape fluttered at the quarry entrance, industrial black and orange plastic ribbon tied around the huge gates. The old sign that said DANGER KEEP OUT still leaned crookedly to one side of the track. It had not stopped Genevieve entering the quarry on the morning of her death. Why had she agreed to go there? Had her lover forced her? Or was she already dead when he brought her to the quarry?

I turned into the drive of Claudia's house and was disappointed to see that the Volvo wasn't there. Obviously, she hadn't picked up my message. The gates were closed. I pressed the button on the post at the side of the gates.

'Yes?'

'Bill, it's me, Sarah.'

There was a buzz and the gates swung open.

I hesitated.

Once I was through the gates, they would shut automatically behind me.

Don't close the gates. Why were those words in my head? What did they mean? These gates? I stepped forward. The gates were open, the sensor that controlled them waiting for me to pass through.

I went through the gap. There was a few seconds' delay, long enough for a car to pass through, and then the gates would begin to close.

Oh, it was stupid, it was just a random phrase, the precursor to a dream.

Don't close the gates.

The words wouldn't go away. *You next. Don't close the gates.*

I knew I was being superstitious and silly, but still I picked up one of Claudia's small lavender pots and put it close to the left gatepost. I watched as the gates swung together again, and the hinged edge of the left gate became stuck against the pot. There was a gap hardly big enough for a person to squeeze through between the tall closing edges of the gates. I could not, for the life of me, see any relevance or point to the exercise, but still I felt an immense sense of relief, a release almost. That was what I had been supposed to do.

I walked slowly up to the house. A large, ornate

wreath of holly leaves and berries and ribbons was nailed to the wooden door. It must have been there before but I hadn't noticed. As I admired it, a gust of wind caught me from the north; it was icy cold, like a punch against my face. I steadied myself, reached out my hand and pressed the bell, and that set the dogs off barking inside the house.

After a moment or two, Bill opened the door. Blue jumped up at me, but I was ready for him – I caught his huge front paws and set them back on the ground. Bonnie came more slowly from around Bill's legs. She was stiff with arthritis. I stroked her head.

Somewhere inside the house, I heard the strains of operatic music – a woman was singing something terribly sad in a faltering soprano.

Bill looked terrible. He had aged a decade in the handful of days since I'd seen him. There were bags under his eyes, and jowls beneath his stubbled cheeks. His hair stuck up and he was wearing a baggy old pair of jeans beneath a striped shirt. He smelled faintly sour.

'Come in,' he said, and I stepped through the door. He closed it so that the dogs stayed outside.

'Are you all right?' I asked.

He looked at me.

'Sorry,' I said. 'Of course you aren't.'

He took my coat and gestured with his hand that I should go into the living room.

'Did Claudia get my message?'

Bill ignored the question.

'Isn't she here?

'No.' Bill shook his head. 'She doesn't want to see you.'

I opened my mouth and closed it again.

'Where is she?' I asked quietly.

'It doesn't matter where she is. She won't see you, Sarah.'

He followed me into the living room. The milky-coloured carpet was grubby, so many feet had passed through the house in the last days. I perched on one of the sofas, on its edge. The Christmas decorations were tired and rather pathetic in the empty house. Nut shells were scattered in the fireplace.

Bill cleared his throat. He said: 'Claudia asked me to give you a message.'

I brightened a little. 'Oh?'

'She wants you to leave the family alone. She wants you to go away and never come back. She wants you to forget about us. OK?'

I shook my head. 'I can't do that. I can't forget about Jamie.'

'You have to.'

'I won't.'

Bill paced over to the window. He scratched his head.

'The thing you have to understand, Sarah, is that I am prepared to do anything it takes to make my wife happy. If she doesn't want you here, I'll make sure you aren't here.'

'I didn't come about Jamie today,' I said. 'I came to tell Claudia that Alexander didn't kill Genevieve.'

Bill laughed. 'Nobody cares what you think.'

'There's proof.'

Bill came back over and stood in front of me, leaning over me. I shrank away from him.

'You aren't listening to me,' he said. 'Claudia doesn't care what you have to say. I don't care. Nobody does. We don't want to know about your little fantasies, your games.'

'No, it's not like that. I . . .'

Bill spoke slowly and calmly.

'We *know* that you're – how can I put it? – fragile, Sarah. Everyone knows you've had problems, and even you would probably agree that you're somewhat obsessed with Genevieve.'

'No, I . . .'

'Your own sister told us that you're still being treated for postnatal depression. Your mind's addled. We know you tried to abduct Jamie. We have absolutely irrefutable evidence.'

I felt myself go cold inside. My mouth was dry as dust, and the old feeling of terror rushed through my bloodstream.

'You wanted him to be your son, didn't you?' Bill asked. 'You wanted to *be* Genevieve.'

'No.' I shook my head, still afraid to say anything that might incriminate me, because I didn't know what Bill knew. Had May mentioned something to him, or to Claudia? Surely she wouldn't have.

Bill must have seen the confusion written on my face.

'CCTV,' he said. 'We installed CCTV over the gates when we knew Damian was back in Burrington Stoke. Just to be on the safe side. When we played the tapes back, we saw you, Sarah. I saw you, Claudia saw you, the police saw you. We have digital recordings. Several of them.'

I shook my head in despair.

'I wasn't thinking straight that night,' I said.

'You haven't been thinking straight for months,' said Bill.

I was trying to keep calm and at the same time think through the implications of what he was saying. Had I done anything to jeopardize Alex's chances of gaining custody of Jamie? What if the Churchills made a case that he'd employed somebody mentally unfit to care for Jamie? Wouldn't that make him a bad father?

Bill said: 'We've spoken to the police and taken legal advice. You'll never be allowed access to Jamie, Sarah. Not while you're considered a threat to him.'

'I'll never do anything to hurt Jamie!' I cried.

'No,' Bill agreed, 'you won't. We're arranging an injunction so that you can't go anywhere near him.'

'Please let me talk to Claudia,' I said. 'Please let me explain . . .'

Bill shook his head. 'Stop it, Sarah. Give it up. It's over.'

He said: 'I'm going to straighten up, then I'll drive you back to the train station. I want you out of here before Claudia returns.'

I was feeling so panicked and upset I could hardly think. I knew the family was powerful and wealthy, and my position could hardly be more tenuous, but it didn't matter. It didn't matter because Alex would soon be free and he'd let nothing stop him from getting Jamie back.

'You can keep me away, but you can't stop Alex from being with his son,' I said. My voice was brittle. I knew I sounded desperate.

Bill sighed, as if he were bored now.

'Alex is going to be in prison for a long, long time.'

'He went to Sicily looking for Genevieve. He was preparing to fight her for Jamie's custody. Why would he have done that if he knew she was dead?'

'It was a way to cover his tracks. He's not stupid.'

Bill turned and went to leave the room.

I took a breath. 'And we know that Genevieve had a lover and that she believed he was going away with her that day. We know his name.'

Bill hesitated.

'Well, part of his name,' I said.

He held up a hand to stop me.

'I'll be two minutes,' he said. 'Stay there.'

He left the room. I sat where I was for a moment or two, my head falling forward. I twisted a piece of hair around my finger like I used to when I was a child; it used to calm me. I thought I'd let Bill take me back to Temple Meads then I'd get a taxi to the prison. I doubted I'd be allowed to see Alex, but it was possible. At least I'd be close to him and perhaps I could get a message to him. The very thought of being near to Alex made me feel a little better. Only bricks and mortar would be between us. We had been apart so long. I felt almost faint at the memory of Alex's body, his presence, his face.

I stood up and wandered over to the window. A stack of post had been left on the sill. I leaned over to look out at the dogs in the garden and, as I did so, I must have disturbed the pile, because the mail fell to the carpet. I picked up the letters. There were a couple of handwritten envelopes that I could tell were condolence cards by the gravitas of the writing and the colour of the envelopes. They were addressed either to the Lefarge Family or to Bill, Claudia and the Girls. There was a circular, a brown envelope addressed to Claudia, and a white one addressed to Mr William Lefarge.

I put the letters back where they had been, on the window ledge, and straightened the pile again. I heard Bill's footsteps on the stairs.

I went back to the settee, and sat down where I had been, in the same position.

Something was bugging me, but I couldn't chase it down.

Something was wrong.

I fiddled with my bracelet.

Bill came back into the room. He looked neater. He was fastening the cuffs on his shirtsleeves. I shrank back from him.

He had washed and shaved and changed. He looked better now, presentable. I stood up, and went behind the settee, keeping an arm's length between us.

'Shall we go?' he asked.

I nodded. He walked towards me. I moved away again, towards the door into the hall. Bill picked up the post from the window ledge, and that's when I realized.

I felt as if I were an upturned bottle full of icy water and somebody had just unscrewed the lid. I felt everything – all my emotions, my optimism, my conviction that we would be all right in the end – drain out of me, and I could almost feel the future puddling about my feet, disappearing.

Mr William Lefarge.

Mr *William* Lefarge.

Will*iam.*

Liam.

Lee.

It was Bill! Of course it was Bill! Someone Genevieve met at university – probably the person who pulled the strings to admit her in the first place. A married man who was close. A family man whose wife had been pregnant a few years before Genevieve was. Someone with everything to lose and only Genevieve to gain. A man whose identity nobody must know. Someone who knew about the quarry. Someone who loved Genevieve but loved his wife and family even more. The man who had said to me only ten minutes earlier that he would do *anything* to protect Claudia.

I thought my knees would give way beneath me, that I would simply faint and fall and the next thing I would feel would be the smack of the hall floor against my skull, and maybe that would be a good thing because then Bill wouldn't be able to see that I knew.

Genevieve had warned me.

You next, she had said.

I turned my head away from Bill and stepped into the hall so my back was to him. I hoped he hadn't seen the recognition dawning on my face but, even if he hadn't, there was a smell about me, a smell I recognized from years back, from school, and the smell was coming from my skin, from my glands, my neck, my armpits, the hot place between my breasts. It was the hormonal, primeval smell of fear. As I saw the dull sunlight falling through the windows, I knew that Bill must smell it too.

'Come on,' he said with a little sigh. 'Let's get this over with.'

CHAPTER SIXTY-NINE

I moved very slowly towards the front door. I patted my pockets, looking for my phone, and then I remembered it was in my coat pocket and my coat was hanging up in the hallway.

I tried to rationalize and reason, but thoughts were chasing through my head so chaotically that I could not sort them. I was safe: Neil knew the truth. No, he didn't, he didn't know that Bill was Lee; he might work it out at some point, but he didn't know now. He might never work it out.

Maybe Bill wasn't going to kill me. Perhaps I was being paranoid. Probably he was just going to do what he said and drive me to the station. I couldn't bear to be with him that long. I'd ask him to drop me at the nearest bus stop, that's what I'd do. Everything would be fine.

Bill took hold of my arm and squeezed.

'Come on,' he said again.

He pushed me in front of him out of the house. One hand was in the small of my back, the other held my elbow. He wasn't exactly being rough, but I knew I did not have a choice. He grabbed my coat from the hook in the hall as we went past and, as he did so, the mobile phone clattered out of the pocket and slid across the floor.

Bill passed me the coat, and put the phone in his pocket.

'I'll look after it for you,' he said.

He wasn't looking at me. It was as if his thoughts were miles away.

I glanced around, but there was no obvious escape route. The gates were still slightly open. That didn't make any difference; there had never been anywhere to run. The lane to the left led directly up to Eleonora House, but it was a good half-mile away and mostly up a steep hill. I was wearing boots with heels that weren't designed for running. The lane to the right led back down to the main road, and to the gated junction to the quarry, but that sheered sharply downhill and was much further and there were patches of black ice amongst the mud and rainwater. Ahead was farmland, but it was hedged, a thick, dense hedge that was impenetrable; even the nimble little deer could not find a way through. Behind was the old quarry.

If I ran, Bill would catch me. If I screamed, nobody would hear me. Bill had my phone and the phone was switched off so it would not be transmitting a signal. The taxi driver had dropped me off at the Spar. That would be the last anyone knew of me.

If I disappeared, nobody would ever know I had been here.

I gave a little involuntary cry of distress.

'Don't,' said Bill. 'Please don't do that. I have such a headache.'

'You don't have to take me anywhere,' I said. 'I'll walk down to the bus stop. I'll go on my own.'

'Oh no,' he said. 'No, Sarah, I can't let you do that. I need to be certain that you're gone.'

'Please . . .' I begged, holding back.

'I'm sorry,' he said, 'but you brought this on yourself. Nobody made you come to Burrington Stoke. Nobody made you get involved. Now you have to face up to what you've done.'

He opened the passenger door of his black four-wheel drive and hefted me up. The seat was cold and hard beneath my buttocks.

'Is that what you said to Genevieve?'

'What?'

Why did I say that? Why did those words come out of my mouth? I was trying to survive, I wanted to save myself, not rile Bill, not turn him against me.

He slammed the door shut. I leaned my head back against the headrest, trying to quell the dizziness that was overwhelming me. My fingers were trembling. I grasped my hands together in my lap. I knew it was important not to show how afraid I was. I had to pretend I was calm.

Bill got into the car beside me.

'What did you say?'

'Nothing.'

Bill sat and stared at me for a moment or two.

'Don't put your seatbelt on,' he said, although I had made no move to do so.

'You know, don't you?' he said.

It wasn't a question. I looked at my hands on my lap.

'Was it you all the time?' I asked. 'Did Genevieve steal the money for you? Did she have the baby for you?'

Bill shook his head.

'I told her not to give Damian a penny,' he said. 'Nobody believed a word he said. And she fell pregnant on purpose, to pressure me into leaving Claudia and the twins. I told her. I told her from the very beginning that nothing would make me break up my family. She wouldn't listen.'

The dogs were clamouring to get into the car, their paws scratching against the side. I watched them through the window glass. Blue's big paws scrabbled at the pane, leaving streaks of mud and claw marks. Bonnie paced behind him.

Bill sounded terribly tired. 'Please would you sit forward.'

I did as he asked. I think I was in shock. My brain couldn't come to terms with the possibility that this gentle, softly spoken American was a threat. He bound my wrists together with his scarf, and then fastened it to the car's armrest. It was tied so tightly I could feel the blood pooling behind it, and my hands immediately ached. There was no doubt in my mind then. I knew what he planned to do – but still I couldn't believe it.

He put the car into gear, turning it slowly towards the fancy wrought-iron gates. He picked up a small black remote control from the dashboard and aimed it at the gatepost. The gates swung open. The wheels squeaked on the pink fishbone paving as Bill lined up the car to go through.

'Why did you have to kill her?' I asked. He inclined his head towards me. He did not notice the small lavender pot, although the wheel of the car knocked it slightly as we passed. It rocked on its base, but did not tip over.

'To make her quiet,' he said. 'She wouldn't stop screaming. I asked her, I warned her, but she wouldn't stop.'

My heart slowed a fraction.

We were through the gates, the nose of the car pointing out on to the lane. Bill turned right, downhill, towards the old quarry. In the wing mirror I saw the gates slide to behind us. The left one stuck on the pot. I saw the dogs watching from the other side.

'Were you in the old quarry when she died?' I asked.

He nodded. 'It was our place,' he said. 'Where we used to go. It was convenient. Private.'

Bill swallowed as he spoke and I noticed that the whites of his eyes were red and glassy. He drove the car carefully downhill.

'She couldn't be happy with what she had. She always had to have it all, everything. And even if she had had everything, if she had everything in the world, she still wouldn't have been happy.'

'Bill . . .'

'Please don't talk,' he said.

We drove, slowly, down the lane. In the wing mirror I saw the dogs watching. They had come through the gap in the gates and were hesitating. They knew they weren't supposed to go out of the garden on their own.

'That morning,' he said, 'she turned up all bright and breezy, but she was in one of her moods. She said she'd left a letter for Alexander, and one to her parents, so there was no going back. She asked what Claudia had said when I told her I was leaving . . .'

He wiped his cheek with the back of his hand.

'And I said I couldn't do it to Claudia, I couldn't destroy her like that. So Genevieve said she would tell her herself. She meant it. It wasn't a threat. She said she'd been trying to tell her for weeks.'

Bill shook his head. Tears fell on to the legs of his trousers, stained the light-grey fabric a darker colour. He sniffed. The car was in too high a gear. The engine complained. He pulled a sour face, as if he still couldn't believe what had happened that morning. From the corner of my eye, I saw Blue bounding down the lane after the car. He must have thought this was some kind of game.

'She sat in the kitchen, on a stool. She was drinking coffee and she was serious,' he said. 'Claudia had taken the girls to school. She was due back any minute, so I suggested we went for a walk. I had to get her out of there. I never thought she'd agree to go with me, but she did. She said we'd walk down to the old quarry together and then I could wait for her there while she talked to Claudia. She knew I wouldn't let her do that! What was she thinking?'

'She was exhausted,' I said. 'Her nerves were shot. She

believed you were going to Sicily. She'd been carrying the dream inside her for months.'

'Yes, yes, but that's exactly it – it was a *dream*! It was never real. It was all in her mind.'

'You played along, Bill.'

'She knew the rules.'

He slowed down as the wheels lost traction on a patch of mud. I felt closed in by the steep hedges on either side of the lane.

When Bill spoke next there was frustration in his voice. 'Gen thought she could make me do anything she wanted if she pushed hard enough . . .' He shook his head and then suddenly, abruptly, swung the car right, between a small gap in the hedgerow, so small I'd never noticed it before. Twigs scraped and scratched at the car and we were plunged into darkness as we drove through brambles. The vehicle lurched from side to side as we bumped over ruts and pits. I banged my head on the window and Bill turned and asked: 'Are you all right?' I almost laughed.

'People have forgotten this track,' Bill said. 'The quarrymen built it as a cut-through to cart stone up to the top of the hill when they were building Eleonora House.'

Even then the history teacher in him came to the surface.

The car swerved and rocked. The track between the trees and the undergrowth was so narrow that there was no room to open a door and the world had turned very dark.

'Nearly there,' he said, as if I were a child who had whinged.

'Bill, please,' I said, trying to hold on to my breath. 'If you push me off the cliff, they'll know. It can't have been Alexander and . . .'

'Maybe you won't be found,' he said. 'I thought somebody would find Genevieve straight away. It wasn't as if I did anything to hide her. People are supposed to keep out of here, but occasionally they come in – walking their dogs, picking mushrooms, having sex, swimming even. I saw them. I've watched them. They've been coming all year, and nobody found Genevieve.'

'But if they do find me . . .'

'Then they do. Alexander is going to be locked up for life. People will say you were bound to be upset. Everyone knows you've been obsessed with Genevieve – wanting to be Genevieve, wanting her house, her husband, her child. Your family knows. The doctor knows. The police know. Our solicitor knows. And now those things have all been taken away from you, and you'll never get them back. Especially Jamie. You wanted him more than anything, didn't you? You wanted him so badly you were prepared to abduct him, but now you know he's out of reach and that we'll all be telling him stories about you. About how you tried to take him away from his family.'

'No!' I cried.

'Nobody will be surprised you jumped. People will see the symmetry in your actions, the poetry, the fatal emulation of the woman you could never be. Do you know what people will say, Sarah? They'll say they saw it coming. They'll say it was a way for you to get your picture in the papers right next to Genevieve's.'

He turned to me and smiled. His tears were gone. He may have wept when he killed Genevieve, but I meant nothing to him.

'I'll be on the CCTV,' I said. 'There'll be evidence of me coming to the Barn this morning, and of us leaving together. If you hurt me, everyone will know it was you.'

'No, they won't,' said Bill. 'I turned the camera off before you came. I didn't want Claudia to know you'd been back.'

I caught my breath and tried to stay calm.

Ahead, I could see the cut-through opening up. I could see the green of holly bushes amongst the winter trees, their finger-pointing branches. We must be at the top of the quarry. I had seen aerial photographs in the newspapers and on the internet. I knew how land overgrown with brambles and shrubs suddenly gave out to a sheer stone cliff, and that sixty feet below was the flooded pool, edged with abandoned and fallen rocks, the rocks that had caught Genevieve's body, and broken it so thoroughly as she fell to the water; the same rocks that had hidden her from view for so many months.

Bill stopped the car. The passenger window was parallel with the cliff edge. It was only a couple of feet away. The drop made my stomach turn.

I tried to move my wrists, but I couldn't. My hands were pressed too far back, my fingers couldn't reach the fabric of the scarf.

Bill didn't look at me.

'You should have stayed away,' he said.

'Please don't do it,' I said. 'Please, Bill. Let me go.'

He shook his head.

'I have to look after Claudia,' he said. 'That's what I must do. That's my job.'

'Oh Bill, please!' My voice was breaking now. I began to cry; there were no tears, it was a terrified, dry cry. I tried to find the words to convince him not to hurt me, but when I looked in his face it was obvious that his mind was made up.

Bill reached out his hand and moved my hair out of my eyes. I recoiled at his touch. His skin was cool and soft, office skin, and I thought of Alexander's rough, warm hands and felt the tears then rush to my eyes. They spilled down my cheeks and down my chin.

I sat stiff as Bill cupped my cheeks and my chin with his hand. I could feel his thumb against my neck. I could feel my own blood pulsing against his thumbprint.

'Sarah,' he said. 'You stupid little headcase.'

I was desperate. I swallowed and said softly, 'I always liked you, Bill.'

He laughed. 'Oh lord! You girls, you think sex is the answer to everything. Genevieve was the same! You think it makes you powerful. It doesn't.'

'Please . . .' I murmured.

'Oh, stop it. *Stop it!*'

He slapped my face, hard. I was shocked. My cheek stung. Tears rolled down my face. My nose was running. I snivelled like a baby.

Bill rubbed the palm he'd used to hit me on the thigh of his trousers.

'Jesus,' he said.

'I'm sorry,' I whimpered.

He opened his door.

I shook my head, I sobbed out loud.

'Please, Bill, please let me go. I don't want to end up here, like this . . .'

He shut the door and came round the back of the car. I saw a little robin fly past. It looked so sweet, all bright-eyed innocence. It was my tiny witness. Nobody else would know.

Bill opened the passenger door and crouched down beside me.

'Oh Bill, please, please . . .' I cried. 'I'll do anything, anything . . .'

'It's ironic, isn't it,' he said, 'how you came along and followed in Genevieve's footsteps all the way? Right here to the very edge of the cliff. You wanted to be her so badly, didn't you?'

'I never wanted to be Genevieve,' I wept. 'I just wanted to be with Alexander.'

'But if you're honest, Sarah, you were glad she was out of the way, weren't you? You didn't really care, did you, what had happened to her?'

'I didn't want her to be dead!'

'Are you sure?'

I sobbed again. Bill pushed me forward so he could untie my wrists.

'As it is, it's all worked out neatly,' he said. 'Jamie can come and live with me . . .'

'You're not his father,' I said. 'You'll never be his father. Alexander is his father and Jamie knows that.'

'Oh, shut up,' said Bill. He was struggling with the knot.

I thought: *This is it, I have just a few more seconds of being alive*. In that instant, I realized how I loved life. My heart was pounding so hard and I liked the feeling of being in my body. Just a few more seconds and feeling and thinking and being would all be over. I could see no way out of the situation. My life did not flash before my eyes but I saw snapshots of people and places and they were all dear to me and I was so glad they had been in my life. I felt a rush of pure, exquisite love and I thought that I'd been lucky.

I smelled the rain in the air above the stink of my own fear. Bill took hold of my elbow and pulled. I tried to fight him off but he was strong and determined and I knew I did not have a chance.

I saw a snapshot of my baby. I remembered how peaceful he was in death, his cheek against my breast, and I thought if he who had never had the opportunity to run through grass or taste a strawberry or hold a lover in his arms or even to feel air in his lungs; if he who had so much less than I could be dignified, then so could I. I thought of my boy's perfect little face and I held on to the thought, because that was the thought with which I would die.

I calmed down in a heartbeat and, as Bill leaned over to heave me out of the car, I gazed up through the gap between the car door and its frame, I gazed up into the sky where white clouds chased across a darkening grey sky. I decided then that I would not look down into the quarry. I did not want to see the jagged rocks or my own reflection hurtling towards me. I would look up to the sky as I fell and I'd die thinking of my baby boy.

I felt the blood rush into my fingers as the scarf was finally loosened and the silky material slipped past my wrist.

'It's nearly over,' said Bill.

He was holding my left hand tightly, twisting my arm across the back of my body. It was pointless, but still I resisted.

And then something happened. One moment Bill was pulling so hard that I thought my shoulder would dislocate, and then he let go of my hand.

He disappeared.

The door swung back against me, trapping my left leg, and I felt intense pain in my ankle, which took the force of the slam. Instinctively, I pulled my leg back into the footwell, pulled the door shut and pressed down the central-locking button. I expected to see Bill's face, any moment, at the window. I buried my face in my arms and braced myself for the onslaught. I expected him to try to open the door. I was waiting to hear the smash of glass, or even to feel the car moving – if he couldn't get me out, maybe he'd push the car over the edge of the cliff – but nothing happened.

Nothing happened for moments. After a long time, when it dawned on me that maybe Bill was not coming back, I reached across and pressed my elbow on to the steering wheel, blasting the horn out across the quarry, and I stayed there, weeping, with my arm on the horn, until they came to find me.

CHAPTER SEVENTY

It was Blue who saved me.

This is how I believe it happened.

He had mustered the courage to come through the gap in the gates and followed us down the lane, along the cut-through, into the quarry. He chased ahead, with Bonnie following behind.

Blue didn't wait for Bonnie. Once he'd started following the car, he began to enjoy himself, panting with excitement and wagging his thick tail low, his paws skittering on the icy patches. He probably thought he was clever and brave. He probably thought he was *supposed* to follow Bill's car. He struggled to keep up as the car went downhill but tracked us through the hidden gap in the hedge following the fumy trail along the old quarrymen's path. Blue, arriving at the end of the track just as Bill tossed the scarf on to the grass and reached over to pull me out of the car, bounded forward to greet his master.

Claudia never had got round to training Blue not to jump up. He threw his considerable large dog's weight against Bill, planting his paws on Bill's chest with his customary exuberance, and Bill, surprised and wrong-footed and not expecting eleven stone of dog to hurl itself into him, went over the cliff. Blue went too.

I don't know how long it took Bonnie to reach the car but, when she did, finding the door shut, the horn blaring and no sign of Blue or Bill, she sighed and turned a few circles and then lay down beside the car, and that's where she was found, whimpering and distressed, guarding me.

It was Blue who saved me, and Virginia, out feeding her horses, heard the car horn and came to find me. I was so terrified of the cliff that I refused to open the door when she rapped on the window with her knuckles and shouted at me through the glass. She didn't realize what had happened. She thought I'd had a breakdown and stolen the car. She assumed, as Bill had predicted, that I was planning suicide. She called the police and they came at once. DI Twyford, who looked over the cliff edge and saw what Virginia hadn't, persuaded me to unlock the doors. He climbed into the driver's seat, released the handbrake and rolled the vehicle carefully back into the undergrowth, talking to me all the time in a reassuring voice. Then he carried me to safety in his arms.

An ambulance came to take me to hospital. The paramedics were kind and jolly. They wrapped me in a blanket and gave me something that went into my veins like alcohol and soothed me. They didn't want to know about the voice in my mind telling me not to close the gates, although I kept trying to tell them. It was a miracle. If I hadn't obeyed the command, I'd have been dead. It would have been Genevieve first and me next, exactly as she'd said. I'd asked her to help me and she'd told me what to do. I kept telling them but they didn't care. They were more interested in my ankle. They gave me oxygen and put my legs up and my head down and told me, Shh, not to worry, I was in shock.

At the hospital, due to my status as a victim of serious crime, I skipped the queues and went straight into a cubicle in A & E. The doctor, who was young, Asian and tiny, nodded when I told her about the miracle of the gates and said: 'Oh yes, dear?' in a disinterested voice, and then a nurse put a mask over my mouth and nose and I could not talk any more.

I spent a nice quiet day in hospital, comfortably numbed by various anaesthetics and tranquillizers. When I woke from the operation to fix my ankle, May was there, sitting in a plastic armchair at the side of the bed reading a well-thumbed New Year's edition of the *Radio Times*. I tried to talk to her about the warning I'd heard in my mind, about how it had saved my life, and she said: 'Honey, sweetheart, you've had a terrible shock. Just rest. You're safe now.' My leg was encased in plaster, right up to above the knee, and it was suspended above the bed like a broken leg in a *Carry On* film. I couldn't sit up.

Some time during the day, Genevieve walked past the open door to my room. She was smiling and holding on to Blue's collar. He was looking up at her, his tongue lolling, his tail wagging. Or maybe I imagined that.

The police came to interview me, two women; I

didn't recognize either of them. They didn't want to hear about the voice and the gates either. They smiled and said: 'Yes, but . . .' and steered me back to their original questions whenever I diverted. I told them about the laptop in the sealed-off well because now I was certain that was a message from Genevieve too. I saw one of them roll her eyes up towards the ceiling and the other struggled to hide her grin and I wished they would listen to me.

Because I knew.

Later, May fed me a cheese salad sandwich, bit by bit, and helped me drink orange squash through a straw. Then she left and I lay, as I had to, on my back, staring at the pattern made by light reflecting on tinsel on the ceiling of my room and I thought of Genevieve and, in my heart and my mind, I thanked her.

May drove me back to Manchester the next morning.

'Promise me one thing,' she asked as we drove up the M5 with my plastered foot on the dashboard, swollen toes sticking out of the blue sock.

'What?'

'Don't ever go back there.'

'I won't,' I said.

A week went by and then another. We went to Mum and Dad's tiny terraced house for Mum's birthday on 18 January, and we had a riotous time. Well, everyone else did. I pretended to be enjoying myself as much as they were, for their sake, but inside I was lonely as the moon. Mum kept putting her arms around me and kissing my cheek and telling me how much she loved me, and every time Dad looked at me his eyes filled with tears.

'When I think of what could have happened . . .' he kept saying, wiping his nose.

'But it didn't!' I replied each time, with a big smile on my face.

I heard them saying quietly, when they thought I wasn't listening: 'Hasn't she done well! Hasn't she been brave! She seems almost back to her old self. Who'd have thought she'd cope with something like this?'

By then, I'd learned to stop talking about Genevieve, and how she'd saved my life, but I never stopped thinking about her.

CHAPTER SEVENTY-ONE

Two feet of snow fell on Manchester on the first day of February and all but the main roads were impassable.

The boiler in May and Neil's flat developed a leak and we had to shower at the sports centre. I looked at myself in the mirror and did not recognize myself. May said: 'Oh, for goodness' sake, stop posing. We can all see how skinny you are.'

The foetus inside her wasn't even as big as the top half of her thumb, but he or she had a beating heart and May had put on weight. In the sports-centre changing rooms I turned to hug her and she said: 'And please stop these spontaneous displays of affection, Sarah. They're freaking me out.'

It was 17 February before the snow went, and then Alexander and Jamie came to Manchester.

This time it was me waiting on the platform to meet them. Their train rolled into Piccadilly station bang on time. There weren't many people on board, and we found one another straight away. I held up my hand

and waved, and they came towards me, slowly at first, hesitantly, and then Jamie broke into a run and he threw himself at me, almost knocking me over. I wasn't using crutches any longer but my leg was still weak.

'Hey you,' I said, kissing him all over his head. He was squeezing so tight I had no breath left for Alexander. I looked up at him and he looked away.

Too much had happened. Neither of us knew where to start with one another. We were too afraid of causing more pain to the other's bruised heart.

They had brought me a present. I opened it in the taxi. It was a framed drawing of a fighter aircraft with flames and smoke coming out of one wing shooting at some kind of monster.

'I drew that,' said Jamie, 'and Dad framed it.'

'It's amazing,' I said.

Jamie leaned across me.

'See, that's a dinosaur who's escaped from the quarry to find a better life and that plane any minute now is going to crash and the dinosaur will stamp on it.'

'Will the pilot escape?' I asked. Jamie shook his head and pulled an expression that denoted it was a shame, but what could you do?

'Wow,' I said.

We all went to the Harvester for dinner that night.

In the ladies, Mum said she wouldn't kick Alexander out of bed and May told her to stop encouraging me.

'He is rather handsome, though,' May said wistfully. 'And the little lad's a darling.'

'Oh, listen to you, you're just as bad!' Mum said, and

she squeezed my elbow and I knew then that they approved. After all that we had put them through, my family would be happy for me to be with Alexander and Jamie.

We sat on the bench by the canal. The canal was frozen. Ducks were waddling comically on the ice. The toes in my bad leg were frozen too, even though I was wearing two of Neil's thick walking socks over the bottom of the cast. Alexander and I sat together like a couple in a painting staring out over the water, together but not touching.

'The police found Genevieve's laptop,' said Alexander.

'Where?' I asked.

'In the well. It was sealed in a plastic bag. She must have left it there in case anything went wrong. It had all her emails on it. Everything. She must have had some idea, some premonition.'

I blew my breath away.

'I knew it was there,' I said.

Alexander picked up my hand and cradled it on his lap.

'I'm sorry,' we said at exactly the same moment, and that was all we needed to say.

EPILOGUE

We married in the summer, less than a year after we met. We had a very quiet register office wedding, just Alexander, Jamie and me with May and Neil as witnesses and my parents sitting next to us. May's baby daughter Anneliese slept in her buggy in the aisle. I wore an old blue dress I'd borrowed from May, and a new necklace of painted macaroni threaded on cotton that Jamie had made for the occasion.

In the evening, we had a party in the garden of the Blue Flame pub. Matt Bryant and his wife and children drove up from Worcester, together with other friends who had lost touch with Alexander. My Manchester girlfriends were there, all except Rosita. Roseanne, Midge, Betsy and Tom hired a car and drove up together from Burrington Stoke.

It was a lovely party. The grass was very green and the garden was lined with lacy heads of cow parsley. Midges danced in the air, and the cool country dampness was tempered by the candles in lanterns strung in the trees and the music played by a couple of my old friends. I sat on a rickety bench sipping cider while Jamie slept on my knee. Alexander wrapped a cardigan around my shoulders and leaned down to kiss me.

He didn't say that he loved me.

He didn't need to.

After that, Alexander shaved off his beard and had his hair cut and I grew mine even longer. We were broke, always. We rented a tiny flat in Bath, which was a good compromise between Manchester and Burrington Stoke. We'd given up any idea of living in Cornwall by then. That had been our pipe dream, our romantic fantasy. Alexander had found work as a stonemason for a company that specialized in the restoration of historical buildings – and there were plenty of those in Bath – and I enrolled on a full-time art-foundation course at the university and worked as a waitress in the evenings. We saved a little money and eventually one of the surveyors who worked with Alexander told him of a little house that was coming on to the market.

We went to see it, Alexander, Jamie and I. It was a pretty house, halfway up one of the hills that overlook the city. It was called Lilyvale. The family who were moving out – two adults and two children – were friendly and happy.

'Why are you leaving?' I asked the woman, who was small, fair-haired and very pregnant.

'We need more room,' she smiled, stroking her stomach.

We don't talk about the past. Now we're settled in our new life, we try not to look back.

Claudia sold the Barn and moved away, with the twins, as soon as she could. The last I heard, she had bought a house in Pembrokeshire, not far from Damian's place in Tenby. I haven't seen her, but I do think about her from time to time and I hope she's all right.

Once a month, Virginia and Philip come to Bath and they take Jamie out for the day. Philip is still going strong. He is made of stern stuff. Jamie's pony has been sold but occasionally we all go together to some major equestrian event where the Churchills can show their beautiful and bright grandson off to their posh, horsey friends. Everyone is kind to Alexander and me, and they find it hard to hide their emotions when they look at Jamie. On the evenings of those family get-togethers, we eat out for supper in one of Bath's myriad restaurants. Philip and Alexander take turns to pick up the bill. Other than that, we have no connection with the Churchill family, although I understand Genevieve's money has been put in trust for Jamie.

My parents treat Jamie as their grandson. He calls May and Neil Auntie and Uncle and refers to Anneliese as his cousin. I think about my baby boy often, but not as often as I used to. It is the living child who demands my attention now. I will never be his mother, but I will do my best, always. Jamie knows.

We have decided not to tell Jamie the truth about Bill. Short of him developing some rare genetic problem – and that seems unlikely, given that his half-sisters are both fit and healthy – there is no reason for him, or anyone else outside the immediate family, to know his real parentage. That part of the story never reached the media, thank God. It's one more secret, one more thing to keep hidden, but what would be the point of the truth? It would benefit nobody and it could do a great deal of harm. Between us, Alexander and I will make sure Jamie is always safe. We'll protect him from his past.

I think of Genevieve all the time, every day. I am not a religious person but, wherever I am, if I come across an open church, I go inside and light a candle for Genevieve. I find a quiet place to sit, and I think of her and remember it was she who saved my life, even though she had lost hers.

I haven't mentioned this to Alexander. As I say, we don't talk about the past. What's important is that Genevieve entrusted me with her boy, and I will do the very best I can for him. I will always be grateful to her.

We're happy now, Alexander and I; quietly, genuinely happy. We are gentle with each other. Sometimes one or the other of us will disappear into their thoughts and we know that this is only a temporary state, that history can only hurt us if we let it. Now we both know the truth and there are no secrets between us – none that matter, anyway – it seems safe to let the past lie.

I am no longer haunted and neither is Alexander.

I look into his face and see its true beauty, and he sees me watching and smiles and he reaches out to take hold of my hand. We fall into one another, as we always have done, and together I know we are better and stronger than we ever were apart.

ACKNOWLEDGEMENTS

This book wouldn't have happened at all without the hard work and support of my agent Marianne Gunn O'Connor, and I'm also immensely grateful to Pat Lynch and Vicki Satlow. It has been vastly improved by my very talented editor, Cat Cobain. Thanks to the lovely Transworld people who have been involved, especially Madeline Toy, Kate Tolley and Kate Samano, and Sarah Day. I know how lucky I am to be working with all of you.

I'd like to thank my parents Janet and Michael and brother Steve for their unwavering encouragement, Kevin for being my hero, Chris, Nick and Mark for being perfect sons; Angie, Callum, Carol, Claire, Henrietta, Judith, Kaela, Martin, Melanie, Milly, Niall, Roger, Roseanne, Sandy and Shelley and everyone at the RNA – in particular the Somerset/Wiltshire chapter.

The Secrets Between Us is steeped in Gothic themes drawn from some of my favourite classic books. Daphne du Maurier's *Rebecca* and *My Cousin Rachel* were particularly influential; also Emily Brontë's *Wuthering Heights* and Charlotte Brontë's *Jane Eyre*. I learned a great deal from Bram Stoker's incredible ability to describe the countryside and build tension, and Henry James's use of psychological drama.

Finally, thank you to you for reading it.

In Her Shadow

Louise Douglas

Before Ellen, things were easier and less complicated. They were either good or bad, right or wrong, black or white and I understood the difference. Since Ellen, everything has been coloured in shades of grey . . .

One ordinary morning at work Hannah Brown glimpses a young woman with dark hair, wearing a green coat spattered with rain. The woman is identical to her childhood best friend, Ellen Brecht. Can it really be her?

For a moment, it is as though the past twenty years have never happened: life becomes dazzling and exciting again and Hannah remembers how she felt when she was young and strong, and without regret. But as she remembers what happened to Ellen and to her all those years ago, she flies into a terrible panic. Because the seemingly idyllic Cornish childhood that she and Ellen shared ended in obsession and betrayal. Has Ellen come to forgive her, or to punish her?

American Wife

Curtis Sittenfeld

On one of the most important days of her husband's presidency, Alice Blackwell considers the strange and unlikely path that has led them to the White House. Thrust into a position she did not seek – one of power and influence, privilege and responsibility – Alice must face contradictions years in the making: how can she at once love and fundamentally disagree with her husband? How complicit has she been in the trajectory of her own life?

American Wife is a beautifully written novel that weaves race, class, wealth and fate into a brilliant tapestry – a novel in which the unexpected becomes inevitable, and the pleasures and pain of intimacy and love are laid bare.

Before I Go To Sleep

S J Watson

Memories define us.

So what if you lost yours every time you went to sleep?

Your name, your identity, your past, even the people you love – all forgotten overnight. And the one person you trust may only be telling you half the story.

Welcome to Christine's life.

WINNER – GALAXY NATIONAL BOOK AWARD
CRIME THRILLER OF THE YEAR

Darkside

Belinda Bauer

It is freezing mid-winter on Exmoor, and in a close-knit community where no stranger goes unnoticed, a local woman has been found murdered in her bed. This is local policeman Jonas Holly's first murder investigation. But he is distracted by anonymous letters, accusing him of failing to do his job.

Taunted by the killer and sidelined by his abrasive senior detective, Jonas has no choice but to strike out alone on a terrifying hunt . . . *but who is hunting who?*